The Mackenzie Trilogy

H.C. BROWN

LUMINOSITY PUBLISHING

LUMINOSITY PUBLISHING LLP

THE MACKENZIE, TRILOGY
Copyright © January 2016 H.C. Brown
Paperback ISBN: 978-1-910899-54-0

Cover Art by Poppy Designs

Dedication

For

Gary—my rock.

H.C. BROWN

CHARMED

The Mackenzie, Book One

Charmed
The Mackenzie, Book One
H.C. Brown

Highlander Drew Mackenzie's double life as a respectable gentleman and the notorious, smuggler, *Le Diable Noir*, comes into jeopardy the moment Lady Adrianna Beachwood's father rejects him as a suitor. He devises an ingenious deception to meet her in secret by using his cousin, the respectable, Lord Rupert as a decoy.

Nothing goes to plan and when the feisty goddaughter of George II is thrust into danger, her only chance of survival lies in the hands of her courageous and deliciously handsome Scottish warrior.

Chapter One

Lady Adrianna Beachwood slid into the shadows masking the terrace, her attention captivated on the tall stranger bowing over Lady Bracken's hand in the receiving line. *At last, a gentleman worthy of my consideration.* He straightened and bestowed a brilliant smile on his hostess before moving through the reception room in her direction. Sauntering past in elegant glory leaving the expensive fragrance of bergamot in his wake, he astounded her. Dangerously handsome and with the hungry countenance of a wolf, he cast a predatory gaze over the silk encased ladies gathering in the foyer. From the enthusiastic titters beside her and the flutter of fans in her periphery, his perfect proportions, and elegant form had attracted more than a few ladies devotion.

She admired tall men and he was indeed the most stylish of gentlemen. His magnificent broad shoulders fit snugly inside a dark blue jacket nipped at the waist and worn over crisp ivory linen with an overindulgence of lace in the French mode. Her gaze drifted in wanton abandon from his expertly folded silk cravat tucked into a heavily embroidered waistcoat to his breeches cut tight enough to enhance his long muscular legs. Lifting her fan to hide her heated cheeks, she gaped after him. Rather than covering his head with a wig, he had queued his glossy ebony hair at the nape without one trace of powder, yet he certainly appeared to be a devotee to fashion by the cut of his cloth, and the expensive lace at his cuffs.

Her attention matched his swagger in the direction of the ballroom and entranced by his devilish countenance, she stepped into the hallway and followed him along the passageway. She picked up her step, but he sauntered straight past the ballroom without as much as a glimpse within and continued in the direction of the card room. *Bother!* Adrianna pressed her lips together and stared after him. Determined not to miss the opportunity to catch his eye, she cleared her throat. The temptation of a man stopped abruptly and turned to face her. His languid gaze traveled over her and as he inclined his dark head, the corners of his full mouth twitched into a secretive smile.

A booming voice, announcing the arrival of her father, broke the spell.

"Ah, there you are Adrianna. Why, may I ask do you find it necessary to dally so close to the card room? It is not seemly for a lady to be in close proximity to gamesters, my dear." He moved to her side then his gaze slid past her and darkened at the sight of the handsome stranger. "Come along, I am sure there are more suitable gentlemen waiting to fill your card." He offered his arm.

Annoyed by her father's untimely appearance, she composed her features into a mask of disinterest, and rested one hand on his arm. "I noticed you in the company of Lord Somerton in the receiving room and assumed you would pass this way so I waited for you, Papa."

His nostrils flared in disgust and he bent his head lowering his voice. His acid tongue lashed over her like a whip.

"You are not a girl on her first come out and should know better than to expose yourself to rakes and ne're do wells."

She turned to him aghast. "Oh, Papa, your worry is unfounded. To be sure, Lord Bracken would not allow scoundrels within a mile of Lady Bracken's soiree."

Her father raised both eyebrows and peered at her thoughtfully through his quizzing glass.

"Adrianna, your naivety astounds me. It would seem I will have to keep a closer eye on you this evening." He tucked an errant curl into her chignon with unexpected skill. "Come along, I have arranged for a number of *respectable* gentlemen to make your acquaintance."

A wave of heat crawled up her neck. Indeed, the delicious man had caused her pulse to race in an alarming fashion but with her father's words, the hope of an introduction to the tantalizing stranger splintered into a thousand pieces. She forced her lips into a smile, raised her chin, and strolled into the lushly decorated ballroom. Moving through the crush, she made her way toward her usual bevy of friends. She inhaled to calm her nerves and wrinkled her nose in distaste. The delicate glass vases perched high upon alabaster podiums overflowed with roses but did little to disguise the foul odor of stale sweat permeating the stiflingly hot air. All at once, the room moved in and out of focus.

"Adrianna." Her father's voice cracked like a whip in her ear. "What is amiss?"

Flicking open her fan, she met his furious gaze. "It is very hot in here, Papa. Perhaps a cordial might help?"

Her father lowered his deep voice to a whisper.

"Very well. Sit down and for heaven's sake do not make a scene. It is imperative you fill your card this evening." He offered a congenial smile to the small group watching with interest and deposited her beside a matron. "I will go for some refreshment, Adrianna."

Her heart sank at her father's direction. She had little choice but to act the dutiful daughter, although the men her father had thrown in her path had become as boring as last week's broadsheets. *How am I to stand another evening like this?* She gathered her wits and smiled. "Thank you, Papa."

The usual old and uninteresting bread puddings of men approached to fill her card. Listening with feigned interest at their nonsensical dialogue, her thoughts returned to the handsome stranger. She swallowed hard and gazed at the group of hopeful suitors. God help her. From this night onward, she would compare all men to him, her phantom of delight.

The desire to catch another glimpse of him consumed her and she ignored the chatter. With effort, she pushed down the overpowering need to lift her skirts and dash back to the card room. She observed the men her father had selected as suitable and none of them cut a dashing figure or had the face of a dark angel. She hid a smile behind her fan forcing her attention to the conversations buzzing around her like a swarm of angry bees, but her thoughts slipped unrestrained to the card room and the temptation within. Good Lord, the man had taken up permanent residence in her mind. One look at him had bewitched her into a witless ninny.

The suffocating devotion from the group of balding, overweight, suitors was unbearable, and waiting for a convenient pause in the conversation, she stood. "Please excuse me for one moment, gentlemen."

She moved through the crush and along the hallway determined to reach her destination by way of the card room. Lifting her ample silk skirts, she weaved through the crowd keen to glimpse the gamester's retreat and the forbidden delights within. Remaining close to the wall, she slipped into the passageway, rounded the corner, and paused beside the card room door. She peeked inside and her heart raced. He sat at a table close to the doorway engaged in conversation with her host, Lord Bracken. From within, she overheard not a Parisian accent as she had expected from his attire, but a deep Scottish brogue as potent as the finest Scotch whisky.

"Aye, I attended King Louis' Court less than a month ago. Du Court is not a man I would do business wi' and he one of the most brutal men I have had the misfortune to meet. He takes great pleasure in decapitating his enemies and displaying their heads on stakes atop the ramparts of his castle." He cleared his throat. "Not to mention the rumors abounding in respect of the suspicious deaths of his two previous wives. The man is a brute and ma advice to ye is to keep well clear of him."

Lord Bracken's deep voice came in reply.

"It would seem the rumors I overheard in Whites held some truth."

She blinked away images of severed heads hoisted upon stakes and took a few deep breaths to calm her nerves. Conversation of such a distressing nature was not for mixed company to be sure. With care not to appear too interested in the contents within, she chanced another swift glance inside and she met a pair of emerald green eyes twinkling with mischief.

Breathless at the sight of him, she pressed one hand to her throat. Heavens above, not only had she caught the deliciously handsome man's attention, but his gaze held an enticing offer of intimacy. Her face grew uncomfortably hot and she raised her fan in a vain attempt to disguise her response to him. Unable to look away from his intense expression, she lingered caught in his spell.

The stranger winked at her and his full tempting mouth twitched into a smile around a gold tipped cheroot holder. Her heart pounded and she froze caught by his sinful attention like a rabbit in a deadly dance with a fox. He lowered deliciously long black lashes, folded his cards on the table, dropped his cheroot into the ashtray, and pushed to his feet.

Anticipation prickled down her spine and her limbs refused the command to move. The stranger strolled toward her with an interested expression on his handsome face. Fighting against the overpowering desire to wait for him, she shut her fan, lifted her nose in a dismissive air, and proceeded along the hallway. His soft footsteps sounded behind her and his hand brushed her elbow. She should not stop but the exotic scent of him enveloped her and all good sense fled. Heart pounding with anticipation, she turned slowly to face him.

He stared down at her from a great height, his eyes a sliver of green beneath hooded lids. His gentle smile sent a tingle of awareness to the junction of her thighs. *Dear God, he is magnificent.*

"Your servant, ma lady." He bowed. "I noticed ye were trying to get ma attention. If ye have something of importance to say to me. This is not the place. Would ye perhaps walk wi' me in the garden?" He offered his arm.

Heat shot up her neck scalding her cheeks. Embarrassed, she bobbed a curtsy and averted her gaze. "I thank you, sir, but as we have not been formally introduced, I fear I must decline."

"A formality easily remedied." He bestowed a devastating smile upon her. "If ye will wait one moment." He bowed and turned back toward the cardroom.

Moments later, he returned with Lord Bracken. Her father's best friend gave her a long considering stare, sighed disapprovingly, and turned to the Scottish gentleman.

"Lady Adrianna Beechwood, may I present Drew Mackenzie from the Clan Makenzie at Badenoch?"

"I am your most obedient servant, ma lady." Mr. Mackenzie bowed low over her hand and brushed his lips across her knuckles leaving a trail of heat then rose. "Now we have been formally introduced, would you, by chance have a space on your dance card for me?"

She lifted her gaze and fell into an ocean of glittering green. "I am afraid my card is full."

He held her gaze and beside him, Lord Bracken cleared his throat.

"I am heartbroken but at least allow me to escort ye to the ballroom." Drew sighed and offered his arm.

Unnerved by the overwhelming desire to melt into his strong arms and damn the consequences, she dragged her senses into a modicum of order, and smiled in her best coquettish manner. "Thank you."

Her pulse raced with every step toward the ballroom. The crush opened like the sea for Moses allowing their passage. People stared and chits dropped open their jaws at the sight of her splendid companion. When they paused on the perimeter of the dance floor, he turned to face her and bowed.

"If ye are not spoken for, I would verra much like to call on ye, ma lady." Mackenzie smiled warmly and met her gaze. "If ye would permit such a thing?"

"I must admit, good sir, you are an intriguing fellow and I would be most happy for you to call on me." She smiled and made her curtsy. "I beg you to excuse me. I find I am late for the first set. Please accept my apologies for disturbing your game."

Unnerved beyond reason, she brushed past him and pushed through the crush spilling from the passageway. The music had started for the first set, and to her relief one of her father's elderly colleagues, Lord Winton, strode toward her, his ruddy cheeks dimpling from a wide smile.

"I believe this is my set?" Lord Winton bowed over her hand dispersing a shower of dust from his overly powdered wig. "May I have the pleasure of escorting you to supper this evening, Lady Adrianna?"

Smiling, she met his gaze. "Yes, I would like that very much, Lord Winton." She gave him her curtsy and laid a hand on his arm.

Standing opposite her partner in the middle of the ballroom, she searched the crowd for Drew Mackenzie, and her heart squeezed at the sight of him. He stood out like a beacon at the edge of the dance floor with one shoulder resting nonchalantly against the wall. He smiled outrageously, then turned and vanished into the crowd.

Her stomach fluttered in an unnerving fashion. In truth, no gentleman had ever looked upon her with desire, after all, her brown curls and fuller figure usually attracted widowers. Indeed, he had caused an unfamiliar curl of desire to blossom inside her and she wanted to experience the thrill again. At last, she had caught a young man's interest. Excited at the thought of their fortuitous introduction, she smiled and could not contain the enthusiasm in her dance steps much to the delight of Lord Winton.

"It is good to see you smile, Lady Adrianna." Lord Winton's violet-scented breath accosted her nose.

She inclined her head and fought back a giggle. "It is a delightful evening to be sure."

To think a dashing young man was interested in her. At one and twenty, she could not afford to lose such an opportunity and making an effort to push his delightful image from her mind, she concentrated on the complicated steps of the dance but to no avail. His handsome face and intimate gaze continued to linger in her consciousness like a forbidden confection.

Drew Mackenzie tried to force his wits into order. Some time had passed since a woman had made such an impression on him. Indeed his heart pounded with a deep attraction that stirred more than his loins. Lady Adrianna was the epitome of his dream lover. She was the essence of a phantom, he craved to love and protect for all time. He could not allow this precious being to slip through his fingers and vowed then and there to throw caution to the wind and pursue her. *I must have her.* He rubbed his chin and stared after her as if he had lost something precious. How could such a beauty be unattached? She had regarded him with a comfortable familiarity and had not flinched at his accent. He wanted her and would do everything necessary to persuade her father he would make a suitable match for her. He would ask his cousin Rupert to make the necessary introductions. He intended to pursue the delightful beauty and discover if his senses had guided him in the right direction and love at first sight really existed.

He inclined his head to acknowledge the arrival of Lord Rupert, the second son of the Duke of Bainbridge, and taking one last glance at the temptress gliding about the dance floor sighed with regret. Business came before pleasure in this instance and Lord Rupert awaited him. He moved through the crush of finely dressed company and made his way toward the elegant gentleman.

Dressed in the height of fashion, Lord Rupert's dandyish attire caught the devotion of both chits and fops. He met his cousin's gaze and wondered if many noticed Rupert's eye color matched his own Mackenzie green and the only trace of Rupert's Highland heritage. Although, now at the age of two and five, he had to admit, Rupert had grown a good breadth of shoulder but the golden curls came straight from his English sire.

He wanted to avoid any undue attention and moved toward an alcove. Not many in society had knowledge of Lord Rupert's Scottish blood and he had no plans to present them with the rumor of a spy in their midst. He bowed. "Your servant, sir. It is good to see ye again, Rupert."

"You are looking exceedingly well, old chap." Rupert bowed and gave him a leg. "Lord Bracken has offered me the use of the library to conduct our business." He led the way through the house and down a passageway. "I must remove myself from the noise. Christ, are my ears deceiving me or have fine ladies so much gossip to discuss they have commenced cackling like a flock of geese?"

Drew followed him along a corridor smelling of beeswax polish. He chuckled. "Aye, would seem they do." He moved to Rupert's side, anxious for some news. "Were you able to purchase some mares for me?"

"Yes, indeed." Rupert stopped beside a pair of double doors and gave the footman standing in the hallway a curt nod. "See that we are not disturbed." He stepped inside the book-lined room and strode toward a table holding a large decanter of whisky and two glasses.

The library had the refinement of elegance, but the lived-in feel was missing. He dropped into a comfortable chair beside the marble fireplace and stretched his legs. "Will they be ready to travel home wi' me? If not, I will arrange for Jamie to meet the ship at Inverness." He grinned. "I have a few ah ... *meetings* to attend to along the French coast in the next month or two."

"Christ, tell me you have refrained from conducting business as *Le Diable Noir*?" Rupert's eyes widened and he groped for the bottle of spirit. "How much longer do you expect to continue in this outrageous fashion before someone of consequence recognizes you?" He poured two drinks then gulped down a glass of whisky in an obvious state of distress "Do stop grinning at me as if you are deranged. Smuggling will see you hanged and well you know it."

"Dinna fash, nayone will recognize me behind the mask. It does not signify. The people I do business with do not move in polite society." He winked. "As *Le Diable Noir*, I do not dress in the mode of *Monsieur* Mackenzie, *le formidable* French wine importer or as a Highlander." He took the glass

Rupert pushed toward him and took a sip. "Now will ye forget about ma affairs and tell me how many mares ye have purchased?"

"Very well, I managed to acquire two mares of excellent breeding from Lord Bradshaw but had the chance to meet with a gentleman from France. You may be acquainted with him, Lord Moreau?" Rupert raised both eyebrows.

Disgust roiled his stomach and he snorted. "Och aye, I ken the wee gomeral. Ye dinna do business wi' the likes of him did ye?"

"No, I am not daft." Rupert sat in the chair opposite. He gave him a look of disdain over the rim of his glass. "I overheard him speaking to Lord Bradshaw about a gentleman selling his stock. Apparently, the Honorable Peter Ramsbottom is the proprietor of a very exclusive breeding establishment in Surrey and Lord Moreau was most inclined to purchase a stallion for his benefactor, one Baron du Court."

"Ye are correct. I would dearly love to obtain one of his verra fine mares." He leaned forward in his chair and gripped Rupert's arm. "Tell me, ye secured at least one of Ramsbottom's mares for me?"

"I would appreciate it greatly if you restrained your enthusiasm. You are breaking my arm." Rupert's face had drained of color.

Drew removed his hand and grinned. "Och, I ken verra well, ye have some muscle protecting your bones under that fine garb. Now stop your blathering and tell me about Ramsbottom's mares."

"Well, I spoke to the gentleman in question and had the pleasure of inspecting his stables. After a considerably long negotiation over four bottles of French wine, it would seem he is not only willing to sell the mares but will have them covered by his Destrier stallion as part of the agreement." Rupert plucked at an invisible piece of fluff on his sleeve then shrugged. "Apparently, Lord Moreau was a little short of the funds required to purchase the stallion or indeed any of the mares at this time. I was most fortunate as Ramsbottom was more than happy to negotiate a sale with me." His mouth curled into a satisfied smile. "In all I have purchased six mares, two from Lord Bradshaw and four of the finest mares from Ramsbottom."

Elation drained from Drew. He did not have the funds available to pay for so many mares. After making a recent investment in a French winery, he would have to wait until next quarter to obtain his share of the profits.

Damnation. He rubbed his chin. "I gather ye will require a wee bit more money to pay for these fine mares?"

"Ah, *well* quite a lot more, actually." Rupert's expression was unreadable.

"I am verra sorry to place ye in such an untenable position, but I will not be able to raise the funds overnight." He had perhaps one hundred guineas in his purse intended for his father on his return to Badenoch. "I did mention my recent investment in French wine, did I not? If ye need more money now, I will have to sell ma townhouse but that could take months."

"No, I would not hear of such a thing. The amount you gave me was ample for the two mares from Lord Bradshaw." Lord Rupert arranged the lace on his cuff before meeting his gaze. "As you know, I have always wanted an excuse to leave London. How would you feel about making me a partner in your stables? I have the means to pay for all the mares and any others you may require." He cleared his throat. "You have the finest stables in Scotland, two fine stallions, and mares of your own. I do understand the imposition, but I would only require a small percentage of the profits."

He gaped at him in disbelief. "Ye mean ye want to leave all this behind and move to Badenoch?" He waved a hand to encompass the entire room. "Have ye gone daft?"

"No, as it happens, I am of quite sound mind." Rupert's mouth lifted in a beatific smile and raised his glass in a mock toast. "Of course, the contract I signed ensured the mares would be covered by the stallion before I settle the account and I would be most happy to escort them to Inverness." He met Drew's gaze over the rim of his glass. "Are we in agreement?"

Astonished, Drew raised his glass. "Aye. *Slainte.*" He emptied his glass and met Rupert's wistful expression. "Why do ye want to leave your home? Are ye in trouble?"

"No, I am *not* in trouble." Rupert smiled ruefully. "What possible attraction does London have for me? I am the second spare, not the heir. At two and five, I have come into my fortune and have no plans to marry or set up a nursery. Life here is fashion, chits on their first come out fluttering their eyelashes at me, and widows trying to get me into their beds." He sighed. "I have fond memories of the holidays I spent with Mother at Badenoch. I miss the freedom and the companionship of my clan—of you and your brothers." He chuckled. "Oh, don't look so appalled, *mo bhilis.* In case it has slipped your mind, my mother made a point of residing at Badenoch for my birth, so in truth, and much to my father's displeasure, I am indeed Scottish, and would prefer to live there."

Many years had passed since Rupert had visited Scotland and it warmed his heart to hear he had not forgotten the Gaelic. He grinned and offered his hand. "Then partners it shall be but an even split, aye? Ye will be verra welcome at Badenoch and aye, I have missed ye too, ye wee fop." He took a sip of his whisky enjoying the rich malt flavor spilling over his taste buds. "I will write to Da and let him ken ye will be returning to the fold. He will be verra pleased to see ye again. What has it been, eight years or more?"

The door flying open and heavy footfalls entering the room prevented Rupert's reply. Drew placed the glass on the table and pushed to his feet to greet the six men regarding him with menace. *Christ, what in Hades have I done now?* The ringleader of the group puffed out his chest like a rooster and his thin mouth turned down at the corners.

"How dare you, sir." The intruder remained ensconced in his company rather than moving to confront him. The gentleman, for he was indeed a gentleman from the diamond pin in his cravat and the heavy gold watch chain attached to one buttonhole of his blue velvet waistcoat, raised a bony finger and pointed at him. "I insist you keep your lecherous intentions away from my daughter or face the consequences."

Chapter Two

Gentlemen." Lord Rupert sprang from his chair and moved between them his hands outstretched. "You must be mistaken, Mister Ma—"

"Get out of my way, Bainbridge, this is none of your concern. My business is with that despicable fortune hunter."

Drew racked his brain for a reply having no notion to whom he had insulted. To be sure, he had not sought comfort with a woman since arriving in London. He bowed. "Your servant, sir, and to whom do I have the pleasure of addressing?"

"*I* am Lord Beachwood, forth Earl of Sussex, physician to His Royal Highness King George."

"Och aye, and ye are addressing Drew Alexander Lachlan Angus James Mackenzie, heir of Laird Mackenzie of Badenoch, and I dinna have the faintest idea to whom ye are referring." He straightened to his full height and the group of men shrank back. He glared at Lord Beachwood. The one thing he despised above all was a man who hid behind his friends during a confrontation. "If it is your daughter ye believe I have disrespected, would it not be prudent to speak on the matter wi' me in private?" He shrugged. "Unless ye believe we are beyond civilized discourse and ye wish to take the matter outside?"

"There will be no discussion, sir." Lord Beachwood scowled at him. "I bring you a warning. The *lady*, you had the effrontery to accost outside the card room happens to be my daughter, Lady Adrianna. I will not have her turned about by the likes of you when Lord Balham has made his offer." He indicated to a thin man beside him of about five and fifty. "I give you fair warning. I do not suffer fortune hunting gamesters sniffing around my daughter and should you so much as glance in her direction, I will inform her godfather, His Royal Highness King George, to send a garrison to

Badenoch or wherever, to exterminate your entire clan. Do—I—make—myself—perfectly—clear?"

Drew cast his attention over the group of men and settled on Lord Bracken. The man had an expression of guilt and refused to meet his gaze. He had followed the desired protocol and Bracken had run straight to her father. The memory of the bonnie lass with the dancing blue eyes and happy smile filled his mind. To be sure, she had held him in an alluring spell from the moment their eyes met and now this pipsqueak would deny him the chance to call on her. Damnation!

"Well, Mackenzie, do you intend to reply, or am I speaking too fast for your sensibilities?"

Somewhat confused by the sudden turn of events, he rubbed his chin. "Aye, Lord Beachwood. I understand ye fine, but I am a trifle mystified as to why ye came charging into a private meeting and made assertions on ma good name wi' out good reason. It was I believe ye good friend Lord Bracken who introduced me to your daughter?"

"No reason? You have overstepped your mark. We English do not behave in such a barbaric manner." Lord Balham preened within the shelter of his friends. "I should call you out."

"I would welcome it, ye wee sparrow." Drew rolled his shoulders. "Outside now if ye please. I have ma second and I am sure one of these fine gentlemen will be more than happy to oblige ye?"

"Stand down, Balham." Lord Rupert moved between them with his lips turned down in a scowl. "This is none of your affair."

Lady Adrianna had welcomed his attendance and no wonder. Her lot in life was not so fine if her father had insisted she consider the likes of Lord Balham. Drew blinked and raked his mind for some reasonable explanation for this man's accusations. He had not mistaken her eager countenance or subtle comment on her pleasure of meeting him. A rush of anger forced him to rethink the situation. To be sure, he would have to protect sweet Lady Adrianna from her intolerable father and dispel any notion of an attraction toward him.

Lord Beachwood puffed out his chest like a rooster readying to signal the approaching dawn.

"Good God man, you can hardly deny insisting Lord Bracken made the introduction nor can you deny forcing my daughter to accept your company to the ballroom." He glared at him spittle forming at the corners of his mouth. "How could she have refused such an offer especially in front of her host? She likely believed you to be an acquaintance."

Drew moved his attention back to Lord Beachwood. "Aye, I do recall having a brief discourse wi' a verra respectable lady and I offered her my arm to prevent her being trapped in the crush. Indeed, she could not remove herself from my side soon enough." He leveled his gaze on Lord Beachwood and raised a brow. "I must admit, I was surprised to find a fine lady dallying in the vicinity of gamesters. Perhaps ye should take better care of her, aye?"

"You impudent pup." Lord Beachwood raised one hand as if to slap him obviously thought better of it and let his arm fall limply to his side.

Drew held the man's angry gaze. "Would ye have preferred me to have left her alone in the presence of gamesters?"

"No, I would not. However, my information differs greatly to your account of events." A satisfied smile crossed Lord Beachwood's lips. "You were, I gather, in a hand of cards with Lord Bracken? He informed me the moment you set eyes on her you folded your hand, and went to her."

He forced his muscles to relax in an effort to control the rising need to teach this arrogant popinjay a lesson in manners. "I dinna have to explain ma actions to ye, but as this is a matter of some importance to ye, I will acquiesce in this instance. As it happens, I agreed to meet Lord Rupert before the first set and merely passed the time in the card room awaiting his arrival. I folded ma hand, the moment the music started and left the room, *not* because I laid eyes upon your daughter." He took a deep breath. "*However*, if the lady in question is affronted, I meant nay disrespect by asking Lord Bracken for an introduction. Indeed, if this is the case, may I attend her and offer ma apology for causing such grievous offense?"

"No, you may *not*." The corner of Beachwood's mouth turned up slightly into a sneer. "In fact, I suggest you leave this residence immediately. Return to the Highlands where scum like you belong."

"Lord Beachwood, I must protest." Lord Rupert stepped between them his hands outstretched. "There is no need for such insults. Mister Mackenzie has told you the truth."

Drew squeezed Rupert's shoulder. "He is a father protecting his daughter and I take nay offense." He met Lord Beachwood's flushed face with a smile. "I am sure ye dinna plan to take this matter further do ye now?"

"I do not have to challenge you to a duel to remove your presence from London." Lord Beachwood gave a sarcastic laugh. "I could destroy you with one stroke of my pen."

Lord Beachwood gave him pause to believe he had a hidden agenda for his daughter and from her reaction to his offer to call on her, one he had not discussed with her. *Without doubt, the poor lass, is a pawn in a game of money or worse, power.* He lifted his chin and smiled. "Will ye now? I think not. Many of your countrymen have business interests in Scotland and ma father is a powerful man."

"You dare to insinuate your father is more powerful than the King of England?" Lord Beachwood scoffed. "I understood the Scots were bacon-brained, but you must have sawdust between *your* ears if you believe such a notion."

"Sawdust for brains, is it?" He straightened and glared down at the man. "Are ye sure ye want to take responsibility for the end of dealings between England and France too? I am a particular friend of King Louis and he holds my counsel in such matters in high regard. Higher, I believe than King George relies on his *physician's* opinion on trade. "

He noticed the flush pinking the tips of Lord Beachwood's ears and straightened. He refused to cower before this inconsequential little man—King Geordie's physician, or no. "Ye are the one wi' maggots in your head if ye believe I would disrespect your daughter. The notion does not signify, so ye may lay down your hackles."

"How dare you speak to me in that fashion, sir?" Lord Beachwood's face had turned an ugly plum color. "You will pay for such insolence."

I would welcome crossing swords with an insufferable dunderhead like you. "You appear to be full of empty threats, sir, but if ye insist, get on wi' it, and select your weapons, because ma time in London is limited." He waited for the space of ten heartbeats then inclined his head. "I thought as much." He turned his back on the group. "Good day to ye."

"There is no need for hostilities, no need at all." Lord Rupert ushered the group from the room. "If you would be so kind as to give us some privacy to conclude our business."

Drew refilled his drink and waited for the sound of footsteps to fade. He emptied the glass and waited for the whisky to steady his nerves. As a Scotsman alone in London, he had little choice but to remain calm and not cause trouble but damn it all to hell, Lord Beachwood's dire threats had not quelled his flames of desire for Lady Adrianna. He had no doubt of her attraction toward him. In fact, the connection between them had burned as if fate had thrown them together. Christ, no other woman had affected his heart with a mere flutter of her eyelashes. He wanted to pursue Lady Adrianna Beachwood and it would seem she belonged to another. *God help me, I am truly cursed.*

"Well, I must say old chap that was interesting." Rupert dropped into the chair opposite. "Did you act like a cad?"

"Nay, do ye really believe I am capable of disrespecting such a fine lady—any woman in fact?"

"No, well *not* intentionally but your reputation with the ladies in France is well known." Rupert raised his glass. "Not that there is anything wrong with such pursuits. In fact, I do believe many gentlemen admire notoriety."

Drew snorted. "I dinna believe ma reputation has anything to do wi' Lord Beachwood's outburst. He called me a 'fortune hunting gamester,' did he not? This is a reputation I have neither earned or desire."

Although, if Lord Beachwood had caught wind of his escapades along the French coast, he would have reason enough to fear his interest in Lady Adrianna. No man of his status would risk his daughter being involved with a notorious smuggler. He sucked in a long breath and let it out slowly. "Why would he believe I am a threat to his daughter? I dinna ken the gentleman and I would assume, he has nay notion of ma business in France."

"Lord Beachwood? Good Lord no. I am the only person in England privy to your business." Lord Rupert looked scandalized. "I would never divulge a word. Perhaps, as you arrived dressed in the height of Parisian fashion, he believes you made your fortune from hellholes and rich French widows." He chuckled. "That being the case, my dear fellow, you would fall well short of his expectations for Lady Adrianna."

Trust a Sassenach to judge a man by the cut of his cloth rather than his honor as a gentleman. He pushed the disagreeable incident aside, in truth, Lady Adrianna intrigued him, and he wanted to discover more about the bonnie lass with the flashing eyes. "Do ye ken Lady Adrianna?"

"Yes, in fact, I do have her confidence." Lord Rupert winked.

"Och aye, why dinna I like the sound of your association wi' such a respectable lady?"

The tips of Lord Rupert's ears pinked.

"For heaven's sake, Drew, I have no carnal interest in her, none at all." He stared at the ceiling as if seeking divine intervention. "If you must know, I often seek the pleasure of her company. We are acquaintances from childhood. My father insisted Lord Beachwood tend my mother during her illness and he resided at the manor for the entire month before she died. He was of the opinion Lady Adrianna would be of some comfort to me as my brothers were away at school. We became close friends. She understands my reluctance toward being leg-shackled, and I her abhorrence of marrying one of her father's widower acquaintances. We have an understanding and I often mark her card at these affairs to give her respite from the old codgers." He smiled. "But I am sure you require more personal information?"

Lady Adrianna had drawn him like a moth to the flame. To be sure, she had befuddled his senses and he had not mistaken her attraction toward him. *I must find a way to see her and know the truth.* Arranging his features in an effort to cover his eagerness for any snippet of information about her, he narrowed his gaze. "Aye, I do but if ye had the pleasure of kenning such a delightful lady since childhood, why in God's name have ye not mentioned her afore?"

Rupert threw both hands in the air and glared at him with an expression of incredulity.

"*You*, my dearest cousin are a notorious smuggler not to mention a *rake* and Adrianna is my particular friend. Why would I risk such a delicate flower with a man of your reputation? If you had once mentioned an intention to enter the marriage mart, she would have been my first consideration for you." He shook one long thin finger at him. "I will not see Lady Adrianna's heart broken. She may not be in her first come out, but she is a kind and genteel lady and deserves better."

Abashed, Drew swallowed the stinging retort to defend his honor and smiled. "I believe I am a deal better than the 'old codgers' ye mentioned, especially, Lord Balham. At least, I would appreciate her as a beautiful woman, not as a means to increase ma fortune." He swirled his drink and forced his anger to subside. "Ye have ma word. Ma intentions are honorable. She is a remarkably beautiful woman and one I would treasure." He lifted his gaze. "I doubt ye will believe me but the moment I set eyes upon her, it was if we had known each other for a lifetime. I asked her permission to call on her and she agreed. Which makes me wonder if she had any notion of her father's intentions. She did not act like a betrothed lady."

"I can assure you, she is not betrothed." Rupert raised a thin blond eyebrow. "But what of your mistresses? I know Lady Adrianna very well and she would expect a significant amount of your attention."

"Aye well, I admit I have had mistresses in France and had one or two fancy bits at Badenoch." Drew smiled. "But I would forgo any mistress for Lady Adrianna's attention." He sighed. "Ma father insists I set up my nursery soon, he wants to see at least one grandson afore he dies. God's truth, I have enjoyed ma life without the trappings of a wife and had not given marriage much thought but the moment I laid eyes on Lady Adrianna every woman I have met afore faded into insignificance. Tell me what ye ken about her." He grimaced. "Although, it would seem I am a wee bit late if the lass is promised to Lord Balham."

"Not at all. Lord Beachwood's mention of a betrothal does not signify." Lord Rupert's green eyes flashed in anger. "I had the pleasure of Lady Adrianna's company this afternoon for a walk in Hyde Park. I have her confidence and would be the first to know if she had received an offer from Lord Balham. In fact, she has declined every gentleman her father has recommended to date." He drummed his fingers on the arm of the chair. "Although, it is possible, Lord Beachwood made a lucrative arrangement with him this eve unbeknown to her." He shrugged. "If he believes you stand to jeopardize his deal it would be a logical reason for him to remove you from the equation."

"Well mayhap, but one would think, he would at least *listen* to my offer." Drew rubbed his chin and brought to mind each detail of the brief meeting. "Unless she did not have time to mention my intention to call on her? Then again, why would he attack my good name without due provocation? It makes no sense."

Rupert's handsome face creased into a frown and he gave a dismissive wave with one hand.

"If Adrianna has mentioned your intentions to her father, I find it hard to believe he warned you off unless he has already made a lucrative match with Lord Balham."

"Or he hates Scots." Drew grimaced. "He had hate in his eyes for me as if I had caused him a great injustice and I have never met the man afore tonight."

"I have never heard mention of his preferences toward Scots." Rupert refilled his glass and sighed. "I agree it makes no sense at all. There was no impropriety on your part and one would think a respectable gentleman such as yourself would make a suitable match for her. You do have an unimpeachable pedigree. On the contrary, I would have thought, he would have been more than happy." He narrowed his gaze. "I am surprised Lady Adrianna has inflamed such desire in you. Are you sure, you are not making too much of this flirtation?"

Drew leaned forward in his chair. "I understand the ways of women fine and she opened to me like a flower in the sun." He smiled at the image dancing across his consciousness. "I caught her eye again during the first set and have nay doubt she finds me agreeable." He rubbed his chin. "She is an honorable woman, aye, and would not have flirted with me if she had accepted an offer and why would she consider a match with Lord Balham? Christ, the man must be close to sixty."

"*Exactly*." Rupert refilled their glasses. "Something is afoot. It makes no sense at all and one would think Lord Beachwood would value her happiness above all things but apparently not." He sipped his drink. "You will need to keep out of sight, but I will remain as close to her as decent for the rest of the evening." He grimaced. "I dare say her father has devised a scheme to force her to marry the old reprobate."

"Force her? Are ye suggesting, he will allow the despicable wee gomeral to *compromise* her then insist she marry him to protect her honor?" Drew pushed to his feet. "Maybe I should be the one doing the compromising?"

"Dear God! Have you lost your wits?" Rupert grasped his arm. "Think man. Beachwood would have you thrown in Newgate. He is very close to the king and has his ear." He sighed. "I beseech you, take my carriage to your townhouse, and stop mooning over this chit."

He glared at his cousin. "I am not 'mooning' over her but for some unfathomable reason I have a powerful compulsion to protect the lass from the likes of Lord Balham." He met Rupert's amused expression with a snort of derision. "Ye can wipe the silly smile off your face, I dinna need a fancy piece. Lady Adrianna is different, aye. I feel it in ma bones."

"You want to *protect* her? Did you by chance hit your head on the way here?" Lord Rupert scrutinized his face for a long moment before his mouth spread into a wide grin. "Dear God you *are* smitten."

"Aye well, if the lass is free to make her choice, I will offer her another option." He rolled his shoulders. Damn, his cousin could read him like a book "Surely ye would agree I am the better man for such a *delicate flower* as ye say?"

"Oh, very well, I will keep a close watch on her this evening and inform you if this is a ruse or not but believe me she is not bacon-brained and will never allow an idiot like Balham to compromise her."

Anger rolled over him at the thought of Lord Balham touching her. He forced down the desire to punch the corpselike weasel into offal and nodded. "Verra well, but afore I leave I must have a wee chat with the lady in *private* ye ken?" He cleared his throat at Rupert's accusing gaze. "Afore I leave, I must discover the way of things between us. Can ye arrange a meeting?" He reached for his drink and swirled the amber liquid around the glass.

"Do you *really* want her for a wife?" Rupert raised his eyebrows. "Or do you find her a contest you must win after being denied her company?" His chest expanded with a deep breath and a puff of air whistled out between his teeth on a grimace. "You could never resist a challenge, could you? I will not risk Lady Adrianna's good name and indeed, heart, if this is your intention."

The image of her flushed face and inviting smile flitted across his mind. Dear Lord, he would carry her image forever. He smiled. "Aye, I would very much like to ken her better and not because her father has denied me, nay not at all. The attraction between us was powerful and I did not imagine it nor do I lust after her." He rubbed the back of his neck and met Rupert's amused gaze. "Aye, well, maybe I *do* a mite but my intentions toward her are honorable." He shrugged. "Lady Adrianna is not a girl in her first come out, she is old enough to understand the way of things. If she is willing, I will court her in secret."

"Indeed, but all such discussion is a waste of time unless you determine if the lady is willing to risk her reputation." Rupert inspected his nails. "I advise you to tread carefully, old chap, if you *do* intend to continue in this reckless manner. Lord Beachwood does not have a forgiving nature. Should one word of this deception reach his ear, he will ship her off to places unknown."

The memory of Lady Adrianna's wide-eyed expression of desire urged him on like an untried lad. "If she agrees to go against her father's wishes and walk out wi' me"—he touched Rupert's arm—"I would be verra much obliged if ye would offer me your assistance and act as chaperone."

A smile lit up Rupert's face.

"Why not indeed? Heaven forbid I should stand in the way of true love. If she agrees to meet you this evening and intends to allow your painful compulsion to woo her, I will make suitable arrangements in your stead." He chuckled. "At least, when the chits believe I have Adrianna on my list of potential brides they will cease pursuing me for a while." He raised both eyebrows. "Of course, I will arrange the meetings within the necessities of decency."

"I thank ye, I would not wish otherwise." Drew sipped his drink and observed his cousin over the rim of the glass. "Do ye think I am a fool for responding so keenly toward a lass I have just met?"

Rupert's expression displayed no signs of chagrin.

"Ah well, life is a concoction of strange occurrences, my friend." He lifted his drink in a toast. "If you are correct and Lady Adrianna is the one destined for you then love will find a way."

"I thank ye. Ye are a good friend and maybe there is more of your mother in ye than ye ken." He sighed. "If Lady

Adrianna is willing, I will see how the land lies between us over the next month." He smiled. "Although, I will have to leave London for a few weeks to take the mares ye have purchased to Badenoch. I will accept your kind offer to accompany the others to Inverness. They are too valuable to travel aboard ship unescorted."

"It will be my pleasure and would suit me well as I do need time to tidy my affairs before leaving London." Rupert rubbed his chin. "Lord Ramsbottom's groom would be an asset to us. I could offer him an inducement to leave his employ to work with us. He would be invaluable to me on the journey to tend the mares. What do you say?"

Drew nodded his acquiescence. "I say a man can never have too many experienced grooms."

"Splendid! I shall inform you the moment the transaction is completed and I have booked passage to Scotland." Lord Rupert strolled to the door, turned the handle, and spoke to the footman. "Have my carriage brought around after supper if you please." He turned back to Drew and smiled warmly. "My carriage is at your disposal on the event you require a swift retreat if the meeting is discovered." He chuckled. "Do not worry too much about all this nonsense with Lord Beachwood, such unpleasantries have a way of resolving in due course."

Lord Beachwood's threats against his clan still rang in his ears and a cold band tightened around his heart. He lifted his chin and sighed. "Aye, they do, but I believe Lord Beachwood is set in his ways."

"Ah, but perhaps *we* can turn the tide of events in your favor. You have lucrative businesses and my father would write a reference, as would my brothers on your behalf to present to Lord Beachwood." Lord Rupert slapped him on the back. "If the lady is willing, I will arrange for a meeting after supper. There is a rotunda situated beside the lake and fortunately concealed by shadows. Wait here until my return and I will take you there." Rupert grinned. "My goodness, I feel like a spy on a mission into enemy territory."

Chapter Three

The evening moved laboriously on without another glimpse of the intriguing Scot, or the opportunity to speak with Lady Bracken about the gentleman. Somewhat distracted, Adrianna failed to take more than a passing interest in the droning conversation of Lord Balham during the course of their set. Indeed, the man spoke without taking a breath as if delivering a long inconsequential speech in the House of Lords.

She glanced at his flushed cheeks noting the hopeful sparkle in his beady black eyes and drew a deep breath. Had she absently agreed to a liaison with him? "I *do* beg your pardon, Lord Balham, I have not heard a word—the music you see is quite deafening, is it not?"

The thin spider of a man sighed and a waft of fine brandy tainted with the reek of foul breath fell over her. He inclined his head and gave her a tight smile, no doubt to disguise his blackened teeth.

"As you are so distracted, my lady, would you prefer to forgo the last set, and take the air with me on the terrace before supper?"

She fluttered her fan to disperse the odor and nodded in agreement. Even in *his* company, the cool evening air, and respite from the noise would be a blessing. Her attention drifted to the grandfather clock in the hallway and the tension in her jaw relaxed. Thank goodness, Lord Winton would be collecting her for supper after the next set, and her time with Lord Balham would be short. She noticed him conversing with her father on the edge of the ballroom and as she moved toward the terrace on Lord Balham's arm, both men smiled at her conspiratorially.

A flicker of impending doom crawled up her spine and without due consideration of the consequences, she pressed her fingers into Lord Balham's arm. He gave her a thin smile and she recoiled releasing her grip. Heaven's above, had he escorted her to the privacy of the terrace with the intention of discussing an offer with her? The hairs on the back of her neck rose in disgust. How much longer did her father intend to thrust dusty old tomes of men at her feet?

"Come along, my dear." Lord Balham tipped his head toward her in a far too familiar fashion.

She compared his pallid countenance and sharp tongue to her new acquaintance. To be sure, Mr. Mackenzie's Scottish brogue had spilled over her like warm honey and the intimate appraisal given from below his long black lashes had undone her. To have such a man call on her would be glorious. Her face grew hot at the notion of swooning in his strong arms and the chance to inhale his intoxicating scent again. He had shown an outrageous amount of interest in her and his absence on the dance floor would indicate he had ignored the bevy of young beauties in their first come out. A glow of happiness engulfed her and she smiled into the darkness.

Cool, fragrant air brushed her cheek and lifted the curls on her neck. She sighed with delight and moved toward the balcony railing to peer into the garden below. Pools of light spilled from the lanterns and illuminated the couples strolling along the garden paths. She stared into the heavens and could not remember a night more beautiful. To be sure, Mr. Drew Mackenzie had given her hope of finding a love match.

Lord Balham's sharp voice at her side snapped her back to reality.

"One must keep one's feet firmly on the ground, Lady Adrianna. Do take your head out of the clouds for I wish to speak with you." He moved closer than propriety considered decent and the sleeve of his brown superfine jacket brushed her hand. "I have spoken with your father and he agrees we would make a good match. He is quite insistent we should dispense with formalities and marry as soon as possible." He slipped one thin arm around her waist. "I will call upon you in the morning to make my offer. We must at least appear to be interested in each other's company."

The image of the handsome Scot shattered. A cry of horror escaped her lips and she stepped away. Rounding on Lord Balham, she pitched her voice loud enough for all to hear. "How dare you, sir. Your actions toward me are well past the point of discretion." She moved beside an astonished matron and her round-eyed charge seeking their protection. "Do not think to compromise me. I have a witness in this good woman. I will not be forced into accepting an offer from you." The rage on his face unnerved her and she stepped behind the matron for safety.

The elderly woman bristled and stuck out her chin.

"Have no fear, Lady Adrianna. I will stand witness against this disreputable fiend."

Lord Balham straightened and his thin lips turned up in a demonic smile.

"As you appear to be a little muddled headed this evening, my dear lady, allow me to clarify the situation before your *witness*. Your father and I have come to an arrangement. I *will* call on you in the morning and make my offer and you *will* accept."

Lord Balham reached nonchalantly into his waistcoat pocket and took out an enameled snuffbox. He placed a delicate pinch on the back of one hand, sniffed the aromatic powder, and sneezed violently. He straightened, and leveled a menacing gaze on her.

"The only words of *agreement* I require from *you,* my dear, is during our marriage ceremony at the church."

She lifted her chin, glad of the small crowd gathering in the doorway. A fine audience indeed to denounce his disagreeable suit. "Are you in your cups, sir, for I can find no other excuse for such intolerable behavior?"

"You *will* accept me or tarnish your father's good name." Lord Balham's face had turned the shade of a beetroot and spittle shot from his mouth. "He *gave* me his word."

Shocked, she pressed a hand to her chest. How could her father consider such a disgusting man as a suitable match for her? She gathered her courage. "My father would not do such thing without first consulting me. Indeed, I would rather lay violent hands upon myself than accept an offer of marriage from *you*, Lord Balham. To be sure, *death* would be a more favorable outcome than to agree to a match with you." She turned and lifting her full skirts glared back at him. "Do not think of following me, sir."

Her head hummed and a pulse thundered in her ears. She turned toward the crowd and the interested spectators parted to allow her to pass. Shock from the encounter had set her knees trembling, but she took a deep breath, straightened, and headed to the retiring room. Word of the confrontation would move through society in seconds. She ignored the women taking respite from the ball, and waving to a servant to attend her, collapsed on a sofa.

A plump round-faced maid approached her and bobbed a curtsey.

"Are you well, milady? Do you require a cloth soaked in vinegar perhaps, or I have some feathers I could burn for you?"

Taking a glass of cordial from a tray on the table, Adrianna forced her trembling lips into a smile. "I thank you for your concern, but I am quite well. I will only require some fresh air. The ballroom is exceedingly hot this evening."

Staring at the gold ornate pattern on the small table, she tapped her fan in the palm of one hand. The memory of the handsome Scott's liquid gaze lingered in her mind. *I do hope my altercation with Lord Balham does not reach his ears. He may have second thoughts about calling on me.*

To be sure, Lord Balham's bold declarations had come without warning and shocked her. The entire affair made no sense. Lord Balham had little to offer. Indeed, his paltry Essex estate offered nothing but boredom. He had no influence over the king, or indeed anyone. His life was as bland as bread and milk. *Why would my father agree to a match with him?* His disturbing words repeated in her mind.

"Your father gave me his word."

To be sure, her father could not force her to accept Lord Balham now, but then again if he *had* given his word, would she be obliged to consider the match to save his honor? *He did not offer me such consideration, did he?*

Resolute, she would refuse Lord Balham no matter what the cost. She placed the glass of cordial on a small table, and addressed the maidservant. "Brandy if you please."

She ignored the woman's scandalized expression. To be sure, she would need more than cordial to bolster her resolve. Taking the drink from a silver tray, she upended the glass, and gasped. The liquid cut a scorching path down her throat, but the throbbing in her head eased and clarity of thought prevailed. Determined to guide her own destiny, she leaned back to form a plan. She would confide her concerns to her good and trusted friend, Lord Rupert, and seek his counsel. He may well be able to introduce her to the Scottish stranger. Yes, if her father was agreeable to old Lord Balham as a match, surely he would give due consideration to a fine young gentleman.

The door opened to admit another housemaid. The girl moved toward her and curtsied her cheeks flushed with excitement.

"Begging pardon, milady, but Lord Rupert is in the hallway. He requests a private word with you. Shall I inform him you are indisposed?"

How fortunate. No doubt, he has come to offer his support. Dear Rupert, I am truly blessed to have such a friend. She bit back the smile hovering on her lips at the girl's flustered demeanor. Lord Rupert had the same effect on most women. "Yes. Please show Lord Rupert to the sitting room and inform him, I will be with him shortly." She waved her from the room.

In her periphery, she noticed a servant wearing white cap and crisp apron, waiting expectantly.

"May I tidy your hair, milady?"

Standing, Adrianna shook out her skirts and moved toward the dressing table. She sat in a white ornate chair before a superbly crafted dressing table of French design and peered with some trepidation into the mirror at her reflection. A woman with an angry disposition and flushed cheeks stared back at her. With considerable effort, she arranged her features into a well-trained expression of haughty disinterest. Powder would cover the irritated blush to her cheeks and years of hiding her innermost thoughts would carry her through the ordeal of discussing her humiliation with Lord Rupert.

A few moments later, curls pinned in place and her gown smoothed, she stepped through the adjoining door into the private sitting room. Lord Rupert stood with his back to the fireplace, his superbly fitted green jacket matched his eyes, and worn over a stylish yellow waistcoat embroidered with rearing horses, he was indeed the epitome of fashion. To be sure, he cut a fine figure of a man, broad of shoulder with a narrow waist, and long legs encased in the finest breeches. His eyes danced with mischief at her arrival.

"My dear Lady Adrianna. I am your most obedient servant." He took her hand and bowed low bestowing a light kiss over her knuckles. He straightened and his gaze flicked toward the maid standing in the open doorway. "As the noise from the ballroom is considerate would you permit me to request a maid or perhaps two remain with us so we may close the door to speak on a private matter?"

She raised one eyebrow in query but he offered no further explanation. Wishing she could read his mind, she nodded in agreement. It would seem Lord Rupert had the ability to mask his thoughts too. She gave her curtsy. "Yes, of course, but I am sure one maid is sufficient to avoid a compromising situation." She turned toward the woman. "Close the door and take a seat over there." She pointed to a window seat at the far end of the room and a safe distance away to avoid anyone eavesdropping on her conversation.

Lord Rupert clasped his hands beneath the tails of his jacket and waited with more than a little apprehension for the woman to retire. On his return from pointing Drew in the direction of the rotunda, he had witnessed the entire outrageous discourse with Lord Balham. The betrayed expression on Lady Adrianna's face as she fled to the retiring room angered him. Her father had treated her more like a chess piece in his particular game of life, rather than a daughter to be loved and cherished. In consequence, he immediately approached Lord Beachwood and requested permission to call on her. After the public denouncement of Lord Balham, her father had dropped his regal façade and practically tripped over his tongue in astonishment.

Lady Adrianna's blue stare and silence unnerved him. He observed her with interest. She gave the outward appearance of serenity as if the unpleasantness with Lord Balham had not occurred. He met her bland expression with a smile and raised his voice for the maid to hear. The below-stairs gossip would be an invaluable asset for his deceit. "My dearest Adrianna, your father has given me permission to call on you." He winked at her dumbfounded countenance. "Would you be in agreement?" He offered his arm and led her to the far end of the room then dropped his voice to a whisper. "May I speak with you about a certain Scottish gentleman?"

Her fan came up to cover her face and the fingers on his arm trembled. Concerned by her distress, he stepped away then noticed her shoulders shook with mirth.

"How fortuitous, I had intended to discuss *him* with *you*." She dropped her fan and her lips curled into a delightful smile. "Surely you do not seek a match with me so what devious plan have you concocted, my lord?"

He drew a deep breath and met her forget-me-not gaze. "I feel for you as a sister, not as a wife and if this offends, I must apologize. However, a certain gentleman who I know to be of good character finds you most desirable and I come in his stead to arrange a meeting." Her cheeks colored and he smiled. "I believe you have given him permission to call on you?"

"Yes, I have but why does he require a go-between and not seek my father's permission to call on me himself?" Both her sienna eyebrows raised in question. "I have given him my thoughts on the matter."

Should he explain her father's threats and risk her immediate rejection of his cousin? No, surely one white lie would do no harm. He shrugged and waved a hand in dismissal. "Unfortunately, at this point in time, I fear he would not pass muster to gain your father's consideration as he has nothing to offer as a prospective match. Although, he is heir to a considerable estate, indeed, he will one day be Laird of Clan Mackenzie and is in a fortuitous business venture with me." He smiled at her astonished expression. "He is not a pauper by any means as I gather you would have noticed by his attire. He comes into a considerable fortune on his majority in six months, is an educated man, and has recently returned from King Louis's Court where he is a confidant of the king."

Adrianna glanced up at him and her eyes rounded in astonishment. She lifted a gold embossed fan to cover her flushed face.

"Is he a rake for he certainly has a way with words?"

Taken aback by her bluntness, he straightened. "I am not at liberty to discuss a gentleman's fancies, but I can convey that his intentions toward you are honorable and should you wish to meet him in the garden this evening after supper, I will act as chaperone."

"A secret meeting?" Her cheeks pinked. "Do you not think that is a trifle unwise?"

He inclined his head and smiled. "I would not condone a meeting with him alone, my lady. I will continue in my role as chaperone to allow you to know him better. Once, he has met the necessary requirements to call on you he will approach your father."

"I *would* like to meet him again and be formally introduced." Adrianna dropped her fan to reveal a brilliant smile. "To be sure, you are a good friend, Rupert." She touched his arm. "My heart is all a twitter to be involved in such scandalous intrigue."

* * * *

Drew paced back and forth along the dark pathway, melting into the shadows each time a couple strolled along the parallel walkway within sight of him. Apprehension shivered down his spine. To act in such a dishonorable fashion with an innocent girl curdled his wame. He snorted in derision at Lord Beachwood's uncharitable words toward him. Christ, did being the son of a Scottish Laird have so little meaning in England, he had to skulk around in the dark rather than openly declare his intentions?

To think King Louis had given him liberty to court any French lady of his choosing and yet he had refused. Indeed, before meeting Lady Adrianna, he had not given a fig about becoming leg-shackled. So why had this particular lass caught his fancy?

He swiped at the swarm of annoying insects buzzing incessantly around his head sending them to join the clouds of gnats hovering around the lamps bordering the pathway. He turned his attention to the lake looming before him, black and dangerous. Weeping willows hung over the water their branches like the bent backs of witches. An owl hooted overhead encouraging the songs of a thousand frogs to sound a warning. The noise and splashes of their dash to safety obliterated the music drifting from the ballroom and left the rotunda in eerie chaos.

He stared at the terrace hoping to catch sight of Lord Rupert and Lady Adrianna moving through the French doors. Would she go against propriety and agree to meet with him? He rolled his shoulders appalled at making such flagitious plans with Rupert. A smuggler he may be, but he placed his honor above all things. Had the chance meeting of one beautiful woman changed his character to such a degree? Disgusted with his lack of chivalry, he dashed a hand through his hair tearing the ribbon from the neat queue. The image of Lady Adrianna in the arms of Lord Balham had infuriated him beyond reason. *I can only hope I am doing the honorable thing by saving a beautiful woman from the clutches of a disgusting old man.*

His attention moved back to the terrace and his heart skipped a beat at the sight of her descending the steps on the arm of Lord Rupert. He moved into the shadows and quickly put his hair to rights. The couple strolled along the pathway nodding and exchanging pleasantries with other couples before slipping unnoticed along the shadowed entrance to the rotunda. As she stepped into view, moonlight poured over her turning her blue eyes into dark, unreadable pools. He drew a deep breath inhaling the floral scent of her and waited for Rupert's introduction.

"My Lady Adrianna, I believe you have met Drew Mackenzie of Badenoch?" Rupert stepped back into the shadows.

Drew reached for her hand and bowing lifted her trembling fingers to his lips. "I am your most obedient servant, ma lady, and I thank you for trusting to meet me in such an unusual fashion."

"Mister Mackenzie." Lady Adrianna bobbed a curtsy but did not withdraw her hand.

Her unexpected boldness unnerved him. He stared down at their linked fingers and for once in his life the witty compliments, he used so frequently to lure a woman to his bed deserted him. Her fingers fluttered in his hand like the uncertain wings of a small bird. He cleared his throat. "Forgive me, ma lady, I suddenly find myself without the words to express how delighted I am ye have agreed to meet with me."

A soft, feminine laugh drifted to his ears and moonlight flooded over her smiling face revealing a flash of perfect white teeth.

"I can assure you, I do not make a practice of meeting strangers under the cover of dark, but I must admit you have me intrigued, Mister Mackenzie." Adrianna giggled. "To be sure, to render a man speechless must be a feat indeed?"

He welcomed the darkness covering the heat rising into his cheeks. "I admit ye are a rare beauty and I hope ye will accept ma apologies for the necessity of meeting ye in such an unseemly manner but nay doubt Rupert has explained why I am unable to approach your father at this time." He moved closer to allow her to view his expression in the stream of moonlight. "However, I am an honorable man so, afore I continue, I must ken the truth of the rumor that ye are betrothed to Lord Balham."

Her small hand closed around his fingers and his heart raced in anticipation.

"A rumor indeed. No, I am not marrying Lord Balham. He attempted to compromise me this evening and I gather with my father's blessing." A flash of anger crossed her countenance and she lifted her chin with a determined air. "I assume you were not privy to the altercation between Lord Balham and myself before supper?"

He met the determined look in her eyes and raised an eyebrow in question. "I did not. I hope the witless idiot dinna touch ye inappropriately?"

"He *did* and I made a public declaration that I would rather commit self-murder than marry *him*." She smiled ruefully and wet her bottom lip in a subtle invitation of intimacy. "To be sure, I would much prefer the attentions of a younger gentleman."

His gaze went to the slick of moisture on her bottom lip and the heat surging to his groin made his breeches intolerably tight. Good Lord, she might yet allow him to kiss her. He forced his dry mouth to form coherent speech. "Well then, if ye prefer a younger gentleman, would ye allow me to call on ye, wi' Lord Rupert as chaperone of course, but I am afraid, without the permission of your father?"

"To what ends, Mister Mackenzie?" She took a single step toward him, tightened her grip, and tilting up her chin scrutinized his expression. "How will clandestine meetings signify if you believe my father will refuse an offer from you?"

"I dare say he will run me out of London if he discovers I met with ye tonight." He covered her hand and bent closer. "Apart from my honor, I have little for him to consider until I reach my majority in six months. I imagine your father would believe I am interested in your fortune and as Lord Rupert can attest, this is not the case, not at all." He sighed. "I asked Lord Rupert to arranged this meeting because I believe there is a spark of something between us and if this is the case then only a fool would want ye accepting a match wi' the likes of Lord Balham."

"You have not answered my question, Mister Mackenzie. To what ends? I admit I flirted with you in the passageway, but I am not a light skirt." Her tongue darted across her lips again as if tasting the passion-filled air between them. "If you do not have noble intentions toward me, there is little point of us meeting again."

"I dinna ken what the future holds for us, but I am an honorable man and do not seek ye as a mistress. However, if ye agree to make ma acquaintance or not, I will abide by your verdict." He sighed and rubbed his thumb in small circles over the back of her gloved hand. "Will ye agree to walk wi' me in the Hampton Court Maze on the morrow and discuss this matter further?"

Rupert's voice came out of the shadows.

"I have received an invitation from the Prince of Wales to attend a garden party and Mister Mackenzie is my guest. I am sure if your father will allow you to accompany me. The maze would be most private."

"Well then, I would like it of all things." Lady Adrianna squeezed Drew's hand. "I will look forward to speaking with you in the sunshine, Mister Mackenzie." She giggled. "As we are acting with such indiscretion, may I use your Christian name?"

"Aye, if I may call you Adrianna?"

He ignored Rupert's snort of disapproval and bent closer to catch her reply. Her words came out on a sigh.

"Please, do." She swayed toward him and pressed one gloved hand on his chest.

"Sweet, Adrianna." Without a second thought, he drew her against him. Rather than pulling away as he had expected, she made soft mewing sounds and gripped the front of his jacket.

He searched her face for any hint of distress then bent to brush a chaste kiss across her damp lips. Her soft mouth opened to him and the taste of white wine and raspberry tart rolled over his tongue. Inexperienced though she was, she responded to him with unexpected passion. The heated feminine scent of her confused his senses, reason fled and he ravished her mouth in a demanding kiss.

"Ah-hem." Rupert gripped his shoulder. "We should be getting back before we are missed or Lord Beachwood will have me leg-shackled to Lady Adrianna by daybreak."

Annoyed by the intrusion, Drew lifted his head from paradise and gazed at her confused expression. Glossy brown curls had fallen from her coiffure to frame her face. Forcing back the desire to take a silken strand and wrap it around his finger, he stepped back and bowed. "I will look forward to our meeting, tomorrow, Adrianna."

Adrianna stared at Drew Mackenzie in disbelief, her gaze traveled over his features blanched gray in the moonlight. His full tempting mouth glistened from their kiss and his eyes watched her with an unnerving intensity. In an effort to take a single breath, she fought the unfamiliar yet desirous emotions surging through her.

He had kissed her.

Heavens above, I kissed him back.

She ran the tip of her tongue across her lips reveling in the taste of him. Goodness, she would not have believed a kiss could be so delightful. The tenderness of his lips sliding so wonderfully over her mouth and the heat from his hard body seeping through her silk bodice had curled her toes. The back of her hand still tingled from his soft caress and her heart raced in a most disconcerting fashion. She caught the flash of white from his smile and swallowed hard.

"Aye, we have an attraction." He bowed then straightened. "The hours will drag unmercifully until we meet again."

Drew's voice washed over her, and Rupert's hand gripped her elbow before she succumbed to a threatening swoon and guided her back toward the house.

"Come along, Adrianna."

The moment they stepped into the light, Rupert regarded her closely.

"Let me look at you." He pushed a curl back into place. "I beg you to hide your swollen lips with your fan before they are noticed. We will take refreshments then go and speak with your father about my intention to escort you to Hampton Court Palace."

She opened her fan and peeked at him over the top. "Thank you. Did you know, my dearest Rupert, I have just experienced my first kiss."

"I assumed so." Rupert offered his arm. "I could not imagine you swooning over Lord Balham or any of your father's cronies." He cleared his throat. "Do be careful, Adrianna. I would hate to see Drew break your heart. As one so innocent, I fear you are somewhat vulnerable to a man of his charms."

She tried to drag her mind from the dreamlike state Drew had induced and smiled. "But did you not insist he is a man of honor."

"He is most honorable." Rupert sighed. "But he is a *man*."

* * * *

In the early hours of the following morning, Adrianna stared into the darkness unable to sleep. She tossed and turned for some hours before slipping from the bed and moving to the window. She threw open the heavy brocade curtains then pressed both hands to the windowsill and stared into the star-filled heavens. From now on, night would hold a special meaning for her. She held the secret of a handsome man bathed in moonlight with soft lips and a demanding kiss. She cupped her breasts and ran the pads of both thumbs over her hard tingling nipples wanting more of him. Drew Mackenzie had ignited a passion in her, a desire she did not understand. Her nurse had failed to describe the delicious hardening of nipples or the rush of damp heat between her legs. Dear Lord, a throb of pleasure curled between her folds at the mere thought of him. Her nurse's instructions on wifely duty had mentioned pain but not pleasure. Sighing, she crawled back into bed and gazed at the sky watching the night fade to a new exciting dawn.

Chapter Four

Each stroke of the valet's brush over Drew's green velvet jacket sent dust motes dancing in the shaft of sunlight streaming through the window of his dressing room. He adjusted his waistcoat and admired his reflection in the standing mirror. The black silk affair with extravagant silver buttons and exceptional embroidery was one of his particular favorites and in the French mode. Dressed in this fashion, he would easily pass for a French lord, especially in the company of Lord Rupert. After two years abroad, his Parisian accent was faultless, so why did he suffer the annoying cramping of his wame? He pulled on his gloves and glared at his image with such distaste his valet dropped the brush with a troubled expression.

"Is there anything amiss, milord?" Rotheram fluttered his arms like a butterfly pinned to a collector's board.

Drew cleared his throat. "Not at all, I had the occasion to dwell on an unpleasant memory is all."

Why on God's Earth had he risen before dawn and paced his study like an untried youth contemplating his first call on a lady? He did not have the slightest concern about meeting the Prince of Wales. As Lord Rupert's guest, Prince Frederick would accept him without question especially as he had the good fortune to speak fluent German, and had the same interest as the prince. To be sure, his malaise came from the prospect of bathing in Lady Adrianna's beauty and traveling in such an intimate fashion with her to Hampton Court. No other woman had lured him into her web of delights with such intensity. His mouth twitched unnervingly and threatened to spread into a smile at the memory of her kiss. He clamped his jaw shut and arranged the French lace at his cuffs. *Rotheram will be convinced I have lost my wits if I grin like a ninny.*

Sweet Adrianna was very different from the women who usually attracted his attention. He did not have to bend double to kiss her and her lush body fitted well against him. Her silken curls reminded him of the rich golden brown of a horse chestnut newly escaped from its husk. Not a dull brown, to be sure, but alive with streaks of gold. Why had the young bucks overlooked her at her first come out? If not for her remarkable countenance then surely her intelligent, witty mind would be favorable. Then again, it would seem the current mode for a *suitable* female in polite English society preordained women to be *petite*, blonde, with the penchant of aimless twittering. No wonder, he had never had the slightest inclination to become leg-shackled to a Sassenach and had spent his time with a procession of widows.

He arranged his features to display his usual dispassionate air and took the hat offered by Rotheram. "It is a beautiful day for a walk in the gardens of Hampton Court Palace and I should not require ma cloak but bring it along. I will be in ma study. Inform me the moment Lord Rupert arrives."

"Yes, milord." Rotheram opened the dressing room door and bowed low.

* * * *

Lord Rupert's carriage, complete with four exquisite grays arrived spot on time. Inside Adrianna leaned against the red velvet squabs, her heart pounding with excitement at meeting Drew again. How bold to think of him in such an intimate fashion. She smiled at Lord Rupert and fingered the ribbons on her pale blue dress. She had taken care with her appearance and worn her most spectacular hat, complete with a daring silk bow and ostrich feather.

"You are the epitome of beauty, my dear." Lord Rupert inclined his head. "I dare say, you will be the talk of the town."

"You always give me the nicest compliments, my lord." She inclined her head. "To be sure, I will be the food of much gossip walking out alone with you today."

"Ah, but we will not be alone." Lord Rupert's full mouth twitched into a smile. "We will be traveling with Mister Mackenzie. Indeed, we are just now arriving at his townhouse." He waved toward a stylish house in a tree-lined street. "Will you excuse me for one moment, my lady?" The door opened and he stepped out.

Moments later, he emerged with Drew dressed in an elegant emerald green affair to match his eyes. Her mouth watered at the sight of the handsome Scot moving toward her in long strides. The door to the carriage opened and in a flourish, he removed his hat, and gave her an elegant bow.

"I am your most obedient servant, ma lady." Drew climbed into the carriage in a cloud of bergamot and sat facing her. He smiled and his eyes danced with mischief. "Ye are a vision of loveliness to be sure. I am honored and much relieved ye have agreed to see me again."

Oh my, you are a vision of forbidden delights and you smell divine. She offered him her most coquettish smile. "How could I refuse such an intriguing offer?"

"Intriguing indeed and one, I might add, fraught with danger." Lord Rupert dropped onto the seat beside Drew and removed his hat. "As luck would have it, the invitations to the Prince of Wales's garden party have been restricted to a few close friends. I know for certain, none of the people attending will recognize Mister Mackenzie."

"I beg ye both to refer to me by ma Christian name, we are all involved in this deceit and are way past the necessities of formality." Drew's green gaze narrowed on her. "For your protection, ma lady, I have decided to be introduced to the Prince of Wales as Lord Alexander and will speak French if we should encounter anyone at all or German if I am required to speak with the prince." He smiled at her. "It will appear I am the one acting as chaperone, as we all ken what a lecherous lad Rupert is, aye."

She smiled. Rupert's ears had turned a delicate rose pink. Her attention moved between the two gentlemen and settled on their eyes. To be sure, Drew was dark haired and tall with broad shoulders while Rupert was smaller in stature and no wig could match his impressive mass of golden curls, but the shape and color of their eyes matched as if they were brothers. The familiar way Drew spoke to him told of a long association or indeed as one might speak with a brother. *An illegitimate brother?* Heavens above, no wonder Drew refused to approach her father.

"Are you quite well, Adrianna?" Lord Rupert gave her a quizzical gaze.

How could she possibly approach the subject? She could not in all honesty continue in this fashion if indeed, Drew was one of the Duke of Bainbridge's by-blows. Dear God, she might as well elope with a groom. Gathering her courage, she met Rupert's gaze. "You seem to be on very familiar terms with Mister Mackenzie, my lord. I find myself wondering why you have never mentioned him to me."

"Mister Mackenzie is it again, lass?" Drew leaned back in the seat and stretched his long legs. One muscular calf clad in an immaculate white stocking, brushed the hem of her dress and her heart raced. He offered a benevolent smile. "I will answer that question for ye. We are cousins, but since ma Auntie Jenny died, the Duke of Bainbridge refuses to acknowledge ma family." He sighed. "I dinna think Rupert would mention me as we rarely see each other anymore. I have lived in France for two years past and afore that, ye would have been a mite too young to discuss suitable beaus. Rupert and I grew up together until he left Scotland to attend school in London." He lifted a dark eyebrow. "I raised the very same question with Rupert about ye."

She relaxed although, his referral to her as "lass" did seem a trifle forward. "I would imagine you have many tales to tell about each other?"

"Aye, I do." Drew's mouth curled into a wicked grin. "Rupert had this wee dog. A frightfully ugly beast, wi' long fur and a wicked bite." He chuckled and grinned at Rupert's obvious discomfiture. "He carried the flea bitten rodent everywhere wi' him, like a wee dolly." He chortled and squeezed his impressive bulk into the corner of the carriage.

She bit back a grin at Rupert's tragic expression. "Is he by chance, referring to Fru?"

Rupert, his face the color of a ripe cherry, glared at her. "Yes, I would imagine he is."

"Och, Rupert, the ugly beastie canna still be alive?" Drew raised both eyebrows in an expression of astonishment. "My God, he must be twenty years old or more?" He chuckled with unbridled mirth. "Please tell me, ye dinna still carry the hairy dung beetle under your arm everywhere ye go?"

Rupert gave him a scandalized look. "Well, *yes*. In fact, I do, but my current Fru Fru is less than two—indeed, a mere pup and I can assure you, he does *not* have fleas."

"Well, I must admit, ye smell a might better than ye did afore." Drew sniffed appreciatively. "Do ye douse the wee beastie wi' your own fragrance? I must admit lavender is a might better than wet dog." At Rupert's moan of distress, he held up both hands in surrender snorting with amusement. "Och, dinna get so testy, Rupert. I ken ye loved the wee beastie, but ye should have had a sword in your hand. A wee dog will not protect ye." He turned his attention back to her. "Do you ken the wee beastie, ma lady?"

The image of the small much loved fluffy dog, crossed her mind. Fru Fru was one of a line of companions of the same name. She had comforted Rupert and attended the garden funeral of his last Fru Fru. To be sure, in a home where Lord Rupert's father regarded him as the lesser son, he needed the friendship of his little dog. She forced down the giggle rising in her throat and gave Rupert an apologetic nod. "Yes, and I happen to love Fru Fru. He is more than welcome to come with you when you attend me, dearest Rupert."

Rupert gave her a courteous nod then rounded on Drew.

"At least I carry my dog under one arm and do not wear it hanging from my waist on a belt to keep my skirts from falling down."

"Och aye?" Drew grinned in a flash of white. "I gather ye are referring to ma sporran? I did not make it from a dog. It came from the pelt of wolf who tried to kill ma horse." He wiggled his eyebrows. "Now then, stop this coarse talk afore ye frighten Adrianna." He turned to her and offered an apologetic smile that did not quench the laughter in his eyes. "I am sorry for ma teasing but as ye can imagine, poor Rupert here, is used to it."

Rupert's mouth twitched at the corners in a hint of amusement.

"Well, we cannot choose our sires and although my mother has the bloodlines of Highlanders, it would seem I favor my father in every aspect apart from the Mackenzie green eyes." He shrugged and smiled at her. "I'm afraid, being a great deal smaller than my cousins did not bode well for me during my time at Foiseil Castle."

"Aye, well for some years we thought ye were a lassie." Drew snorted and slapped Rupert on the knee. "Ye can imagine the shock when we dragged back those golden curls and caught sight of his face."

Adrianna glared at him. To be sure, Lord Rupert was a most handsome man. Although, fair of face and without the sharp features of most men, she could not condone such a statement. "I find Rupert's countenance most pleasing. Indeed, he is looked upon kindly by every woman in my acquaintance." She stiffened and flicked open her fan to display her annoyance. "To be sure, *Lord* Rupert does not have to sneak around in order to meet women like you do *Mister* Mackenzie."

"Oh, well met my lady." Rupert preened and raised a fair eyebrow.

"Och, I *am* sorry, Rupert." Drew looked anything but apologetic. "I never said ye were ugly. I ken ye have women swooning at your feet. I should have explained how much ye resemble your father." He turned to gaze out of the window. "Ah, our journey is at an end. I can see the lions atop the gates of Hampton Court Palace in the distance." He smiled at her. "Will ye accept ma apology, for my bold talk in your presence, ma lady? We will be arriving soon and we canna have ye arriving indisposed."

She cleared her throat and met his gaze. "I am not at all indisposed, in truth I find your conversation stimulating. I would like it of all things for you to continue the stories about your childhood exploits but not at Rupert's expense, if you please."

Drew's intense expression heated her cheeks and flamed a path between her thighs. She cleared her throat and to avoid his flirting paid attention to closing her fan. "I am afraid I have no such wonderful tales of childhood to share. You are a most interesting companion and I crave to know more about you."

"I am?" Drew leaned back and observed her for a long minute. "I want to ken everything about ye too."

As the coach swept through the majestic wrought iron gates and rattled down the long wide driveway, she leaned back into the squabs and sighed. Hampton Court Palace had always been a favorite place to visit, but of late, her father had preferred to keep her well away from the Prince of Wales and his decadent womanizing. She had no doubt, he trusted Rupert to protect her. She covered a smile with her fan. If he discovered the truth of it, he would have an apoplexy.

The coach stopped before the long red building and a footman approached to open the door and let the steps down. Moments later, she mounted the sweeping staircase on Rupert's arm and they joined the queue and waited for the footman to announce them before she made her curtsy before the Prince of Wales.

Rising, she swallowed hard at the prince's candid gaze. Heaven's above, he was actually assessing her. When he addressed her in broken English, she straightened her spine, and forced her mouth into a small smile.

"You are most beautiful. I am holding a masquerade ball at the end of the month. I do hope you will attend, my dearest Lady Adrianna?"

She inclined her head. "I will be honored, Your Royal Highness."

"Splendid! I will look forward to taking the floor for the first set with you." The prince waved a hand toward Lord

Rupert, and lowered his voice to a whisper. "I will find someone to occupy him so we may become better acquainted, my dear."

At the prince's outrageous declaration, Drew stepped closer to Adrianna and very nearly forgot his deception. The hair on the back of his neck bristled at the thought of the prince touching her. When the footman announced him as Lord Alexander, he gave his bow, and replied in German to His Majesty's questions about the delights of French courtesans. Noticing the scandalized expression on Adrianna's face, he cut short his expressive dialogue, and moved away from the prince as soon as possible. *Ah, the sweet lass, speaks German, and French too no doubt. I will have to mind my tongue.*

He strolled into the gardens and followed his companions to a marquee with a refreshments table and a small group of musicians. His attention moved to the sway of Adrianna's hips and the determined tilt of her chin. His heart sped. Soon he would spend time with her in the maze and in two weeks, he would dance with her at the masquerade ball.

Damn propriety, and the prince, he would fill her card and prevent him from monopolizing her time. It was, after all a masquerade ball, not a soul would know him or care how many times they took to the floor together. The Prince of Wales's guests, so far, consisted of widows or gamesters, and not the elite society usually frequenting Lady Adrianna's circles. God help him, she aroused him and he did not want to frighten her. Indeed, most of his conquests had been anything but innocent. Bold Adrianna may be, but her first kiss had given him the impression she remained pure as driven snow.

Not wanting to appear too anxious to explore the maze and his need to taste her soft, sweet mouth, he encouraged Adrianna to take refreshment, and seated beside Rupert, they listened to the music. He noticed Rupert examining the small gathering with interest and touched his arm. "How did ye manage an invitation to this gathering? These people canna be your usual acquaintances or have I been mistaken about ye?"

"Ah, *no* I do not usually find myself in such interesting company." Rupert lifted his chin toward a young man with large brown eyes and pouty lips. He dropped his voice and spoke in Gaelic. "I assume His Majesty has invited me because he believes I am of a particular persuasion and not because I enjoy a game of cards." He cleared his throat. "Even more so as I requested to bring you along as my particular friend."

"Ah, now it all becomes clear." Drew smiled at his cousin's flushed cheeks. "He made the most outrageous enquiries about my exploits with French courtesans. I gather he had red lips over yonder picked out for your entertainment fore by?" He grinned. "Or is he not to your taste?"

"*Duin do bhuel!*" Rupert glared at him. "This is not something to discuss in mixed company, nor any of your concern."

"Are you arguing again?" Adrianna placed her plate on the table and blotted her lips with a fine linen napkin. "What on earth does, *'Dùin do bhuel'* mean? It is not a language I am familiar with."

"I must apologize, my lady." Lord Rupert inclined his head. "I am afraid I told Drew to ah … 'be quiet,' so I may hear the music." He sighed. "The language is Gaelic."

Drew grinned. He had noticed the subtle byplay between Rupert and the young man the moment they entered the marquee. *He tells me to shut my mouth and yet he must know Adrianna is aware of his preferences. She feels safe with him as she would with a sister.* He sipped his drink avoiding Adrianna's gaze not wanting to offer an explanation. Without doubt, if she ventured to Scotland, she would learn the Gaelic fast enough without his assistance. Placing the glass on the table, he turned to her. "Would you do me the honor of accompanying me to the maze?"

"Indeed." Adrianna smiled. "Are you coming, Rupert?"

"Yes." Rupert got to his feet and offered her his arm. "Some fresh air would be invigorating." He gave Drew a knowing look then led her from the marquee and along a wide pathway toward the maze.

Adrianna placed her fingertips on Rupert's arm and heart racing in anticipation, forced her mind to concentrate on his discussion about the various flowers in the palace gardens, although her mind had other notions apart from the beauty of nature. Having Drew so close beside her, indeed a mere hand span separated them, sent her normal calm exterior into disarray. She flared her nostrils to inhale the delicious scent of a freshly bathed man, oblivious of the late summer rose bushes spread out on each side of the pathway.

As the entrance to the maze came into view, she noticed with some distress the amount of guests milling around. How could she possibly speak in private with Drew with so many others in plain sight?

"Are you familiar with the maze, my lady?" Lord Rupert raised one perfect blond eyebrow and smiled at her.

The memory of her father's teasing at her distress caused her to reply rather sharply. "Yes, I do recall finding myself completely lost inside some years ago and my father made quite a jest of the affair."

"Have no fear. I know this maze like the back of my hand. In fact, there is a small section closed to guests. The groundskeepers are making repairs to the pathway but will not be bothering us today. We will go there and avoid being disturbed or indeed overheard." Rupert led the way onto the grass and she followed him toward the tall clipped hedges surrounding the maze.

Some distance away from the other guests, they turned a corner to find an entrance blocked by a stepladder. Drew moved forward and with an angelic smile lifted the obstacle for her to enter. Once inside the maze, he replaced the ladder and turned his intense gaze on her.

"Will ye walk with me, Adrianna?" He offered his arm. "I have so many questions to ask ye."

"And, I you." She gave Rupert an apologetic smile. "Do you mind?" She placed the tips of her fingers on Drew's green velvet sleeve.

"No, I will remain here and wait for you" Rupert indicated to a nearby bench. "I am sure I can trust Drew to behave like a gentleman." He gave Drew an austere stare.

"Ye can indeed and I thank ye." Drew led her deeper into the shady dark maze. "I do believe there is an arbor at the end of this row." He smiled. "Ah, there it is." He moved into a cozy nook set inside the hedge, took a white silk kerchief from his sleeve, and dusted the wooden bench. "Ma lady." He waved her toward the seat.

She sat down and smoothed her skirts not sure what subject she should offer in conversation. He sat beside her and his muscular thigh brushed her leg sending her heart racing. The heat of him seeped through the material of her dress, the petticoats below, and her shift to warm her in a most disconcerting fashion. When he reached for her hand, she lost all sense of propriety and answered the caress of his thumb with a gentle squeeze of encouragement. Her boldness startled her, as did the heat in his eyes.

Heavens above, he gazed upon her with an expression of sensual delight, his green eyes almost hidden under long black lashes. She could not waste what precious time they had together in idle conversation. In truth, she craved the taste of him and with wanton abandon placed one hand on his chest. Wetting her lips, she caught his sharp intake of breath and lifted her chin. The ostrich feather perched on her hat dropped between them brushing Drew's nose. His eyes crossed for a moment then he snorted with amusement.

"I thought a large blue spider had fallen from the bushes." His teeth flashed white in the dim light. "Would you mind verra much if I removed your hat?" Without waiting for her reply, he skillfully removed the hatpin and lay the offending garment on the bench.

She wanted to offer an apology, but the next moment his mouth closed over her lips. He placed one large hand on her waist and slid her onto his lap. Perched in a precarious position with the heat from his muscular thighs searing her bottom, she gripped his broad shoulders, and melted into his embrace. He traced a path along her lips with the tip of his moist tongue demanding entrance and the delightful taste of sweet wine spilled over her taste buds. She pressed closer moaning in delight and opening her mouth for him. He flicked his inquisitive tongue inside to caress and tease, driving her to insensibility.

He trailed ardent kisses across her chin, down her neck then paused over the neck of her low cut gown and flicked his emerald gaze to her in a subtle request. Gasping, she tipped back her head in acquiescence and heart racing waited for the pleasure to come. However, none of his kisses brushed her bare décolletage. Instead, without taking his gaze from her face, he dipped his long fingers inside the front of her gown and cupped her breast. Flames of need licked her folds and the now familiar wetness leaked between her thighs. She gasped out his name. "Drew, I–I … "

"Hush, sweetness." He skillfully exposed her breasts to the cool air and gently squeezed each throbbing nipple. "I will not hurt ye. Is ma touch pleasurable to ye?"

She gasped her acquiescence then stared at him incoherently as if he held her in an erotic spell. Blinded by lust, she arched into his hand wanting more of his forbidden touch. Aware her legs trembled and not wanting to slip from his lap, she took a firm grip of his shoulder. "This is madness. I hardly know you, but it would seem you have driven all sense from my mind."

"Do I now? Well, that is as it should be between a man and a woman that have a fierce attraction." His husky voice had dropped a full octave. "I have acted inappropriately, but God help me, Adrianna, it is as if we have known each other for a lifetime." He examined her face. "Tell me it is not the same for ye?"

Denial spent a fleeting moment in her mind then melted like the snow in spring. She lifted her chin to meet his hooded gaze. His expression held such tenderness toward her, tears stung the backs of her eyes. God help her, his delightfully slow caresses would see her undone but held with such tenderness in his strong, powerful arms, respectability fled.

She wanted Mister Drew Mackenzie and damn the consequences. "Yes, I feel the same toward you and it is thrilling as well as most disturbing."

"Ye are so verra beautiful." Drew's attention dropped to her exposed breasts. "So white, and full, and your nipples are like ripe cherries begging for me to taste them."

A breeze rustled through the hedges hitting her bare flesh and her nipples tightened but inside she burned for him. Her cheeks flamed. No other man had seen her so uncovered or spoken to her in such an outrageous manner, but she did not want him to stop. She swallowed hard and regarded him with curiosity. "You want to *taste* them? Do tell, is that a normal request?"

"Och, lass, it is a beautiful experience and nothing to be ashamed of, it is the way men pay devotion to women they desire. I am sure ye will find the experience most pleasing." He caressed her aching nipples with his rough thumbs, and she gasped with delight.

He observed her intently, then as if waiting for her to refuse his advances paused his exploration, and rested his hot fingers on her neck. Panting with need, she grasped a handful of his raven hair and boldly kissed him. He made a low growling sound deep in his chest and breaking the kiss bent his head. The moment his mouth closed over one hard bud, flames of passion licked her core. Dear God, she would die of such wicked delights. In abandon, she pressed his head to her and wallowed in the wonderful sensations each lash of his inquisitive tongue produced. She pressed into his embrace, demanding he give his attention to the other breast and he complied with a low satisfied chuckle.

As he suckled, nipped, and grazed his sharp teeth over her sensitive flesh, spirals of delight curled deep inside her soaking core. She clung to him driven to the point of insanity by his lusty attentions and wriggled to relieve the insistent ache between her thighs.

He let out a moan akin to pain and lifted his head.

"I would bid ye to remain still, *mo nighean donn*." He rearranged her position on his lap. "Do I please ye?"

She pressed her thighs together in an attempt to quell the delightful throbbing in her groin and pushed her words out on a moan. "You take me to a strange place indeed. I admit I have never felt so wonderful and yet so bereft."

"Aye, I ken the way of things, but although I yearn for ye too, I will not take this further, not now."

She touched his face, wanting more of the delights he offered. His words of restraint silenced the little worry worm inside her head. "I thank you for your consideration although, I must admit, I do so enjoy your most ardent kisses." She sighed and rested her head on his shoulder. "Your touch makes me restless and long for more, yet I am worried this delight you offer is sinful."

"What ye feel is not wrong when it is with a man who cares for your well-being." He nuzzled her cheek. "I would not dishonor ye by taking ye afore we wed, nor be so low as to have ye on a park bench nay matter if ye begged me. I dinna have to bed ye to ease ye but I will not do so yet. Not until we have an understanding." He brushed tender kisses to the corners of her mouth. "In truth, I have seduced ye. I ken verra well how to please a woman, but I dinna come here to take advantage of ye. Ye are not compromised and may walk away wi' nay harm done."

She cupped his nape and gazed into his liquid emerald eyes. "No harm, you say? Do you believe I would allow any other man to touch me so?"

"Nay. We are verra well matched and ye have responded to me as ye should." He caressed her breast in his large, warm hand. "I also ken ye are new to a man's touch and I have awoken your womanly lust, but I am willing to offer ye so much more than kisses. I *want* ye, Adrianna, but afore ye say anything, ye must ken more about me."

"I know all I need to know. Rupert has informed me of your weakness for mistresses and of your business." She fought against the flames of desire licking between her thighs for coherent words. "I do not want a suitor who beds mistresses, and although your touch drives me to the point of madness, I am seeking a love match."

"So am I and if ye will allow me to call on ye, I will not visit ma mistress, ye have ma word. Indeed, all are in France and I have no reason to return for some time." He glanced toward Lord Rupert waiting inside the entrance to the maze then shrugged. "I am surprised Rupert told ye of ma business, he must trust ye not to speak a word of it to anyone especially your father."

She stared at him blankly for some moments in an effort to get her mind around his declaration. Rupert had mentioned a business concerning horses. Heavens above, could he be involved in racing his beasts? Her father would not approve of such activities, to be sure. No wonder he required time to establish a respectable business before approaching him. Taking a deep breath to steady her racing heart, she smiled. "You have my confidence."

He nodded slowly and met her gaze with a serious expression.

"If who and what I am does not trouble ye. Will ye agree to accept nay other gentleman's attention until I am able to speak wi' your father?" He frowned. "It will mean continuing in this fashion until I am able to obtain references from The Duke of Bainbridge and documentation regarding my business in France. I canna remain in London for more than a month. Much as I desire to remain here and court ye, I will have to return to ma home in Badenoch for a short time." His expression turned to one of deep longing. "I did so want to call on ye in the respectable way ye deserve, but I had to act now because the thought of your father insisting ye wed an old widower makes my blood boil. Will ye do me the honor of waiting for me to return, sweet Adrianna?"

She cupped his chin and met the longing in his emerald eyes. "I would wait forever for you, Drew Mackenzie."

Chapter Five

The following week sped by in a whirlwind of forbidden romance, although Drew's attentions went no further than kissing under the scrutiny of Lord Rupert. Flowers arrived from Drew daily, filling Adrianna's bedroom with the heady scent of roses. The attached cards, unsigned but filled with endearments littered her dressing table. The bouquets of red blooms had become the talk of society with all believing Lord Rupert was on the cusp of making an offer. Indeed, her father greeted him on his arrival and would insist, he take drinks with him in the study. Dear Rupert carried on the ruse in splendid fashion and their *romance* had become the current topic of conversation at every gathering.

When the invitation to the Prince of Wales's masquerade ball arrived she stared at the royal seal, and her heart raced in anticipation. Once again, she would be with Drew in public but to ensure their secrecy, he had decided to cover his long black locks with a wig. No one would recognize him as Drew Mackenzie, not when the Prince of Wales had accepted him as *Monsieur* James Alexander confidant to King Louis.

When the day of the ball arrived, unable to rest after luncheon, she paced the decorative Chinese rug on the bedroom floor wishing the hours would pass and she would be in Drew's arms once more. A knock on the door brought Betty into her room carrying a silver tray adorned with a small box and one single red rose.

"This came for you, milady." Betty smiled. Lord Rupert is such a generous suitor. Do you not find him most handsome?"

She removed the rose and inhaled the sweet fragrance ignoring her servant's impudent question. "This will need water." She replaced it on the silver tray and lifted the box. "Off you go, Betty."

The door closed behind the indignant maid. She smiled. Of course, she would indulge the girl by showing her the contents of the box on her return, but she required a few moments of privacy to enjoy her gift. With care, she unpicked the red ribbon and peered inside. "Oh how charming." She lifted out a silk mask decorated with blue gemstones and admired the superb quality. Pressing it to her face, she turned to the mirror.

Her reflection showed cheeks flushed with excitement, eyes sparkling with love. She lifted the card and read the familiar hand.

Only such gems do justice to your exquisite eyes. I crave your presence. You warm my heart like sunshine on a summer's day.

Until tonight.

A familiar wetness, pooled at the junction of her thighs at the memory of his intimate kisses. Indeed, his ardent devotion of her breasts had near made her beg him to ease her restlessness. In his stead, Rupert called on her almost every day to escort her to their rendezvous. They had strolled every secluded spot available in London then moved further afield. She had fond memories of rambling through the woods at Box Hill with Drew and stealing kisses behind giant oaks.

Her maid, thought her most inconsiderate of Lord Rupert for leaving him cooling his heels in her company. Indeed, the sweet girl could not fathom her sudden desire to be alone to pick wildflowers or to examine a certain exhibit at the museum unattended. To be sure, her extended visits to the necessary had brought raised eyebrows on many occasions. No matter, she would do whatever was required to spend precious time alone with Drew. Later, at the masquerade ball with the guests believing her to be in Lord Rupert's company, she would leave him in plain sight, and sneak away in the pretense of visiting the retiring room to meet Drew.

How delightfully scandalous.

* * * *

Drew stared at the letter in disbelief. He read his brother's rambling scrawl once more and sat down heavily in the chair before the desk. In one fatal blow, Jamie's disastrous news had shattered his bid for respectability, and any chance to offer for Adrianna's hand. He must sell his townhouse at once, to raise the necessary funds to aid his clan and leave for Scotland.

He took the glass of brandy offered by Rotheram and swallowed the contents then lifted his chin to meet his valet's concerned gaze. "Three hundred of my clan are ill with the bloody flux including the healer and now my father has succumbed. Foiseil Castle is defenseless. Seeing our clan so diminished, Clan Munroe conducted a few well-planned raids. They fired our crops, burned the tenant's houses to the ground, and ran off our livestock. I must return home and pray I am in time to help. Pack my bags I will leave at first light."

"I thank God, you are so skilled a healer, sir, I am sure you will put things to right. Do you wish me to purchase any medicinals?" Rotheram raised a brow. "I would imagine the stocks at the castle will be depleted."

Drew took a slip of paper from the drawer and placed it on the desk. His mind in turmoil, he steadied his thoughts, and reaching for a quill, considered what herbs he would need to tend his clan. "Yes, send a footman with this note to the apothecary and tell him to wait." He sanded the document then handed it to him. "It will be necessary to make arrangements with you regarding the staff."

Rotheram's eyes opened wide. "The staff, sir?"

"Indeed. Pack all my personal belongings and set the housekeeper to prepare the house for sale. Instruct Mister Dander, I want all valuables packed, and sent with the remaining staff to Badenoch within the next two weeks." He gave him a tight smile. "Inform them we are returning home."

"Yes, sir." Rotheram carefully folded the note. "Will there be anything else, sir?"

Dear God! He must inform Rupert and Adrianna he would be leaving. He pushed to his feet and turned to his valet. "I am going out, have my carriage brought around and lay out my clothes for the masquerade ball tonight."

Damnation, he had planned to return to Scotland but not now, not so soon in his relationship with Adrianna. What would become of him, if his father died would he ever be able to return to her? As laird, or indeed with his father incapacitated, he would carry the responsibility of protecting the Badenoch tenants. A severely depleted clan would make the defending and running of his estate difficult. He would require assistance but would have to wait until the sickness passed before sending out a calling of the clan.

He rubbed his chin searching his mind for a solution. With the clan's livestock stolen and the crops burned, he would require substantial funds to buy supplies to feed the clan and re-build the tenants houses. He had funds and trusted Rupert to sell his townhouse, but he would have to return to smuggling in the meantime, and not in France, in Scotland. He glanced back at the letter and snorted. Without doubt, Angus Mac Bride, his father's right hand man, would try to gain the clan's backing to appoint him laird in his stead. His only hope lay with his brother, Jamie's determination to ensure his rightful place as the next laird. Although, not yet twenty summers, Jamie had a good head on his shoulders and held the respect of his clansmen. *Aye, Jamie will keep the clan safe in ma stead.*

* * * *

Drew arrived at Lord Rupert's residence in time for afternoon tea. Ushered into the study, he flopped into a large wing-backed chair and handed Rupert the letter from Jamie.

"Christ, if your father dies, do you really think Angus will attempt to gain support as laird?"

"I dinna ken, but if Jamie is worried, he has reason, aye, and the clan will need ma presence to ensure Angus has nay claim. This is not ma only purpose for returning wi' haste."

He rubbed his chin trying to order his thoughts. "I am the only member of the clan able to raise the substantial funds necessary to rebuild and feed the clan until we can replant and harvest the crops. The moment I arrive in Scotland, I have nay choice but to assume the guise of *Le Diable Noir,* and seek a suitable business arrangement."

"And how, pray tell do you intend to achieve such ends after being absent from Scotland for more than two years?" Rupert inclined his head allowing a golden curl to fall over one eye.

"Ye ken verra well *Madame* Josephine is ma go-between in Inverness. I have sent a letter on the mail coach and she will contact a French privateer, by the name of Captain Jacques. He is presently moving along the English coast and should arrive in Inverness afore I do. Although, the blackguard, Baron du Court owns the ship, Jacques is under direct orders from King Louis." He smiled. "I have done business with him afore and I dinna think I will have too much trouble arranging a meeting, there are coves aplenty along the coast."

"Do you have goods to trade in Scotland?" Rupert wrinkled his brow. "Then why not sell them locally and forget this *Le Diable Noir* nonsense?"

"Och, if it were not for the taxes, I would. As luck would have it, I have a warehouse at Inverness, containing a good quantity of the finest brandy. I can trade a quantity of it to Captain Jacques for gold, *if* I can keep it away from the excise men." He grimaced then shrugged. "Then I will make shift to haul twelve barrels of aged whisky from Badenoch and trade them with Jacques the following month for goods I can sell in Inverness. I ken King Louis has a fancy for the Mackenzie whisky." He scratched his chin and turned over the plan in his mind. He would require a substantial amount of money to ensure his clan's welfare. He sighed and met Rupert's concerned gaze. "I need coin and have nay option other than to sell ma townhouse, but that will take time. Can ye arrange the sale in ma absence?"

"Yes, of course. I will set my man of affairs to the task at once." Lord Rupert handed him the letter. "What will you do if the Monroes have taken the whisky too?"

"They would not have found a drop, well mayhap a barrel or two of the raw alcohol in the distillery. To be sure, we have hidden caches of whisky going back a hundred years or more and nayone but ma father and brothers ken where they lie. I would say we have maybe two thousand barrels of aged liquid gold in verra safe places."

"Well, I must say that is somewhat of a relief, however, in the meantime, I will arrange a transfer of funds to the Bank of Scotland and send a missive to Jamie. At least, the clan will be able to replenish their larder in your absence." Rupert snorted and held up one hand. "Do not dare insult me by telling me I am not allowed to help my clan in times of need? I will not hear any objections."

"Aye well, I thank ye." Drew raised his eyebrows. "I am not a pauper yet awhile. I have one hundred guineas but will have to leave a substantial portion with ma butler to pay ma outstanding bills and transport ma belongings and staff to Badenoch."

"Do you want me to inform Adrianna you are leaving?" Rupert grimaced. "She will be heartbroken." He moved to his desk and filled two glasses with whisky. "I do believe she is in love with you." He placed the drink beside the plate of cucumber sandwiches on the side table, and took the seat opposite him.

A deep pain of loss curled around Drew's heart. He swallowed the lump in his throat, and lifted the drink to his lips. He sipped the aged whisky and allowed the warm malty elixir to sooth his wame. *Adrianna*. Leaving her would tear out his heart. He met Rupert's troubled gaze over the rim of his glass. "Aye, there is an attraction betwixt us and I ken my leaving will trouble her. She will nay doubt believe the worse and I will not spoil her time at the ball tonight by mentioning my problems although, she is aware I planned to return home next month. Nay, I want to see her happy and will give her a night to remember. Once we have completed the supper set, I will take her aside to explain why I must return to Badenoch. Hopefully, she will be willing to wait for me." He narrowed his gaze. "Ye will not tell her I have returned to smuggling fore by?"

"I beg your pardon? What do you mean by, 'returned to smuggling'? I have never mentioned such a thing to her. Christ, Drew, do you believe me to be so addle-brained to even mention such a thing?"

"Ye did not tell her? Then how does she ken?"

"I have no notion. You must be mistaken for I only made mention of our business in the stables as a recommendation of your worth, and of course, as a friend it was my duty to make her aware of your mistresses." Rupert shrugged and patted an errant curl into place. "There was no reason for her to know you are *Le Diable Noir*. Before this disastrous news, you planned to put that part of your life behind you. Indeed, you have invested your ill-gotten gains in a profitable business in France. Any gossip toward your intent to be in France for any other reason would be quelled once your involvement in French wine is made known." He shrugged. "Before you return to London I suggest you put *Le Diable Noir* behind you. Lady Adrianna will never hear the like of it from my lips. I am sure your co-conspirators are sworn to secrecy?"

"Aye, no one in France has seen my face. I wear a mask ye ken?"

Should Adrianna discover his life as a smuggler, love may not be enough to persuade her to marry him. He could not take the chance she would be disgusted and turn from him. *She will never find out about Le Diable Noir—will she?* He swallowed hard. "I will not contact her until my business is concluded. I cannot lie to her, not now or ever."

"When *Le Diable Noir* is dead and buried that consideration will not signify. No man is required to disclose *all* his sins to his future wife prior to marriage, but to sooth your conscience, make your confession and peace with God then move on in grace." Rupert lifted his Mackenzie green eyes and glared at him. "And as to why I informed Adrianna about your mistresses, you must remember, she happens to be my *particular* friend, and I did not want to see her hurt by you or indeed any man. She deserved to understand the ramifications of being involved with a man of your reputation." He cleared his throat. "I would do the same again so strike me now if you must and be done with it."

"Och, Rupert, I ken she is your 'particular friend' and I am pleased ye informed her about ma wicked ways. Although, she is nay a wilting flower but a braw lass wi' a mind of her own. If I am able to convince Lord Beachwood I am a suitable husband for her, we will make a fine match." He grinned at his cousin's bravery. "Ye are a good man, Rupert, and I could not wish for a more competent man to protect her during ma absence."

"Then you will have to resolve matters at Badenoch as soon as possible. Has it slipped your mind that I will be removing to Scotland with your horses in the near future? I will not be able to delay my departure for more than two months or I will be obliged to oversee one of my father's estates. I have had a deuce of a time avoiding him and if not for your request to call on Adrianna, I would now be living in perpetual rural boredom."

Drew snorted with laughter. "Och aye, so what does the wet and wild Highlands really have to offer a wee fop like yourself then?"

"You mean, for a man with my *varied* fancies?" Rupert raised his glass in a toast. "Let me just say, *Madame* Josephine's excellent brothel is a *go-between* for me as well."

* * * *

The evening arrived filled with expectation but the moment Adrianna stepped onto the dance floor with Drew, she experienced a strange sensation in the pit of her stomach as if a disaster was imminent. He had been most attentive since her arrival, yet the emerald eyes peeking through his silk mask held regret and not his usual devotion toward her.

Dressed in black with cream ruffled linen and black silk cravat, he was indeed the epitome of style. For a man of his size, he moved through the complicated dance steps with elegant grace. At each turn, she could not fail to notice the admiring glances and coquettish appraisal of the women seated on the edge of the ballroom, indeed, it would seem he had gained the approval of every lady present. The set finished and he returned her to Rupert's side without uttering a word. She gazed up at him and spoke in French to keep the illusion of his identity. "I thank you, *Monsieur* Alexander, for a most enjoyable set."

"The pleasure was indeed mine, my lady." Drew bowed then turned on his heel and vanished into the crush.

She turned to Rupert and placed a trembling hand on his arm. "What is amiss? Is he angered over my set with the prince?"

"Not at all, but you should brace yourself for some unpleasant news." Lord Rupert covered her hand and his handsome face lit up with a smile. "Please do not look on me with such a devastated expression, people will believe I am being a cad." He bent his head toward her in a confidential manner and lowered his voice. "Unfortunately, Drew's father is ill and he will have to return home. I will take you to him so he may explain. He is waiting in the garden for you." He led her from the ballroom.

How much time did she have left to spend with Drew, one week, one day? The thought of him leaving London made her heart ache. She straightened, determined to deal with the situation. She *would* cope without him—somehow.

Although, Rupert made great progress guiding her through the crush, a number of small groups of inquisitive friends halted their progress. She answered polite questions and paused to take refreshment with the Prince of Wales. Not wanting to dance another step with him, she took out her fan and gripped Rupert's arm. "I do beg pardon, my lord, but I find myself indisposed. The heat is making me quite giddy. May we retire to the garden for a breath of fresh air?"

"Of course, my lady." Rupert turned to the prince and bowed. "If you will excuse us, Your Highness?"

"Yes, yes, go along. The night is yet young." The Prince of Wales gave them a dismissive wave.

She moved with Rupert through the French doors and onto the long elegant terrace. A wave of delightful rose fragrance from the vast gardens below filled the breeze caressing her face, but the beauty of the late summer blooms faded into insignificance with each step toward the garden. A woman on the way to the gallows could not have felt worse. To be sure, the thought of Drew leaving her turned her stomach in a most dreadful fashion.

Unable to appear in a hurry to escape the attention of the other guests, they strolled along the path in a languid fashion. She wanted to scream, to run and find Drew and beg him to stay, but how could she expect him to place her above his father or his clan?

Distraught to distraction, she did not notice Rupert had led her around the main building and down a dark path toward the dowager's residence. To her surprise, a candle glowed in the window, although, no one had occupied the house for many years. She stopped mid-stride and glared at Rupert. "Why are we here?"

"*Monsieur* Alexander mentioned to the prince, he was seeking a safe place to conduct a secret rendezvous with a married lady. Of course, the prince thought it a capital idea and put this residence at his disposal." Rupert opened the door and she slipped inside into darkness. "The candle in the upstairs window is the signal that Drew is within." He closed the door behind them and led her down a dark passageway. "He will be in the sitting room. I will enjoy a few glasses of French wine in the study and wait for you." He opened a door and light flooded into the hallway.

She wet her lips at the sight of Drew standing before the fire. He had removed his wig and gazed at her with such intensity her heart missed a beat. When he held out his large hands, she ran to him. Enclosed in his muscular arms, she could not prevent the tears stinging her eyes. "Oh, Drew, I am so sorry to hear about your father."

"Aye, so am I." Drew stroked her hair and bent to brush butterfly kisses over her cheek. "I am heir to Badenoch, but during ma father's illness it would seem the clan has appointed ma godfather to run things in ma stead over ma younger brother, Jamie. I must return at once. Should ma father die and I am absent, Angus has every right to challenge ma place as laird and I will not have ma clan's future given to a man who does not carry the Mackenzie name."

She lifted her chin and stared into bottomless pits of grief. "Take me with you."

"Oh, ma sweet lass, dinna ye ken how much I want to have ye by ma side?" He kissed her with gentle passion then raised his head and met her gaze. "I will not dishonor ye, not any more than I have already by sneaking around like a thief in the night to spend a few precious moments wi' ye." He sighed and pressed her hard against his chest. "Ye must trust me to return to ye. I canna say when I will be able to return to London, but ye have ma word. I want ye, Adrianna, and nay matter what is thrown in ma path to stop me, I *will* come back to ye." He gazed into her eyes with a frightening intensity as if willing her to believe him. "I will not be so far from ye. If ye look at the moon each night at nine o' clock, ken that I will too."

He was so romantic but had not once said he loved her. Could this be his declaration, the promise she must cling to in the lonely times ahead? As he swung her into his strong arms and carried her toward a red satin chaise lounge, all doubt vanished. She sprawled across his lap and devoured his ardent kisses, savoring the delicious taste of him, his exotic scent, and the solid strength of him. She wanted to give herself to him in wanton abandon. "I will miss you so much, you have stolen my heart. Take me, here, now. I beg you give me something to remember, a moment to cherish until we can be together again."

His long fingers fumbled on her buttons and in moments, he had stripped her gown and corset leaving her trembling in her shift. She met his hooded gaze and flames of anticipation licked her folds in erotic heat. He lifted her with gentle care from his lap and placed her on the seat then stood to remove his jacket. He gave her a smile of such tenderness her stomach clenched before he turned to pick up her discarded dress and lay it neatly over a chair. He sat beside her and traced her chin with the tip of one elegantly manicured finger.

"Och, Adrianna, ma sweet innocent lass, I will miss you too and although I would treasure the gift you have offered, I will not take your maidenhead. I would never use you for ma own satisfaction and leave ye ruined, but I will ease your restlessness." He lifted the hem of her shift and pulled it over her head. "I want to look on ye and brand ye in ma mind for the lonely days ahead. Ye are so beautiful, so verra soft wi' skin like the marble statues in Rome. I want to touch ye, and taste every inch of ye. Will ye allow me?" He kneeled beside the sofa.

Her face grew hot and she forced down the urge to cover her breasts from his admiring gaze. She trusted him and ached to have him buried deep inside her, but she understood the need to wait. For now, she would enjoy anything he had to offer. He had promised to return for her and she would cherish their time together and look forward to a future by his side. She held up her arms to him and forced her trembling lips into a smile. "I would like that very much."

"Ye will not be sorry." He trailed his cool fingertips over her breasts and bent to capture her mouth.

She arched into his caress and opened for his exploration. The taste of whisky exploded across her tongue and she moaned kissing him back with passion. His touch set her aflame, her nipples hardened to painful peaks, and she gripped his shoulders in an effort to drag his mouth down to sooth them.

"Ye will make a demanding lover. Ma dream is to have ye in my bed and make ye scream out ma name in desire, but I will not have ye without the sacrament of marriage." He lowered his head and used the tip of his inquisitive wet tongue to circle each tingling nipple. "Mmm, you taste better each time." His attention moved downward in slow deliberation. "You have such an exquisite navel." He circled then plunged inside making her tremble with anticipation.

Heat filled her cheeks. "Am I not a deal larger than most women? Indeed, my height and fullness are my downfall as is my hair. Most gentlemen prefer petite blonde ladies."

"I dinna like skinny women and your hair is magnificent. A man would be blind to now see ye are perfect in every way." He raised one dark eyebrow and smiled. "Grasp the arm of the chair and dinna let go until I tell ye. I want to see your perfection stretched out and open for my touch."

Restless, she tossed her head from side to side but complied and gripped the arm of the chair behind her. A wave of panic hit her. Heavens above, would the wetness coating her inner thighs disgust him? She pushed all thoughts aside, the moment his mouth closed around one nipple and then the other. "Oh!"

"Do ye like ma touch?" Drew lifted his head, his lips wet, and glossy. "I would hope so because ye taste verra fine."

She blinked and tried to make sense of his words. The art of conversation had fled and she nodded.

"Ye are so beautiful, so verra beautiful." He palmed her breast in one hot hand and scraped his nails across her sensitive buds.

Each of his movements, each gentle caress, or teasing pinch drove her mad with desire. When he cupped her mound, she rolled her hips to meet the tantalizing strokes of his long, skillful fingers, and as the tips slid between her folds and circled her swollen nub, she gasped in delight. Shimmers of sublime sensation unfurled within her building and surging in wonderful erotic waves. She clung to the chair panting. *Dear God! My head will surely explode if this continues.*

His low chuckle broke through the haze of delirium and his warm breath on her most private parts startled her. She dropped her arms and clamped shut her thighs. "You surely do not intend to taste me there?"

"Aye, I do and as with your breasts, ma touch will only bring ye pleasure. Open your legs for me, Adrianna, and allow me to savor every part of ye." He pushed her knees apart and she dropped one of her feet to the floor opening her to his gaze. "Ye are the most beautiful woman I have ever seen. So wet and needing ma attention. Now, lass, hold onto the chair for I will not stop until ye have reached your conclusion."

She blinked at him unable to understand but did as he commanded. "My what?"

"Hush now and enjoy what I offer ye." He gripped one breast in his large hand then bent his head.

His soft kisses to her mound brought forth instant rolls of tormenting delight tunneling deep inside her. She dug her fingernails into the silk fabric of the chair heedless of the damage and lifted her hips caught in wave after wave of incredible sensations. When he pinched her nipple and tormented the throbbing nub between her folds, she bucked. "Oh, please, I cannot stand such pleasure. It is too much to bear."

Drew held her hips in his large hands then slid them under her to squeeze her bottom in a most delicious fashion. She could do nothing but squirm under the forbidden delight of his expert ministrations. Caught in the flames of rapture, she gasped for air. Heat raced up her thighs and the erotic sensations expanded then flowered into a confection of exquisite delight. Tremors wracked her and her legs jerked uncontrollably, but she wanted more. Placing one foot firmly on the floor, she pushed her aching folds toward his deliciously tormenting mouth.

"Drew, dear God ... I—"

He circled her throbbing nub with the tip of his wicked tongue, then with a feral groan closed his lips over her and suckled hard. Spots danced behind her eyes and with muscles twitching, she rode the crest of erotic euphoria and hovered there on the brink of delight before crashing into lustful oblivion. Floating on a cloud of pleasure, she lay back reveling in his soft kisses. He gathered her in his arms and his damp lips closed over her mouth. She opened to him, accepting the possessive and demanding kiss he offered.

"Ye are *mine*. Nay other may touch ye." Drew growled against her mouth. "Do ye hear me, Adrianna? Ye are *mine*."

She gazed into eyes filled with passion. He had given her a gift to treasure and yet taken nothing for himself. "Yes, I am yours and I will wait for you, I promise."

When he stood, a cold chill brushed over her. Bereft of his heat, she hugged her chest. Pain of loss as deep as mourning gripped her and she took in the sight of him memorizing every inch of his handsome features. How would she survive without him now? She loved him with every part of her being. Heavens, he would see her unhappiness and believe she had not enjoyed their encounter. She would bury the turmoil raging inside her and force her expression into one of blissful happiness. His memory of her must be of love and devotion. When his gaze moved over her face and his lips curled into a satisfied smile, she sighed in relief.

Drew took a jug of warm water from beside the hearth and filled the wash basin. He washed and dried using a thick cloth. Adrianna's face shone with love and contentment. The times they had been together, he had prepared her for his touch, and she had responded well. Her declaration to wait for him had tied an unbreakable knot around his heart and he would do everything in his power to become a suitable match for her. He wanted her father's blessing for her sake and not for her fortune, but whatever the outcome, Lady Adrianna Beachwood belonged to him.

He swallowed hard, hoping the ache deep in his balls would subside. Christ, his beautiful Adrianna's ardent response to his touch had pushed him to the brink of insanity, and how he had abstained from sinking into her liquid heat, he had no idea. Indeed, the madness to have her and damn the consequences had waged war in his head from the moment he touched her. He had overstepped by easing her, but had wanted to demonstrate what she could expect from him in a loving relationship. In truth, he desperately wanted to prove his desire to make her happy in and out of the bedchamber. She perhaps thought of him as a rake, who only sought his own gratification, and he hoped he had rid her of that notion.

He wrung out the cloth and strolled toward her. "Will ye allow me to wash ye?" He unfurled her legs and pressed kisses to her hard pink nipples then lifted his head and smiled at her wide blue gaze. "Will ye remember me now?"

"I will never forget you and not for the exquisite way you made me tremble, but for *you*, the most honorable of gentlemen." She cupped his face and her eyes filled with tears. "I will miss you more than I can say."

He swallowed the lump in his throat and turned away to wipe away the remnants of his lustful advances. She trembled under his touch and the need to comfort her welled up again. He must keep his head, Rupert would return soon and his advances had gone far beyond genteel kisses. His cousin would be well within his rights to be angry. He turned back to her. "Rupert is waiting. I will help ye dress." He stood and gathered her corset and gown. "How will ye busy yourself during ma absence?" He offered his hand and pulled her to her feet.

"I am sure Rupert will keep me company and away from any of my father's acquaintances." Adrianna turned to allow him to tie her laces. "As your clan is sickly, perhaps I should spend some time with my father and at least obtain some knowledge of healing." She stepped into her dress and pulled it over her arms. "To be sure, there are many children, orphans, and street ruffians I can help too if I have a little knowledge of such things."

He buttoned her gown then went about pushing a few dangling curls back into her coiffeur. He turned her to face him and smiled. "I ken about heeling too. Aye, ye should learn as much as ye can from your father. To be sure, we would make a fine pair working side by side." He brushed a kiss across her lips and sighed. "Rupert will continue to call on ye for as long as he is able. Now, I want ye to promise me, if your father makes plans for one of his friends to wed ye, I beg ye to inform me by way of Rupert. He will get word to me and whatever the cost, I will return." He frowned. "Ye ken I canna write to ye, it would not be seemly to do so."

"Yes, I understand and it would be doubtful my father would allow me to read such correspondence. Will you write to Rupert?" Adrianna chewed delightfully on her bottom lip, her blue eyes filled with despair. "Perhaps you could send news of your father and details of your expected return to London?"

He pulled her into his arms. "I will write to Rupert as soon as I am able and send notes to ye. He will show them to you, but they must be destroyed directly." He sighed. "Until I am able to speak to your father, we must keep our secret or all will be lost."

A sharp knock sounded at the door and they sprang apart. Drew grabbed for his wig and pushed it onto his head then turned to face the door. "Yes, who is it?"

"It is Lord Rupert." The door opened and he sauntered inside raising both eyebrows at Adrianna. "It is the last set before supper and you have been absent for over an hour." He smiled and winked at Drew. "I returned to the house and made comment that Lady Adrianna was indisposed. Although, I gather a few matrons have been scouring the palace looking for her." He sniffed the air and his nostrils flared. "I do hope I will not be accompanying the pair of you to Gretna Green?"

Drew glared at his cousin. "What are ye suggesting? Ye have ma word we dinna need to elope. Although the idea has merits, I dinna care for King Geordie sending redcoats after us and to be sure, her father would go straight to him should she go missing."

"No, he would not because Lord Beachwood believes she is with me." Rupert rubbed his chin and stared blankly at the wall. "No, eloping is out of the question. I would return alone and believing the worse, my father would most likely shoot me for dishonoring the family."

"Christ, Rupert, have ye got sawdust between your ears? I dinna say we planned to elope." Drew straightened his waistcoat. "Now take Adrianna back to the house afore her father insists ye marry her. If that should happen, cousin or not, I will be the one doing the killing." He shrugged into his jacket.

"Very well." Rupert moved around Adrianna inspecting her with a critical eye. "You will do." He offered his arm. "Come along."

Tears welled in her beautiful eyes and Drew pulled a handkerchief from his sleeve and handed it to her. "Ye have ma word, Adrianna. I will come back for ye or die trying."

Adrianna's gaze searched his face for long moments and although her lips trembled, she smiled.

"I know you will. Goodbye, Drew. Godspeed and may you find your father recovered." She gave a curtsy.

He bowed and fought the lump closing his throat. "I will not say 'goodbye,' Adrianna. *Au revoir, ma cherie.*"

Chapter Six

Three months later

"I most certainly made an error of judgment by allowing you to attend my patients with me." Lord Beachwood's mouth formed a thin line. "A very grave error indeed and one I regret."

Adrianna stared at her father in disbelief. "I enjoyed visiting the sick with you, Papa." His angry gaze unnerved her. "I am most grateful for the opportunity to learn from you and I must offer an apology if I have overstepped my mark. You see, I have found great satisfaction in helping the sick and needy. I do believe it may be my calling."

"Indeed! If I had known the truth of your intention, I would never have allowed you to accompany me." His lips curled in disgust. "I cannot dare to imagine what will happen if the king gets wind of his goddaughter sneaking out unescorted, let alone discovering you have engaged in treating the pox infected rabble."

He took out a blue enameled gold snuffbox and tapped it as if deciding to indulge. His penetrating gaze sent shivers down her spine.

"Really, Adrianna, I am at my wits end with you. This very morning, Lord Rupert confided, he does not intend to make an offer for you after all and in truth, I do not blame him. Who would take you after reading this?" He slammed a crumpled broadsheet on the table before her depicting an exact representation of her standing in a crowd of scantily clad prostitutes outside a brothel.

She glanced at the headline: *Lady Light Skirt* and her face grew hot. *So they think I am a whore.* "I can ex—"

"How many gentlemen of consequence do you believe will offer for you now?" He grabbed the paper and waved it under her nose. "Not one would dare tarnish his good name with the likes of you, madam."

She gaped at him unable to breathe and waved a hand dismissively as if the article held no consequence. "*Really,* Papa, how could you think such a thing? My giving succor to the sick was not the reason Lord Rupert failed to make an offer. Indeed, Lord Rupert believed my involvement with the sick was a noble gesture."

"*A noble gesture*, you say?" Her father rounded on her eyes blazing. "Yet, he thought it necessary to deliver the damning evidence into my hands?"

She squeezed her eyes shut in an effort to prevent the tears threatening to spill. "Lord Rupert would never do such a thing, not *ever*."

"Look at me." Her father rapped his knuckles on the arm of the chair. "Lord Rupert is so concerned the gossip will ruin his reputation, he is planning to leave London for the country." He snorted with disdain. "My God, and to think you have been friends since childhood."

How difficult it must have been for dear Rupert to speak with her father on such a delicate matter. He had stood beside her in Drew's stead for three months and had discussed how he would respond should her father demand to know his intentions toward her. Not with a disgusting broadsheet but with the excuse, he did not look upon her as a wife but as a sister. She lifted her chin and glared at him. "He told me he would be leaving London on his father's bequest. My working with the sick had nothing to do with his leaving or this filthy rag." She grabbed the broadsheet from her father's hand and tore it into shreds dropping it heedlessly on the Chinese rug. "I have lost *nothing*, Papa, because I would have refused Lord Rupert as well."

"What is wrong with you, Adrianna?" His lip curled into a snarl. "Have you spent so much time wool-gathering you have not noticed the bloom of youth has left your face? Have you not seen the wealth of beauties in their first come out? By the end of the season, you will be too old for consideration by any gentlemen of consequence." He sighed. "Not that it matters now after this public humiliation."

She flinched under his cruel words and dropped her gaze to her lap. How she wished she could mention her love for Drew Mackenzie but she dare not. Since meeting him, she had wanted to yell his name from the rooftops but had given her word to Rupert to remain silent. After all, Drew had promised to return and his many notes had confirmed his devotion. She understood the problems he faced with his clan took time to resolve and she had a lifetime to wait if necessary. For now, gazing at the moon at nine o' clock each night would have to do. She met her father's furious gaze. "I do not care to marry at this point in time, Father."

"Indeed? Is it not bad enough you have become an embarrassment to me?" His expression hardened. "How do you think society will react seeing your face plastered across a broadsheet? You have made me a laughing stock at Whites and I will not tolerate this situation a moment longer. It is time for me to take a firmer hand in the best interests of all concerned." He took a miniature from his pocket and placed it on the table before her. "Fortunately Baron Jean-Pierre du Court has made an offer, so it would seem your reputation has not yet reached France."

Baron du Court? The name sent a shiver down her spine and the memory of Drew's conversation detailing his barbarianism flooded her mind. She swallowed hard searching for a way to make light of the situation. "An offer? He has never laid eyes on me." She peered at the miniature portrait of the ugly French baron and suppressed a grimace.

"Nevertheless, he sent his man of affairs with his offer and is very keen to wed you as soon as possible." His eyes sparkled with triumph and her stomach roiled in fear.

She had made her choice and would take no other but in an effort to appease him examined the portrait closely. The splendid luncheon of eel pie turned to a brick in her stomach and threatened to rush up the back of her throat. Nauseated, she flicked open her fan to cool the growing warmth flooding her cheeks. Her father's consideration of an offer from such a distasteful old man concerned her.

The image of her handsome Highlander crossed her mind. She remembered his kisses, the soft caress of his lips, his promise to return to her. *He will come and end this farce.* Fear curled in her chest making it hard to breathe. Dear God, if Rupert departed for Scotland, she would have no way of contacting Drew to explain her situation. She pressed her lips together in an attempt to focus on how to deal with the intolerable situation. She required more time and would not allow her father to force her into marriage. Changing her expression to one of disdain, she met her father's unyielding expression. "I *am* sorry, Papa. I cannot accept this gentleman's offer."

"I *insist* you accept his offer, Adrianna." He scowled at her. "Or you will suffer the consequences."

Her mind reeled with the implications of a forced marriage with Baron du Court. Her skin prickled and she flicked the ornate gold frame across the table then sat back in her chair to await her father's wrath. She had to convince him the necessity of finishing the season to allow Drew time to return to London and make his offer. Surely, after refusing so many gentlemen, her father would agree to a match with him. She lifted her chin. "Do as you may, Papa. I will not marry Baron du Court."

Her father's expression had changed from anger to bewilderment. He cleared his throat and his mouth turned up in a benevolent smile. The sight sent a shiver of apprehension scuttling down her spine. Heavens above, he had decided to change his gambit.

"My dear Adrianna, there is no negotiation in this matter. Your come out was four seasons ago. Do you want to die an old maid?" He leaned back in his chair and assumed a less threatening posture. "Baron du Court will introduce you to the French court. Most ladies would jump at the chance to be involved in such distinguished society." He brushed lint from his breeches and smiled. "I suggest you give his suit due consideration because although I cannot hold a gun to your head, I can have you secreted in Bedlam. I am sure most of society believes you have lost your wits."

Anger flared and then flowed into a wave of panic. She drew a breath to steady her nerves and fiddled with the tassel on her fan unable to look at him. Appeasing her father would require her acquiescence. She flashed look at him from below her lashes and could not prevent the sour tone in her voice. "What has the baron offered to make you rush me to the altar against my will?"

"That is none of your concern." He raised one eyebrow in question. "Do you have another solution for the scandal you have caused? Do you have *anyone* on your list of prospective husbands? One who is a deaf mute perhaps?"

She swallowed hard. Dare she tell her father of her promise to wait for Drew? No, she could not. She did not give a fig about her reputation, but one mention of her clandestine meetings with Drew and society would shun Lord Rupert. She groped for another excuse, anything to extend her time in London. Lord Rupert's acquaintances have been very attentive of late and all would make a better match. I will finish the season and then make my decision."

"No one will offer for you after reading the broadsheet. The gossip mill is already turning and you will no longer be seen in public." He frowned and his narrow shoulders shook with anger. "You will stop wasting time and accept Baron du Court's offer and have done with it."

Oh, Drew, I need you. I do not know what to do. "Have you thought of my feelings in this matter? Baron du Court will not do." She rubbed her temples. "Are you blind to the cruelty in his countenance, Papa?"

Her father's dark eyebrows rose to his hairline and he glared down his aristocratic nose at her. One hand came down hard on the arm of the chair.

"I've had enough of this nonsense." He peered at her through his quizzing glass. "You will do as I say."

She flicked her fan to cover her expression of distaste. To be sure, her depiction in a broadsheet did not give him the excuse to treat her in this appalling fashion. Taking a deep breath to steady her fragile nerves, she met her father's glare. She had to give Drew time to return. "Will you at least give me a few days to consider his offer?"

"No, I will not." He wiped a hand over his flushed face. "I have accepted Baron du Court's offer for your own good. You will remove to France and I will not hear another word about it." He glared at her. "This morning I met with his man of affairs and signed a settlement. You will retain your grandfather's inheritance and your mother's estates in Gloucestershire. I have instead provided Baron du Court with a substantial dowry."

Gaping at her father in disbelief, she dropped her fan, and clasped her trembling fingers together in distress. *Drew, oh Drew, I will lose you forever.* Images of Baron du Court's displeasing countenance flooded her mind causing her vision to waver at the edges. The room swayed and an unpleasant taste filled her mouth. What had she done to deserve such treatment? Lips pursed on the edge of a retort, she caught the flash of anger in her father's gaze. Arguing with him when his mind was set would achieve nothing. Instead, she arranged her expression to one of disinterest. "You have made decisions on my future happiness without consulting me and would send me away in dishonor. I am not to blame for a scribbler's fancies."

"It is too late to worry about your honor but society may well forgive you once you are married to a baron." He glared at her. "To redeem my reputation, your betrothal will be announced in the newspapers on your departure." He snorted. "To ensure respectability on your arrival in France, the Countess D' Cologne has offered her home for your convenience and will act as chaperone. Baron du Court will call upon you to make his offer which *you will accept.* You will be married in France at his castle at Muzon. I will be there in good time for the nuptials." He leaned back in his chair and pressed the tips of his fingers together. "When the Baron's ship sails for France you will be on board. He has sent his man of affairs to escort you and your maid. In fact,

Monsieur Moreau is waiting in my study." He pushed to his feet, strode to the door, and spoke to the butler.

She stared at her father in disbelief. He had never intended to consider her thoughts on the matter and the proof waited in the study. She stood on trembling knees and smoothed the skirt of her pale blue morning gown before moving her attention to the insignificant man entering the room. Although, dressed in the height of Parisian fashion, the fine garments did nothing to improve his appearance. Indeed, if she had come across the man prone on a pallet, she would have assumed him dead. A powdered black wig framed a cadaverous face with dark circles cut deep beneath soulless eyes set in a scull-like face. Her gaze slid to a black beauty spot in the guise of a rearing stallion adorning one, sunken ivory cheek in the mode of the French Court.

"*Monsieur* Moreau, may I present my daughter, Lady Adrianna." Her father smiled congenially.

She gave her curtsy and against her better judgment offered a hand. At his touch, ice filled her veins. To be sure, the baron's man of affairs appeared merciless and dangerous. As his kiss lingered on her hand, she set her expression to one of bland disinterest. Good Lord *this* man was to escort her. She stared at him in disbelief and her nostrils filled with the disgusting odor of stale sweat covered by an overindulgence of lavender water.

Monsieur Moreau spoke in a thick Parisian accent.

"Your servant, my lady." He straightened and his amusement of her distress unnerved her. "I will look forward to our trip together. It is an adventure, *non*?"

She had the overwhelming desire to wipe her hand on her skirt, or better still take a long hot bath. His touch revolted her. "I have yet to agree to this match, *Monsieur* Moreau, and I still have much to discuss with my father."

"Ah, I *see*." *Monsieur* Moreau inclined his head and shot a puzzled glance toward her father. "Then I will return to the study and await your decision." He bowed. "My lord."

Agitation flowed from her father and the tension between them crackled in the air. He waited for *Monsieur*

Moreau to leave the room then rounded on her with his eyes blazing.

"There is nothing more to discuss and your rudeness toward *Monsieur* Moreau is unwarranted. Sit down, Adrianna."

The possibility of losing Drew forever slammed into her and unable to stand, she collapsed into a chair. Without his imminent return, all hopes and dreams of a life with her Highlander would crumble to dust. She closed her fist, determined to fight for the man she loved. Setting her attention to pleating her skirt in order to gain time to think, she searched her mind for as many excuses as possible to cause delay.

She drew a deep breath to steady her frayed nerves and straightened. "May I ask why *you* have no plans to escort me, Papa? It would be most unseemly to travel alone with *Monsieur* Moreau." She lifted her gaze. "You do, I assume, intend to view the Baron's estate to ensure my well-being?"

"You make no sense child." Her father stood and towered over her with his hands locked under the tails of his superbly tailored brown velvet jacket. "Baron du Court is one of King Louis's advisors." His dark brows furrowed. "Traveling with your maid at the age of two and twenty is well within the bounds of respectability. I cannot leave London for some time as you know full well, I have patients to consider."

Swallowing the bad taste in her mouth, she regarded her father's expression with interest. She understood the determined set of his jaw, oh yes, he had made up his mind, and any words of protest she uttered would be meaningless. With effort, she ordered her thoughts. If she contacted Rupert immediately, he would have time to inform Drew of her plight. Indeed, her life depended on Drew's presence to change the outcome of her demise.

Forcing back a sigh, she reached for her untouched glass of cordial and sipped meeting her father's thunderous expression over the rim. "Very well but I hope you do not expect me to leave at once. I will need time to prepare for the journey."

"Yes, you will have plenty of time. The voyage will be lengthy as Baron du Court's ship will be delivering goods along the coast as far as Scotland before returning to France."

Scotland? The Baron's ship would lodge a manifest and perhaps Lord Rupert could inform Drew. Mayhap, she could make an excuse to go ashore and meet him. With her reputation already in tatters, eloping with Drew did not signify. She offered her father a small smile. "Who will run the house in my stead, Papa? Will you not miss me?"

"Do not concern yourself over me. I have told you a dozen times or more of my intention to offer for Lady Amelia Duffy and set up a nursery. She is of unimpeachable pedigree and I need a male heir." He raised his quizzing glass and made a noise of soft derision. "I am not getting any younger. My wife will be the mistress of Beachwood Manor."

The enormity of her situation curled around her in a frigid grasp. Her appearance in a broadsheet had not placed her in this intolerable position after all. He had planned a new family and her presence had become redundant. She swallowed the lump in her throat and inclined her head. "Are you sure she will do as a replacement for Mother?"

The familiar tick in his cheek indicated his patience with her was at an end and to persist would cause an irreparable rift between them.

"Enough go to your room, Adrianna."

Aghast, she bent to retrieve her fan and fought back tears. For now, she must act the part of a dutiful daughter, board the ship to France, and hope Drew would rescue her. Straightening, she bobbed a curtsy. "I must apologize, Papa, for placing you in such an intolerable position."

"You have, but all will be forgiven the moment you set foot in France." His thin victorious smile broke her heart.

She arranged her skirts and moved her attention back to the baron's portrait to give her father the impression she had reconsidered. Forcing her lips into a smile, she laid one hand on her father's arm. "Very well, I will go with *Monsieur*

Moreau to France and give consideration to Baron du Court's offer but it is with the greatest reluctance, Papa."

"Thank you. I never intended for us to quarrel." He covered her hand. "You have to believe, I do want what is best for you."

No, Papa, you have only considered what is best for you. She withdrew her hand knowing the truth of it. No amount of good intentions would heal the pain of rejection. She meant nothing to him. Lifting her chin, she bolstered her resolve. She would send a letter to Lord Rupert, but she required more information to relay to Drew. "I gather you have organized a departure date and might I ask on what vessel will I be traveling?"

"The baron's ship goes by the name of *The Black Turtle* and I have yet to make the final plans for your departure." He waved a hand dismissively. "Within the next two months, I would gather."

She clamped her lips together to smother a sigh of relief. Two months would give Drew time to return to London and if he decided the only course was to elope then she would need freedom of movement without her father's constant vigilance. Meeting her father's considering gaze, she spread her hands wide. "Well, Papa, you must understand, I will require new dresses made in the mode of the French Court. You cannot possibly expect me to arrive in France dressed as a pauper."

He straightened as if making a decision.

"Very well, I suggest you visit *Madame* Boucherie this afternoon. Lady Amelia insists on using her. I believe she follows the latest mode."

Biting back a snort of resentment, she inclined her head in resignation. "Thank you, Papa." She lifted her skirts and swept from the room.

Her father had treated her like a girl in her first come out and had not taken into account her intelligence. She would use the generous portion left to her by her grandfather to escape his plans. Very well, he wanted her from his life, and she would leave England. She snorted. *Scotland, not France is my destination.*

The image of Drew's smiling face filled her mind. He had promised to return and time had run out. In the hallway, she waved away her maid, and slumped against the wall. She pulled Drew's linen handkerchief from her pocket, and pressed it to her nose. The scent of him bolstered her courage. *I will see you again.*

She straightened thanking God for her ability to keep her head in a crisis. Lifting her skirts, she made her way to her room, and as she climbed the stairs, the memory of her mother opened in her mind like the petals of a rose. She smiled. The precious stones and gold coins her mother had entrusted to her on her deathbed would see her immediate destiny secured. She would find Drew and return to England to claim her mother's estate. She giggled. *I will look forward to seeing the look on your face, Papa when I return with a husband of my own choosing.*

* * * *

After concluding business with *The Black Turtle* and other vessels along the coast for the past two months, Drew entered the gates of Foiseil Castle with enough food to feed his clan for a month. Finding the keep in chaos, he strode directly to the laird's chamber to discover his father on his deathbed. His brothers, Ian and Jamie stood in the dim light as if guarding the bent figure of his mother sitting beside the bed. In that moment, all hopes and dreams of returning to London and Adrianna fled. The once strong man's skin clung to his bones and the smell of sweat hung heavy in the air. Drew flung open the windows to air the stagnant room. He stared down at his father in disbelief. News had come that his illness had passed and rather than returning to Badenoch, he had spent his time gathering much-needed supplies. "What in Saint Bride happened to ye, Pa?" He touched his pallid damp skin. "Ye dinna look as if the bloody flux has returned. What ails ye?"

His father's voice came out in a cracked whisper, but his eyes held the same determination as ever.

"The Monroe poisoned the wells, I am sure of it. Ma wame is burning and I am coughing blood."

"Aye well, rest easy and I will brew ye a ptisan to sooth the pain."

His father gripped his arm and a determined expression met his gaze.

"It is too late for me, aye. I ken ye will argue, but ye must use what time I have left to make ye presence known." He coughed and a trickle of blood ran from the corner of his mouth. "Angus is gaining favor with the clan, I overheard him planning to make himself laird on ma passing."

Drew patted his shoulder and prayed for the necessary strength to watch his father die. Tears pricked his eyes, but he smiled. "Aye, Jamie told me about the bastard. Dinna fash, I arrived with food aplenty. All ken I have returned home and gave me a fine welcome."

"Good, then bide awhile and tell me about your travels."

Drew sat beside him through a long night and offered what skills he had as a healer to aid his suffering. His father said little but as the first rays of morning spilled through the tapestry covering the window, he turned to him, and twisted the clan ring from his finger.

"Come closer, my sons." His father's green eyes searched the faces of his three boys. "I have been murdered and ask ye to seek vengeance on the Monroe. Guard your mother wi' your lives." With a trembling hand that broke Drew's heart, he pressed the ring into his palm. "I declare ye laird now, go down first thing and call a meeting of the clan, they will swear fealty to ye." He smiled displaying bloodstained teeth. Ma only regret is I dinna see ye wed afore I died."

Drew squeezed his hand. "I have found a bonny lass, wi' hair like the shell of a chestnut and eyes the color of a loch in summer. I will settle things here and then fetch her. Ye will like ma choice, Da."

His father coughed and gasped for breath, red spittle leaked down his chin.

"Aye, well I will die a happy man." He turned his head and reached for his wife's hand. His last words came out in a whisper. "I am *sorry*."

* * * *

The following morning every clansman swore fealty to Drew, and he walked from the Great Hall as Laird Mackenzie. He pushed down the overwhelming grief of losing his father and so many dear friends and relatives, and led the funeral procession to bury his Da beside three of his cousins. He glanced across the lines of kerns in the graveyard and shuddered. With so many dead, the priest had needed to consecrate an additional acre for the burials.

With a heavy heart, he returned to the keep and made his way to his father's study, his sanctuary now. He needed a few moments alone to organize his mind. Opening his father's journal, he skimmed through the pages but found nothing of significance. However, his father had been correct by not placing the blame on the bloody flux for taking his life. All to a man had died of poisoning. He recognized the symptoms the moment he laid eyes on his father's pallid, sweating skin, and purple, swollen, bloodstained tongue. Thank God, Jamie had come to the same conclusion and boarded up the wells then instructed the tenants to haul water from the river.

His father blamed Clan Monroe for poisoning the water and by Jamie's account not three days after the first Mackenzie clansman fell ill, they arrived to burn and pillage. Afore, apart from the odd border raids of a few Mackenzie cattle, they had not dared attack his clan. The men at Badenoch once numbered four hundred clansmen—two hundred of these fine men and many wives and children had died immediately when the poison was at its most potent. The rest had barely escaped with their lives. He could have saved his father if he had returned home a month earlier. He gazed into the heavens. "I am but one man, Lord. What am I to do?"

The door crashed open and Jamie stormed into the study, his green eyes flashing with anger. "Ye ken the houses we built in Downleigi? Jock Murray is in the courtyard wi' three men, he says his son informed him riders wearing Monroe colors burned down the houses, and took the women."

Drew slammed a closed fist on the table overturning a pitcher of ale. The contents pooled then ran over the edge of the desk and dripped to the floor. He dragged his attention away from the dark liquid then gathered his wits. "And where were the men? I gave them explicit orders they were not to leave the village unguarded."

"Aye, ye did true enough." Jamie rubbed his chin and gave him a considering look. "They went hunting. As it has been more than a month since the last raid they thought the women would be safe." He sighed and tossed a dirty piece of paper on the desk. "The Monroe intends to hold the women to ransom."

"Och aye, *ransom,* is it?" He lifted the note between finger and thumb and peered at it dubiously. "Ten women for two casks of ma finest whisky, aye?" He lifted his gaze to his brother and grimaced. "It is obvious we have a spy in our midst. Someone poisoned the wells and told the Monroe when to strike and now they want to discover the direction of our whisky cache." He grinned. "I will give them their due. Fill two barrels with piss and arrange a meeting at the base of Craig Dubh at noon tomorrow. Ye will take a few men and carts to carry the women to safety. I will take twenty men and leave afore dawn. We will hide in the rocks and wait for the misbegotten arse wipes."

Anger blackened his vision. Laird Monroe had misjudged him if he thought he would cower to the likes of him. He pushed to his feet. "You will make the bargain then leave wi' the womenfolk. I am going to kill them all and leave their murdering carcasses to rot on the road, but they can keep their piss, aye."

"Are ye planning a raid on the Monroe?" Ian strolled into the room and gave him a quizzical stare.

Drew straightened and met his younger brother's curious gaze. At sixteen, the lad could hold his own on the battlefield but lacked the ruthlessness of both him and Jamie. "They have murdered our father and taken our women to ransom. Aye, the debt will be paid in blood—their blood."

The boy paled but gave a curt nod of agreement.

"Aye, I would like to join ye to rid the world of Munroe scum."

"And leave the castle unprotected? Nay, lad, not this time. I will need ye here in my stead. Clan Mackenzie has declared war!"

* * * *

Drew rolled his shoulders to relieve the stiffness following the altercation with the Monroe clansmen foolish enough challenge him. Blood splattered his plaid and boots but overcome with exhaustion he sought refuge in the solar. He clenched and unclenched his right hand, glad he had trained with his broadsword daily during his time in France.

The Monroe clansmen had ridden into his trap, dragging the Mackenzie women on ropes behind their horses. Once the women had driven away atop the cart, he had led the charge and cut down the murdering Monroe pigs where they stood. He snorted and collapsed into the chair before the desk. A bottle of his great grandfather's whisky sat on the table before him. He lifted the bottle and ripped the cork from the opening with his teeth then filled a glass. He held the drink high. "Ye are avenged Da,"

A movement caught his eye in the hallway and he noticed his brothers heading toward the door. Ian stepped inside and waved a document in one hand. He motioned him forward. "Did ye want me, lad?"

"A messenger came afore wi' a missive. He said it was urgent business from Lord Rupert." Ian strode into the room and handed him the letter.

"Ye better get in here too, Jamie." He broke the seal and spread the document on the desk. "Close the door, aye and we will see what is so urgent for Rupert to send this by messenger."

He dragged a hand through his hair and re-read Rupert's note. Despair rushed over him with such hopelessness, he moaned in distress. *Oh God, I am, but one man and yet ye force me to choose between ma clan and the woman I love.*

"What has happened?" Jamie leaned forward in his chair. "Drew, for the love of Bride, say something."

He waved a hand at Jamie in dismissal and stared in horror at the letter written in Rupert's flowery scrip. By the end of the month, his beautiful Adrianna would be unwillingly thrust into the hands of Lord Moreau, henchman of Baron du Court, and set aboard a ship he knew well—*The Black Turtle*. He snorted with incredulity. Of all the damnable ships and people Lord Beachwood could have chosen to transport his daughter, he had chosen a pirate with more notoriety than him.

He lifted his attention back to his brothers' pale faces. An explanation was in order but how could he explain his promise to a Sassenach lady? He pushed to his feet and paced up and down before the hearth. The study still held the rosemary and lavender scent of father. The desk was scattered with his discarded quills, and the leather chair held the outline of his massive body. He swallowed the lump rising in his throat. Dear God, he had not had the time to mourn him.

Resolute, he turned to face his brothers. "Ye ken I went to London to arrange the purchase of some mares with Rupert?"

"Aye, but I dinna think a few mares has ye in such a lather? Ye mentioned a lass to Da, has she got your wame in a knot?" Jamie eyed him with suspicion. "What mischief have ye got yourself into this time?"

"Verra well. Give me your word not to mention this to the clan." He waited for both men to nod in agreement. "I met a fine English lady but her father made it verra clear I was not to pursue her." He sighed and raised a brow. "I encouraged Rupert to arrange secret meetings wi' her and I gave her ma word I would settle ma affairs and return to speak wi' her father."

"A Sassenach? Ye want to wed a Sassenach. Have ye lost your wits?" Jamie glared at him. "Now what? Is she wi' child?"

Scandalized, he rounded on Jamie. "Nay, Rupert acted as chaperone I dinna compromise the lass but maybe I should have. Her father, Lord Beachwood, physician to King Geordie, is forcing her to wed Baron du Court and she will be traveling to France on none other than *the Black Turtle*." He snorted in derision. "Under the *protection* of Captain Jacques and Lord Moreau."

"Holy Mother of God." Jamie shot to his feet. "Are ye sure?"

"Aye," He forced down the overpowering need to jump on his horse and ride hell for leather to London to save her and tried to think. "I will need to leave at once and make my offer to prevent this happening."

Jamie eyed the document and his brows knitted.

"Rupert says here, the lass is betrothed to the baron." He lifted eyes filled with sorrow. "Ye canna barge into London and make demands. Her father will not listen to anything ye have to say. What do ye have to offer him against the wealth and position of a title? If ye want this lass then we must be devious, and snatch her out from under his nose, aye."

Drew rubbed the back of his neck. His brother's words cut through his panic and calmed him. He nodded. "I want her for ma wife and she made it plain she is of the same mind."

"Then we must plan our next move but how will ye inform the lady of your intent?" Jamie handed him back the missive. "Mayhap we can use *Le Diable Noir* to cover her escape?"

Could he arrange a meeting with *the Black Turtle* as *Le Diable Noir* and steal Adrianna out from beneath Lord Moreau's nose? He stared at the document in his hand and smiled. "Aye, you may well have the beginnings of a fine plan, Jamie. Rupert mentions that Jacques has business along the coast afore he returns to France and has sent me *the Black Turtle's* manifest. Although, as a privateer I ken he lays anchor off the coast for his clandestine meetings. I have time to arrange a meeting wi' the weasel again." He rubbed the back of his neck. "I will send a missive to *Madame* Josephine to arrange the trade of whisky wi' Captain Jacques. She will get a message to him at his first port of call." He turned to Ian. "Do ye ken if the messenger is still here?"

"Aye, he wants to leave by first light."

"Good, I will send the message wi' him." He ran his gaze over Ian and the thought of sending a young lad in his stead curdled his wame. "I will need your help. *The Black Turtle* will be in London at the end of the month to collect Lady Adrianna. If I send ye wi' *Madame* Josephine's messenger, will ye meet the ship at its first port of call in Scotland and sign onto *The Black Turtle* as a deckhand?"

"A deckhand?" Ian frowned. "I dinna ken a thing about ships."

"Aye, I ken but I need someone I can trust to watch over the lass and I will need Jamie to move the whisky to the meeting place." He took in Ian's shocked expression and smiled. "A short trip, aye, so ye can inform Lady Adrianna of ma plan for her escape. Dinna fash, Captain Jacques treats his men well, ye will be fine."

"And when exactly did *ye* meet him?" Jamie scowled at him. "If I remember, ye remained on the beach and it was me and Angus who conducted business wi' the wee gomeral."

"Och, I have met him afore but as *Monsieur* Alexander but then I wore a fine wig and powdered ma face." Drew grinned. "Nayone kens *Le Diable Noir* is a Highlander and the ruse is necessary to keep the clan's good name out of ma business. This time, he will be dealing wi' *Le Diable Noir* the wicked brigand who stole the Mackenzie whisky." He turned to Ian. "Can ye do it, lad? Will ye help me rescue Lady Adrianna?"

Ian straightened and a determined expression crossed his young features.

"Aye, ye have ma word but are ye sure there is not another way?"

Drew sighed. How could he possibly explain his need to have Adrianna safe by his side? He opened his arms holding his hands palms up in supplication. "Nay, lad, and trading our whisky wi' Captain Jacques will feed the clan this winter and as to the lass, I gave her ma word I would return for her. Ma word of *honor*, Ian, ye would not have me foresworn would ye now?"

"Nay." Ian straightened suddenly looking older than his sixteen years. "I will do whatever is necessary to protect her in your stead."

Drew lifted his chin and met Jamie's puzzled gaze. "Ian has pledged his word to help me. Now will ye stand by ma side, brother of ma heart?"

"Aye well." Jamie shrugged and let out a long sigh. "I suppose someone has to keep ye out of trouble."

Chapter Seven

Light-headed from lack of sleep, and with eyes raw from crying, Adrianna smothered a sob. She had departed before word arrived from Drew and had no choice but to remove to France and the uncertain future awaiting her. Pushing the image of her handsome Scot to the back of her mind, she gathered her wits. Drew would expect her to be strong and find a way to his side and she had a plan of sorts. On arrival in France, she would slip away from Monsieur Moreau and book passage to Scotland on the next available ship. Once in Inverness, she would ask the direction of Foiseil Castle and hire a coach and four.

Although, bolstered by her intent to find Drew, rising in darkness and taking her leave before sunrise like, a thief in the night had disturbed her. More so her father's absence on her departure. She had wept before leaving her home but determined not to show her anxiety to *Monsieur* Moreau she straightened and schooled her expression into one of disinterest.

She stepped down from the carriage and moved through the gloom to the dock. Evil smells accosted her and she pressed a lavender-scented handkerchief to her nose to suffocate the foul odors of rotting fish and night soil buckets. Waiting to board, her attention moved to a group of sailors moving sure-footed along a bouncing strip of soaked glossy wood.

Shivering in the chilled air, she tightened her cloak against the breeze lifting her skirts and seeping through her clothes. In the murky light, tales of ghost ships and giant octopi invaded her mind. *Lord, keep us safe on this journey.*

As if a prediction for the future, the weather had turned foul to mourn her departure and the band of dark clouds looming overhead promised the journey would be treacherous.

She understood the dangers of traveling by sea having read grisly tales of shipwrecks during inclement weather. Storms changed the oceans from a flat azure expanse one moment and into a raging firmament the next. She glanced at her maid's ashen face. Betty had not uttered one word of complaint about accompanying her to France but removed from country, family, and friends, she would be lost. Adrianna smiled to encourage her and silently vowed to return her to her home.

Loud voices caught her attention and she turned to find a line of burly sailors carrying her trunks. The men moved from the dock to disappear into the thick fog surrounding *The Black Turtle* and their voices muffled into silence. A movement of air twirled the obscuring mist around them into pirouetting ghosts above the water and bearing a chilling reminder of the many souls lost at sea.

Monsieur Moreau's mouth turned up into a semblance of a smile and he waved her toward the gangplank. The next moment a strong gust of bitter wind swirled her cloak and pulled at her clothes. Distracted, she gripped her cloak tighter to prevent the rush of air raising her skirts.

"Ah, there she is"—*Monsieur* Moreau rubbed his hands together—"a most impressive vessel, *n'est*-ce *pas?*"

The sudden squall had dissipated the blanket of fog and a stream of weak sunlight illuminated the ship. She pressed a hand to her stomach gaping at the apparition before her in disbelief. Icy tendrils crawled up her back and fear held her motionless. Convinced she had fallen asleep in the coach and a nightmare had her in its grip, she came abruptly to her senses at Betty's squeak of terror.

"Come away, milady, that's a devil's ship that is." Betty gripped her arm.

Adrianna clamped her jaw shut to smother a scream. *Heaven's above, a pirate ship.* She pinched her arm and winced at the pain confirming wakefulness. Gaping at the vessel in disbelief, she stepped backward, and her chest constricted with fear. *This cannot be so.* She blinked, speechless at the sight before her. The vessel was black from bow to stern with matching sails and a row of polished cannon's deadly snouts peeked through hatches along the side. Her gaze moved to the horrific figurehead looming out of the fog in the guise of a black wolf with fangs dripping blood. Floating on an unearthly gray mist, the vessel appeared to have sailed directly from Hades. Her skin prickled with apprehension and she glanced back to where the hackney had let them down. Perhaps, she had time to escape. At once, *Monsieur* Moreau's necessity to leave at dawn became abundantly clear.

She turned and glared at him. "Have you lost your wits? I will not step one foot on that vessel." She lowered her voice under the weight of his stare. "That, *Monsieur,* is if I'm not mistaken, a *pirate* ship. Is this some kind of jest?"

"Not at all. *The Black Turtle* is a privateer, Baron du Court has King Louis' gratitude for the wealth this ship brings to France." *Monsieur* Moreau gazed down at her in an intense unnerving fashion and offered his arm. "Come along, my lady, Captain Jacques is most anxious to catch the high tide."

Unnerved and giddy with uncertainty, she ignored his arm and moved closer to Betty. Searching her mind for some excuse to avoid boarding, she refused to move. Her intention to remain calm and in control of the situation rapidly dissolved into panic but taking in the flippant disposition of the man beside her, she strengthened her resolve. As *Monsieur* Moreau was in the employ of the Baron as her protector, surely he would not see her harmed. Indeed, if du Court intended marrying her for her fortune, he would have to get her safely to the altar. She lifted her chin and met his anger with a shrug. "I think not. I will seek alternate passage. Have no fear I have the funds to pay for our fares on a more suitable vessel."

"You are acting as if you are still in leading reins. This ship and the men aboard are under the command of the Baron's own man, Captain Jacques, and you will come to no harm. Come along, *allez! Vite!*" *Monsieur* Moreau's mouth curled into a snarl. He took a firm grip of her elbow and dragged her toward the gangplank.

She dug in her feet and glared at him. "Unhand me."

Sighing, he inclined his head and gave her a quizzical stare.

"Walk or I will carry you aboard. I cannot understand your reluctance, are you not anxious to rush into the arms of your betrothed?" His suggestive smile flashed yellow against his pallid complexion.

Blast his impudence! Lifting her chin, she gave his amused expression the disdain it deserved. "I do believe I can contain my enthusiasm, *Monsieur* Moreau." She pulled her arm from his grip and stepped away.

"Your father will not be pleased if you refuse to board the baron's vessel." He folded his arms across his chest in an insolent manner. "Stop this childish nonsense at once."

She took one last glance toward the road leading to freedom but to her dismay, the coach had disappeared into the morning fog. Her fate sealed, she disentangled Betty's grip and moved forward refusing his assistance. She could walk the gangplank very well on her own two feet. Placing one foot on the shifting gangplank, she shuffled toward the ship.

A grinning sailor greeted her at the end of the gangplank and encircled her waist with impropriety. She bit down hard on her tongue to prevent words of disdain spilling from her mouth. He lifted her onto the deck of *The Black Turtle* and then had the audacity to wink at her. She immediately averted her gaze and turned away to smooth her skirts. Betty arrived at her side moments later, wide-eyed with terror. She gripped the girl's thin arm. "Stay by my side, Betty."

"Oh, I will, milady." Betty moved as close as her shadow.

A sharp voice drew her attention. A man dressed in unusual garb strutted toward her barking orders to a nearby sailor in a guttural French dialect. *Captain Jacques?* She met the man's inquisitive gaze with a haughty stare and waited for *Monsieur* Moreau to introduce her. The uncouth captain ignored her, his interest settling on Betty. She shuddered in disgust at his slow smile. His lascivious attention toward Betty disturbed her. To be sure, she would keep her maid at hand and well away from Captain Jacques. She reached into the pocket of her cloak, took out her fan, and with a practiced flourish, fluttered it in front of her face to indicate her annoyance.

"My lady, may I present Captain Jacques." *Monsieur* Moreau waved toward the man. "Captain Jacques, may I present your most honored passenger, Lady Adrianna. She is Baron du Court's betrothed." He grinned at the captain. "So cast your appetite elsewhere. The Baron wants her untouched, *comprendre*?"

"So I have—how do you say in English—*free reign* with the maid?" Captain Jacques tilted an enquiring eyebrow toward Adrianna. "What do you say, my lady?"

Adrianna's face grew hot. The impudent lout. She straightened and glared down her nose at the pair of degenerates. "How dare you say such a thing in my presence?"

Not waiting for a response, she snorted with derision, grasped Betty's arm, and turned away. The sound of *Monsieur* Moreau's chuckle followed her, like a passing bell to her ears. What insignificant protection that beast of a man offered. She strolled along the deck refusing to listen to their bawdy dialogue. Indeed, the conversation was not for mixed company and had curdled her stomach. *Good Lord, I have stepped into madness.* Bending as if to inspect the cannon, she peeked at the captain from below her lashes. He certainly did not resemble a respectable ship's captain. Indeed, Captain Jacques' dirty blond hair hung loose about his shoulders and the hoop of gold in one ear gave him the appearance of a vagabond.

She examined his strange assortment of garish clothes with distaste. He had no care of his appearance whatsoever by the soiled purple silk pantaloons tucked into knee high boots. He wore a yellow shirt embroidered with daisies below a knitted waistcoat in red and blue stripes—a dandy he most certainly was not! She moved her gaze to *Monsieur* Moreau and shuddered at the sight of his amused expression. To think, the baron had trusted her safe passage to France with this lecherous man. *A murderer and a fool.* A swing of the small coin purse in her reticule would offer more protection. It would seem she had to survive a sea voyage with two despicable men before she could vanish without a trace in Scotland. She could not give *Monsieur* Moreau any reason to doubt her intention to meet Baron du Court either. If he caught wind of her plan to flee once on French soil, the captain might well throw her in irons.

"The Lady Adrianna speaks French, so you have no need to worry about your command of the English language." *Monsieur* Moreau's Parisian accented French indicated a long time in close proximity to King Louis' court, although, it would seem he understood the dialect of the lower classes well enough. "Make it clear she is to follow your orders. I have no intention of acting as her nursemaid."

She straightened and turned to face Captain Jacques confident jeer. Instinct insisted she should flee back down the gangplank and seek refuge in the closest church. Instead, with leaden feet, she moved closer and fixed her attention to his string of garbled French. She sighed with exasperation. The guttural dialect he used made no sense at all. Holding up one hand to still the man's incoherent ramblings, she addressed *Monsieur* Moreau. "May I have a word, *Monsieur* Moreau?"

"Of course, what is it *now,* my lady?"

She lowered her voice to a conspiratorial whisper. "I am having difficulty understanding the Captain. I believe the tongue is unknown to me. Fortunately, I do understand every word *you* say in French. Would you be so kind to translate?"

Monsieur Moreau inclined his head in a respectful gesture, but she caught the devil lurking in his expression. With an obvious intention to mock her, he slowed his precise French.

"You are to remain below and not walk on deck unescorted or he will not be held responsible for his crew's actions. Do you understand?"

Oh yes, monsieur more than you imagine. She glared at him. "As you mentioned, I am not a child and I do understand perfectly well." Her face heated and he had the audacity to grin at her discomfiture. To be sure, no good would come of any additional discussion with *him*. She sighed. "I thank you for clarifying the situation, *Monsieur* Moreau."

"Very well, now if you will follow me, I will escort you to your quarters. Fortunately, your cabin has a small window and is close to the galley." *Monsieur* Moreau led the way through the milling crew and down a small flight of steps. He paused beside an open hatch and motioned Betty to move down the ladder into the darkness. "Wait below for your mistress."

Betty let out a small cry of mortification and gazed at her with incredulity.

"Down *there*, milady?"

Adrianna stared into the blackness and swallowed hard. Dark places frightened her too, but she refused to cower before *Monsieur* Moreau. Gathering her courage, she forced her mouth into some semblance of a comforting smile and patted Betty on the arm. "Go along, I will follow directly."

She flared her nostrils at the abhorrent odor seeping from the inky depths. Mayhap the fear of Captain Jacques chaining her in the hold had not ventured far from the truth. As Betty moved down the ladder and disappeared into the unknown, her attention went to the crew, all to a man busy preparing the ship to set sail. They appeared little more than beggars, dressed in rags and adorned with the most unusual tattoos, from gaping eyed soulless skulls to the naked forms of women. The crew did not resemble the smartly dressed sailors of an English Baron's vessel. Good Lord, had her father any notion of the extent of Baron du Court's indiscretions? Not only a tyrant and murderer, but also she could add privateering to his list of profligacy.

She stared at the black hole destined to be her home for the next few weeks and taking one last look at her beloved England, turned to grasp the small handrail. Forcing down her fear of dark places, she backed down the narrow wooden rungs taking cautious steps into the unknown. At the foot of the procession of wooden rungs, she blinked into the darkness. The outline of Betty came into view and she moved to her side. Amidst the rank smell of night soil wafting from places unknown, she could distinctly hear the bleating of goats. She tugged on Betty's arm. "Is this the way to the cabins?"

"I have no idea, milady, but I would guess by that awful smell the hold is in that direction and they keep goats on board for fresh milk and meat." Betty waved a hand in front of her face. "It stinks somethin' terrible down here."

Adriana pressed the handkerchief to her nose again. "One would think we were going to the Indies rather than across the Channel."

"*The Black Turtle* spends most of its time at sea." *Monsieur* Moreau dropped down the ladder with practiced ease and landed beside her. "She is a trading vessel. This is why we will be sailing up the coast to Scotland and visiting some of the more remote islands before we return to France."

She gazed up at the shadowed figure, his expression hidden in the darkness. He continued to address her in rapid French no doubt to test her language skills. *Are you contemplating a language duel Monsieur?* She bit back a smile. Her Parisian tutor would be proud of her. "Then why did I not board the ship on the return trip rather than having to endure a long sea voyage?"

"We will not be returning to London." He moved so close the cloth of his coat sleeve brushed her arm. He lifted his chin toward Betty. "Your maid, does she speak French?"

She stepped away, bumping into Betty, who let out a surprised squeak. She laid a hand on her arm to comfort her. "No, she does not."

"Then perhaps, to make certain she does not construe some liaison between us, from now on, our conversations should be in English. Baron du Court will likely interrogate her on our arrival. He is possessive, you understand. " He moved past her along the passageway.

A possessive murderer, how quaint.

"These are your quarters, milady." *Monsieur* Moreau threw open a door and light from a small window filtered into a tiny room. He waved her toward the entrance. "I will leave you to get comfortable." He turned and climbed back up the ladder.

Comfortable? She gazed in dismay at the cramped cabin. The stained linen strewn over the small bunk had the foul odor of unwashed bodies. Thank goodness, she had the good sense to pack her own linen. The very thought of sleeping on filthy sheets made her skin itch. She straightened and cast a critical eye around the small area. Metal braces secured a small table, two chairs, and a washstand to the floor. Empty bottles and other refuse littered the rough wooden planks and a hammock, presumably for her maid, swung above her trunks.

Pressing a handkerchief to her nose, she raised both brows and turned to Betty. "Help me collect up this mess and throw it overboard, Betty. We will have to make haste if we are to make this place livable."

* * * *

A loud noise jerked Adrianna from her nap. Heart pounding, she drew a deep breath and glanced around to find her cabin empty. A slash of white light from the small window tore a gap in the gloom, followed by a thunderclap so loud she feared for her life. She stared at the cabin door willing it to open to admit her maid.

Heavens above, how many more storms must she endure? Treacherous squalls had whipped the sea into madness for seven days since leaving home. Another flash of lightning illuminated the cabin before hail hit the wall like gunshots. *Drew, I beg you. Come for me soon or I will surely perish on this dreadful vessel.*

The ship listed then reared up only to crash down with a sickening thud tossing her about the bunk. Terrified, she pressed the pillow hard against her ears to block out the commotion. An icy wind whistled through the small cracks in the wooden beams above her head, chilling her to the bone. She stared in horror at the wall of water outside the insignificant window and grasped the edge of the bunk to gain purchase. "Dear God preserve us."

The next wave pitched her to the floor. She landed hard and pain scored a path up one thigh. The unforgiving waves rolled her across the floor before she had time to catch her breath. With effort, she pushed to her knees and reached for the bunk rail only to find air beneath her grasp. Another surge sent her sliding across the rough floorboards. As she raked the wooden surface for purchase, splinters cut deep into her flesh, and her skirts tangled about her knees.

Disorientated, she struggled to sit but the next wave had her colliding hard with the leg of the table. As metal hit bone, she forced her muddled brain to work. "Ahrrr!"

I must get up. I could die on this filthy floor. With effort, she slung one arm around a chair as an anchor and shook her head to dispel the black spots dancing across her eyes. Gritting her teeth against the pain, she used the fixed furniture for handholds and struggled to her feet. Taking stock of her soaked dress and bloody hands, she dismissed the injuries. She would survive a few scratches well enough. Moving slowly, she staggered across the cabin and flung open the door. She raised her voice above the noise. "Betty, where are you?"

A splash of water leaked under the door, spilled across the wooden planks, and pooled around her bare feet soaking the hem of her gown. In the walkway, a river of debris sloshed back and forth in disconcerting waves. Fear of being below deck if the ship was sinking gripped her and she peered toward the galley but not one soul lurked in the dark corridor. Surely, Betty or someone would have woken her if the ship had been in danger. In the hope of attracting the attention of someone, anyone, she peered into the gloom. "Betty, *Betteeeeee.* Is anyone there?"

No one answered.

Icy tendrils of apprehension crawled up her spine. She listened intently, but the usual banter of the sailors had vanished. Had everyone abandoned ship or perished? Her mind filled with images of great octopi rising up from the depths and snatching people from the deck. Pressing a hand to her pounding heart, she dragged a breath past the tightness in her chest. *I must find out what has happened.*

With care, she stepped over the partition at the foot of the door into foul ankle deep water. Pushing distaste aside, she took a few cautious steps into the corridor. "Betty, are you there?"

The Black Turtle rolled again and the single lantern in the walkway near the entrance to the galley winked out. She turned instead toward the soft stream of light from the hatch and gripping the wooden wall trimming, edged toward the opening. Her skirts swirled in the freezing water and in a few steps, the sodden garment had wrapped tightly around her legs. Panting with effort, she fell against the ladder and clamped her lips shut against the icy rain pouring over her from above.

She thrust one arm through the rungs and moved up to peer through the hatch. Observing the chaos on deck, relief flooded through her. Waterlogged sailors tethered with ropes around their waists fought to secure the ship. Others wrestled with sails flapping like dragon's wings. *I am not alone. Thank God.*

A flash of lightning lit up the sea and she gaped in terror at the monstrous waves rising above the ship to blend with the angry clouds dashing across the sky. The wind howled with a banshee's cry through torn sails and tousled her sodden hair.

As sailors passed orders down the line, she caught intelligible snatches of conversations. She turned her head to find Captain Jacques strapped to the helm, his expression fixed in a mask of grim determination. He stood feet apart braced against the wind, his hands white-knuckled on the spokes. Dressed in oilskins, with his wet blond hair plastered to his face, he spun the great ship's wheel. Behind him, a tremendous wave rose up, higher than the mainsail and she froze unable to move. *God help us.*

The ship climbed the mountainous seas then rode atop the crest for a heartbeat before plunging downward into a hell of swirling white. She clung to the ladder, her feet trailing behind her as if she had taken flight. A shadow crossed her vision and a scarred face appeared before her with the mouth stretched in a terrible grin. The sailor's large hand came down upon her head and thrust her below. The hatch slammed shut and she fell. Searing pain shot into her temple and her hip burned. Darkness surrounded her and breathless, she curled into a ball in the churning water gasping for air.

Something scurried over her legs and wet claws scraped her bare flesh. Rats! She scrambled to her knees and pawed the wall for purchase. The next wave tossed her back into the filthy water and she slithered to a stop outside *Monsieur* Moreau's cabin.

The unmistakable smell of opium leaked from Lord Moreau's door overpowering the stench in the corridor. Oh yes, she had experience of the foul concoction. Many a time, her father had administered laudanum to a patient and the sweet sickly smell lingered in her memory. Indeed, Lord Moreau's frequent use of the pipe was evident by the dark circles under his eyes and gaunt appearance.

She dragged her aching legs under her then staggered through the rodent-infested water to her berth and flung open the door. The room moved in and out of focus and a wave of nausea clenched her stomach. She gripped the edge of the bunk and braced against the rolling motion of the ship. Each movement caused the wooden bed rail to cut into the skinned flesh of her palms. She stared down at her ruined hands angry for being such a fool.

Watery sunlight burst through the window and the boat steadied. Relieved, she glanced around the gloomy cabin to assess the damage. Apart from the damp floor, nothing seemed amiss. In an effort to control her nerves, she moved with care to the washstand and concentrated on her injuries.

She would need more light to remove the splinters. Turning away she stared at the cabin door her mind reeling. To be sure, a few splinters held little significance in the scheme of things for she had bigger problems to navigate.

Her situation had changed significantly since boarding *the Black Turtle*. Convinced at first, her impending marriage to Baron du Court would keep her safe until Drew rescued her or she arrived in France, she had accepted the Captain's daily invitation to take dinner in his cabin accompanied by *Monsieur* Moreau. However, after overhearing a disturbing conversation in German concerning their lascivious plans for Betty, she had remained in her cabin pleading *mal de mere.*

Thank God, her father had insisted she endure the long and time-consuming lessons in languages as a child. Better still, not knowing of her skill the two had spoken freely about many things of interest. Most particularly, Baron du Court's reason for offering for her hand. Indeed, as she had suspected, the Baron did not desire a wife and planned to do away with her once he had secured her fortune. The information steeled her resolve. If Drew did not arrive soon, she must find a way to escape *the Black Turtle* before it sailed for France.

The cabin door flew open and Lord Moreau hung in the entrance like a large black bat. She stiffened and her attention shifted down to the exposed limbs beneath his breeches before meeting his black gaze. "Is it customary in France for a gentleman to enter a lady's chamber without knocking? What do you want, *Monsieur* Moreau?"

He ignored her question instead raising one dark eyebrow.

"Ah, I thought I heard someone outside my door." He gripped the doorframe, his eyes intent on her disheveled appearance. "I thought mayhap you would require company during the storm."

She gave him her most haughty glare. "The storm is over and Betty is all the company I require. Did you pass her in the hallway?"

"Ah *non*, my lady. Perhaps, she waited out the storm in the galley."

As a man of insignificant height and painfully thin, *Monsieur* Moreau's dark hair and pallid completion gave him the countenance of a hawk. Indeed, with his frequent use of the opium pipe, it was a wonder he had the ability of cognitive thought. Since leaving London, the dreadful man had watched her every move. She stepped away from the washstand unable to conceal a wince of pain.

He examined her with a perfunctory look.

"Are you indisposed? The baron will be most displeased if I deliver you in a damaged condition."

His thin hand rested on the hilt of a silver snake's head cane. He carried the stick on his person at all times, but more likely to keep his balance than for protection. Pasting an affable expression on her face, she met *Monsieur* Moreau's scrutiny. "I am sure it will take more than this squall to take me to my reward, but I thank you for your concern." She straightened. Although he disgusted her, she refused to cower to him. "While I have your attention, *Monsieur* Moreau, may I have a word?"

"Of course, my lady, what is it you require?"

The floor rolled beneath her feet and taking a firm hold of the side of the bunk, she waved a hand toward her pile of belongings. "I have made every effort to cram everything into this small space, but I am afraid this cabin will not do. There is not enough room to turn around without catching my gown on one thing or another and the smell is abhorrent."

"Captain Jacques had no idea of your attendance on this trip prior to our arrival, my lady. My cabin is no less cluttered. This one is luxurious in comparison and you have a window, do you not? Mayhap you would prefer a hammock in the hold. *Non*? Well then, you will have to make do."

She met his dispassionate expression with a frown. "I fear my safety is at risk and as you are well aware, this passageway leads to the galley and is frequented by uncouth sailors."

He bowed, but his dark rimmed eyes regarded her with contempt.

"None of these ruffians have harmed you. They are all aware of the baron's wishes concerning your safe arrival in France." He sighed in a dismissive fashion and glared at her. "Although, I would not want you informing the baron of my lack of protection and will move into the cabin next door then if you are concerned you may bang on the wall." He stared past her to the small window. "The journey will be over soon. The Captain has one more rendezvous at the dark of the moon and if the weather cooperates, we should sail for France within the week."

His attention moved to the front of her wet gown and his lips curled in a predatory smile.

"Mayhap you should remain in your cabin during bad weather, unless, of course, you desire me to tie you to the mainsail for your protection." He made a great show of examining her disheveled appearance from head to toe and chuckled. "If you feel inclined, do knock on the wall, my lady, and it will be my pleasure to escort you topside."

The bacon-brained lout had the audacity to laugh at her predicament. How dare he? She did not consider her intolerable position the least bit comical. "I am sure Baron du Court will be most displeased at the way you address me. May I remind you I am a lady and not a tavern wench? Now get out of my sight."

Monsieur Moreau's jaw clenched and a nerve twitched in one cheek. He raised himself to his full height and glared at her.

"Ah, *non, non, non*, milady. I am not how you say, a *servant* for you to dismiss at will. I am a member of the court of King Louis and you may refer to me as Lord Moreau." His expression turned to stone. "I will send a bonded servant to attend you in my stead. Perhaps you should think long and hard on how to behave in *my* presence. It will be good practice, *non*. You see, Baron du Court has no patience with disagreeable ladies."

She stared at him in disbelief fighting back the instinct to slap his arrogant face. "I am *not* betrothed to Baron du Court. Marrying him or not will be *my* decision and one I will make after I have received his offer at the Countess D' Cologne's residence."

"Ah, *non*. In fact, we will be going straight to the baron's castle at Muzon and you *will* be married before a priest the moment we arrive. Do you think Baron du Court requires your acquiescence? Your father has sent your dowry with me along with his written permission for the match. Lord Beachwood is glad to be rid of you and I am quite sure you will never see him again."

Aghast, she shrank back. "How dare you, sir. My father would never do such a thing and no man on this earth will force me to marry against my will."

"Lord Beachwood is fully aware of the particulars of the arrangement. Indeed, he suggested all of them." Lord Moreau's mouth twitched into a sadistic smile. "You are no longer in England, my lady. In France, you will have no choice in the matter." He inclined his head, turned, and swayed down the passageway.

She swallowed the lump in her throat and unable to believe her father had betrayed her, tears threatened to spill. She pressed one hand to her roiling stomach and drew a few deep breaths. The image of her handsome Scot filled her mind. *Drew.* His strong, delicious countenance haunted her dreams and filled her with determination. She sighed. The bump on her head may have made her bacon-brained but, in truth, her secret desire had become an anchor of late, a beautiful dream to cherish. She missed Drew and blinked away tears but then her heart leaped with anticipation at the thought of him sailing to rescue her. He had given her his word, her knight in shining armor. *He will come for me.*

H.C. BROWN

BETRAYED

Betrayed
The Mackenzie, Book Two
H.C. Brown

After her handsome Scot is forced to leave London, Lady Adrianna's father arranges her betrothal to a French Baron known as *The Murderer of Muzon*. She reluctantly boards his vessel and finds herself on a pirate ship under the perilous protection of an opium smoking deviate, by the name of *Monsieur* Moreau.

With the captain, hell-bent on her seduction, the feisty goddaughter of George II's only chance of escape lays in the hands of her courageous Scottish warrior.

Preface

Drew Mackenzie's double life as the Mackenzie heir and the notorious, smuggler, *Le Diable Noir,* comes into jeopardy the moment Lady Adrianna Beachwood's father rejects him as a suitor. He devises an ingenious plan to meet her in secret by using his cousin, the respectable, Lord Rupert as a decoy. Nothing goes to plan and Adrianna's father forces her into a betrothal with a French Baron known as The Murderer of Muzon. She reluctantly boards his ship, under the protection of the opium smoking deviate, Lord Moreau in the hope her dashing Highlander will find a way to rescue her.

Chapter One

Outside, the wind had dropped and at last, some semblance of normality prevailed. Lady Adrianna's attention went to the sound of splashing in the passageway. She tensed and reached for a damp cloth to press against the throbbing pain in her brow. *What now?*

She collapsed in the chair and leaned her head into the soothing coolness of the wet rag. As a shadow approached the doorway, the outline of Betty came into view.

"There you are, milady." Betty negotiated the dim entrance with a basket in one hand, shoes, and stockings in the other.

Relief flooded over her. "Oh thank heavens. I thought I had lost you."

"I found myself stuck fast in the galley and had to wait for the bad weather to pass. The cook says the storm has blown itself out for now, so I have brought a bite to eat." Betty smiled. "I will wait a bit for the men to pump the water from the hallway then I will go back for a pot of tea." She shut the door and placed the tray on the table. "We are lucky the cabin has that step to keep the water out. The floor in here is practically dry. Now what is amiss? Are you quite well, milady?"

"I will do but I have had a fall and hurt my head and my right leg is quite sore too." She leaned back in the chair. "Thank God, the ship has stopped pitching back and forth. Perhaps now we may light a lamp or two."

"Goodness, I should never have left you, milady." Betty placed the basket on the table and went at once to light the lamp. She turned, lifted the lantern, and stared at her mistress wide-eyed. "You are soaked through and filthy to boot. Did *Monsieur* Moreau have anything to do with this?"

"No! He did not lay a finger on me but the man is a beast and we are to refer to him as 'Lord Moreau' from now on."

She squeezed the rag into a ball in the palm of one hand. "He made my position very clear." She narrowed her gaze at Betty then went on to give her details of her disastrous situation and explaining Drew as Lord Rupert's trusted friend.

Betty's dark eyes rounded and her mouth turned down. "Oh, milady."

Adrianna pressed the back of one hand to her aching head. "I trusted my father to assure my safety and respect my wishes concerning Baron du Court. I was sorely mistaken." She stood to allow Betty to unlace her sodden gown. "Unless I have help from Mister Mackenzie, I do believe it will take a miracle for me to escape from Lord Moreau."

"Do not worry yourself about that now. My Grandfather used to say, 'where there's life there's hope.' If he is a good friend of Lord Rupert as you say, Mister Mackenzie may well find a way to rescue you. He might be waiting in Inverness with his clansmen to free you. If not, I am sure we can leg it the moment we arrive." Betty turned to fill a bowl with water. "You sit down and I will wash the dirt from your legs."

Where there is life, there is hope. The words had merit to be sure. She blinked. *I wonder if Betty's grandfather has actually read Cicero.* She dismissed the notion and sat to allow Betty's ministrations.

Washed with a fresh gown and her wet hair brushed, she ignored the twinge of pain in one hip and struggled to her feet. "Thank you, Betty, now hurry along and fetch me that pot of tea. We will discuss what we have to do. I believe we will need a cunning plan to slip this noose."

"That may be, milady but mind you lock the door the moment I step outside. From the way the men are lookin' at me of late, I would not trust the crew as far as I could throw them. Pirates are not to be trusted, milady. You must continue to keep well away from the men on deck."

Adrianna met her gaze. "Indeed, we are in a dreadful situation. Do you believe Baron du Court hoodwinked my father?"

Betty's hands balled into fists and her shoulders shook with anger.

"No, milady. Lord Beachwood is no fool and I overheard him speaking with Lord Moreau when I was waiting in the hallway." She heaved a deep breath, dropped her lashes, and chewed on her bottom lip. "Beg pardon, milady."

"Oh, for goodness sake, I will not scold you for listening. What did he say?"

"It was before Lord Beachwood spoke to you, milady. His lordship came into the hallway from the library and shook Lord Moreau's hand. He told him he would have your dowry by the morrow along with his letter of consent." Betty lifted a concerned gaze. "He said, he had no intention of giving you an excuse to refuse the baron and would not be traveling to France to see you wed."

Her heart twisted in the pain of betrayal and she stared at Betty in disbelief. "You waited until now to tell me this?"

"I had no idea what you had discussed with Lord Beachwood nor am I in a position to ask you." Betty wrung her hands. "I *am* sorry, milady. I assumed Lord Beachwood had explained everything."

Gathering her senses, she straightened. "Thank you, Betty. Now at least my path ahead is clear. We must form a plan to outwit Lord Moreau. If only we had a friend on board to help us."

"There is a young lad working in the galley I have had occasion to speak to. He came on board as a deck hand at our last stop. He was set to work in the galley and during the storm he asked me all secret like, if he could have a word with you."

Adrianna blinked. Why would a kitchen hand want to speak with her? "Who is this lad?"

"His name is Ian, milady. He has been helping me to order your meals from the cook as you know they all speak French, so he has been a great help. He says he came aboard looking for work and ended up as Lord Moreau's slave."

"Slave?" Adrianna swallowed hard. "I have heard of this despicable practice. Good Lord, Betty, Lord Moreau is more of a hound than I thought. What are we to do?"

"Calm yourself, milady. There is no good getting upset, now." Betty handed her a fresh wet cloth. "Hold this to that nasty lump and I will go and fetch you a dish of tea." She opened the door and glanced nervously both ways before proceeding down the dark passageway.

Adrianna stared after her into the gloom. Desperation hung over her shoulders. *I have to find a way to escape.*

Chapter Two

Drew tightened the plaid across his chest and turned into the freezing wind. He peered at the horizon searching for a signal from *The Black Turtle*, but the night was as black as the Earl of Hell's waistcoat. His stomach roiled in fear for the safety of Adrianna and Ian in the company of pirates. Had the ship survived the ferocious storm? The fates had dealt him a cruel blow by removing him from her side at the most delicate part of their relationship. Mayhap, Ian would be able to convince her of his devotion and she would agree to leave *The Black Turtle* and escape with him to the Highlands. *Will she be willing to leave her lavish life behind to come to me, an impoverished Scottish Laird without her father's consent?* A crack of lightning streaked across the sky and he bit back a wave of despair. *Dear God, keep them safe, my sweet Adrianna, and Ian.*

The change in weather came with speed and ferocity. Rain threatened and vicious winds lashed his men since leaving Badenoch, but he had pushed onward in the hope they would beat the storm. It would seem, his plan to meet Captain Jacques's ship at Burghead on the dark of the moon had changed, although, dealings with pirates were often fraught with problems. He had no choice but to wait. He shook a fist at the sky. "Why canna ye work in ma favor for once in ma life?"

Not only had the delicately balanced plan to save Adrianna from the clutches of Baron du Court come asunder, the exchange of the clan's prized nectar for goods was essential for their survival this winter. Turning at the sound of boots crushing gravel, he greeted, Jamie.

A flash of white from his smile broke through the gloom.

"I dinna just see ye threatening the gods did I?" Jamie hugged his plaid around his large frame and lifted his wind-tousled head to stare into the sky. "Not a good thing for ye to do standing alone on the edge of a cliff with a storm threatening."

A shiver crawled up his spine and he returned his brother's smile with an apologetic grimace. "Aye, maybe I did."

True enough, ghosts of the long dead walked on nights such as this. He searched the black clouds for bloodsucking ghouls speeding across the evening sky, and the hairs on the back of his neck prickled. He grinned at his stupidity. No beasties sought him out for revenge but in the distance, a storm raged whipping the sea into a firmament of crashing waves and white foam. Where the horizon once sat the ocean blended with the swirling heavens into one dark roaring mass. Lightning streaked the sky, illuminating the black water in a flash of brilliance, followed by endless peals of thunder to shake the ground beneath his feet. He inhaled and the taste of ozone rolled over his tongue laced with brine. He hunched in disappointment and turned his attention back to his brother. "Where is the damn ship, can you see it?"

"Nay, I canna and I dinna believe any ship's captain who would dare risk dropping anchor in this weather." Jamie stared into the distance. "I hope Ian and your fine lady are safe, I dinna trust Captain Jacques."

"Och, Ian will be fine, if all goes asunder, he can jump ship when *The Black Turtle* arrives at Inverness. Captain Jacques always makes his presence known at *Madame* Josephine's establishment." Drew chewed on his bottom lip. "As to the lady, aye, I dinna believe Baron du Court would be too pleased if she arrived in France damaged in any way. He would have Moreau's head. Nay matter, I must save the lass, or she will not live long. Rupert mentioned she is to marry Baron du Court"—he sighed—"but what I did not tell ye is, I believe he murdered his last two wives on their wedding night. It would seem he makes a practice of marrying heiresses that die soon after."

"Jesus, Mary and Joseph." Jamie gaped at him. "Ye will be the one murdered if he discovers who is stealing *his* betrothed."

He winked at his brother. "She will not be the first lass I have stolen from a lord." He sobered. *Adrianna will be in fear of her life.*

"What about Ian? How will ye face our mother if he is drowned?" Jamie brushed a strand of hair from his eyes and turned his back to the howling wind.

Responsibility for Ian's welfare weighed heavy on his shoulders. "Aye well, Ian is a braw lad and he can swim like a Selkie, so dinna fash." He shrugged nonchalantly to give his brother the impression all was well. "Ye ken sailing is not a precise practice, we may have to bide here for ten days or more depending on more factors than the weather. *The Black Turtle* might well be facing similar delays along the coast."

Wind rushed past him howling through a line of trees standing like sentinels behind him and sounding as if a pack of wolves bore down on him. He covered his head with one end of his plaid to prevent the salty spray lashing his face and waited for the next streak of lightning to break through the darkness. No ship appeared on the horizon or rode the raging sea's white foam. His wame curdled with worry. Rescuing Adrianna had become his greatest worry, but he had other concerns. He had made a number of business dealings with customers in Inverness relying on him for bolts of silk, cambric, French wine, and spices from the Orient. He would exchange the twelve barrels of the finest aged whisky hidden in the caves along the beach for these goods. Each day they lingered here, they came closer to running afoul of the excise men patrolling the coastline. With him and his men under arrest, Adrianna would be lost forever. The government would confiscate the whisky and the Monroe would seize the Mackenzie land.

He rubbed his chin and stared into the unforgiving sky. With luck, the storm would pass overnight and Captain Jacques would arrive on the morrow or perhaps the following day. They had provisions, the game was plentiful, and he doubted his men would refuse a few days respite before they continued on to Inverness. They could rest easy in the castle ruins disguised as a hunting party taking shelter from the storm. If necessary, he would bide in the ruins for one week to secure Adrianna's safety and if *The Black Turtle* failed to arrive, he would make shift and sail to France. Captain Jacques had other ports of call before sailing home, and he would arrive in France before *The Black Turtle*. During his time in Versailles, he had traveled the roads between Calais and Muzon. He would wait at the coach house and God willing be able to steal Adrianna away under cover of darkness.

He shivered and stared into the gloom. On nights like this, he could almost believe in the tales of the Fin Folk or imagine a herd of ghostly Nucklelavees, the mythical demonic horses, charging along the cliff edge, manes flying, and red eyes blazing. He grinned into the darkness at his stupidity and pushed away such thoughts. Large raindrops splashed his face and trickled down his neck in an icy stream. Beside him, Jamie made an exaggerated shudder.

"I dinna care for the look of that storm." Jamie pulled his plaid over his head. "Come away. I have nay intention of being struck by lightning or sleeping in wet clothes."

Drew slapped him on the back. "Well then, we had better get out of the rain." He sighed and turned away from the cliff and headed up the rocky trail. The wind buffeted him, clawed at his hair, and tangled his plaid around his legs with each step.

His boots crunched on an overgrown pathway leading to the deserted castle ruins. He made his way through the blackberry and honeysuckle bushes growing in abundance. The matted branches entwined and spilled over the once neat garden. He stared at the door to the keep and a shiver of awareness quickened his heart. The darkness of a stormy night often played tricks on a man's mind, or perhaps knowing the blood spilled in the battle for this small piece of ground had enhanced his imagination. Ahead a blackened tree stood like a gargoyle guarding the once majestic gatehouse.

He blinked drawing a deep breath to clear the wandering fancies from his head. Glad of his brother's company on such a night, he moved through the shadows and hooted like an owl to announce their arrival. He lifted the covering from the opening, and stepped inside. A horse snorted and the sound of a voice soothing the disturbed mount came from the darkness.

He led the way through the darkened courtyard and into the Great Hall. This part of the castle was untouched by time and war. He pushed open the massive studded door and inhaled the musty odor mingled with the sweat of men and beasts. A familiar voice greeted him.

"Is that ye Drew Mac?"

He snorted. "If it was not us, ye would be slaughtered in your beds by now."

A flint scraped and a small fire burst into flames. He glanced around the room at the faces peering at him through the gloom. From deep inside the hall, horses whinnied a greeting. He shook the rain from his plaid and straightened to his full height to address his men. "There's a fearsome storm brewing and I canna see *The Black Turtle*. We will bide and wait for the weather to clear."

"I dinna think it wise to stay." Angus Mac Bride loomed out of the gloom with his red hair ablaze in the firelight. "Ye ken full well the government men pass by here. They have been shadowing our every move of late. Each day we dally we are in danger of being caught with twelve barrels of illegal whisky."

Drew spread out his damp plaid, then sat down and rested his back against the wall. "Dinna fash yourself, godfather, I doubt verra much the customs men will be out in this weather. We are in a good position here and can keep watch for the vessel and any unwelcome visitors traveling along the road. The new moon and the cloud cover will hide us well enough for a good few days yet." He warmed his hands over the fire and lifted his gaze to his men "Captain Jacques is nay fool and will wait out the storm then anchor off shore as planned. He has orders for the whisky. Mark ma words, he will not return to France empty-handed and disappoint King Louis. We will bide until he arrives. The forest yonder is plentiful with game. We will not starve."

"I dinna agree. It is too risky." Angus crouched beside the small fire. "Your father would not have made such a bargain. Who do ye think will protect the clan if we are all in prison marked with the lash or worse, hanged?"

Drew sucked in a breath. The pain of his father's death and half his clansmen weighed on his conscience without his men having doubt in his leadership. He made a sound of derision and glared at Angus. "Was I dreaming or did ye kneel afore me and swear fealty? You gave me your life to command, aye. Yet ye question ma decisions when I have led ye on raids many a time afore ma Da died. Do ye doubt me, for if ye do, take yourself back to the safety of Badenoch and maybe help the women tan the hides?"

The room fell deathly silent. He flicked a glance around the ashen faces of his clansmen. With their bodies obscured by deep shadows, they resembled decapitated sculls with the firelight reflecting in their eyes. Turning his head in a deliberately slow gesture back to his godfather, he tempered his anger and waited for a reply. To some extent, he understood Angus's frustration. As second-in-command, he had tasted leadership during his father's illness. His return had snuffed out his godfather's power over a severely depleted clan. *Ah well, he will do, so long as he does not plan to kill me in ma sleep.*

"Och, ye have been spoiled, lad. Ye have spent nay time at Badenoch, but ye spent three years with Lord Lovett preaching rebellion in your ear. Ye might explain away the need to attend King Louis and bed French mistresses as youthful excesses but becoming a smuggler is not the required preparation to becoming laird." Angus glared at him. "Ye should have been home, lad, when your father needed ye."

"Och, Angus, hold your tongue, ye ken verra well, I returned the moment I received the letter telling of my father's illness." Drew snorted. "And I dinna see ye refusing the food I purchased from the coin made by ma smuggling?"

"Aye well, explain to your men why ye dinna return from France straight away and spent your time attending fancy balls in London." Angus cast a slow glance around the hall. "And why ye plan to risk our lives wi' a harebrained scheme to kidnap a Sassenach lady from the verra pirate ye are doing business wi.' Have ye lost your wits?"

Adrianna. He sighed at the recollection of the heady time in London and the brown haired beauty who had stolen his heart. Her bonny vision filled his thoughts and since spending time with her, his desire for any other had waned. He wanted her and yes, he would risk his life to save her from Baron du Court's clutches. Not that he could divulge his intention to take a Sassenach wife to Angus. He had yet to convince Adrianna to have him, and a penniless laird with a near starving clan was hardly a good match for such a fine lady.

Turning his gaze back to Angus, he shrugged. "It is a matter of honor, aye? I gave the lady ma word I would rescue her from *The Black Turtle*. Would ye have me forsworn, Angus?"

"Verra well, but ye have yet to explain why ye thought it necessary to attend the balls, when your clansmen were dying by the dozen?"

"Jamie's letter went first to France and I came as soon as the news reached me. By the time, I arrived in Inverness I received word ma father was weakened but in nay danger and the bloody flux had done its worse. It was under your watch the Monroe poisoned our wells and ma father, not mine." He glared at Angus and rested one hand on his dirk ready for confrontation. "I would like to ken how that happened? Ye were ma father's second-in-command. If Jamie had not boarded up the wells, I would have returned to a castle filled with corpses."

"If ye had been here, your father may still be alive." Angus glowered at him.

"Do ye really believe I would have tarried if I had known ma father was dying? Have some sense, man." He glared at him in disgust. "I went to London to meet Rupert to make payment for the mares, he purchased on my behalf to breed with my stallion. Warhorses are needed if we are to protect our clan in the future and all others we can sell for a fine profit."

"Aye well, I still believe being away from Foiseil Castle has removed ye from the concerns of your clansmen. Ye should have been here to prevent Clan Munroe causing a blood feud. Men and women died during your absence." Angus searched through the saddlebags. "Ye spent two years fornicating in King Louis' court rather than attending to your clan's needs?"

Apart from Angus, he had no doubts about his clan's loyalty but the man did have a way with words. He lifted his chin and stared at his accuser. As laird, he did not intend to allow any clansman to speak against him. He lowered his voice and enunciated each word to make his intent clear. "I was not laird during ma time away. Ma father, God rest his soul, prepared me for every aspect of leadership including establishing business relationships in both England and France." He glanced at his men watching stone-faced then moved his attention back to Angus. "Ye are not a Mackenzie and the way ye speak of ma Uncle George with such an evil tongue concerns me. Must I remind ye he is Chieftain of Clan Mackenzie? It was he who provided the finances for ma education and trained me well in combat as ye well ken." He leveled his gaze on his godfather. "I am not an addlebrained lad and have nay intention of being drawn into another rising, so ye can dismiss that notion from your thoughts." He shrugged. "We will have enough to do to ensure the clan survives the winter with so few men to tend the fields, let alone be dragged into another of Lord Lovett's fancies."

Anger tightened his gut. He had not caused the feud with his neighbors and doubted he alone could have prevented Clan Monroe from poisoning the wells, or destroying the houses and crops. He stared at Angus and noticed with some pride, Jamie and three other clansmen had moved to sit beside him. "I ken ye had aspirations of becoming laird but ye should put that notion from your mind. I am laird now and wi' Jamie and Ian to follow should I not sire an heir, your only claim to Mackenzie blood is by your marriage to ma auntie." He removed the dirk from his waist and rested it on one knee. "Nay, Angus, ye did nothing to protect the clan. I was home not two days afore I took revenge against the Monroe and cut his men down where they stood. I did not see any blood on your hands. Now unless ye wish to challenge me here and now, I will hear nay more of your babbling, do ye hear?"

"Aye well, but tarrying here is a fool's errand. We are targets for the excise men and ye well ken it." Angus's mouth drew down in a frown.

Drew pushed both hands through his hair. "I am nay fool, why do ye think I insisted we hide the whisky in the caves? Enough of your blathering, man." His stomach growled notifying him it had been twelve hours or more since he had last eaten. "Is there anything to eat?"

"Nay fool is it? Ye have placed Ian's safety in the hands of a pirate. What do we do if all goes asunder or the wee man has changed his mind?" Angus passed him a few bannocks and a wedge of cheese.

"Dinna fash yourself. If Captain Jacques does not arrive in a day or so, Ian will jump ship at Inverness. If he does, I will meet she ship to ensure he is safe."

"And the woman? Ye will risk your life for her too—a damn Sassenach?"

"Nayone is risking their lives, but I will ask ye to accompany me. I will need to distract Captain Jacques so ye can get the lass and Ian ashore. If ye fail, well, I will go to France to meet the ship. I have many acquaintances in France to assist me. If the needs be, Jamie can sell the whisky to a brothel in Inverness. I ken of at least another two establishments who will be more than happy to buy from us and they will have coin aplenty. Not the amount I gain from Captain Jacques but enough." He sighed, bored with his godfather's constant complaining. "I doubt verra much I will gain passage to France straight away and will have time to speak with a few other people I ken who will trade with us as well."

"I dinna come wi' ye to sit here twiddling ma fingers for weeks on end." Angus gazed around the room as if trying to gain support but none came.

Drew smiled inwardly. His men avoided Angus's gaze.

"It is not so bad, we can use the time to bag a few deer, and fresh meat will bring a good price in Inverness. We will hunt on the way home and have meat aplenty to spread between the tenants." He speared the cheese with his dirk and took a bite of the stale bannock. The taste of mold rolled over his tongue. He grimaced and stuffed the cheese into his mouth.

"We will not have time to hunt, have ye got maggots in your head?" Angus glared at him, his eyes flashing with anger. "More likely we will be set upon by the Grants or the McGregors afore we reach Mackenzie land."

Drew swallowed the dry mouthful and coughed then narrowed his gaze on him. His godfather had overstepped his place more than once this eve and his actions had caught the notice of his clansmen. He needed to put a stop to his insolence and lifted his chin. "Aye, we *will* hunt on our way home and it is by my choice as laird *not* yours." He glared at Angus. "Rupert is waiting in Inverness wi' ma mares and I will not be rushing them home and chance they slip their foals. I take it ye dinna think these fine men are capable of fending off a raiding party? Well, *I do*." He surveyed the faces around the fire glad to see the heads nodding in agreement. He scratched his chin and raised his voice for all to hear. "I have purchased a herd of cows and some sheep from the Frasiers to replace those stolen. We are to meet Douglas on the boarder of Frasier's land at Badenoch Pass. I will send a messenger ahead to make the final arrangements. We will be moving slowly and have more than enough time to hunt. Jamie, lad, mind ye buy enough salt for the curing." He turned his attention back to Angus. "Or would ye rather we do nothing now and try to hunt in the snow later? Ye do ken the first snow will be on us afore we reach Badenoch?"

Angus drank from the wineskin and his Adam's apple bobbed with each long gulp. He wiped a blood-red trickle from his chin. "Are ye sure the brothel will take the whisky?"

Drew rubbed his chin and winked. "Och aye, *Madame* Josephine has been verra accommodating of late and if Captain Jacques lets us down, she will see us right."

Laughter filled the room and the tension vanished. His shoulders relaxed and he grinned at his clansmen. "Get on wi' it, ye bunch of lecherous fools. Ye will not be using one dram of ma whisky to pay for slaking your desire."

"Had dealings with those lasses afore have ye?" Jaime dropped down beside him and handed him a jug of beer. "And ye the laird too." He grinned like a donkey.

He winked at his brother. "Maybe I have and maybe I have not. *Madame* Josephine is ma go-between for a number of smugglers trading along our coastline. She trades in more than petticoats. Likewise, I have had the occasion to do business with Mrs. Dalrymple's house on Piton Street."

Relieved the tension had dissipated he took a long drink from the stone bottle of beer and wiped his mouth on his sleeve. The passage of moving from close friend to laird in a blink of an eye had not been an easy task and he had yet to prove his worth. He had stepped into the shoes of a mighty warrior and one who had fought against the English. His father's word had been law. To be laird and gain his clan's confidence, he needed respect, and of late, Angus had become a burr under his tunic. Aye, he walked a fine line indeed. He must gain their trust but not with his title alone.

One day, his men would follow him with pride and have confidence in his ability to keep them safe. He took out his pocket watch and angled it toward the fire to read the time. "Get some sleep. We will change the lookout every two hours. I will take the first, Angus, ye will take the next, and then Jamie followed by Dougal."

"*I* will take first watch." Angus tossed a pile of blankets at Drew's feet. "Get your head down for a few hours, laird. I will make sure to wake ye if I see a ship's signal."

"Wake me in two hours." Jamie grinned. "The laird will need his beauty sleep if he plans to deal with *Madame* Josephine afore he sails for France to rescue his Sassenach wench."

The camaraderie offered by Jamie warmed his heart. He tossed the remains of his bannock at his brother. "Then ye had better get your rest too, because ye will be coming along to the brothel wi' me."

Chapter Three

Adrianna leaned against the wooden paneling in her cabin and stared through the window at the expanse of ocean. Hate for Papa, welled up overflowing in a rush of anger. Why had she complied with his wishes and boarded *The Black Turtle* like a lamb to the slaughter? Damn it all to hell, if he had he given her the choice, she would have gladly slipped away to rusticate on her country estate and waited for Drew's return.

She gazed into the cloudy sky and considered her situation. The protection of the baron had rapidly deteriorated. Indeed, he would not care how she arrived if her fortune was his only consideration. She must make an excuse to leave the ship at the next port of call and make her escape. Shaking her head, she limped back and forth in the confined space. The idea had merit, but Lord Moreau would be an obstacle. She pressed both hands on the nightstand and closed her eyes. Grave doubts of her ability to slip his clutches assailed her for he had the attention of a hawk and would follow her every move.

Picturing the map in Papa's study brought the coastline of Scotland to the front of her mind. She counted the numerous ports along the shoreline and sighed. Inverness would be the last port of call before the ship returned to France and if Drew had not rescued her by then she must act alone.

Her only chance of escape would be to convince Lord Moreau she needed to go ashore to purchase a gift for her betrothed. Escaping the despicable man would prove difficult, but once on Scottish soil she would send a missive to Drew and inform him of her whereabouts.

She fell to her knees hissing with pain and flung open the lid of her chest. The smell of roses surrounded her reminding her of home and a sob caught in her throat. *Home.* Never again would Beachwood Manor be her sanctuary. She swallowed the pang of regret and with renewed resolve delved inside the rich mahogany box. She clicked open a secret compartment and retrieved a container holding a small fortune in gold and silver coins. The sight of the modest hoard bolstered her courage. She had more than enough to see her well away from any port by coach and settled in a tavern in a Scottish village to wait for Drew. Any town far away from Baron du Court's clutches would be suitable.

She frowned and ran her fingers over the coins. Traveling alone would be a problem in itself and many coaches fell foul to raids by highwaymen. She tapped her fingers on the side of the box and searched her mind for a solution. If she secured the gold in the hem of her petticoats, the silver coins in Betty's garments, and placed the rest in a purse inside her pocket, no highwayman would find a penny.

A scratch on the door had her shutting the lid of the chest. Heart pounding she stared at the door afraid Lord Moreau would discover her fortune. "One moment."

With effort, she struggled to her feet wincing in agony. She composed her features and patted down her hair. "Who's there?"

A soft Scottish brogue drifted through the door and her stomach clenched in remembrance.

"It is Mackenzie, ma lady. Lord Moreau sent me to assist ye."

A Mackenzie maybe but that was not Drew's melodic voice. Dear Lord, the very name made her heart race. She frowned. Lord Moreau had mentioned sending a roughneck to care for her needs. She bristled. *His needs more like.* Mister Mackenzie would not step one foot inside her cabin without Betty present. She lifted her voice to be heard clearly though the door. "*I see*, Lord Moreau sent you to do *what* exactly, Mister Mackenzie?"

"It is a long story, aye and one I will divulge soon enough. For now, all ye need to ken is that Lord Moreau offers me for your convenience. I am your bond servant, ma lady."

Bond servant? She frowned at his abrupt manner. No servant she had encountered before would dare to speak to her in such a bold manner. To be sure, Mackenzie's speech with his educated Scottish accent reminded her so much of Drew's soft brogue. Her stomach gave a little twist of longing and she swallowed hard. "I do not believe Lord Moreau would send you here without first introducing you. Go away."

"Dinna fash yourself, ma lady. Betty mentioned ye would be worried, but I have not come to do ye harm. I bid you to open the door. I do not desire our conversation to be overheard."

Uncertain, she wedged one foot against the door and opening it a crack pressed her ear to the gap. "Very well, go on and be quick about it."

The soft brogue dropped to a conspiratorial whisper.

"I am Ian Mackenzie of Badenoch, ma brother Drew sent me to help ye escape, and in the meantime, I will do ma best to keep ye safe. Ye have ma word and the oath of a Highlander cannot be broken."

Drew? This must be trickery. "Indeed, and why would he send you in his stead?"

"This vessel is armed for war. Do ye think it would be an easy task to board such a ship let alone steal Baron du Court's betrothed from under Moreau's nose?" Ian made a sound of derision. "Drew has a plan, aye to get ye safely away wi' out Moreau being any the wiser."

"Well met, Mister Mackenzie, but why have you not shown yourself to me before?"

"I had not expected ma request to join the crew would end up in slavery, ma lady." He let out a long tired sigh. "Indeed, I would have come to ye sooner if I had been able."

She opened the door a little wider and peered into the gloom. Disappointment washed over her at the sight of a lad standing before her in the dim corridor. How could one so young assist her in escaping the clutches of Lord Moreau?

Mackenzie bowed and gave her a leg like a man of breeding.

"Your servant, ma lady."

Charmed by his courteous approach, she flung open the door and offered her hand, then withdrew it. Heavens, had she lost her wits and fallen into a trap? She regarded him with interest. He did not dress in the same manner as the rest of the motley crew on board *The Black Turtle*. Somewhat flustered, she straightened and squinted at him, trying to make out his features in the gloom. "Let me look at you." She stepped to one side to allow the light from within to spill over him.

As Mackenzie lifted his chin, the lantern illuminated his face. Her heart raced at his resemblance to Drew. Indeed, he had sent a brother much like him apart from the color of his eyes. This lad's intelligent royal blue gaze met her examination with a defiant not beaten expression. The lad although big for his age, at closer inspection could be little more than sixteen. His jacket of green velvet was of good quality and fashionably cut. Although his breeches flapped about his legs, the silver buckles on his leather shoes shone from constant polishing. Her heart went out to the forlorn lad and she smiled encouragingly. "If you are Drew's brother, then tell me, what color are *his* eyes?"

"They are green, my lady, but he has hair the same color as my own, and we share my father's dimple on our chins."

She inclined her head. "Yet *you* are a bond servant?"

His cheeks pinked and he lowered long lashes.

"So it would seem. Although, these papers imply I am a slave." He held out a folded document. "Lord Moreau instructed me to give ye ma bill of sale, ma lady."

"Very well, but I will take it with the greatest reluctance. I cannot imagine what your brother will make of me being involved in your misfortune." She unfolded the paper and moved closer to the lamp to read the flowery handwriting. Indeed, Captain Jacques had forced this young lad into servitude against his will and she hated slavers with every part of her being. She swallowed hard at the nausea roiling her stomach. *I own a human being. Dear God forgive me.*

She lifted her attention back to him. He had suffered and put his life at risk to save her. "Come inside." She sat down gingerly on the lid of the trunk and took out her fan. "You appear to be telling the truth and I do indeed see a resemblance. "I abhor any form of slavery, Mister Mackenzie. I assure you the moment I am on Scottish soil I will tear up this appalling document and return your freedom. I would do so at once but as my servant you come under my protection whatever that is worth aboard this ship."

"I thank ye for your generosity, but first I must discuss Drew's plans for our escape. It will not be easy and ye will be in constant danger."

Mackenzie gripped his hands under his coattails and stared at the floor. He slowly lifted his gaze and his expression displayed a lad with experience older than his years.

"Nay matter what happens from this time forward, I will need your word ye will follow ma orders and do what is necessary to get safely to shore."

Her heart squeezed. She could only imagine the hardships he had endured under Captain Jacques's whip. "You have my word. I will do as you ask."

"I thank ye." He glanced nervously into the dark hallway. "May I close the door, I dinna want Lord Moreau overhearing our conversation."

"Please do." She stood and moved to sit on the edge of the bunk. "Do sit down and tell me everything. Is Drew well and your father, has he recovered?"

"Nay, Pa died by poisoning. This is why Drew could not return to England, but he is well enough. Ye ken as laird, he has nay choice but to place his clan above matters of the heart."

The tight band around her heart relaxed. She smiled at him in an attempt to offer comfort. "Yes, I do understand. Drew is an honorable man and his duty to his people will always come first."

"Many of our clan have perished." Ian sat and rubbed both hands over his face. He lifted a mournful expression to her. "That is not the least of our worries. The neighboring clan also raided our stock and burned our fields. It was only by the grace of God ma brother, Jamie had the good sense to bring the tenants into the castle or we would all be dead." He sighed. "By the time, Drew returned we were near starving. Then he received a missive from Rupert and sent me straight away to meet *The Black Turtle*."

Excitement sent shivers walking up her spine and she leaned toward him. "What plans does Drew have for my rescue?"

"It is fortunate Drew has had recent business dealings with Captain Jacques. The moment he heard ye were bound for France aboard *The Black Turtle*, he sent a messenger at once to organize a meeting." Ian stood, rolled his shoulders, and moved to the window. "He plans to meet with Captain Jacques in a secluded cove near Inverness, but I dinna ken *where* precisely. I left afore the meeting was set."

Drew is risking his life for me. She pushed the words over the lump in her throat. He *was* her knight in shining armor. "What excuse will he give for boarding a pirate ship?"

"Ah, ye see, the clan needs food for the winter and he has agreed to trade our whisky for goods we can sell in Inverness." He flicked a concerned gaze back to her. "Ye see, if we try to sell the whisky in Scotland wi' out paying the taxes, the excise men will confiscate the entire load. It takes ten years to cure a good whisky and we have barrels fifty years old."

She stared at him dumbfounded refusing to believe her distinguished Scottish gentleman would do anything underhand. There had to be a reasonable explanation for his behavior and she chose not to ask the lad. "Will he offer payment for my release? I am sure a pirate is bribed easily enough."

"Oh, nay, ma lady." Ian swallowed, his eyes shifted around the cabin and his Adam's apple moved up and down. "He intends to distract Captain Jacques and his crew to give us time to escape. We will take one of the boats lowered to carry the goods ashore. Under cover of darkness, nayone will see us, and Angus will come aboard to help row us to shore." Ian grinned. "Dinna fash, Angus is a man of honor and will see us safe. Ye will not have to endure Lord Moreau's company much longer. Drew plans to meet *The Black Turtle* on the dark o' the moon." He met her gaze and raised one dark eyebrow in question. "Are ye willing to go ahead wi' the plan, my lady?"

Drew is coming to save me. She grinned. "Yes, I agree. That is a very sound plan, Mister Mackenzie."

"Aye, it would be if I had any notion when the dark o' the moon is expected. I spent some time in the hold and lost track of the days." He sighed. "I will need to get topside tonight to see the phase of the moon to ken when the meeting will take place. As I am your servant, I should have a wee bit more freedom to move about the ship."

She gave him an encouraging smile. "Splendid."

"Although, wi' all the storms, I dinna ken *where* we are either." Ian peered out the window and shrugged. "I canna see any land and we should be nearing the rendezvous by now but maybe the captain has avoided the coast because of the storms." He rubbed his chin thoughtfully. "I will flap my ears in the galley and see if I can find out our direction."

She smiled. "Fortunately, the last time I dined with Captain Jacques I overheard his conversation with Lord Moreau and I am privy to that information. The ship is heading to for a rendezvous at Burghead, a remote cove not far from Inverness, however, I did not hear mention of your brother's name. To be sure, Captain Jacques is set to meet the notorious French smuggler *Le Diable Noir*. I am afraid this band of good-for-nothings may place Drew and Angus in danger."

A deep blush ran up the lad's neck to flood his face. He shuffled his feet then as if making a decision, cleared his throat, and regarded her with a sweet guileless expression.

"Aye, well, as it happens Drew is *Le Diable Noir*. I gather ye dinna ken Drew was a smuggler? Afore the trouble wi' our clan, he worked wi' pirates along the French coast."

A smuggler? She blinked at him unable to grasp his meaning. Her handsome, modish Scottish gentleman was the notorious French smuggler, The Black Devil. Suddenly faint, she lifted her fan eyeing Ian over the frilled edge. Dear God, had she moved from one misfortune to another? Although, being in the company of a handsome smuggler was more comforting than enduring a forced marriage to a murderer. Hoping her voice remained at a calm even tone, she met his embarrassed gaze. "I was of the impression he traded in the finest of horseflesh."

"Aye well, he does but he did not make his fortune from horse trading but he will when his stables are established." He sighed. "Only three people outside our clan ken Drew is *Le Diable Noir.* Smuggling is a hanging offense ye ken?"

"Yes, I am aware." She snapped her fan shut. "I have to admit for a notorious smuggler he is indeed a gentleman."

"Aye, a fine gentleman, to be sure. Dinna allow his smuggling to sway your impression of him. He is honest in his dealings, smuggler or no." Ian lifted one dark eyebrow. "Now ye ken the truth about Drew are ye still willing to escape wi' me?"

Her knight in shining armor, the deliciously handsome Drew Mackenzie was on his way to save her and no, she did not give a fig about his escapades. Indeed, her heart raced with the anticipation of being in his strong arms once more. She gave Ian an encouraging smile and the tension in the lad drained away. "Thank you, Mister Mackenzie. I assure you, his secret is safe with me." She chewed her bottom lip deep in thought. "Why do they meet in the middle of the night?"

"Privateers usually weigh anchor some ways out and meet smugglers at night to avoid the excise men. Captain Jacques lowers boats to transfer his contraband to one of the coves. Rest assured, Drew and Angus will be coming aboard. Ma brother is taking a mighty risk of Lord Moreau recognizing him. He kens the man from King Louis' Court."

An icy chill shivered up her spine. If discovered, Lord Moreau would not hesitate to expose Drew. "How does he usually conduct such business?"

"He does not like working the Scottish Coast and in France uses a go-between to arrange the details of his meetings wi' *The Black Turtle* and other vessels. He remains on shore and always wears a mask, not even his men ken his identity. He usually has a band of Frenchmen to exchange the cargo. They are safe enough. There is honor amongst thieves ye ken?" He swept a speculative gaze over her and the tips of his ears pinked. "Ye are lucky Drew was able to arrange a meeting wi' *The Black Turtle* on this side of the English Channel. He must think verra kindly of ye to place himself in such danger."

She bit back a smile. "I would say he is my particular friend."

"Aye, I thought as much but if there is affection between ye, he has not informed the clan so go canny. Some may not appreciate their laird taking a Sassenach to wife."

Doubt reared its ugly head and her stomach gave a squeeze. *He had not informed his family about her.* "Oh, I see. Very well, I will keep a good distance between us and not acknowledge our friendship."

"That would be for the best." Ian sighed. "Well then, we will need to be waiting above at the appointed time, in readiness for him to cause a distraction. The hardest part will be getting ye on deck, over the edge and into one of the boats wi' out any of the crew spying ye." His eyes narrowed and he stared into space for some moments then sighed. "Bide here for a while and I will work out a plan. Ye will need a disguise of sorts."

Splashes echoed in the hallway and holding a finger to her lips, she moved toward the door, opened it, and peered into the dim corridor. To her relief, Betty came bustling toward her carrying a large tray. She turned to Ian and lowered her voice to a whisper. "It is Betty. She is unaware of my ... ah personal *acquaintance* with your brother but I have confided his name to her."

Betty flounced into the room, gave Ian a broad smile, and moved inside to set the tray on the small table.

"Ah, I see you have met Ian, milady."

Adrianna moved to the door and turned the lock. She indicated to Ian to take a seat at the table. "Yes and it would seem he is our answer to this intolerable situation. Do take tea with us, Mister Mackenzie."

Betty pursed her lips and gave Adrianna a disapproving glance.

"Best you be callin' him 'Ian,' milady. Not many slaves are given the consideration of a title."

"Very well, but *Ian,* is not my slave and never will be. He is the son of a Scottish Laird and sent by a dear friend to aid in my removal from this vessel." She glanced at the indenture in her hand and revulsion roiled her stomach.

Sitting opposite him, she indicated to Betty to serve the tea. Nauseous from the pain in her leg, she waved away the plate of biscuits and turned to Ian. "Has Mister Mackenzie informed you of the reason I am in this predicament?"

"No, milady, he only told me ye needed to be away from this vessel and I was to protect ye from Lord Moreau." Ian perched on the edge of the seat as if expecting to flee at any moment. "Although, I must admit, ridding yourself of that flea is reason enough to jump ship."

"Well, there is a little more to my story and if you are prepared to risk your life for me, you should be informed of the reasons. Although, I will give you the details with the greatest reluctance. Do I have your oath this information will not leave this room?"

"Aye, ye have my oath." Ian pressed his hand to his heart. "I will never betray your trust, ma lady."

Relieved, she gathered her thoughts. After divulging an abridged version of her dilemma, leaving her affair with Drew out of the equation, she regarded Ian's reaction with interest. "Oh do not give me that look of disapproval. I realize I was addle-minded to board this ship, but I had little choice in the matter."

"That was a big decision, ma lady." Ian's brow creased into a frown. "It is no wonder Drew wants you far away from here."

Not wanting to answer any questions on the distasteful matter, she glanced at Betty. "Do unpack that basket, I am suddenly famished."

"I am honored ye would trust me with this information, milady." Ian straightened. "I will get ye ashore or die trying."

She took in the breadth of his shoulders. Oh yes, he was strong enough to row a boat. The lad would grow to be a fine figure of a man like his brother. "You are very tall and so like Mister Mackenzie. Are all the men in your family of the same stature?"

"Aye, they are indeed. We are Highlanders, milady. We tend to be larger than Outlanders."

She smiled. "Yes, I have heard tales of Highlanders and their barbarism. Yet you appear to be of genteel upbringing as does your brother, so I imagine this rumor is an untruth."

"Aye, the English do have that opinion since the rising. We are a threat to King Geordie, but we are men of honor. We have an aristocracy as ye do and are well educated. I am to begin studies at the University of St. Andrews in the New Year." He cleared his throat. "We believe the English are the barbarians. Did they not destroy the church at a whim of a king who murdered his wives in order to take another to his bed? Then King Henry had the audacity to put himself in the place of the Pope." His intent gaze flicked toward her. "The English hang men for stealing bread and make it public entertainment, yet call us barbarians. It is not so difficult to understand the reason we would prefer a Scottish king on the throne."

The loyalty of the young man impressed her. He had a strong mind and put his case forward in a forthright manner. Conversations with him would be lively indeed. She took a freshly baked ginger biscuit from the plate and smiled at him. "I find it hard to believe the Scots do not commit punishable crimes."

"Aye, they do and heinous ones too." He placed a biscuit on his plate and lifted his chin. "We deal a little differently with criminals than the English."

She lifted her cup and saucer and gazed at him. "How interesting. Do tell."

"We belong to clans yer ken? If a clansman is caught doing something wrong, he is taken afore the laird or chieftain to plead his case. If the laird decides he is guilty, he must take his punishment in front of the entire gathering. Women are punished the same way, aye." Ian met her gaze. "All are required to watch from the youngest lassie to the oldest man. If ye ever have the occasion to watch a man's skin flailed from his back ye will never feel inclined to break the law." He swallowed. "To lose your honor in front of the clan would be a punishment worse than death."

Adrianna swallowed hard. "Have you witnessed this justice many times?"

"I have not seen more than two floggings in ma life." Ian dropped his gaze. "Nayone would dare break the laird's law."

She sipped her tea noticing the loose fit of his jacket. He would need all his strength to row them to shore. She turned to Betty. "Collect large portions of food on each visit to the galley. From now on, Ian will take his meals here. I must ensure he eats well." She turned her attention back to him. "Now, Mister Mackenzie, do tell what the phrase 'dark o' the moon' means to you?"

"That would be the night of the new moon, ma lady." Ian rubbed his chin. "I am worried it may have been last eve but I canna be sure."

She closed her eyes and drew a deep breath. What else could possibly hinder her escape from this vessel? Storms had most likely delayed *The Black Turtle*. Perhaps Captain Jacques had changed his mind and had decided forgo the rendezvous and return to France. Good Lord, if so, she would have little hope of escape and be forced to marry du Court. She opened her eyes and sighed. "If the time has already passed then the jig is up."

"Not necessarily, ma lady. The ship would not drop anchor in a storm. Mayhap, Captain Jacques means to meet with Drew tonight or perhaps tomorrow. It will be as black as pitch with the cloud cover and a new moon." He rubbed his chin. "Whatever the day of the meeting we must be ready and need to find disguises for ye and Betty."

She raised an eyebrow. "Yes, as the only women aboard this ship we would stick out like two left thumbs if we attempted to board a boat."

"Aye ye would dressed in all your finery but the weather is not so fine yet awhile. If ye removed your shoes and covered your shifts with oilskins, ye would blend in with the crew just fine. Begging ma pardon for mentioning such a thing but ye should be better wearing men's breeches under your skirts because it will be verra cold." Ian frowned. "I will steal a few bags from the hold to carry a few of your necessities. It will be pitch black in the boat, so if ye keep your heads down, nay one will notice ye." Ian pushed to his feet. "I will go topside to see if we are heading toward the coast, if Captain Jacques questions me, I will say you sent me to check the weather."

Adrianna placed her cup on the table and gazed up at him. "How will you know if you cannot see land?" She admired this young man's courage. Indeed, he almost made sport of escaping. "It is cloudy from the storm and the visibility will be limited."

"Seagulls, aye." He flashed a white grin. "I will be back in a while." He moved his attention to Betty. "The crew will be busy making repairs to the ship, so ye will be safe to move around. I noticed one of the sailors storing oilskins in a chest under the ladder below the hatch, go and collect three. I will bring ye a few canvas bags but take only what is essential, aye. Remember not to make them too heavy, ye will have to carry them down a rope ladder and into the boat." He stuffed a biscuit into his mouth and headed for the door.

"And how am I supposed to obtain a pair of men's breeches? From what I have seen most of the sailors are dressed in rags." Betty pushed her hands on her hips and glared at him. "Milady is not wearing filthy rags."

"I have yet to hear Lord Moreau returning to his cabin. Knock on his door, if he is out, might I suggest ye remove some of the clothes from his chest? Mind, one of ye keeps watch in case he returns." He unlocked the door and slipped outside.

Adrianna stared at the door for some moments before pushing to her feet. Her skin pebbled at the thought of wearing Lord Moreau's clothing. She dropped her voice into a conspiratorial whisper. "I will knock on Lord Moreau's door, if he does not answer run along to the galley to make sure he is not within. If the coast is clear, I will wait at the bottom of the ladder. If he approaches, I will insist he escorts me above for some fresh air. Collect what you need for your own use from his chest. I have a pair of woolen drawers I can wear."

"Yes, milady."

Adrianna drew a deep breath and straightened. She opened the door and hobbled the short distance to Lord Moreau's cabin. She sniffed and not detecting the pungent scent of opium, knocked on the door. "Lord Moreau, may I have a word?"

Fear made her voice come out in a squeak and she had not considered what to say if he replied. Fortunately, no sound came from within. She beckoned her maid forward. "Off you go Betty and check if Lord Moreau is in the galley. I will take a look under the steps for some oilskins."

 Ignoring the ache in her hip, she shuffled toward the ladder. In the dim glow of a single lantern, she made out the outline of a large box hidden in the shadows. With care, she lifted the heavy lid and peered into the dark recess. A large rat hit the floor and scampered over her feet heading toward the galley its long tail held out behind it like an arrow. She pushed down the well of disgust and reached inside the box. Her fingers brushed over the slippery outside of a pile of folded oilskins. She collected three and shook each one to dislodge any hidden rodents then waited in the shadows for Betty to return. Long moments passed before the girl arrived and dashed inside their cabin. A few painful steps had her back to the safety of her room. She deposited the oilskins on the bunk and eased down beside them. "Well?"

Betty's face flushed with excitement. "Lord Moreau is with Captain Jacques and for a while it seems. They ordered a fresh bottle of wine and had a meal sent up."

"Good, we must act now, before he returns." She waved Betty toward the open door.

She struggled from the bunk to follow and pain burned a hot trail down one leg. Moving cautiously along the hallway to Lord Moreau's cabin, she glanced both ways before turning the knob, and edging the door ajar. A blast of opium-tainted air washed over her and she peered into the untidy cabin. Beneath a lamp on his desk, she spied the trappings used to keep him in his opium-induced stupor

"Good, he has left a lamp burning. I will find a pair of his britches, milady." Betty stepped inside.

Adrianna lifted her skirts and biting back a gasp of agony dragged her feet back to the ladder to keep watch. To her dismay, the hatch opened pouring light into the corridor and voices drifted down to her through the opening. Above patches of blue sky, peeked between sails stretched with wind. She edged up the rungs enough to see the crew repairing torn sails and removing debris from the deck. The ship was riding at full sail and cut through the water at a great pace racing the confection of white meringue clouds streaking the sky.

Salty fresh air tempted her and she gripped the rim of the hatch and eased her shoulders into the open. A delicious breeze brushed her cheeks and she turned toward the stern of the ship. Elation swept over her at the sight of Ian moving toward her. As he pointed to a flock of seagulls soaring in the wind above the ship, his young face creased into a wide smile. *Land!*

The meeting would take place soon.

Chapter Four

Drew pulled on a pair of gloves and eased each finger into the tight leather. With a degree of contempt, he clenched his fists and eyed the dark shadow of *The Black Turtle* anchored off shore. He feared for Adrianna's safety and found it hard to believe a father would do such a thing to his only daughter. He did not trust Captain Jacques and the thought of Lord Moreau recognizing him curdled his weam. Not for his sake but Adrianna's whereabouts would become common knowledge and no doubt, Lord Beachwood would have him hanged for smuggling and she would be defenseless.

His last dealing with the Captain Jacques had resulted in a number of items missing from the agreed transaction, but he could use this oversight to his advantage. Indeed, an argument would make a fine distraction.

He eased the crudely made mask over his eyes to keep his identity secret and let his hair fall loose around his shoulders. For the first time in his smuggling career, he would oversee the loading of his merchandise. If he made enough noise about compensation for the missing items, he would keep the attention on him and with luck, not a soul would notice Angus and Ian escorting Adrianna to shore.

Her sweet face and trusting smile filled his mind. Panic for her safety welled up inside him in an angry rage and one hand went to the dirk at his waist. *If they have hurt her, I will kill them all.*

A number of small lights glowed above rowboats bobbing beside the vessel. On deck, *The Black Turtle's* lanterns illuminated a line of men carrying cargo to the nets marching back and forth like ants in the shadows. At the water's edge, his men moved around in restless anticipation. All to a man had complained bitterly at his instructions to remove boots and plaid and don breeks to cover their naked arses. He grimaced at the thought of wading into the freezing water to land the boats. The wind alone cut through his shirt chilling him to the bone.

Captain Jacques' usual practice of sending two men to row each boat left his men the task of unloading the cargo and replacing it with barrels of the clan's finest aged whisky. He smiled into the darkness. Jacques would not be expecting *Le Diable Noir*—to board *The Black Turtle* to inspect the cargo.

A small lantern swaying above the waves caught his attention. As usual, Jacques dispatched one empty boat. His men would use the excuse of rowing ashore to pick up a passenger if the excise men had laid a trap. As the small craft rode the shore break toward the beach, he beckoned to Angus to follow him then plunged into the freezing waves and waded to the boat. The craft bobbed before him carried back and forth by the waves. He called out in French. "Bring it closer, you fools."

The men used the oars and the swell brought the boat within reach. He grasped the edge of the boat and turned to drag Angus beside him. His godfather swore a string of Gaelic curses and fighting against the pull of the ocean's currents spun the boat toward *The Black Turtle*. Drew gazed at the wary expressions of the sailors. In the darkness, their eyes reflected a demonic glow from the red flames of the lantern's flicker. Pushing aside his notions of the Fin folk and the like, he continued to address them in French. "I am *Le Diable Noir*. I need to have a word with Captain Jacques." He flung his soaking body into the boat.

"As you wish." One of the men grabbed his arm and dragged him aboard.

He crawled to the side and offered a hand to Angus. As the big man slithered over the edge, the boat rocked wildly threatening to toss them into the black water. At the sight of Angus's wild appearance, the sailors cried out in distress. With his long hair stuck to his face, Angus had risen like Poseidon from the inky depths.

Drew settled in the bottom of the boat and ordered the men to row back to the ship. Icy wind lashed through his wet clothes and he clamped his chattering teeth together. He waved a hand toward *The Black Turtle*. "Did the ship suffer from the storm?"

"It did, but we are used to such things." The sailor picked up an oar. He grinned. In the light from the lantern, his teeth appeared to be no more than a line of blackened stumps. "You have had business with Captain Jacques before, surely you know he is no novice when it comes to sailing and we have survived worse."

Drew propped his back against the bow and grimaced into the salty spray. The unforgiving blasts of icy wind plastered his soaking clothes to his skin. He shivered and wrapped his arms around his knees in an effort to keep warm. His mind filled with images of Adrianna drowning in the churning sea. He touched Angus's arm and addressed him in Gaelic. "No matter what happens tonight, give me your word, you will keep the lady and Ian safe."

Angus gave him a long considering stare then nodded.

"Aye, foolish as your plan is to rescue a Sassenach wench, ye have ma word." He pushed a lock of soaking hair from his face and grimaced. "I hope ye ken what ye are doing. Ye risk them discovering ye are a Mackenzie. Continuing to use a go-between would have been safer on this side of the Channel."

"Nay, I will deal with Captain Jacques from now on, he kens well enough *Le Diable Noir,* is held in high regard with King Louis. Moreau does not usually set foot outside of France." He slapped Angus on the back and grinned. "Stick to the Gaelic at all times on board and get away to find Ian as soon as you are able. He will hide in the shadows toward the stern."

He turned and smiled at the men pulling on the oars, sweat beading their brows. Mayhap they would allow him to row to keep warm. He smiled at the sailors and addressed them in French. "We would be happy to row and save your backs."

"And get the cat for disrespecting *Le Diable Noir*. No, I think not." The sailor moved the craft through the waves with practiced ease.

The Black Turtle loomed before him, a dark shadow in the gloom and an intimidating sight to be sure draped in its black glory. A ladder hung over the railing and the moment the small boat came alongside, he stood, grabbed the rope and swung his feet to gain purchase on the rungs. He led the way up the ladder ignoring the roiling of his wame caused by the worry of his plan going awry. Reaching the top, he determined the positions of the crew and noted what weapons they carried. Many had pistols tucked into the belts of ragged pants and the hilt of daggers glinting at their waists. All to a man drew weapons and glared at him.

He dropped onto the deck with Angus close on his heels and raised both hands. Angus scowled and made a sound of derision but followed his lead. Pirates surrounded them and made demands in guttural French. Picking out the largest man in the group, he turned his attention toward him. He urged frozen lips into a semblance of a smile and dropped his hands. "Gentlemen, I am *Le Diable Noir*. Inform Captain Jacques I wish to speak with him if you please."

A man with a long scar down one cheek waved a pistol toward him.

"Wait over there. I will send someone to inform the captain. Do not wander. I will be keeping an eye on you." The man pushed the pistol into the top of his britches and turned to speak to a member of the crew.

Drew backed up into the shadows until his legs hit a powder barrel. He heard a soft voice speaking Gaelic close behind him.

"Do not move or give anyone reason to discover ye ken me, brother, nor ye, Angus."

Ian. Relief poured over him. He flicked a gaze into the shadows then turned and spoke as if addressing Angus. "Ian? Thank God. How fares my Lady Adrianna?"

"She is as well as can be expected being wi' this bunch of foul mouthed louts."

Drew bit back his sigh of relief. He had not rescued his bonny lass yet. "She will not have to suffer much longer. Are we set?"

"Aye, and ye should thank the Lord, I am alive too. The bastard Jacques had me in irons for two days. I have lowered a boat not ten paces away, but you will have to make a fine distraction for me to get the women overboard and down the ladder wi' out being seen."

Drew straightened, his heart pounding with excitement. "Ye ken I will." He cleared his throat. "I wish I was the one carrying her from this vessel. She is my responsibility, not yours."

"Dinna fash, ye are doing your part well enough and she kens the risk ye are taking to save her." Ian moved closer keeping to the shadows. "I will have nay trouble moving them into the boat during the loading of the cargo, but I will need Angus's help to get them ashore."

"Aye, I ken you will. When I am speaking to Captain Jacques, I will make an excuse for Angus to go ashore. When you get the women to safety, head toward the south of the beach, and follow the path to the castle ruins."

Adrianna's sweet face drifted into his consciousness and he blinked the image away. She had etched a deep longing in him and no other had come close to replacing the lass in his mind. His heart squeezed with the recollection of intelligent sky blue eyes set in a bonny face and framed with a mass of curls the color of a burnished hazelnut. Jolted back to reality by Angus's growl, he flicked a gaze at his godfather. His face had turned a disturbing shade of purple.

"I can see you lust after the lass." Angus's eyes had turned to black pools of hate. "Ye canna be thinking of stealing this lass for your own pleasure? I will not be a part of such a thing."

He had not wanted anyone to discover his regard for Adrianna. He shook his head and glared at him. "I told ye afore. I gave ma word to rescue her and that is the truth of it."

"I will not lift one finger to help ye destroy the clan's business. King Louis will not hold ye in high regard after this or do business with you again if ye steal one of his baron's brides."

Ian's voice turned to granite behind them.

"Dinna fash, ye old misbegotten idiot. I will manage fine on ma own. I gave ma word too and I will not go back on it to please ye, Angus MacBride."

Drew touched Angus' arm. "Have ye got maggots in your brain? Ye dare to argue when ma brother and I have both promised to help these lasses? The women are in danger, aye—Sassenachs or no makes nay difference. Would ye do nothing and allow these devils to use these women without their consent?"

"Nay, but ye ken verra well the Sassenach women will be trouble. They will ken we are trading wi' *The Black Turtle* and God only kens whom they will prattle to for coin. Mark my words, ye will rue the day ye agreed to help them." Angus jutted his chin toward the shadows. "And I will deal wi' your insolence later, lad."

"I am sixteen and ye canna tell me what to do. I only answer to the Laird now." Ian's voice rose. "Christ! Dinna ye understand the lady is set to marry Baron du Court in France and wants nothing to do with the match."

"Aye well, I canna argue wi' your reason." Angus scratched his beard. "If we keep to the shadows in the confusion of loading the cargo, we will be able to slip away unnoticed."

Drew rubbed his arms to warm the chilled flesh. "I will keep Jacques and his men occupied as best I can. Waste nay time. Move the lasses ashore and have them well hidden afore Captain Jacques notices they are missing, aye." He caught sight of movement in his periphery vision. "Now get on with ye, the captain is on his way to speak wi' me."

"Well, well if it is not *Le Diable Noir*?" A brightly dressed man strutted across the deck and addressed him in French. "So, we meet at last. My man said you needed to speak with me?"

He recognized the man's guttural French dialect from the docks in Calais. He stepped forward and dropping into a similar French dialect, inclined his head. "Your servant, sir. I wish to speak with you about the missing merchandise from the last shipment." He turned to Angus. "This is *Monsieur* De Lange, my assistant."

Captain Jacques flicked an inquisitive glance at Angus then returned his attention to Drew.

"Ah, well you must understand some of the items you ordered were unobtainable at the time. In hindsight, I should have compensated you with something else but as you know, time is of the essence in such matters." He led the way toward a stack of crates piled in the middle of the deck. "As you see, I have wine, tea, as well as the finest bolts of silk and other fabrics as you ordered. You shall have the pick of my cargo. The king is very partial to the whisky you supplied and informed me to spare no expense in obtaining your entire cargo."

Drew straightened. Both he and Angus stood head and shoulders above the crew, and had intimidated many a man in their time. He held Jacques in the palm of his hand if King Louis had requested his entire stock of whisky. He smiled at the diminutive man, who resembled a peacock more than a pirate. "Very well, but this time, I will personally oversee the loading." He turned to Angus, gave him a meaningful stare, and dropped into the Gaelic. "Go down to the stern and check the loading there, aye."

"My laird is a loon. How do ye say that in French?" Angus slouched into the shadows.

"Is there a problem?" Jacques gave Angus's retreating form a quizzical gaze. "I do not understand his unusual tongue."

Drew laughed returning to French. "No, he suffers with seasickness and is ashamed he will disgrace himself. I will send him back with one of the boats."

"Very well, come and inspect the goods I have for you, although my men have already loaded a few barrels of wine." Captain Jacques led the way to the crates. "You do understand it is necessary to move swiftly if I am to catch the tide."

Men surrounded them and a shiver slid down his spine. He straightened and turned his head slowly to glare through his mask at each one in turn. "I am sure this could be accomplished if your men returned to work rather than examining my every move."

"You must excuse my crew." Captain Jacques grinned. "They are in awe of the notorious Black Devil."

* * * *

Adrianna's heart raced fast enough to burst through her chest as she slipped on deck amidst the shadows. At the opposite end of the ship, a group of sailors lowered bulging nets to the waiting boats below. As the crew worked, a sea shanty fit for the inside of a dockside tavern lilted on the air. She pressed against Betty and dropped her voice to a whisper. "Stay in the shadows, Captain Jacques may be very close."

Ian moved beside her, and with a hesitant touch to her elbow coaxed her around a pile of crates waiting to be loaded and toward a gap in the ship's railing.

"Dinna fash yourself, ma lady, they will be loading from the other end first and Drew will keep them busy. We will have more than enough time to slip over the edge of the ship and into one o' the boats tied up below. I have already opened a hatchway and dropped a ladder and not one soul tried to prevent me."

She stared into the small circle of light for any sight of Drew but a pile of goods hoisted from the hold obscured her view. She grasped Ian's arm to get his attention. "Is Drew here?"

"Aye, he is close by and I hope distracting Captain Jacques and Lord Moreau."

Dragging the canvas bag filled with a few necessities over one shoulder, she beckoned Betty to follow. A massive shadow loomed from the darkness and she cringed away smothering a scream. Behind her Betty squeaked then slapped one hand over her mouth.

Ian's comforting voice came out of the darkness.

"Hush now, this is ma clansman, Angus MacBride, he has offered to help us, ma lady. Hurry to the ladder afore we are discovered." Ian moved to the edge where a gap in the ship opened into inky blackness. "Turn around and follow me. I will not let ye fall and I will guide your way. Hold onto the rope and dinna look down, aye."

As if recognizing her hesitancy at contemplating such a compromising position, he raised both eyebrows.

"I dinna think ye should worry, ma lady. I have nay intention of peeking at your ankles. It is verra dark down there and I doubt I could see ma hand in front of ma face."

The big stranger loomed in front of her and when she shrank away from him, he gripped her arms in his large hands then held her on the edge of the gaping maw. She glanced wildly around not wanting to risk falling into the sea then caught sight of Lord Moreau strolling slowly in her direction. Her throat tightened and unable to form words, she tipped her head frantically in Lord Moreau's direction. Angus turned at once shielding her with his huge body. To her relief, the buffeting wind carried a voice in French demanding Lord Moreau's attention. The big man holding her grunted something unintelligible. Concerned, she lifted her chin and met his hard gaze. His eyes narrowed to slits and hate radiated from him, good Lord, she could almost taste his disgust.

"The wee Frenchman has gone and if ye thought he posed a threat to *me*, ye were sadly mistaken."

His mouth flattened into a thin line and he jutted a chin covered in red bristles toward the gaping hole and indicated she move backward. In trepidation, she grasped the rope each side of the ladder and stepped into the night feeling around gingerly with one foot for the first rung. The oilskins flapped about her and the ladder swayed underfoot with every movement of the ship. Fear gripped her and unable to move, she clung in midair. Angus's angry face dropped into view. He glared at her and spoke in a low menacing whisper.

"Ye would have us all killed? Stop acting like a fool and get yourself into the boat or do I have to throw ye into the sea and be done with it."

His anger spurred her on. She ignored the searing pain in her hip and backed into the chilled night taking care to place her bare feet squarely on each rung. With each tentative step into the unknown, blasts of icy wind lashed her legs. Betty followed her chanting *The Lord's Prayer* in a small breathless voice. Inky blackness surrounded her and roar of the ocean muffled the singing from the sailors filling the boats. Her eyes became accustomed to the dark and she chanced a glance along the side of the ship.

Wet and glossy, *The Black Turtle* resembled a huge black whale rolling back and forth in the waves. She paused to take a breath to ease the rising nausea and squeezed her eyes shut. Determined not to lose her footing, she continued down the ladder at a steady pace. From below the welcome sound of Ian's voice reached her.

"Ye are doing verra well. Just a few more steps, ma lady."

She dared a glance down and her vision blurred. Ian grasped her waist in his firm hands to steady her. Turning, she caught sight of his pale face. "How much further?"

"Let go of the rope now and I will lift ye the rest of the way." Ian grasped her waist and swung her into the boat.

Her legs flew in midair and the canvas bag slid from her shoulder and landed with a small thud on the bottom of the boat. Under her feet, the wooden planks moved in a most unnerving fashion. Acting on instinct, she dropped to her knees and gripped the piece of wood traversing the middle, a seat of sorts for rowing perhaps. The vessel rocked from side to side and sea spray splattered her face. Unsure of how to proceed, she turned to Ian for instruction and he smiled down at her, his teeth a faint flash of white in the gloom.

"Crawl up to the bow and hunch down. Take the bag wi' ye." He turned and reached for Betty. "Follow your mistress, Betty. Nay talking, aye."

A wave carried the boat against the rolling mass of *The Black Turtle*. She gasped and bit back a scream. Dear God!

The boat would capsize and toss them all into the murky depths. As if sensing her concern, Ian made soft shushing sounds. She scrambled forward and throbbing agony joined the waves of red-hot pain searing her hip. Biting down hard on her cheek to keep silent, she curled into a ball and waited for the agony to subside.

Her attention settled on the Ian, his outline barely visible in the gloom. He stood in the middle of the boat, his legs set wide apart to balance the small craft. She had trusted Ian this far, now she must have faith in his ability to keep her safe. Moving with slow deliberation toward the bow on hands and knees, she dragged the canvas bag behind her. The boat stunk of tar and fish and the foul odor sent bile rushing up the back of her throat making her gag. She sat with her back to the hard wooden surface and Betty loomed before her with her young face set in a determined expression.

Adrianna gathered the oilskins around her freezing legs and lay down then indicated to Betty to curl up beside her. The boat rocked again and Ian strolled purposefully toward them. Behind him, Angus, moving as silent as a cat, dropped into the boat and cast off. She had no liking for Angus and the giant of a man frightened her. She had heard tales of barbaric Highland warriors, and from his expression of disgust, he had no time for English women. In fact, she would wager, he would have preferred to throw her into the sea rather than row her ashore.

Ian's dark shape hovered over her examining her face and she fought to control the quiver in her bottom lip. "I find I am frightened of boats, Mister Mackenzie."

"Ye will be fine." Ian smiled and piled the bags around them. "Dinna move and nay matter what happens do as I say." He sat beside Angus and they took up the oars.

The boat slipped into the night, rising and falling with the swell of the ocean. Soon the sounds of voices from *The Black Turtle* drifted away to be replaced by the splash of oars and the soft grunts of the two men rowing. To her relief, no call of alarm came from the ship. With luck, they would be well away before Captain Jacques discovered her missing.

She had locked her cabin door and tossed away the key. Lord Moreau would think her sleeping and perhaps not bother to check on her for some time. After all, he had charged her care to Ian.

She gazed up at the few stars peeking between the clouds and a wave of exhilaration washed over her. They had escaped—but into what? Had they moved from a pirates den into a precarious position with a band of Scottish smugglers? Drew had organized her escape, but she did not know him as *Le Diable Noir*. The fine gentleman, she had fallen in love with had been a sham, a falsehood of the highest degree. Could she trust him? Had he used his kisses and experienced touches to lure her away from her father in an attempt to gain her fortune? Dear God! Did her dearest friend Lord Rupert know about Drew's smuggling antics? *Has he deceived me too?*

The hairs on the back of her neck rose. Drew's need to meet her secretly became apparent. Good heavens, Drew's band of smugglers might well be in league with Captain Jacques and plan to ransom her. *Dear God, let there be honor amongst thieves.*

Chapter Five

Drew moved between the sailors raising his voice to keep their attention and insisting he check the contents of each crate. He glanced surreptitiously toward the stern and sucked in a deep breath before moving his gaze to the boats moving toward shore. By now, Angus should have Adrianna to safety. Turning his attention to the bolts of fabric rolled in oilskins, he stopped the sailor hoisting one into the net. "Open it so I may see the contents, if you please."

Captain Jacques appeared at his elbow heavy with the stink of sweat.

"For a smuggler you are very brave. I cannot recall anyone having the gall to challenge my honesty. It is good we are *not* men of breeding. Such men would demand justice over a slight on their character by dueling, would they not?"

Drew laughed drawing attention from the crew and dropped his French into a cultured Parisian accent. "Good luck for *you*, as I happen to be an excellent shot." He narrowed his gaze and snorted his discontent. "A smuggler I may be, but I also have the acquaintance of King Louis. You would know he holds the whisky I supply in high regard."

Captain Jacques grinned and his gold earring glittered in the lamplight.

"So if you *are* a gentleman as you profess why not trade through the normal channels rather than skulking around at the dark o' the moon wearing a mask?"

"I do not intend to be robbed by the English crown's notion of fair taxes and this way is financially rewarding for me and King Louis." He peered at the bolt of fine cambric. Happy with the contents of the oilskin, he waved the sailor away. "I am satisfied with our bargain. Thank you. When the last boat is loaded, I will return to shore and order my men to load the rest of the whisky."

"As you wish." Captain Jacques smiled. "When the next batch is ready for shipment, send me a list of your requirements through *Madame* Josephine."

Drew tensed at the shadow looming at his side. A Parisian accent cut through the noise.

"Whom do I have the pleasure of addressing, *Monsieur*?" A small dark haired man strolled into the patch of light. "Ah yes, you must be the famous Black Devil." He bowed and gave him a leg with a Parisian flourish of one hand. "Your servant, sir. I am Lord Moreau."

Drew flared his nostrils at the distinct smell of opium oozing from the man and stared at his dead eyes. Lord Moreau, yes, he had made his acquaintance afore in King Louis' court and once had been more than enough. This man held the position of lackey to the Baron du Court. He ground his back teeth in anger. To think Lord Beachwood gave his precious Adrianna into the hands of this despicable man. The snotty-nosed gomeral posed no threat to him and he relaxed. He forced his attention to Lord Moreau rather than move out to sea to confirm Adrianna had escaped. He inclined his head. "Likewise. What brings you to Scotland, Lord Moreau?"

"Ah, I would not dream of setting one foot on land hereabouts. As to *why* I am on this vessel. I am merely escorting Baron du Court's betrothed to Muzon." Lord Moreau waved a lace handkerchief under his nose and gave him a pious gaze. "A thankless job but not difficult as the lady prefers to remain in her cabin rather than take the air with me."

Biting back a retort, Drew raised a brow. "I have had the occasion to meet English ladies and they are not keen on stepping out in such weather. They value their fair skin far too much."

"So it would seem." Lord Moreau's mouth turned down at the corners in obvious distaste.

Drew inclined his head toward Captain Jacques. "It would seem our business is concluded. I will be on my way. Good evening to you, sir." He gave Lord Moreau a curt nod and swung onto the net carrying the bolts of silk. Giving the men a wave, he rode the cargo down to the waiting boat.

He dropped into the bow and straddled the bolts of cambric. The boat moved off and he scanned the distant shoreline in the hope of glimpsing Ian and Angus. His godfather was very canny and would have landed the boat well away from the others to enable her to disembark undetected. He would take them to the old castle and they would be safe.

Without his thick woolen plaid to protect him, the freezing wind cut him to the bone. His teeth set to chattering again and he rubbed his arms vigorously in an attempt to warm his chilled flesh. No matter, soon he would be back on land and leaving for Inverness at first light. The thought of seeing Adrianna again send his heart racing. Maybe his life as a smuggler could end now she had arrived. The sale of the cargo would see his clan set for the winter. He would be able to support the clan well enough from his investment in French wine, and the foals from the mares Rupert had purchased would see his future set. He smiled. His greatest task would be convincing his clan he wanted a Sassenach for his wife.

He stared at the distant shore and his good mood dissolved. Captain Jacques would soon discover Adrianna's escape and place the blame on *Le Diable Noir*. Lord Moreau would not give up his valuable charge without a fight and without doubt, would lead a band of armed pirates to search for her. If Lord Moreau discovered his true name or clan, he would notify Lord Beachwood and would have King Geordie's troops on his doorstep.

He had to sell the contraband, and Adrianna and her maid would be in plain sight the moment they arrived in Inverness. He would secure her somewhere safe, finish his business then take her to Badenoch. *Sweet Adrianna, will you still care for me now you know the truth?*

With no time to explain his duel identity, or the reason he could not reveal his affection toward her in front of his clan, she may well reject him. Christ! A woman scorned and privy to enough information to see him and his men hanged. Apprehension washed over him. Why had she promised to wait for him then boarded a ship for France? Baron du Court's offer must have come on the heels of Rupert's interview with her father. Yet Rupert had made Adrianna aware of his plans to remove to Scotland. Perhaps Lord Beachwood had forced her hand. Yet, Lady Adrianna was strong-willed, and he would have thought, she would have taken the first mail coach to Scotland to be with him. *This is not your fault, Adrianna, it is mine.* Regret squeezed his heart. He should have been in London to prevent this injustice toward his love.

Weariness engulfed him. His life had become a game of chess and every move he made had consequences. He stared at the shadows of his clansmen moving along the beach and rubbed at the vein throbbing painfully in his temple. Circumstances had thwarted his intention to keep *Le Diable Noir's* band of smugglers far from Scottish shores. God help him, he had saved Adrianna but if the excise men discovered his identity, they would all meet the hangman or face a lifetime in prison. He swallowed hard. Being laird, it would seem, had become more troublesome by the day.

* * * *

Lifted from the boat, Adrianna gripped the damp cloth of the shirt stretched across Angus' shoulders. The Scot moved through the shore break and deposited her none too gently on the sand. Taking her bag from his outstretched hand, she met his angry gaze. "I thank you, Mister MacBride."

She turned to see Ian's face creased into a mask of concern. He splashed through the water with Betty hanging over one shoulder like a wet sheet, and carrying two canvas bags. The lad stumbled onto the beach gasping for breath and dropped the baggage.

"I am verra sorry I had to carry ye in such a distressing fashion, Betty." Ian placed her gently on the sand. "Come along now, we need to find a place to hide."

"Up yonder, lie the ruins of a castle." Angus lifted his chin toward a rocky incline. "Follow the path to the keep. Our provisions are inside if ye need a bite to eat. We will be along shortly." He flicked an angry glare at Adrianna. "I ken ye are in fear of Lord Moreau, but he will not trouble ye now. So if ye have a mind to run away think verra hard on how displeased the laird will be, ye kenning our business and all."

Her stomach squeezed and her throat constricted. How dare this man make such threats? She lifted her chin and gave him her best haughty stare. "We both have our secrets, Mister MacBride. Do you imagine I would make mention of any of this? I hold your clan in the highest regard for the assistance you have given me."

"Well, if ye plan to stand here any longer the jig will be up. Get away with ye afore Captain Jacques spies ye standing here and sends his men after ye." Angus leveled a black gaze on her, turned, and headed back to the boat.

"Give me the bags." Ian held out a hand. "Follow me and mind ye stay close, aye." He hoisted the bags over one shoulder and made his way toward the shadowed rocks.

She straightened her back, lifted the cumbersome oilskins from around her legs and followed him. Ian negotiated the pathway with apparent ease. She gaped after him. *He must have the sight of an owl to move so swiftly in the darkness.* In agony, she dragged her bare feet through the sand stumbling on the loose footing. Sharp sticks and pebbles cut into her flesh with each step up the incline. Betty followed behind muttering something unintelligible under her breath. Hidden from view by the rock wall rising high on each side of the passageway, none of the sailors from *The Black Turtle* could witness their escape.

She limped steadily upward, wrinkling her nose at the stink of seaweed and dead fish. She set her gaze on Ian's outline, but he disappeared into nothing more than a black figure in the distance. The path widened at the summit and ahead a ruined castle loomed out of the darkness, its damaged ramparts creating a jagged horizon against the indigo twilight sky. Exhausted and unable to catch her breath, she bent over hands on knees, and gasped at the unbearable pain searing through her leg.

"Look, the castle is just over there, it is not much further." Ian moved to her side, his expression unreadable in the darkness.

Adrianna straightened and sucked in the clean, crisp sea air. She could hardly inform him of her injuries and strengthening her resolve took a hesitant step toward the castle on the sodden ground. "Very well, Mister Mackenzie, lead on." She turned and smiled at Betty. "Come on, Betty."

Swathed in oilskins Betty moved to her side. Hair had fallen from her cap and tangled in the wind. The girl met her gaze. "Let me help you, milady, you are favoring that leg something awful. Maybe these good men will have herbs to make a poultice?"

"Are ye hurt?" Ian stopped and turned his attention to Adrianna. "Ye should have told me."

Her face grew hot. "I should do no such thing. It is not polite to discuss such things in mixed company, Mister Mackenzie."

"Aye, it is. We have a long way to travel and if ye are hurt, it will only get worse untreated. My brother, Drew, is verra good with herbs and the like. He will have ye well in nay time at all." Ian peered at her. "Do ye want me to carry ye the rest of the way?"

"No, I can manage." She touched his arm. "I thank you for helping us escape. I am in your debt."

"Nay, it was Drew's plan. I understand ye dinna ken he was a smuggler, but dinna hold it against him. Ye ken risked everything to rescue ye, ma lady." Ian moved onto a gravel path. "Mind ye keep on the grass, aye, these rocks are sharp underfoot."

"Indeed, but how did he come to meet Lord Moreau?"

"He met Lord Moreau at King Louis' court but as *Monsieur* Alexander. Should he discover his true identity and I ken King Louis is privy to it, he would use the information to his advantage, especially now." Ian frowned.

"He would ken you are with Drew and inform the authorities. We would all be hanged for smuggling."

She swallowed the lump in her throat. "Heaven help us all."

Outside the ruins, Ian ordered her to wait with Betty out of the wind. As he moved away, panic gripped her and she laid a hand on Betty's arm. "I am sorry to involve you in my troubles. I will find a way for you to get back to England as soon as I am able."

"I will never leave you, milady." Betty moved closer and a strand of her unruly hair brushed Adrianna's cheek. "You have saved me from a life on the streets."

"This way." Ian loomed up in the darkness. "The Great Hall is still intact and there is a fire burning. I will see ye safe inside then I will stand guard to give ye time to tend your wounds."

She smiled at him. "I thank you, but I have nothing to use to treat my injuries. I am sure if you could find me a little water to wash the sand from the cuts it will be sufficient."

"There will be a water skin inside. I will search for it but keep the oilskins wrapped around ye. It will get verra cold tonight." He led the way into the darkness.

A door creaked and the warm glow of a fire illuminated the space and glistened in the patches of damp on the walls. She covered her nose at the acrid stench of horse manure, roast meat, and sweat. How long had the men stayed in this room? Did Scots ever bathe? "My God, Mister Mackenzie, this place smells like a pig sty."

"But it is not so cold in here and sheltered from the wind. Sit by the fire and warm yourself. I will find ye some water." Ian disappeared into the shadows, his boots clattering on the stone floor.

She moved toward the light. The massive fireplace held a spit complete with a pig roasting over hot coals. On one side of the hearth hunched a very frightened lad of about ten years old. Her mind insisted she had imagined him and she blinked into the gloom. Two round eyes peered up at her and the boy's red hair glowed in the firelight. He wore a kilt, long knitted stockings and fine leather boots. He muttered something in a foreign tongue and she glanced around to search for Ian. "Mister Mackenzie. There is a boy here. Perhaps you should speak to him?"

Ian's face broke into a wide smile. He handed a water skin to Betty and greeted the boy in the same garbled language. Adrianna gazed back and forth between the two with surprise. The boy was chattering ten to the dozen.

"This is Angus's boy, Dermot. Drew left him behind to tend the fire. I have explained the situation, ma lady." He rubbed his chin. "Ah, he will not understand ye and neither will many of ma clan, most of them only speak the Gaelic."

She tasted the word on her lips before repeating it. "Gaelic? Ah yes, Drew spoke to Lord Rupert in the same language. I gather it is native to Scotland?"

"Aye, like the Welsh and Irish we have our own language. So did ye afore the Romans conquered England." Ian grinned. "Ah well, nay matter. Drew speaks many languages and Angus speaks the English fine. Ye dinna have to worry, most likely ye will not need to speak to any of the lads."

"And the womenfolk?"

"Some do, aye and ma mam speaks French so ye will be fine." Ian pushed his hair away from his face and caught it in one fist to retie the ribbon. He glanced toward the door and frowned. "I hear the men coming. Bide beside the fire and dinna say a word until Drew explains why he saved ye."

The door to the Great Hall creaked open and the raucous voices of men and the tramp of boots echoed in the hallway. She took a firm grip of Betty's arm and sat down bedside the fireplace giving the Highlanders her back.

Drew strode into the Great Hall and ignored the two women bundled up in oilskins beside the roasting pig. He did not intend to run to Adrianna gather her in his arms, and suffer a public rejection. He would need the opportunity to explain his situation to her. There would be time enough to atone for his sins on the journey to Inverness. For the time being, he would keep his true intentions from his clan. He forced his attention on Ian. "Och, Ian. God man it is good to see ye safe on land." He gripped his brother in a hug. "Ye did verra well. I am proud of ye."

"Aye well, it was a might more difficult than I had imagined. Captain Jacques was not one to take his eye off of me for more than a second." Ian grinned. "The women are a might distressed. Do ye want a word with them now, or should I allow them to rest a while?"

"Let them bide, I will speak with them later but I want ye to take them outside so the men can change out of their wet clothes unless—do they have a fancy to watch, do ye think?" He winked at his brother.

"I dinna think so and ye should ken the answer being you are Lady Adrianna's *particular* friend. I will bid them wait in the hallway for a bit, aye?" Ian slapped Drew on the back and went to the women.

Drew shivered and lifted the hem of his soaked shirt. He heard a snort of derision from Adrianna and chuckled. Sassenach's believed Scots to be barbarians and living rough, aye, they came very close, but he waited until Ian had herded them from the room before he removed his shirt and breeks.

Ian returned, his cheeks flushed and he grinned at him. He had embarrassed the lad. "Ye are acting like a mother hen, Ian."

"Nay, ye dinna understand. Lady Adrianna is injured and limping badly from being tossed about in the storm aboard ship last eve." A frown masked his handsome features and he glanced down at the wineskin dangling from his fingertips. "She has suffered cuts on her feet from the journey here too. Will ye tend her, brother?"

Christ, she is hurt and I must act as if she means nothing to me. He tempered his anxiety and narrowed his gaze. "I doubt verra much a fine Sassenach lady is going to allow me to treat her and especially not in front of ma men. *Particular* friend or no."

"There must be a room off this hall you can use away from the men." Ian met his gaze. "Surely you can at least offer her your assistance?"

He pulled on his shirt. "Hand me ma plaid afore my parts fall off wi' the cold." He took the thick woolen strip of tartan and wrapped it around his waist. "And the belt." He secured the kilt and sat on the cold ground to pull on his stockings and boots. "As soon as the men are decent, I will have a word with her." He slid his dirk inside one boot and stood then glanced around the room to make sure his men had dressed. "Go and get them now if ye please and take them well away from the men. I will need a private word wi' them, ken." He ran both hands through his damp hair. *I have not a clue what to say to the lass.*

Dismayed and shaken by the ordeal, Adrianna limped back into the Great Hall. In truth, she had expected Drew to come to her at once. Bad enough, he had neglected to inform her he was *Le Diable Noir* before seducing her beyond reason, but to ignore her arrival was unforgivable. Where was he? Not with this band of foul smelling brigands to be sure. She would complain about his men's blatant disrespect toward her, one had acted like a scoundrel and dared to expose his back in her presence.

Lifting the heavy oilskins from her battered toes, she followed Ian to a dusty alcove and stopped mid-stride causing Betty to bump into her. Somewhere in the miasma of sounds, she heard Ian's voice but her attention fixed on the man strolling toward her. Good Lord! Surely, this vision of male perfection could not be Drew Mackenzie? She gaped at him. Oh yes, she would know him anywhere even with his hair all about his shoulders and dressed in a kilt. His handsome countenance, unforgettable emerald eyes, breadth of shoulder, and hair with a raven's blue-black shine haunted her imaginings.

Unsure of the turmoil of emotions he evoked, she swallowed the lump in her throat and with due consideration to the pain in her hip gave him her best curtsy. Rising, she offered her hand and smiled. "So we meet again, Mister Mackenzie."

He lifted a large hand toward her cheek and she flinched away. A strange, uncertain expression flitted across his face. He dropped his hand and stood stiffly before her. His green gaze narrowed.

"It is *Laird* Mackenzie now, ma father died." His voice dropped to a conspiratorial whisper and stepped closer, sending a hint of bergamot laced with fresh male sweat over her. "Why on God's earth did ye board *The Black Turtle* and not take a coach to Scotland?"

Her heart sped and she had to bite the inside of her cheek to avoid leaning toward him. She inclined her head. "I am sure Rupert explained my situation to you in detail."

"Ye *situation?* Aye, lass, I ken verra well ye are betrothed to Baron du Court." He snorted and gazed into the distance for some moments before returning his indignant gaze to her. "Why did ye agree to such a thing? There was nay need to accept the Baron's offer. I asked ye to wait for me and gave ye ma word of honor I would return. Did ye not believe me?"

The scent of him, so delicious, made her want to swoon and be caught in his strong arms, but she lifted her chin determined to make her situation very clear. "When Lord Rupert informed my father he had decided to remove from London and would not be making an offer things moved very quickly. I barely had time to send him a letter informing him of my situation." She swallowed the lump in her throat. "I had nowhere to turn nor any excuse to offer my father to prevent the betrothal. I could not give him your name as a possible suitor. He had already made the settlement with Baron du Court and given Lord Moreau my dowry before he informed me. I protested most strongly, but you have no idea how difficult my father can be—I had *no* choice."

"Aye, ye *did.* Ye had wits enough to contact Rupert afore ye left. Ye could have taken shelter in any Inn betwixt London and Scotland but nay, ye allowed Lord Moreau to escort ye to *The Black Turtle.*" His magnificent green eyes flashed with anger. "Do ye have nay idea what that man is capable of doing to a woman alone?"

"Yes, I do *now* but I had thought to escape at a port along the way. I had no idea *The Black Turtle* was a pirate ship until I boarded." Disillusioned, she dropped her gaze. "I cannot believe it was my father's intention to place me in danger."

Ian, his face contorted with rage, gripped Drew's arm and gave him a quizzical stare.

"What has got into ye brother?"

Drew rounded on him, his mouth turning down.

"I ken the lass well and would have called upon her in a respectable fashion, but her father warned me most soundly not to cast a glance in her direction or he would have the English army on our doorstep." He made a low sound of derision. "Nay doubt, he believed a murderer a better match than a Scottish Laird."

My father betrayed me—again. Pain stabbed at Adrianna's heart. Could he be speaking the truth? "You h–have met my f–father?"

"Och aye, I met him the same night I met ye but he was not man enough to speak to me wi' out six or more of his friends present. He made his position verra clear. Why did ye think I asked Rupert to arrange our meetings?"

Unable to make sense of the implications, she gaped at him. "Rupert did mention his concerns. I was of the opinion my father would not accept your offer until you had come into your fortune and I do believe you made the same excuse for our charade." Her mind in turmoil, she pressed one hand against the wall in an effort to remain standing. "It would seem I am the recipient of a foul jest for both of you lied to me."

"Aye well, nay a lie more an *exaggeration* of the truth. I dinna want ye accepting the likes of Lord Balham and I *had* planned to go to your father once ma finances were in order." He shook his head slowly. "But ye did not give me the opportunity, did ye? Why when I gave ye ma word of honor to return did ye accept Baron du Court's offer?"

The pain of rejection subsided into irritation. She straightened and glared back at him. "I am *not* betrothed to Baron du Court. In fact, I have *not* accepted a match with anyone. I had to make my father believe I went to France to *consider* Baron du Court's offer. Do you really believe I wanted to leave England and chance never seeing you again?"

"To be perfectly honest, I dinna ken what to believe. Ye should have trusted me, Adrianna."

How could he understand the way her father had treated her, abandoning her into the hands of a murderer? How she wished Drew would hold her in his strong arms rather than chastising her. Tears welled and she dashed them away. "Trust had nothing to do with the way of things. I am an unwed woman and as such, compelled to do my father's bidding."

"Aye, but ye were able to leave the house to meet me." He dashed a hand through his wet hair. "Ye could have taken the mail coach to a safe place and I would have come for ye. Surely ye ken that or ye would not have asked for me to rescue ye from *The Black Turtle*." His voice dropped to a whisper. "Dinna ye ken how much danger ye put me in?"

She dropped her hand from the wall and stared at him in disbelief.

"Put *you* in danger? *You*? How so may I ask? *You* are not the one dragged onto a pirate ship and forced to marry against your will—and to a murderer no less." She refused to wilt under his stare. "And you know full well about the Baron du Court's reputation because I heard the truth of it from your own lips—I overheard your conversation about how he displays the heads of his enemies on stakes *and* your suspicions about the deaths of his wives."

"Och, did ye now? So ye kenned verra well the Baron is nay better than a demon and yet ye thought it fine to go ahead and board *The Black Turtle* along wi' the wee gomeral Moreau, aye?" He balled his hands on his hips.

"You—you—beastly man." She struck him hard across the face. "I had no choice but to do my father's bidding."

"Aye, ye did." He did not flinch, but his green eyes blazed enough to scorch her and his mouth turned up very slightly in one corner as if she had amused him.

Her attention moved to the palm print emblazoned on his cheek. Her outrageous attack on him had unsettled her and she clasped her hands in an attempt to appear in complete control. He must not know how hard her heart thundered in her chest or how badly her knees trembled. With effort, she dropped her voice to a calmer tone. "My father made it perfectly clear my presence was no longer welcome in his home. I had little choice but to comply with his wishes. I had nowhere to go and if I had taken flight to an inn, my father would have given chase. In truth, if you had not rescued me, I thought to ask the Countess D' Cologne to find me a suitable residence in France but then—"

"The Countess D' Cologne happens to be du Court's elderly aunt, so I canna see her offering ye assistance. Dinna ye have any notion of the trouble ye were getting into?"

Ian, his face white to the bone, stepped to her side.

"Nay she did not until she overheard Lord Moreau discussing plans to take her straight to Muzon Castle." He met his brother's hard gaze. "I gave her ma word to protect her, aye, and she in return promised to burn ma slave papers."

"She—What!" Drew rounded on his brother. "Tell me ye have not sold yourself to a Sassenach?"

"I had nay say in the business. When I met *The Black Turtle* and made enquiries about joining the crew, Captain Jacques laughed at the notion, and had me chained in the hold. The next thing I kenned he had sold me to Lord Moreau. Moreau gave me to Lady Adrianna as a bondservant. She had nothing to do wi' it so stop screaming at her. Ye are loud enough to wake the dead, and ye are frightening her. She has been through enough. Canna ye see she is barely able to stand?"

"The papers." Drew opened his hand palm up, toward her. "Now! I canna believe ye would not have destroyed them at once." The delicious man she had dreamed of had vanished to be replaced by a hardened warrior.

She glared at him. "How dare you, sir!" He loomed over her and fear closed her throat, but she straightened. "I abhor slavery. Dear God! What do you take me for?"

"I dinna ken but unless ye want me to strip ye in front of ma men to find them, I suggest ye do as I say." Drew towered over her.

She lifted the oilskin and retrieved the documents from her reticule. No sooner had the papers cleared the opening, he closed one large hand around her wrist and shook them from her grasp. Afraid, she stumbled and fell against him. Agony shot up her leg and she gripped the front of his shirt for purchase. He slid one strong arm around her waist and pulled her hard against him, but his countenance remained impassive giving her not one notion of his intentions. Why had she mooned over this man and wanted him above all others? She could plainly see Laird Mackenzie was a cold-hearted smuggler in league with Captain Jacques and not the fine gentleman, she had believed him to be.

Her gaze settled on Angus and noted his flaming red hair. She swallowed hard. The remembrance of reading about the outlawry of Rob Roy in a broadsheet screamed in her mind, good Lord, had she fallen into the den of the famous brigand? Without thought of the repercussions, she opened her mouth and words fell unfretted. "I gather I have fallen into the hands of Rob Roy's band of reprobates. Was this your plan? Do you intend to hold me for ransom or perhaps sell me into slavery too? That is what people like you and Captain Jacques do, is it not?"

The amused expression on Drew's face unnerved her. Could he be trying to deceive his men about their previous relationship? She wet her lips and pink flushed the tips of his ears.

"Ye believe ye are *insulting* me by insinuating I am with Rob Roy, The McGregor?" His green gaze moved over her and the man she loved emerged. "Ye ken nothing about me or ma clan, lass." He kicked the scattered documents toward Ian "Burn the papers and leave us. You too maid." He turned back to her and his expression turned to one of tenderness. "I will deal personally wi' Lady Adrianna."

More than a little surprised by his change of demeanor, she gave him her best coquettish smile and dropped her lashes. "How personally, Laird Mackenzie?"

"Och, lass, ye ken I needed a deception for ma men." He pushed her into the shadows, cupped the back of her neck, and lowered his head. "I am *sorry* for frightening ye. Oh, God, Adrianna, I thought ye were lost to me."

Overcome with desire, Drew took her mouth and she yielded to him, opening her soft lips and allowing him to explore her mouth. Under his caresses, she melted into his embrace. He sipped and nibbled telling her in his actions what he could not say aloud—not yet. He wanted to be alone with her and make her understand the way of things between them but with twenty men not ten paces away he must hold his tongue for a bit longer.

Her floral scent drove him to distraction and sliding his fingertips into her silken locks, he shook free the pins. She made a soft mewing sound and he reluctantly pulled back to gaze into eyes glazed with lust. "Ye are so beautiful. It seems I have waited a lifetime to hold ye once more. I am sorry ye have had to endure such hardship and I fear there will be more to come. I also had nay choice but to do ma father's bidding. Ye must believe, I wanted to return to ye straight away, but ma clan relies on me now as their laird."

"I do understand. Although, I am afraid you are correct I *will* bring trouble to your clan. Baron du Court will never give up looking for me." Adrianna sighed and rested her head on his shoulder. "Lord Moreau holds a document signed by my father. It is an agreement to a marriage between me and the Baron du Court." She gripped his shirtfront. "A paper that forces me to marry against my will and one I knew nothing about until I had boarded *The Black Turtle*." She drew in a sob and her bottom lip quivered. "My father betrayed me."

"Aye, he did. It is hard to believe a father capable of such a despicable act." He cleared his throat. "I thought your father was up to nay good. Lord Rupert overheard your altercation with Lord Balham. Nay doubt your father would have insisted ye wed that weasel too."

"Yes, Lord Balham endeavored to place me in a compromising position and by doing so believed he could force me to marry him. It would seem my father did not care whom I married."

"I am at a loss to ken why he prevented *me* from attending ye." He pressed a kiss to her unruly curls. "Did he mention me at all?"

Adrianna chewed on her bottom lip as if deciding how to reply.

"No, he did not and I am at a loss to say why he threatened you unless he had reservations about a Scotsman taking up residence in my mother's house. You see her vast estate will pass into my hands on the day I marry and you must be aware of the … ah … current politics?"

He slid his hands under her oilskin and rubbed her cold back. "Aye, maybe, but why dinna he want ye around? Did ye cause him embarrassment or have ye done something to shame him?"

"It would seem I am an embarrassment to him in many ways." She sighed and lowered her long lashes. "We argued about my desire to help the less fortunate and my willingness to work with them has caused him embarrassment." She trembled against him. "Although I believe he used this excuse to his advantage. You see, my mother died many years ago and he plans to marry again and set up his nursery. I am an only child and he desires a male heir above all things."

He wanted to kiss away the tears wetting her lashes and comfort her. She trembled in his arms and he pulled her against him. "And Lord Rupert tells me, ye have rejected every gentleman who offered for ye." He gave her a speculative gaze. "Were ye waiting for me to come along, lass?"

Adrianna glared at him. "I am *not* a 'lass.'"

"Och aye, ye are." Drew's wide mouth twitched at the corners. "Will ye answer ma question?

Would he ever cease making her knees tremble? "I had hoped to meet someone like you, yes that is true. You see, I decided long ago to marry for *love* and refused to accept an old smelly man of my father's choosing."

"Will it make a difference, now ye ken I am a smuggler?" Drew raised one dark eyebrow.

She swallowed and gaped at him. "That is beside the point. You have never once mentioned you love me."

"Have I not? Well, I will have to remedy that oversight." He chuckled and the low, rich sound made her knees weak. "So ma being *Le Diable Noir* does not disgust ye?"

Her face grew hot and she stared at her feet. "No. Although we do need to discuss this subject at length." She sighed. "At least *you* are not a murderer—are you?"

He moved closer and his warm breath brushed her cheek.

"Nay, I am not. Tell me what ye want from me, Adrianna, and ken I will never betray ye."

She gripped his arm and met his fascinating gaze. Dear Lord, she could fall into his eyes and remain there forever. "I would like to go with you but if it means trouble for your clan then escort me to Inverness and I will find a place to stay."

"Aye, I want ye by ma side and tell the world ye are mine, but first I must speak to ma men. They dinna ken we met in London or of ma intentions toward ye and because of the current unrest within ma clan, I canna give them the truth of it yet. I care for ye, Adrianna, but I must ask ye to wait for me a little bit longer."

"I have waited this long and I understand the reluctance of your clan to accept me." She bit her bottom lip. "I am sure I will gain their favor once they know me better, but I fear my way will be difficult with Baron du Court's men searching for me."

He rubbed his chin thoughtfully.

"Ye are correct Lord Moreau will set out to find ye, and I dinna want him discovering *Le Diable Noir* is Drew Mackenzie. Although, he will assume ye are traveling with carts heading for Inverness. If he arrives afore we do, likely he will ride out with his men to search for ye on the road. "

His gaze drifted over her from bare feet to the smelly oilskin covering her gown. "Ye will need a disguise. Wear a plain skirt if ye have one and I will give ye ma spare plaid to cover ye head." He touched her cheek. "Now, will ye allow me to escort ye to the fire so ye may warm yourself and get a bite to eat? I will speak with ye again soon."

Bereft of his warmth she took his arm, but with each step into the Great Hall, pain burned deep in her leg but she refused to limp or show any signs of distress to his men. Small fires glowed throughout the room sending a waving black forest of shadows against the castle walls. The men turned to stare at her, and not one of them smiled. A shiver of apprehension ran down her back. "Laird Mac—"

"Ye must refer to me as Drew if ye are to make it to Badenoch unnoticed. We will all refer to ye as Adrianna. Using an English title on the road will cause ye undue attention and if we meet anyone, best ye keep hold of your tongue." He dashed a hand through his hair and sighed wearily. "Now, I suggest ye eat and get some rest as we move out at sunrise." He turned to face the onlookers. "What are ye all gawking at? Get away wi' ye."

Groaning, she carefully lowered her aching body beside Betty. The girl had filled a plate with roast meat and pushed it into her hands.

"My goodness, milady, you are quite flushed. Did Laird Mackenzie offer to treat your wounds?"

She pressed one hand to her boiling forehead. "No, and I did not ask him. As soon as we have a little more privacy I will see to the cuts myself." She sighed and smiled at Betty. "These are good men and we will be safe under Laird Mackenzie's protection. We will be leaving for Inverness at daybreak."

"If you say so, milady." Betty wrinkled her nose. "I do hope the stink will be less noticeable in the open."

Adrianna stared at the plate of succulent roast pig but had no appetite. Reluctantly, she forced a few morsels into her mouth and reached for the wineskin. She would need her strength to survive the journey. Fever from the putrefaction of her leg heated her flesh and her vision often blurred around the edges. Without the assistance of a doctor to tend her wounds, she feared her injury might well kill her.

Chapter Six

Drew dragged his saddle to one of the small fires set around the Great Hall and lowered his aching limbs to the cold floor. His heart still raced from kissing her. He snorted. Christ, he had never met a woman with such tenacity. A smile tugged at his lips, God, he admired her spirit. He gazed across the room at her. *Not to mention her full, luscious lips and rounded arse.*

Angus came to his side, pushed a plate of roast pork into his hands, and raised both red brows in question.

"A Sassenach shrew to be sure." Angus dropped to the floor beside him. "I dinna think I will be able to stand much more of her squawking."

Drew reached for his dirk and sighed. The delicious aroma of the succulent dish made his wame rumble. He dug the tip of the blade into the meat, lifted it to his mouth, and sighing chewed with contentment. "Nay, not a shrew, she is verra braw to attempt an escape from *The Black Turtle*, and then stand toe-to-toe wi' the likes of me. I admire a strong woman, not so much in muscle, aye, but in their conviction. Although, she *is* nicely rounded, not skinny like most of the Sassenach women who pick at their food then wonder why they swoon the moment they take more than a few steps. Most are too weak to stand let alone escape by dropping down the side of a ship." He met Angus's gaze. "I will tell ye the truth of it. I have met the lass afore, some months ago at a ball in London. If her father had not warned me off, I would have called on her. She is a bonny lassie, aye?"

"*She* is trouble and if ye canna see that ye are blind. Ye should not have involved the clan in her problems." Angus narrowed his red brows. "I ken why Lord Beachwood dinna want the likes of ye near her."

"Och aye, and how would ye ken such a thing?"

"It was Lord Beachwood who offered for your mother and your grandsire sent him away wi' a flea in his ear." Angus chuckled. "Then ye showed interest in *his* daughter and ye the image of your grandsire. It was not ye, he dinna approve of, I believe, he was getting his own justice, ken?"

Unable to believe his ears, Drew stared at Angus in disbelief. To think, Lord Beachwood would make his daughter suffer in order to settle an old score. *Arse wipe.* "Nay I dinna ken, he had met ma mother."

"Aye, he did. The idiot got himself turned about on a visit to the Highlands and wandered into Foiseil Castle. Your ma was tending the sick alongside your grandmother and being a surgeon he offered assistance." He grinned and his blue eyes twinkled. "Ah well, once the Sassenach dandy laid eyes on your ma, and I might add she was nay more than fifteen, he wanted her, aye. Ye Grandsire put up wi' him pestering her for a wee while then told him, his daughter would marry a Highlander, not a Sassenach weakling and that he had promised her to a the Mackenzie."

Drew grinned. "Aye, he is nay bigger than a lad of twelve."

"I would take his threat seriously and keep well away from Lady Adrianna. Ian told me she is promised to a baron and it is none of your business if she wants to marry him or not." Angus waved his dirk to cool the meat pinned to the tip. "Ye have nay notion if Baron du Court is a favorite of King Louis and your interference may prevent our trading with Captain Jacques in the future."

"Dinna fash yourself, du Court has nay friends and least of all King Louis. Du Court may own *The Black Turtle*, but Captain Jacques is under orders from Cardinal de Richelieu, the king's chief minister." Drew wiggled his eyebrows. "In fact, it is *me* Louis holds in high regard."

"Cackle away, but how long do ye think it will take Moreau to come after her? Ma guess is he will come ashore the moment *The Black Turtle* drops anchor at Inverness. The ship will be there more than a day afore we arrive. Are ye prepared to meet this man in a duel and risk your life for a Sassenach besom because this is a verra likely outcome?" He indicated toward the huddled figures of the women. "The wee Moreau weasel was in charge of her and I doubt verra much he will be planning to return to France wi' out his master's bride. The baron would have his head."

Drew snorted and grinned. "It would be worth the trip to France to see the wee gromeral's head atop a pike on the baron's castle ramparts." He reached for the wineskin, bit out the cork, and raised the opening to his mouth. He drank the rich brew and corking the top met Angus's intent gaze. Now was not the time to inform his godfather, he cared deeply for Adrianna. "I am going to help her. It is a matter of honor, aye?"

"Aye well, I will have your back nay matter." Angus raised both brows. "If ye have made up your mind to protect her from du Court ye will have to take her wi' us to Badenoch."

"Aye, I will." He stretched to ease his cramped muscles. "Although, I do not imagine the journey will be easy for a fine lady like her."

"I never thought I would hear myself saying this about a Sassenach but in truth, ye need to go easy on the lass. Braw she may be but ye dinna have the experience with womenfolk as a married man might." Angus held up one grease-streaked hand to prevent his retort. "I am aware ye have tupped all the available widows in Scotland and maybe France as well, but there is more to a woman than carnal desire. Canna ye see she is in pain and it is not with the discomfort of leaving home. Mark ma words there is something verra wrong wi' her. She is burning with fever and I will wager she will not live long enough to reach Badenoch."

Drew narrowed his gaze at his godfather. "Do ye think I dinna ken she is suffering? She kens I am a healer but has not asked me to tend her."

His gaze flicked to Adrianna huddled by the fire. To be sure, the moment she had set eyes on him, her astonished expression had unhinged him. She had not expected a Highland smuggler to be sure. He dropped his gaze to prevent Angus noticing the glow of desire crawling up his neck to heat his cheeks at the sweet memory of her kiss.

He rubbed his nose, Christ, her scent lingered, and his lips still tingled from their kiss. The simple touch of her flesh had heated his groin. He had taken advantage of her in the darkness and snorted, disgusted with his outrageous behavior. Yet, she had returned his attention freely. He smiled at the remembrance of their first meeting then quickly moved his attention to his meal to consider the immediate situation.

Adrianna's presence in his clan would undoubtedly cause trouble, but she would require his protection. Would she be prepared to travel with him in dreadful conditions to the safety of Foiseil Castle? Would she survive? To be sure, she had courage aplenty but inner strength was no cure for the fever.

Damn it, I will have to insist I treat her. He rubbed the back of his neck and pushed the last morsel of meat into his mouth. He glanced around for Angus's lad. "Dermot, will ye fetch me a lantern, lad?" He reached for the bottle of whisky in his saddlebags then searched around for the small bottle of feverfew juice and his bag of herbs. He had a few clean rags and a jar of comfrey ointment. If the silly lass had a mind to die on him, well, he would not allow it pride be damned. He left the small pile of items on the ground, pushed to his feet, and strode toward Adrianna.

Squatting in front of her, his attention moved from the plate of untouched meat to her face. Dark circles cut deep beneath both eyes, her pallid complexion, and the spots of pink high on her cheeks informed him her condition had deteriorated rapidly in the last hour. Pushing down anger at his own stupidity, he touched her cheek to get her attention. "Ye are in pain. Will ye allow me to treat your wounds? If not, at least take something for the fever, aye?"

He took the lantern from Dermot placed it on the floor and spoke to the boy in Gaelic. "Thank ye, now go fetch the whisky and other things I left by the fire, and follow me."

She lifted her fever blotched face to him.

"If I may have a little water and perhaps a rag, I can do for myself. I have Betty."

He gripped her elbow. "Come wi' me, bring your maid. I will take ye to a place where she can tend ye in private."

"I thank you"—Adrianna pressed a small trembling hand to her neck—"but I am not sure I can stand at the moment. Perhaps after I have had a little time to rest?" She straightened and winced. "In fact, I am *quite* sure I cannot move. If you would be so kind as to—"

He scooped her into his arms. "Hush your blathering."

Ignoring her protests, he headed to the back of the Great Hall. The wildflower scent of her muddled his senses, and as if to test his resolve, a lock of her soft brown hair caressed his chin. His thoughts filled with taking her to his bed. *Oh, Jesus.* He ground his teeth and forced the wanton image of her writhing under his touch to the darkest recesses of his mind. She weighed a might more than he remembered and with each step, the hem of her dress struck his shins with considerable force. Aye well, the lass would be canny enough to carry gold hidden in her petticoats. He grimaced. The weight would be placing an extra burden on her injured leg. He glanced over one shoulder to her maid. "Bring the lantern." To his relief, the girl offered no protest, grabbed a large canvas bag in one hand, picked up the lantern with the other, and followed.

Exhausted, confused, and in agony Adrianna sought comfort from Drew. Relaxing against his strong, hard chest, she inhaled the intoxicating masculine scent of him laced with the smell of wine. She sighed, indeed being so close to the male perfection she had desired for so long sent quivers of desire thrumming through her. Daring had her in its hold. All rational thought fled and she slid one hand inside the neck of his shirt.

She brushed his bare chest brazenly and allowed the tips of her fingers to linger in the soft curls. To be sure, the glowing ember of deep longing, she had experienced for so long burst into flames. As if reading her thoughts, Drew pressed her against his hard chest. His intimate touch heated the junction between her thighs and without considering the consequences, she melted into his embrace and traced small circles over his smooth skin. Catching his sharp intake of breath, she removed her hand at once. "Oh, I do beg your pardon."

"I crave your touch, but this is not the place nor the time. We both want more than decency allows, aye? Dinna ye ken I want to kiss ye again and have ye quiver under ma touch?" His mouth turned down at the corners. "I understand your need for comforting so we will have to go canny." He rubbed his face against her cheek and his unshaved chin cut a rough yet exhilarating path across her flesh. "It does not mean I do not burn for ye."

Her face grew hot at the implication and she gazed at his handsome profile. "I may well enjoy your touch, but I have no intention of allowing any impropriety."

"Christ, Adrianna, what sort of a man do ye take me for? Have I not considered your pleasure above ma own at all times?" He let out a long weary sigh. His grip tightened around her and his breath brushed her ear in a whisper. "Ye are verra bold for an innocent. Your eyes and body tell me what your lips deny. I burn to have ye under me, calling out ma name in passion."

Abashed, she aimed a feeble punch at his chest. "You, sir, are no gentleman."

"Did your mother explain to ye the consequences of taunting a man and how a lady should not offer what she is not willing to give?" He tightened his grip. "Now stop fighting me, aye. Ye will only hurt yourself."

In truth, his gaze had penetrated her defenses, sunk down into her baser instincts, and filled her with desire. Fatigued and desperately thirsty, she rested her head on his shoulder. She appreciated his willpower, indeed without it her virginity would not survive long under his intimate attention. How could she forget the forbidden touch of his hands, his delicious kisses upon her most intimate parts? Glancing at his long straight nose and square chin, she sighed. Oh, yes indeed, she would gladly risk fire and brimstone to have Laird Drew Mackenzie.

"Here, this is more private, aye?" Drew set her down gently before an alcove. "I will have one o' the carts filled wi' hay and brought inside. The oilskins will make it more comfortable for the pair of ye. I have a spare plaid ye can use to keep ye warm and I will ask ma brother, Jamie for his as well." He cast a critical gaze over her. "Bide here. Dermot will be along with warm water and soap." He turned to speak to Dermot in Gaelic.

Her legs trembled in a most disconcerting fashion and she leaned heavily against the wall for purchase. Drew took her elbow with one warm hand and slipped the other around her waist. She gripped the front of his shirt and stared at him. "I do beg your pardon. It would seem I am a little unsteady on my feet."

"When did ye last eat?" Drew examined her face intently. "Ye are as white as chalk."

"She has not eaten a bite since before the storm, milord." Betty gave a little bob. "She banged her head and I have yet to see the damage she has suffered to her leg."

Adrianna bristled and glared at her. "I am quite capable of answering Laird Mackenzie's questions myself, Betty. Go and assist Dermot with the water."

"Nay bide." Drew straightened and smiled at Betty. "I do appreciate ye telling me of your mistress's injuries and I ken ye are doing this out of concern for her well-being. Ye must not repeat what ye have heard to anyone about ma previous acquaintance of your mistress. Do ye understand?"

"I would never betray milady's confidence, not ever." Betty's cheeks flamed.

"Good, now mind ye give her the feverfew and whisky for the pain. I will send Dermot wi' some herbs to help wi' the healing but dinna leave your mistress, I want ye to bide close by to ensure propriety." He bent to address her his eyes filled with concern. "Ye must have Betty wi' ye at all times and we must avoid being too close. The thought of kissing ye teases me unmercifully and I have nay experience wi' maidens."

What does he mean by 'teasing' him? She stiffened. Surely, their brief kiss had not awakened his carnal nature.

"You have proved to be honorable in the past. What has changed? Am I to be afraid of you now?"

"Afraid, nay never, but ye ken verra well I desire ye." Drew dashed a hand through his long black hair and his tortured expression bore into her. "Dinna look at me as if ye canna understand what I am saying, ye ken full well. What do ye expect from me, Adrianna?" He snorted. "Ye ken I am nay Saint and the way ye regard me would strain the endurance of the Pope."

She blinked up at him speechless. Heavens above, had she stoked an uncontainable fire in him. Drawing a deep breath, she forced her mind to consider the implications of his words. She would answer him honestly and hope he would respect her truthfulness. "I am sorry to have acted inappropriately. You see, I do not understand the ways of men. I do admit our time together has awakened a longing I cannot explain."

He touched her cheek and she forced back the desire to press her face into his palm.

"Adrianna—"

"Please, I beg you to allow me to continue." She swallowed the lump in her throat and examined his handsome face seeing only compassion. "You see, I am two and twenty, well past my prime, and my options to date have been bland puddings of men. Then I met you and for the first time in my life, I felt attractive." She dropped her gaze to the floor. "However, I will not be your mistress. All I have left is my pride." She blinked forcing the tears away. "I would rather throw myself off a cliff than live in trepidation of being tossed aside for another more youthful mistress."

Drew let out a long sigh and lifted her chin with one long finger.

"Ye are innocent, lass, and dinna ken how desirable ye are." He sighed. "I dinna need a mistress, and Christ, I would rather cut ma own throat than cause ye to commit self-murder." His brow furrowed. "Ye must understand, I am a *man*, aye and it has been some months since I took a woman to ma bed." His gaze traveled over her in a frank inspection.

"I dinna think ye are 'past your prime' nay, not at all." His green eyes softened. "There is a connection between us. I sensed it the first moment I laid eyes on ye." He let his hand drop and one side of his mouth lifted in a rueful smile. "More so after we spent time together but ye are correct, ye are verra innocent and dinna understand the ways of men."

She swayed, caught in his gaze like some unfortunate fly in a spider's web and fought to preserve some modicum of dignity. "I have never been exposed to such a man as you before."

"As I expected, and we can use this time to ken each other better, seeing me as a Highlander ye might well form a different opinion of me." He grinned and his eyes danced with amusement. "Keeping Betty close by will ensure your reputation remains unsullied." He pushed a strand of hair from her cheek. "Ye are verra beautiful." His green gaze swept over her. "I have missed ye, Adrianna, more than I can say."

"I have missed you too. "She lowered her gaze to rest on his chest. "I am worried being here will put you all in danger."

"Aye, Lord Moreau is like a dog wi' a bone. We have to make sure he does not find ye in ma company."

Heavens above, not only Lord Moreau would cause a problem. To be sure, if her father got wind of her direction, he would make a request to King George to send a battalion of troops from the barracks at Glenelg to kill them all. She met his gaze. "Had I known about my father's threat, I can assure you I would not have asked for your assistance."

He chuckled and the sound came like a roll of thunder from deep in his chest.

"Dinna fash, because I am verra glad you did." He bowed then straightened and amusement glittered in his eyes. "Get well, *mho creagh*,"

She swallowed hard, his soft words sounded like an endearment, to be sure. She stared into his fathomless gaze. "I am sorry I do not understand. Would you repeat that in the King's tongue for me please?"

"The *English* king's tongue? Aye well, *mho creagh,* means 'my love.'" He turned and strode into the darkness.

Adrianna gaped after him speechless. At last, the term of endearment she had craved to hear but now with an assurance of his feelings toward her, keeping him at a respectable distance in front of his men would be difficult. He had such strong arms and the scent of him had comforted her like a warm hug. She bolstered her resolve and turned her attention to the matters at hand. If she neglected the pain in her leg, she may not survive to witness the outcome of her journey.

Using the wall for support, she waited for Dermot to deliver the bucket of water and soap to Betty. The lad kept his attention fixed on the floor as if looking at her would turn him to stone. "Thank you, Dermot."

The boy's ears pinked at the sound of his name and he turned and scurried away. She glanced at Betty. "Remind me to ask Laird Mackenzie the Gaelic word for 'thank you.' It seems Dermot is more than a little afraid of me. Perhaps addressing him in his own language might help."

"As it happens I asked Ian, it is *'tapadh leat,'* milady."

Betty moved deeper into the alcove and secured the lantern to a hook in the wall.

"There is plenty of room in here for me to tend you and it is a might warmer than the Great Hall." She turned and smiled at Adrianna. "Allow me to remove your dress and see what is amiss."

Adrianna surveyed her surroundings with interest. Would hiding in castle ruins with a group of smelly men be her lot in life from now on? She examined the alcove. The small chamber, although ruined by centuries of neglect, held a glimpse of its former glory. Intricate iron sconces remained attached to the walls each depicting an acorn surrounded by oak leaves and stains from their dripping wax candles still marred the floor below.

Her attention moved over the damp, moss-covered stone walls to a small threadbare remnant of a once rich tapestry. Moving toward the back of the room, she stepped with care over a covering of thick dust and debris. She grimaced and batted away a miasma of dusty spiders' webs as thick as lace curtains.

"This will have to do, Betty. This room gives us far more privacy than in the Great Hall with the men." She dragged the oilskin over her head and spread it on the floor. "Once I have washed the grime off my feet and rested, I will be fine."

As Betty removed the wax paper surrounding the small bar of soap, the rich smell of bergamot with a hint of lavender filled the alcove. Adrianna drew a deep breath to fill her head with the delightful fragrance. It would seem Drew had given her his own supply of the expensive French extravagance. To use it and surround herself with the scent of him would be a temptation impossible to resist. She stepped out of her gown and waited for Betty to remove her stays.

"I can manage now, thank you, Betty. Take the soap back to Laird Mackenzie and offer my thanks. I would prefer to use my own."

"Yes, milady." Betty searched a canvas bag and retrieved a bar of floral soap. She handed it to her. "Do you want me to return it now because Laird Mackenzie insisted I remain with you at all times?"

"Yes, Betty, go now. I will be quite safe."

A dark shadow loomed in the entrance and Betty cried out in alarm.

"Nay ye will not." Drew bent to pick up the discarded petticoat and stays. "I will return these after I have removed the unnecessary weight." He handed the garments to Dermot. The boy chanced a terrified glance at her and scurried away with the strings of her stays dragging in his wake.

She gaped at Drew in disbelief. How could he possibly have known she had secured a fortune in her clothes? "I bid you to return my garments at once."

"Nay, lass, I am trying ma best to take care of ye and I refuse to allow ye to carry this extra weight with an injury." Drew held out one hand toward Betty for the soap then dropped it into his sporran. "Dinna fash, I will not steal from ye." He met Adrianna's gaze and lifted his chin. "Ye have ma word."

She blinked unable to form a reply then made a slow inventory of the powerful man standing before her. A warm glow curled around her heart for he was her knight in shining armor and she would trust him with her soul. He was, after all a laird and had treated her with an abundance of kindness. She smiled and attempted to explain her concern. "I *do* trust you, but the jewels are—"

"There is nay need to give me a reason. I ken ye have them in case of trouble and I will make sure ye have a few back just in case, but I am wi' ye now. Ye are safe wi' me, Adrianna." His gaze moved down the front of her shift to her aching nipples and back. His mouth twitched at the corners. "Ye trusted me in London and ye can rely on me now." He inclined his head and regarded her for a long moment. "I desire ye, sweet Adrianna, and have made the fact clear, and I believe ye want me too."

Standing in her shift with her legs exposed for the world to see, she wanted to hide. How could she deny her deep craving for his touch, his delicious kisses? Heat blistered her cheeks and she met a gaze filled with longing. She swallowed hard. "I *do* want you."

Catching Betty's scandalized expression she stepped away from him, and a burning flame cut deep into her hip. Unable to disguise a gasp of agony she turned away and reached for her.

"Christ, how much longer are ye planning to suffer? Ye ken verra well I am a healer." Drew's attention moved to her bruised leg. He uttered a string of unintelligible words under his breath and leveled his gaze on her. His lips flattened into a determined line. "Lift your shift. I insist on examining the damage to your leg."

"I will not. I can manage well enough." Seeking something to cover her, she bent for the oilskin. Pain shot through her temples and the room moved in and out of focus.

"It is not as if I have not seen your legs afore and more besides." Drew caught her in his strong arms and lowered her gently to the oilskin. Sharp, hot agony stabbed to the bone cutting off her protest. Tears dampened her cheeks and unable to resist his ministrations, she rolled over onto one side.

He gave a grunt of derision, kneeled beside her and lifted her shift to examine her leg.

"Saint Bride!" He lifted his gaze to Betty. "Bring the lantern closer, aye." He squeezed Adrianna's shoulder. "Ye are foolish to leave this unattended. There is a splinter, the size of ma thumb, buried in your thigh with poison leaking into your hip. Canna ye smell it putrefying?" He pulled the dirk from his boot and handed it to Betty. "Tell Angus I need him and to place the tip of ma dirk in the fire. He is to have Dermot ready to bring it to me the moment I call, aye."

His expression filled with compassion and he moved his cool fingers over her examining her leg with the gentlest of care. She inhaled his familiar masculine scent and refrained from fighting the inevitable. Cold air hit exposed burning flesh and in a wave of panic, she grasped a handful of her shift and attempted to push the thin fabric over her bare bottom. He stilled her with one large hand and thrust a bottle of whisky under her nose.

"Drink as much as ye can, it will help with the pain. I will remove the splinter and drain the pus." He guided the bottle to her lips. "Drink, Adrianna, and for once do as ye are told, aye."

She understood the procedure having witnessed the lancing of boils and the like, but her father always administered laudanum before the process. A shiver of apprehension slipped down her spine and curled in her belly. Why did he need his dirk hot from the fire? Did he plan to burn her? Her father used a sharp knife but never burned his patients. She took a mouthful of whisky and red-hot flames shot down the back of her throat stealing her breath. Coughing, she pushed the bottle away. "That is disgusting."

"Aye well, it is ma clan's twenty-year-old whisky but it is all I have. Drink again and then twice more." Drew upended the bottle into her mouth. "Do it now."

She blinked back tears and drank more of the foul liquid. A warm glow filled her belly and slid agreeably to her toes, but the throbbing pain in her leg persisted. Embarrassment at her intolerable predicament heated her cheeks and she leveled her gaze on him. "I do understand what you are about but why does Angus have to witness my shame?"

"It is nay shame to need help wi' an injury such as this. Ye canna deal wi' it yourself. Angus is the only married man wi' me and I will need someone to hold ye while I tend to your leg. The wee lassie is not strong enough, but I will see she bides close by." Drew's eyebrows met in the middle in a deep frown. "Is it considered dishonorable in England for women to ask for your father's care in such matters?"

She dashed a hand over wet cheeks and shook her head. "No, of course not but *he* is a physician."

"Aye well, in ma clan so *am* I." Drew pressed the bottle back to her lips. "So I will try ma best not to disgrace ye." He reached into his sporran, took out a dark strip of something, and pressed it into her hand. "Bite on this, aye."

Her face burned and a pulse throbbed behind her eyes, but she managed to focus on the thick piece of leather indented with bite marks, he had thrust into her trembling fingers. Of course, he was correct and struggling would only make things worse. She lay back and squeezed her eyes shut allowing tears to stream down her cheeks unrestrained. Under her, the rank smelling oilskin did nothing to prevent the cold seeping through the floor and chilling her to the bone. She shivered and Drew gently pressed a rough linen rag to her cheeks dabbing at the tears.

"Bide awhile. I will fetch ye a blanket." His footsteps faded into the low hum of men's distant conversations.

She clutched the bottle of whisky to her chest and drifted in a muddle-headed state. She started at the sound of voices then Betty kneeled beside her and wrapped a warm blanket around her shoulders. She raised her head and Betty's face swum before her.

"I am afraid."

"It will be all right, milady. Laird Mackenzie says it will be all over in a matter of minutes." Betty pressed the opening of a small bottle to her lips. "Have a sip of this for the fever and take a little more of the whisky to help with the pain."

Betty gave her a quivering smile and smoothed the hair from her face.

"I have some herbs steeping to help with the healing so you will be as right as rain before you know it."

Convinced nothing would help with the pain or ease the fear paralyzing her, she lifted the bottle of whisky and swallowed, gagging at the sharp burn. Good Lord, to think men drunk this foul concoction for pleasure. Moments later, Drew returned with Angus and their shadows moved in an eerie procession across the walls. Indeed, she must have fallen into hell because the men's use of the Gaelic sounded demonic even spoken in hushed tones. She pressed a hand to her forehead in an attempt to quell the awful throbbing and glared at them. "Will you *please* speak English? I am afraid and convinced you are hiding the truth from me. D–do you intend to a–amputate my l–leg?"

"Nay, I may be strong, but I doubt I could sever your leg wi' ma dirk." Drew squatted beside her. "Dinna fash, I will have the splinter out in nay time at all."

"Then I beg you explain what you plan to do so I may ready myself."

"Aye well, ye will have seen it done before, aye?" Drew took the bottle of whisky and poured a quantity over a blade in his hand then splashed some on her leg. "Well, in ma experience the best cure for purulent skin is whisky and fire. I will be making a small cut to remove the splinter and wash the wound wi' the whisky then I will wi' use the tip of ma dirk to cauterize it. Dermot will bring it to me red-hot when needs be." He laid a hand on her back. "It will hurt like buggery but if I leave the splinter to fester, ye will die of the fever."

"Will ye allow me to hold ye still?" Angus loomed over her. "I have been married twelve years, so I will not be taking notice of ye."

"Are ye ready, Adrianna?" Drew's voice drifted to her soft and encouraging.

The heat from his palm seeped through the blanket sending comfort. She clasped Betty's hand. After all, she had little choice and nodding her consent placed the leather between her teeth then bit down hard.

Drew soaked rags in alcohol and ignoring Angus's descriptive Gaelic curses for the waste of good whisky on a Sassenach, packed them around the inflamed area on Adrianna's hip. Her screams of pain tore at his heart, but he bit down hard on his cheek and continued. The heat radiating from her worried him, as did the red lines spreading down her thigh from the injury. He shook his head in disbelief. The pain she had suffered would have toppled a warrior let alone a lass.

He pressed one hand on her hip to stretch the skin, took his dirk in the other, and sliced the length of the splinter. She shook violently under Angus's firm grip and her screams sent the horses inside the Great Hall into a panic. He spoke in Gaelic to Angus insisting he increase his hold on her trembling thigh and moving swiftly scraped the wound, removing the splinter and debris. After excising the damaged flesh, he splashed the cut with whisky.

"Aaaarh! Sweet Jesus." Adrianna spat out the leather strip and turned her ashen tear streaked face toward him. "Stop... *please,* Drew. I beg you to cease, I cannot stand a moment longer."

Christ! Her begging near undone him. He wanted to hold her close and whisper words of comfort but instead, he touched her cheek. "Ye are verra braw. Not much longer, *mho creagh.*"

He caught Angus's expression of incredulity at the Gaelic endearment and shrugged, Adrianna understand the meaning of the phrase and needed his comfort. He strengthened his resolve and called to Dermot for the scalding dirk. The boy came running and skidded to a halt at the entrance. He lifted his gaze to him. "Bring it here."

Taking the blade, he wiped the red-hot tip across the open wound sending blue flames dancing over the raw, whisky-soaked skin in a sizzle. The small room echoed with Adrianna's screams and the smell of burning flesh rose up in a curl of white smoke.

"There, it is done. Ye have been verra braw. Hold still and I will dress the wound to ease the pain."

Not wasting time, he covered the wound with a thick layer of comfrey salve. He lifted her thigh to bind the wound and all gallant intentions vanished. His attention riveted on the glimpse of soft golden curls at her apex and her delicate feminine allure. Captivated, he paused in his ministrations.

Angus's Gaelic cursing slapped him back to reality.

"Get on wi' your work and keep your lustful gaze away from the lass." Angus glared at him. "Ye are a healer, aye? Then act like one and stop allowing your cock to rule your head."

Drew bit down hard on his cheek and set to his task, apparently his godfather had not missed the direction of his lustful attention. He ached for her. Christ, she was everything he desired in a woman but his duty to protect her came before his own needs. In truth, he would wed her in a heart's beat. His clan would object strongly to him taking a Sassenach for his bride, but her natural charm would soon win their hearts.

Will she have me now? I am not the fine gentleman, she expected. Would she accept his offer after experiencing the hard life of a Highland laird or leave him to pursue a new life of her own? *Apart from ma horses, and a fledgling company in France, I have not one thing to offer her. No doubt, Rupert, with his fortune would be a better match.* The thought of the two together made his wame curdle. Sighing, he tucked in the end of the strip of linen to secure the bandage then pulled down the shift to cover her bottom.

Had he done enough to save her? Her skin burned with fever and the escape had exhausted her. How could she possibly have enough strength to fight the poison from the wound let alone be fit enough to travel in the morning? Sobs and fever tremors racked her, but he dare not offer comfort in front of Angus. He wrapped the blanket around her and patted her back then lifted his chin to meet his stern expression. "Do ye disapprove of ma healing, godfather?"

"Nay, but I will be speaking to ye in private, aye. Come away from the lass and let her rest." Angus folded his arms across his broad chest and glared at him.

He did not have the slightest inclination to argue with Angus and pushed to his feet. "Fine, but I will need to check her during the night. Go along now, I need to speak wi' Betty afore I seek ma rest."

"Verra well." Angus stomped out of the room, his footsteps echoing in the hallway.

Drew turned to Betty clearing his throat to get her attention. The young lass's shoulders drooped with exhaustion. If she fell asleep, Adrianna may die. He could not risk leaving Adrianna's side no matter what Angus thought about his intentions.

"Leave her to rest for a wee while. I will have the men fetch the wagon. Try and stay awake for another two hours then I will come and take care of her so you may seek your rest." He smiled to calm her terrified expression. "Your mistress will be fine and will not have more than a small scar to show for it but mind ye keep giving her the herbs. I will send ye another bottle of whisky for the pain. Ye might have a wee dram yourself ye look a bit peaked."

Betty bobbed a curtsy and her dark hair spilled around her shoulders. He cleared his throat. "Do you have a cap to cover your hair? It is not seemly for a woman's head to go uncovered in Scotland. I want ye to make sure her ladyship wears a plain gown and is well covered with ma plaid, aye."

"Yes, milord. I will see to it right away." Betty's eyes became round. "Beg pardon, milord?"

"Aye, what is it and call me laird if ye please?"

Betty drew herself up and with a determined expression on her face, jutted out her chin. "You know very well, she may die of the fever but if she survives, you cannot expect milady to travel in the morning. She is suffering great pain. Beggin' your pardon, sir, but only a beast of a man would expect such a thing."

"A *beast* would have left her to suffer, aye? Dinna fash once she is over the fever I have a verra strong medicinal to help wi' the pain." He stared down at Adrianna's chalk white skin. "If I had time to wait for her to rest dinna ye think I would? Apart from Lord Moreau hot on our heels, dinna ye ken the customs officers watch this coastline? If we are discovered with smuggled merchandise, ye will both be hanged along wi' us. By morning, we will have the carts filled and our goods well hidden under straw and animal carcasses. God willing, as a clan taking their kills to market, we will not draw the attention of the excise men or Lord Moreau. We leave at first light." He strode out without a backward glance and called to Dermot to bring him water to wash his hands.

"Will she live?" Ian's face appeared out of the gloom. "She was screaming something terrible."

Drew shrugged trying to dismiss the need to return to Adrianna and sit beside her to aid in her recovery. He glanced at Ian. "She might."

"What do ye mean she might? If she is so close to death, ye should be tending her not leaving her wi' that slip of a lass." Ian narrowed his eyes. "Ye used to care for the ailing. Has becoming laird turned ye into a cruel sod?"

"Nay." Angus moved to Ian's side. "But he lusts after the Sassenach and is in nay fit state to be left alone wi' her."

"Ye told Da, ye had found a lass to marry and I gather Lady Adrianna is the one, yet when she arrived, ye acted like ye despised her." Ian scowled at Drew. "Now ye want to spread her thighs wi' out the sanctity of the Church?"

Indignant he glared at him. "I will not have ye speak about Lady Adrianna in that fashion. I told Da the truth. I do care for her, aye, but it is not what ye think. I made her acquaintance in London." He sighed. "If ye want the truth, if her father had not warned me off I would have made her an offer."

"Acquaintance be damned." Angus's eyes flashed. "I have seen wi' ma own eyes the way ye lust after the lass."

Anger flared and he grasped Angus by the throat and squeezed until his godfather's face turned purple. "Who I lust after is none of your business. Ye have overstepped your place. *I am laird* and ye have nay power over me." He glared at Angus. "I promised the lass ma protection and she will have it and ma skill as a healer too. Ye will have nay say in the matter." He glared at him. "Christ, I canna believe ye think I am so depraved I would force maself on a woman dying from the fever?" Exasperated he dropped Angus and turned to Ian. "Take another bottle of whisky to Betty then lay your head down."

Shaking with fury, he waved the men away and drew a deep breath to steady his nerves. He would rest for two hours before returning to Adrianna's side. The night ahead would decide many things. She may not survive the fever or the pain he had inflicted. Confusion foxed his mind and he moved away from his men to lean against the moss-covered wall. He needed time alone to think, to distance himself from the spell she had woven over him.

In her presence, all logical thought ceased to exist. His attraction to her had not faded since their last meeting. He stared at the glow of light pouring from her room and bit back the desire to return and offer comfort. Pushing away from the wall, he scoffed. Christ, he had started to behave like an untried youth lusting after a petticoat. Adrianna's face filled his mind and his heart squeezed. He wanted her.

He straightened and moved deeper into the Great Hall, then paused to gaze at his men, lying in rows and appearing in the half-light like lines of corpses covered with blankets. Without doubt, Lord Beachwood or Moreau would eventually discover he had Adrianna. He could never allow them to take her and would fight to the death before allowing Baron du Court to deflower then murder her. For now, she would require his healer's skill to overcome the fever and his sword arm to protect her. He made the sign of the cross. *Lord, I offer my life willingly if you will only keep her safe.*

Chapter Seven

ord Rupert Bainbridge issued a few final instructions to the stable master and strolled along the row of stalls to inspect the mares. The warmth inside the stable heated flesh chilled from standing dockside in a wind intent on freezing him to death. He had taken Lord Bradshaw's groom into his employ, one Sam Greeks, a most fastidious man who had raised the mares from foals. What better surety for their comfort and needs during the voyage and a guarantee his prized horses reached Scotland without incident.

They were indeed the most splendid mares he had ever had the fortune to own. Each had a most agreeable temperament and superb bloodlines to complement Drew's stallion. He moved into the first stall and ran his hand down the mare's sleek neck inhaling the comforting smell of horse and leather. "What a beautiful creature you are."

The mare huffed a greeting then continued to munch from a manger filled with oats as if a long sea voyage happened to be a regular part of her life. He smiled and moved along the line, checking each mare's condition before moving to the next. Satisfied his charges had not suffered during the unloading, he nodded to Greeks. "They all appear in the very peak of health. I thank you, Greeks."

"Thank ye kindly, milord." Sam bowed then straightened. "Will I be returning to England or stayin' on 'ere?"

Rupert rubbed his chin. Where had his mind been of late to forget to consider the fate of this poor man? After receiving news of his uncle's death on his previous trip to Badenoch, his focus had been directed toward selling Drew's assets including his townhouse in Berkley Square and obtaining a good price for a quantity of the clan's family jewels. He cleared his throat. "What would you prefer? I am sure there are very fine grooms at Badenoch, but you do have a history with these mares."

"I would be more 'n 'appy to stay, milord."

"Very well, then see the stable master about finding you a place to sleep. We will be leaving the moment Laird Mackenzie arrives." He sidestepped a pile of manure and headed toward his stone-faced valet, Joseph Bent.

He first met Mr. Bent in a dark alley behind his favorite gaming establishment in London. Rupert had left by the back door after winning a substantial amount of money and a group of vagabonds had attempted to steal his watch and whatever else he had on his person. Out of the gloom, Mr. Bent had arrived like an avenging angel to beat them off. Discovering him to be starving and homeless, he offered him the position of footman at his London townhouse. Having proved his loyalty and being handy with his fists and big to boot, his promotion to personal valet had been inevitable.

Joe handed Fru Fru to him then glanced furtively over one shoulder and shuddered.

"Are yer sure yer want to stay here, milord? They look to me like untrustworthy coves and I cannot understand one word they are sayin'."

"Yes, I am quite sure, and have no fear, Mr. Bent, you will soon understand the dialect." He tucked his dog under one arm and smiled. "I would advise you to be mindful of what you say. You may not be able to understand them, but I can assure you they will know an insult if they hear one."

He led the way from the stables glad to be in the sunshine. "Go along to the inn and have a bath sent up to my room. I am carrying the stink of the cargo ship." He raised a brow and appraised his valet. "As do you." He waved a lace kerchief under his nose. "Lay out the blue and arrange a bath for yourself, if you please, before attending me."

"Yes, milord." Joe sniffed under one arm and frowned. "I am thinking my clothes need to be burned they stink somethin' awful. Was just as well we kept most of the trunks in the hold or we would not 'ave a thing to wear."

"That is precisely the reason why I instructed you to pack old clothes for the voyage. Discard anything that cannot be laundered to my satisfaction and select clothes from the other trunks." He sighed. *When will I find a valet that will do the job without need for instruction?*

"But do not unpack any more than essentials because Laird Mackenzie might well arrive on the morrow to escort us to Badenoch."

"Very well, milord." Joe straightened then glanced around suspiciously. "But be careful walking around alone. I hear tell of press gangs all along the docks. What would I say to Laird Mackenzie if yer went missin'? He would 'ave my hide for not keepin' an eye out for yer safety."

Rupert touched the hilt of his sword. "I do appreciate your concern, but I am sure I will be quite safe in broad daylight—and I have Fru Fru. He will sound the alarm should anyone try to sneak up on me." He indicated in the direction of the inn with his chin. "Off you go. I will return within the hour." He took a few coins from his pocket and handed them to him. "Buy a pie from one of the street vendors for luncheon and we will sup in the inn after we have bathed."

"Thank you, milord." Joe bowed then turned and marched purposefully toward a woman with a tray of freshly baked pies.

Glad to have solid ground beneath his feet after weeks at sea, he strolled out into the crisp morning air and inhaled the flavors of the city, from the delight of fresh baked bread to the foul odor of unwashed bodies. He gazed into the distance familiarizing himself once more with his surroundings. The main road held the usual bustle of people going about their business but unfortunately, no large group of travelers moved in his direction.

Worry over the safety of Lady Adrianna had dogged his thoughts since leaving England. Had Drew managed to rescue her from Lord Moreau's clutches? If so, surely he would have arrived in Inverness by now unless something had gone amiss. He gazed into the sky and rubbed his chin. The weather had been intemperate these past weeks and may have delayed the rendezvous or perhaps, Drew had taken her directly to Foiseil Castle. He would wait, whatever the outcome of the rescue, one of his cousins would arrive to escort him and the precious cargo to Badenoch eventually.

Glad to be in Scotland once more, he strolled along the busy street, and inner peace surrounded him with a tranquility he had not enjoyed since his last visit.

Cries of, "Buy ma rabbits, fresh killed today," "Fresh fish," or "Hot pies" brought back memories of his mother and wonderful times at Badenoch away from a father whom he constantly disappointed. All at once the smell of rotting flesh accosted his nostrils and he pressed a kerchief scented with oil of cloves to his nose and increased his pace past a man selling fly-blown rabbits on sticks. He tried to ignore the creature's sightless eyes and blood-soaked lips and made a decision never to consume a rabbit pie again.

Pushing through the crowd, he reached the town square and sat on the wall surrounding a fountain to soak in the atmosphere. Scottish voices rose and fell in English and Gaelic like music to his ears. The crowd swirled with the muted colors of woolen kilts and the feeling of being home engulfed him. *Christ, it is good to be here.* He grinned, the action drawing the attention of a matron passing by with two chits. The woman regarded him with disgust from below a crisp white mop cap and dragged her charges past him as if he might ravish them on the spot.

He stared after her much to the delight of the charming young women who gave him inviting smiles. Moving his attention to the other direction, he concentrated on the journey to Badenoch. The mares would be fine if they moved at a steady pace and took breaks along the way. Drew would be pleased with the purchases he had made for him. Each of the horses bore the pleasant roundness of breeding and the foals due in spring would delight his cousin. Their sire was a fine creature to be sure.

A cloud covered the sun and a freezing wind cut through his clothes chilling him to the bone. He examined the heavy clouds dominating the horizon and got to his feet. He would return to the inn and if he found no word from Drew, he would enquire after a gaming establishment or perhaps visit a brothel to pass the time. He placed Fru Fru on the ground. "Time to stretch your legs."

The tiny dog lifted both front legs in disdain and gave him a soulful look.

"Oh, I gather you heard the word 'bath'? Yes, I am afraid you must indulge me. We will be meeting Drew in a day or so and he already has an unfortunate opinion of you. Although, I am sure the dogs at Badenoch have fleas a plenty."

Convinced the small dog understood every word he uttered, he lifted the distressed animal and kissed him on the head. "Do not worry about such things. I will keep you safe by my side and away from his beasts."

* * * *

Lord Moreau rested his aching head on his hands and stared at the plate of slop the ship's cook had placed before him. The smell of fish stew wafted from the galley and his stomach roiled from an overindulgence of the finest whisky he had ever had the pleasure of tasting. He grinned and pain shot through his temples. His indisposition was a direct result of Captain Jacques' ingenious ruse to tap one barrel of *Le Diable Noir's* finest whisky. Jacques' excuse to taste the quality of the merchandise rather than risk King Louis' health had seemed sound at the time. Ah well, it would not be his neck on the block if the king was displeased.

He tore a piece of bread apart and stuffed a portion into his mouth. He needed to have his wits about him. Last eve, when well in his cups, Jacques had threatened to take Lady Adrianna to his bed at the first opportunity and if he allowed such action, Baron du Court would have his head. He may allow him to share in the deflowering of his wives but offering anything less than a virgin would not please his master. Fortunately the ship would dock at Inverness on the next tide, weather permitting, and Jacques would be able to slake his lust at a brothel but in the meantime, he would have to guard Lady Adrianna with due care.

Perhaps, he could lure Lady Adrianna's pretty maid to the captain's cabin on some pretense. After all, she had no value to his master. He could sell any child she bore male or female to any of the brothels in Paris and make a fine profit. He frowned. Keeping Lady Adrianna out of Captain Jacques' clutches would prove difficult on the trip to France. He rubbed his chin then smiled at the sudden notion of convincing two whores to join the ship at Inverness. Yes, most brothels would be able to supply two suitable whores for a few pounds and they would be more than enough to entertain the captain for the completion of the trip.

He motioned to the cook to attend him and drummed his fingers on the scrubbed wooden bench in agitation. The large man moved toward him with undue slowness carrying a pitcher of cider. He covered his goblet with one hand and met the man's enquiring gaze. "Has Lady Adrianna sent for her luncheon?"

"No, milord. I have not seen her maid since after the storm, but she did carry enough food to her ladyship's cabin to feed her for a week." The cook rubbed his chin. "I have not seen Mackenzie come to think of it either." He laughed. "He is a bit young to bed both of them, do you think?"

"I would think with all the fine Frenchmen available, she would choose a *man* rather than a boy to serve her needs." He pushed his plate toward the cook and smiled. "Likely she has the boy cleaning her cabin, she is fussy and nothing is good enough. It will be most enjoyable to see her under my master's whip. He will beat the pride from her." He pushed to his feet.

Straightening his waistcoat, he strolled along the passage to Lady Adrianna's cabin. He knocked and listened intently for any sound of movement inside.

"Open the door. I need to speak with you." He hammered again then pressed one ear to the aged wooden panel.

Nothing, not one sound came from within the cabin.

Anger rolled over him clenching his fists. How dare she ignore him? He reached for the door handle and finding the door locked grimaced. He had given her explicit instructions not to go on deck unescorted. *Damn it all to hell.* He had slept like the dead and dallied in his bunk until noon. Captain Jacques might well have deflowered her by now.

He ground his teeth and strode toward the hatch. Once on deck, a gust of wind lifted his wig and it hovered for a second or two before covering his eyes. With a curse, he dragged the matted hairpiece from his head and blinked into the glaring sunlight relieved to find the captain at the helm. He moved toward him and lifted his voice above the noise of flapping sails and crashing waves.

"Have you seen Lady Adrianna this morning?"

"No, I have not." Captain Jacques grinned and the foul odor of stale whisky and onions escaped from his mouth. "Alas, she is not in my bed, nor her sweet maid." He winked a bloodshot eye. "Have you by chance mislaid her, milord?"

"So it would seem." He rubbed the back of his neck. "The slave is missing too. Order your men to search the ship."

"As you wish." Captain Jacques issued orders to his first mate and turned back shrugging nonchalantly. "She will be found. Where could she possibly hide? No lady of her breeding would be with the goats or risk losing a toe or two below with the rats." He grinned. "Mayhap you should lock her in her cabin, or perhaps mine?"

The captain was a fool. Had he forgotten who owned *The Black Turtle*—who owned their very lives? He gaped at him with incredulity.

"Have you lost your wits? This lady is a prize for the baron. She has a fortune, land, and connections and is of great value to our master."

"Like the others?" Jacques grimaced. "It would seem our master has no appreciation of a fine lady. I would hate to see this English rose die on the eve of her wedding too."

Recollections of pain and torture flooded his head and he smiled.

"I was at the bedding of both his previous brides. It was necessary for me to bear witness to the consummation for the baron to gain his bride's fortune without any claims of foul play from her father." His groin heated at the memory. "The baron and I enjoy the sport of inflicting pain and it was never his intention for his bride ... either of them, to survive the wedding night." He raised a brow. "The 'English rose' will no doubt outlast the others and it will be my pleasure to watch her beg for her life."

"He allows you to watch?" Jacques scowled. "Dear God! I knew you treated whores roughly but—my God!" He lifted his chin. "And what of the maids?"

He waved a hand dismissively. "Ah, well after we have taken our pleasure with the bride, the master usually beds the maid the next day—if they are virgins. He prefers not to kill a maid as they are useful pets for the garrison." He shrugged. "Wives you see are disposable. Once the baron has their fortune and virginity, they are of no further use to him."

"I see." Captain Jacques raised both brows. "I suggest you make sure the lady is unaware of your plans. Are you sure she does not speak German? When we discussed the availability of her maid, she gave me the impression she understood our intentions. "

He snorted. "I am no fool. She is ignorant of what lies ahead."

Sometime later, the first mate followed by two sailors came to him.

"There is no trace of the women. I used the spare key to open the cabin door. The trunk is there, but they have vanished, milord."

He glared at him. "Search again."

"Mayhap they fell overboard." Captain Jacques shrugged. "It is possible."

"I do not think so, but they could have stowed away in a cargo boat during the meeting with *Le Diable Noir*." He stared at the coastline anxious to go ashore. "I admit the lady was reluctant to marry the baron and I took away her choice by informing her she would be wed with or without her permission." He shook with anger at the thought of her escaping him. "The rendezvous with *Le Diable Noir* would have given her the means to escape. He may well be involved. A man like him would listen to the pleas of a lady in distress."

"No, my friend that is impossible. I was with him the entire time he was on board and my men rowed him ashore. He did not speak to anyone, let alone a lady. If any of my crew had seen the women trying to escape they would have informed me." Captain Jacques rubbed his chin. "Two women would be hard to miss in the cargo."

Anger clenched his fists. "If not *Le Diable Noir*, it must have been the damn Scottish slave."

"Well, I did not lock him in the hold last eve because you gave him to Lady Adrianna. They could have taken one of the boats and escaped under cover of darkness." Captain Jacques turned to his first mate. "Count the boats."

"I always count them, Captain. They all returned, but two of the men complained they had to row the cargo back single handed." The first mate frowned. "I did not think too much of it at the time."

Moreau ground his teeth and glared at Captain Jacques. "It would seem our time in Inverness is going to be longer than planned. No doubt, they will arrive there in a day or so. I am sure the lady has the money to purchase a means of transport."

"Finding her will be like finding a needle in a haystack." Jacques scratched his head. "It is a big place, to be sure."

"Ah, I think not." He smiled confident of his understanding of the Scotts. "I have one thousand guineas at my disposal in the form of Lady Adrianna's dowry and it will not take me too long to bribe the innkeepers of the whereabouts of one Ian Mackenzie. She has to eat and lay her head down somewhere. The moment she arrives I will know." He rubbed his hands together. "Have no fear the moment she is back on board I will chain her in the hold. She will not escape me a second time." He glared at Jacques. "And *you* will not touch her—do I make myself clear?"

"Of course."   Captain Jacques turned his attention toward the coastline. "I happen to value my head."

Chapter Eight

Lady Adrianna pushed the damp rag away from her eyes and moaned sending a white cloud of steam into the candlelight. The frigid air did nothing to relieve the pounding in her head or diminish the constant throb of red-hot pain searing her thigh. A fuzzy memory of a dream seeped into her mind. Drew was mopping her face and arms, his voice drifting over her in a soothing stream of Gaelic. When shivers racked her body, he had laid beside her warming her and offering comfort. *What a wonderful dream, to be sure.*

She moved her fingers and a warm hand closed around them strong, and protective. *Drew?* He stroked her palm with his rough thumb and his long sigh pulled her from the edge of delirium. Heavens above, he *had* remained at her side throughout the night and, she had clung to him like an anchor to reality. Indeed, no other had offered her such comfort. As a child, she had suffered with the measles to the point of fever terrors. Her nanny had not cared one fig and she had never received as much as a glass of water from her father.

Water. She rasped a dry tongue across cracked lips and her stomach roiled at the taste of whisky. The straw beneath her prickled her bare flesh, but a thick blanket covered her keeping the chilled air at bay. She attempted to lift her head and a large hand pressed her shoulder.

"Dinna try to move." Drew's face came into view. "Best ye rest a wee bit longer. Ye barely made it through the night, lass."

She blinked at the vision before her. He was no dream to be sure. The scent of him washed over her in a reassuring embrace. Concern etched his countenance. His green gaze searched her face and when he bent to examine her, strands of black silken hair brushed her cheek. Her face grew hot at the memory of his ministrations. Her flesh still tingled from his intimate touch on her bare hip and when he lifted her leg to bandage her—oh, my—his lustful expression had branded a most delicious image in her memory. *He still finds me desirable.*

Meeting his troubled expression, she offered a smile. "I need water, if you please." Her voice came out in a strangled croak.

"Verra well, I will give ye a drop, but ye are verra pale." He offered her a small cup of water. "Sip this slowly. I dinna want ye to vomit."

She sipped the cool metallic tasting water and sighed. He had wanted her to be fit and ready to leave by daylight and she did not intend to let him down. She offered him a reassuring smile. "Thank you. The fever has broken and my limbs no longer shake. I must commend you on a job well done."

"Thank ye. How is your pain?"

"I do suffer a little, but I am sure it will pass directly." She swallowed hard at the thought of riding a horse. "We will need to be on our way soon. Would you be so kind as to call my maid to assist me? I will make ready for our departure at once."

"I would prefer ye to rest until daybreak and then I must insist ye ride wi' me." He ran a hand through his hair and one side of his mouth turned up in a crooked smile. "Are ye sure ye are not of Scottish blood? Ye are verra braw for a Sassenach. I would wager not many fine ladies would have the stamina to attempt to ride wi' such an injury." He frowned. "Do ye understand it will be maybe two days afore we reach Inverness?"

"I am sure I will manage. I overheard your conversation with Betty last eve. To be sure, I would not want the excise men to catch us."

A day or more riding with Drew would be heaven no matter how much her leg pained her. The scent of him alone made her weak at the knees. She attempted to sit and Drew placed one strong arm around her back to support her.

Agony stabbed deep in her thigh stealing her breath and the room moved in and out of focus. Panting she gripped the side of the cart, bent over the edge and vomited. Heavens above how much whisky had she consumed? The disgusting taste lingered on her tongue and filled her nostrils. More than a little embarrassed, she wiped her mouth with a handful of straw. "I do beg your pardon. It would seem I have trouble tolerating spirits."

"I will mix ye a ptisan. It will calm your wame and be a kinder way of relieving your pain. I could not give it to ye afore as it is verra strong and might have poisoned ye." Drew wiped her face with the damp rag. "Then I will change your dressing. Ye will need more comfrey ointment on the wound to ease the burn. Dinna fash the wound is small and it will not leave much of a mark." He smiled. "Dinna try to move. I will go and fetch ma things."

Frowning she narrowed her gaze at him. "I am sure Betty is quite capable of changing my dressings and I will require her assistance."

"Nay, she is sleeping." Drew shrugged. "I could wake her, but she will nay doubt fall off her horse with exhaustion afore we cover a mile. She remained by your side most of the night and I sent her to rest less than two hours past."

"Laird Mackenzie." She cursed the heat blazing in her cheeks. "I need Betty and some privacy to retire and as soon as possible if you please."

"I will find ye a pot to use. Ye are not wandering outside alone in the dark and I doubt verra much ye could manage on your own."

Dismay and helplessness fell over her like a shroud. There would be no arguing with him, but she would at least try. "You have me at a disadvantage, sir, but I must ask that you refrain from humiliating me further and call my maid."

"I have sat with women of ma clan during illness many a time. Our midwife died and as the only healer available, I delivered two bairns albeit with the help of the womenfolk. Not one of them believed I shamed them." More than a little agitated Drew rubbed the back of his neck and fixed his gaze on her. "I would not think to embarrass ye. I happen to care for your well-being because if for nay other reason, *I am a healer.*" He turned to walk away then paused and glanced at her over one shoulder. "Ye will not be traveling until I have examined the wound." He rubbed one hand down his face in a gesture of exhausted exasperation. "Did ye not study the Bible, lass? Dinna ye ken pride comes afore a fall?"

She gaped at him striding away. Pride? Dear God, with her derriere and legs on display for all to see, she had lost every ounce of dignity during his ministrations. She chewed on her bottom lip and stared at the open doorway. The passageway held a single lantern and the Great Hall beyond lay quiet. How long had she slept and how many hours would pass before dawn? She picked straw from her hair and longed for a soak in a long hot bath. In truth, she would be content with the opportunity to bathe in freezing water and put on a clean shift. Footsteps crunching on the debris littering the floor brought Drew back to her side. He made a sound of derision and covered her with the blanket.

"Roll onto your back, take a good grip of the sides of the cart and I will slip a bowl under ye." He bent to retrieve a copper bowl.

What? "I beg your pardon? You cannot possibly expect me to—?"

"Dinna give me the evil eye. I have done the same thing to womenfolk many times. It is nay shame to need to take a piss." He lifted her and slid the bowl under her bottom. "Ye should not be embarrassed by ma presence. Not now, after I have loved ye."

Oh really? This is a different matter entirely. Gripping the side of the cart, she glared at him. "It would seem I have no choice in the matter. Turn around and walk away if you please."

He grunted something unintelligible, turned his back, and stomped to the entrance of the small room. With his hands resting on his hips, he filled the entrance. Candlelight reflected in his long, glossy hair and the cloth of his shirt accentuated his muscular back. To be sure, Laird Drew

Mackenzie was the most exquisite of men. Dragging her gaze away from temptation, she tended to matters, then eased the copper pot from under her bottom and covered it with the damp rag used to cool her forehead. Dizzy from the small movement or mayhap the herbal remedy, she rearranged the blanket and cleared her throat. "I have finished."

Drew moved into the room with a blank expression on his face. He removed the bowl with swift efficiency and placed it on the ground. Angus appeared at the doorway, his face hidden in the shadows. At Drew's nod, he moved toward her, holding a bucket in one hand, and balancing a plate of food and a cup in the other

"Drink then eat something, lass." Angus pushed a horn cup rimmed with silver into her hands. She recognized the intricately decorated rim and warmth enclosed her heart. Rather than the tin mug, Drew had supplied her with his own cup.

Angus turned to him and raised his tawny eyebrows.

"I will check on the watch and take one hour's rest afore dawn. Ye will remember what I said to ye, aye?"

She sipped the pleasant, warm brew and gazed speculatively at Drew over the rim of the cup. Why would Angus speak to him in English unless to make a point of some kind? She noticed the tips of Drew's ears redden and bit back a smile. It would seem Angus had noticed his lustful gaze on her too.

Drew's eyes flashed with anger and he snorted.

"I am not a lecher, now away wi' ye to your bed." He placed a pot of ointment and fresh rags beside her then lifted his attention to her. "Have ye finished the drink? Good, it will ease the pain swiftly and make your stomach stop churning. Roll onto your side so I may tend ye, aye." He pulled back the blanket exposing her legs and avoided her gaze.

She gasped and grinding her teeth, complied. Burning pain seared her leg and she bit down hard on her bottom lip to smother the groan rising up the back of her throat. With her eyes squeezed shut, she endured the swift, efficient way he cleaned the wound, applied a good amount of ointment, and changed the dressing. Relieved when the sharp pain receded, she opened her eyes. "Please, I need my maid."

He ignored her plea with a shake of his head and pressed one hand to her forehead.

"How is your pain now?"

Embarrassed beyond reason by the need provoked by his touch, she could not look at him and ducked her head. "Much better, thank you."

"Good. Your shift is wet though from the fever. Ye will need to change into something dry afore ye catch a chill."

Before she had time to object, he gently scooped her into his strong arms, and dropped her with care to her feet.

"I will help ye bathe."

The agony had eased considerably but giddy from the ptisan, she swayed against him and gripped the front of his shirt. "If you refuse to call my maid, please leave me. I am quite capable of washing myself."

"Nay ye are not. Allow me to assist ye and care for your well-being, Adrianna. Ye will feel more comfortable as soon as ye are clean and dressed." In one swift movement, he had pulled her damp shift over her head and tossed it to the floor.

She covered her breasts and glared at him. "No, please it is not proper for you to do such a thing."

"Ye canna stand unaided. The ptisan is verra strong and ye will feel the effects for some hours. Ye have allowed me to touch you afore, Adrianna. We are alone and nayone will ken."

A warm, wet rag ran down her back and she nearly swooned. With her legs, arms, and back most thoroughly cleansed and dried, Drew gave her a crooked smile then pushed the rag into her hand.

"Best ye do the front, aye?"

She lifted her chin and peered over one shoulder at him. "Do me the courtesy of turning your back to give me some privacy."

"And see ye fall flat on your face? Nay, lass." He grinned and his gaze sparkled with mischief. "I will shut ma eyes if it pleases ye, but the vision of your naked flesh is already branded on ma mind from our last meeting."

Too weak to argue another moment, she washed her face. Dipping the rag into the bucket of hot water he held for her, she bathed keeping her attention anywhere but on his face. His warm breath brushed her neck followed by a soft kiss and she melted against him.

"Och, lass, I *have* missed ye so and to hold ye in ma arms again is like a dream come true." Drew sighed and moved his head away. "I want ye so much and I can wait for as long as it takes for ye to accept me for who I am."

Her nipples hardened as if reaching for his caress, she lifted her gaze, and caught his expression of deep longing. "Who you are inside is what matters to me, Drew."

"I thank ye and I will prove I am worthy of your trust."

To his credit, he did not move a muscle other than to hand her a piece of linen to dry herself. "I will need something to wear. I cannot spend the entire journey wrapped in your plaid."

"Wee Betty set out some things for ye to wear, but ye will not be wearing your stays. They will keep safer buried in a wagon. The jewels ye have hidden will keep better inside, aye?"

She let out a long sigh and shrugged. "As you wish."

With exquisite gentleness, he dressed her and wrapped her in his spare plaid. Calmer now, she cleared her throat. "How is it you know how to dress a lady?"

"Och, I ken how to *undress* a lady well enough, it is just the other way around, aye?" He lifted her with tender care and placed her in the wagon.

Shocked by his candor she rounded on him. "Did you have to remind me of your rakish behavior?"

"Och, lass, ye ken I have enjoyed the pleasures of a number of mistresses." His handsome face broke into a wide smile. "I am happy ye are ready to fight wi' me again so soon, it would seem the draft I gave ye has eased the pain." He tucked the plaid around her legs. "I ken Betty should have helped ye but the lass was falling asleep standing up, aye. Your other choice was Angus and I understand how ye feel about him." He patted her shoulder. "Eat afore ye fall asleep, the draft is verra strong."

She fought to keep awake. Indeed, the draft he had given her had muddled her senses but she might not be alone with him again for some time and had questions. "When we met in London, did you intend to seduce me then leave me ruined?"

"Nay, lass, did I not give ye ma word I would return?" He pushed a strand of hair behind her ear. "I will not lie to ye and pretend ye dinna fascinate me from the first." His breath brushed her cheek. "Ye ken verra well how much ye arouse me."

Oh, Lord, she wanted to melt into his arms and taste his delicious full lips. No, she must not fall into temptation again. Gathering her last ounce of strength, she met his gaze. "Why do you continue to taunt me with such words? It will be difficult enough trying to avoid looking at you in front of your men."

His eyes crinkled at the corners and his lips twitched as if he suppressed a grin. Dear God, he was laughing at her. She pointed to the entrance of the room. "I think you should go."

"Nay, lass, ye need me." He rubbed one hand down his face and regarded her with interest. "Ye ken verra well ma intentions toward ye are honorable or I would have taken your maidenhead at the masquerade ball."

Her face grew hot. He had spoken the truth. She would not have prevented him taking his pleasure. Unable to meet his gaze, she stared at her hands. "Then I commend you for keeping your head. However, that was then and this is now. I will require time to discover if this attraction between us is more than lust." She sighed. "I would ask that you give me that time."

"I *would* keep ma distance, if that is your wish, but there is nayone else here with the healing skills to tend ye. Worrying about if we are suited or not will not aid in your recovery, although, I will look forward to setting your mind at ease when ye have recovered. Will ye, at least allow me to care for ye until ye can fend for yourself?" He raised a dark eyebrow in question.

Heavens above, did he have to look so smug? "Very well."

"A wise decision." He bent and searched inside her bag before bringing out a hairbrush. "Ye ken I am not a scoundrel or ye would not asked me to rescue ye from Lord Moreau." He straightened and turning the silver handled hairbrush over in his hand, lifted his hooded gaze to her. "Now then, will ye allow me to remove the straw from your hair?"

"If you give me your word you will not take liberties. Since taking the draft, I am not of sound mind."

"We have an agreement, remember? Look, lass, there is nothing amiss when two people are drawn to one another or nayone would wed." He sighed. "Ye have lived a sheltered life if ye believe a lass canna be aroused by a man afore she weds. There is nay sin in that. Indeed, God made us this way so we may find our one true love." He moved behind her and ran the brush through her hair.

She bit back a moan at his touch and pleasant weariness weighted her limbs. Very well, she would comply with his wishes. "As you are a man of experience, do tell how does one make a suitable love match?"

"Afore ye make your choice, ye need to ken what ye want from a husband. If it is love ye desire well, nay love happens overnight, lust maybe but for enduring love, ye must spend time wi' a man to discover his faults as well the things ye admire about him." He touched her cheek. "Have ye ever spent time in a man's company other than mine and was I the first man to kiss ye?"

Captivated by his deep baritone voice and the slow slide of the brush through her hair, she sighed. "No, you were the first man to kiss me. Not that I had the slightest desire to as much as stroll the garden with any of my suitors. All of the gentlemen I have met, apart from Lord Rupert, are in their dotage." She sighed. "Although, I have never considered Lord Rupert as a suitable match. He is more like a brother to me and has no plans to marry for at least ten years."

"Rupert is a fine man to be sure." He chuckled. "I am verra glad he offered his assistance or I would not have been able to spend time wi' ye."

"I find it amusing that you are cousins. He does not resemble you, apart from the eyes. He is so … well, *foppish*." Turning her head, she met Drew's amused expression. "Not like you at all … *you* are a chameleon. One moment you present as a stylish gentleman, the next a notorious smuggler. Rupert attracts women like flies around a pot of honey and yet he does not have any inclination to make a match." She smiled. "Why is that do you think?"

Drew's gaze darkened.

"I will not discuss Rupert's fancies wi' ye but aye, I have enjoyed the company of many women, although I dinna frequent brothels or make it a habit of seducing maidens, so I am not as depraved as many English gentlemen who make sport of such practices."

She snorted. "How forthcoming of you but I find it hard to believe."

"I will not argue wi' ye. Think of me what ye may. Ye will find out the truth soon enough and make up your own mind." He picked straw from her hair. "Get on wi' your questions if ye must and stop fighting the draft, ye need your rest."

Adrianna bit down hard on her bottom lip. She had to ask the question burning on the tip of her tongue. "Have *you* ever been in love?"

"Aye, I have." His dark eyebrows furrowed. "Why do ye ask?"

A pang of regret or perhaps jealousy clamped her heart. "Do tell, how you knew when you fell in love and not as you say 'in lust'?"

"Aye well, it is not proper to discuss such things with a lady, ye ken."

She chewed on her bottom lip. The pressing need to know everything about Drew outweighed her modesty. "I have not had the opportunity to discuss matters of the heart and feel lacking in my education." She met his gaze. "I cannot promise not to be embarrassed, but it would please me of all things if you would consider giving me this information. I am completely unaware of such things."

His mouth twitched at the corners and he closed his eyes as if gathering his wits.

"Och aye, I kenned as much. When ye are in love ye crave to be wi' them all the time and ye enjoy their company." He cleared his throat. "And when ye touch them, ye want to cherish them forever."

A warm glow engulfed her from his gentle attention to her hair and she relaxed closing her eyes. "That's nice and how different is love from unholy lust?"

"That is not something a lady of breeding should be asking a man."

She turned and stared at him. "I am two and twenty and hardly a girl in her first come out. I might mention that *you* have not only viewed but have *kissed* a good deal of my person. We have already moved beyond polite conversation so I beg you to continue."

"Verra well, ye wee besom." A deep growl rolled from Drew's chest and he cleared his throat. "Lust is fleeting. It is more of an animal instinct to rut without worrying about the consequences. Ye ken there are many widows who prefer a lover and dinna want to wed again. They enjoy a variety of lovers and nayone in society would dare to cast aspersions on them." He sighed and his voice became agitated. "And aye, afore ye ask as I had nay intention of entering the marriage mart, I preferred to take the young widows in King Louis' court to ma bed."

She sighed. "I see. To be perfectly honest, I was of the impression men and women had the same necessities but would seem I am mistaken. Are most men driven by lustful desires like tomcats?"

"I would think *most men* have the same urges, but we all have a choice, aye. Ye may well believe I am nay better than a beast driven by ma needs, but I had the utmost respect for ma lovers. When I wed, I will seek nay other for ma bed." He snorted. "I will not disgrace ma wife by taking a mistress."

She giggled and wet her lips. "At last, we are in agreement."

Drew swallowed hard and forced his mind to concentrate on the silken mass of hair slipping through his fingers. Talk of lust had heated his groin and the evidence of his desire pressed hard against his sporran. *Christ.* After leaving London, Adrianna had dominated his thoughts. He had drifted in sexual oblivion but now after watching her fight the fever and touching her soft white flesh again, he wanted her more than ever. Not for his mistress but cherished as his wife.

Before receiving Rupert's letter detailing her plight, he had made plans to return to London the moment he had settled his clan's business. He had wanted to seek an audience with Lord Beachwood to request permission to call on Adrianna in a respectable fashion. He had hoped his new position as a laird with considerable land holdings might sway the obstinate man in his favor.

He needed to convince his clan to accept a Sassenach noblewoman as their mistress. The clan's agreement had a codicil, his men would have lay down their lives for her because if Lord Moreau had caught the slightest notion Adrianna had joined his clan, the wee gomeral would notify Lord Beachwood. He would arrive home with an English battalion waiting on his doorstep.

He cleared his throat. "Lord Moreau may well be waiting for us to arrive at Inverness, nay doubt accompanied by a party of Captain Jacques' men wi' the intent of taking ye back on board *The Black Turtle*?"

"Yes, you did mention he would cause trouble as would my father. I *am* sorry." She turned to look at him. "I wish I could do something to help but other than give myself willingly into Lord Moreau's hands I am at a loss to know what to do."

"Do ye believe your father kenned about Baron du Court's plans?"

"That he planned to kill me?" She shrugged. "No, I do not believe he would send me to my death."

He rubbed his chin in an effort to evaluate the situation. "Then ye must write a letter to your father informing him of everything ye ken. Tell him why ye escaped but dinna inform him about being with me. I will send one of ma man ahead to Inverness and wi' luck ye father will receive the letter afore Moreau contacts him."

"I will, but I doubt any such information coming from me will make a difference. My father is a hard man to convince." Adrianna pursed her lips. "He believes I am stubborn and willful." She narrowed her gaze. "I think he may be correct."

Glad to see her fight return, he smiled. "Ye are a warrior and I happen to admire your spirit."

Christ, the sight of her mussed and wrapped in his plaid sent heat straight to his groin. He ran a final brushstroke through the mass of curls but wanted to linger. God help him the desire to drag her into his arms and ravage her soft sweet mouth near overpowered him. He ground his teeth. Angus had been correct, the lass was trouble and he would have to explain the danger she posed to his men afore they left at first light.

He handed her the hairbrush and moved to her side. "Get your head down for a bit. It will be daylight soon and I will send Betty to tend ye." He curled a silken curl around one finger and waited for her to complain, but she made no demure. With reluctance, he allowed the soft hair to slip from his grasp. "I have quill and ink in ma saddlebags so I will ask ye to write a letter afore we leave in the morning. Remember, I will not be able to show affection toward ye in front of ma men, not yet awhile but soon, aye?"

Adrianna wrapped her small hand around his arm.

"I understand, but before you go, I must thank you for saving my life." She wet her lips.

"I would walk through fire for ye, lass." He bent and pressed a kiss to her forehead.

"Then I do hope my letter resolves the problem with Lord Moreau but I have grave doubts my father will take direction from me." Dark lashes dropped over her devastated blue gaze. "I beg you to believe when I asked you to help me escape Lord Moreau I had no idea doing so would cause you or your clan trouble."

"I ken ye had nay notion of your father's threats toward me."

A tremble went through her and he forced back the need to offer comfort by stepping away to break her sensual allure. Perhaps God had decided to test his ability to be laird. As if losing his father and inheriting a starving clan was not enough, he had to fight the French and British aristocracy for the woman he loved. He straightened. "Adrianna, I want ye by ma side and nay matter what happens, I promise I will keep ye safe. Now, I must insist ye get some rest."

Exhausted, he strode away to wake his men and explain what was to come. He sighed. Many could die due to his decision to take her from the Baron du Court's clutches.

H.C. BROWN

SEDUCED

The Mackenzie, Book Three

𝔖𝔢𝔡𝔲𝔠𝔢𝔡
The Mackenzie, Book Three
H.C. Brown

After escaping a pirate ship and an unwanted betrothal to a French baron, Lady Adrianna Beechwood may well be safe on land but is alone with a band of smugglers running from the law in the wilds of Scotland.

Finally reunited with the love of her life, she is distressed to find a rugged Highland warrior has replaced the refined, stylish Drew Mackenzie she fell in love with in London.

With her betrothed's men hot on her heels, she must flee with her Highlander, but will their love survive the troubles to come?

Preface

ighlander, Drew Mackenzie's double life as the Mackenzie heir and the notorious, smuggler, *Le Diable Noir*, comes into jeopardy the moment he meets Lady Adrianna Beachwood. Disobeying her father's warning to stay away, he devises an ingenious plan to meet her in secret by using his cousin, the respectable, Lord Rupert as a decoy. The romance is in full swing before fate intervenes, and hearing of his clan's sudden illness, he returns to Scotland to find his clan at war.

Drew's father is on his deathbed and his godfather is trying to turn the clan against him. Clan Munroe is waging war and his clan is losing the battle. Sick and near starving Clan Mackenzie looked to Drew to save them. His plan to leave his smuggling days behind and marry Adrianna quickly becomes an impossible dream and he must return to his life as *Le Diable Noir*, to finance his clan.

In London, alone and without the support of Lord Rupert, Lady Adrianna's heartless father forces her into a betrothal with a French Baron known as *The Murderer of Muzon*. Unable to inform her father about her secret love affair with Drew Mackenzie, she has no option but to accept. In fear of her life, she writes to Lord Rupert to inform him of her situation and begs him to notify Drew of her impossible position and to ask him to help her escape.

Time is running out and without word from Drew, Lady Adrianna reluctantly boards a pirate ship, *The Black Turtle*, and finds herself under the protection of the baron's man of affairs in the form of the opium smoking deviate, Lord Moreau. In fear of her life or losing her honor from the threats of the unscrupulous Captain Jacques, she has little option but to wait in the hope Drew will find a way to rescue her.

After receiving Lord Rupert's letter, Drew plans a risky escape. He sends his brother Ian to join the crew then boards *The Black Turtle* as the masked *Le Diable Noir* and by using, Ian and the cover of darkness rescues Lady Adrianna.

Safe on land and alone with a band of Highlanders in the middle of nowhere, Adrianna is distressed to find a rugged Highlander has replaced the refined, stylish Drew Mackenzie she fell in love with in London.

Chapter One

Adrianna hobbled from the small room in the castle ruins with one arm draped across Betty's shoulder for support and gaped at Drew in astonishment. Dressed in a clean shirt with his plaid attached to one shoulder by an exquisite brooch and a glistening claymore on his back, and a short sword strapped to his waist, there could be no doubt of his position in the clan. Drew straightened to his full impressive height at her entrance and rested one hand on the gold handled dirk on his belt. He held an aura of respect and was defiantly not the vagabond barbarian he led her to believe.

Her Highlander was indeed a chameleon, for before her stood a confident Highland warrior as did the tall, handsome man standing beside him. Drew's gaze drifted over her and a glimpse of the man she met in London surfaced for a brief moment before his expression hardened to one of disinterest. *An act for his clan no doubt.*

She glanced over the restless group of clansmen and all to a man glared back at her grim-faced. A shiver of apprehension slid down her spine. By the wave of Anglophobic hatred directed toward her, Drew had informed them of the trouble her presence would cause. The grunts and Gaelic mutterings combined with unusual hand gestures from the men clearly indicated their attitude toward her. To be sure, they would have preferred if the fever had taken her.

Limping the short distance to stand before him and ignoring the less than welcoming manner of his men, she offered him the letter. She had detailed the reasons for escaping Lord Moreau and informed her father of her reasons to remain in Scotland without mention of Drew or her whereabouts. She had folded the paper neatly and placed her father's direction in bold print on the front then sealed the missive with a crude blob of soot-streaked candle wax. "I do hope this will set matters straight."

"As do I." Drew took the letter and broke the seal eyeing her with a steady confident gaze.

She gaped at him in disbelief and grabbed at the paper in his hand but to no avail. At the twitch of a smile on his lips, indignation rose and she glared at him. "Laird Mackenzie, I find it hard to believe you have the effrontery to examine a private note to my father."

"*Effrontery* is it to keep ma clan safe or maybe I am too canny for ye, aye?" Drew gave her such a look of disdain that she took a step backward. He grabbed her arm drawing her around to face him. "Do ye really think I would be stupid enough to allow anyone with enough information to see us hanged, free reign to inform Lord Beachwood of our whereabouts, and destination?" His gaze moved over her face assessing her. "If ye are so against me reading the contents of your correspondence, ye must have something to hide."

The group of men mumbled in agreement and indescribable dread fell over her. Swallowing her pride, she inclined her head in an attempt to exhibit calm and a regal manner. "Then read on Laird Mackenzie, for there is nothing in that missive that you do not already know about me, I'm sure." She swallowed the lump in her throat. "I do not intend to cause you or your clan trouble with the authorities. You have my word. Nevertheless, I do understand your clan's hesitancy to believe an English woman."

Such an attempt at bravado had not quelled the fear bubbling to the surface. Why had she written to her father and given her explanation for leaving *The Black Turtle* as one to search for true love and with the intention of finding a husband of her own choosing? If Drew read her note to the clan, they would without doubt believe she had designed her escape in an attempt to force him into a compromising position and would regard her with contempt. An English lady would not be a suitable match for their laird, especially one with King George as a godfather. She gazed at him from below her lashes and her heart pounded with the implications. She prayed he would not read the missive aloud. Her ears peeled in the fashion of St. Paul's Cathedral at Easter, and she swallowed hard. Fisting her hands until the fingernails cut deep into her flesh, she stared into Drew's eyes daring him to reveal their secret.

"Aye, if ye want ma protection and expect ma clan to lay down their lives for ye, then ye have to earn their trust." Drew unfolded the letter. He moved to a shaft of light to read the contents and raised both dark eyebrows. He folded the paper then turned to Dermot and thrust the document into his hands. "Light a candle and seal this again." He strolled back to her and gave her a long considering stare. "Verra well, lass. I thank ye, the letter will do nicely."

The tightness in her chest relaxed and could breathe once more. Indeed, Drew's disposition toward her had not changed to one of smug satisfaction or distaste. He gave no hint to his thoughts and had the ability to mask his feelings toward her, yet beneath his warrior persona lay the kind, gentle man who had cared for her overnight.

Oh, you are very good at deception, Drew Mackenzie. I hope you have not deceived me as well. She lifted her chin and met his emerald gaze searching for the man who had stolen her heart. His attention had not moved from her and when his expression softened, the need to throw herself into his arms heated her cheeks. Empowered, she pressed her trembling legs together, and in an effort to appear nonchalant arranged her dark brown woolen skirt. He had insisted she must *earn* his clan's trust and she would if it took the rest of her life. She inclined her head and offered him a hint of a smile. "I thank you, Laird."

Drew took the resealed letter from Dermot and handed it to one of his men. "Ride like the wind and get this on the first mail coach to London. I will meet ye at the Glen Albyn Inn in two days. God's speed." He slapped the man on the back then turned to her and indicated to the man at his side. "May I present, ma brother James Mackenzie, kenned by most as Dubh Jamie."

The man beside him stepped forward and bowed over her hand.

"Your servant, ma lady." Jamie met her gaze. "I do hope the morning finds ye well rested and in better health?"

She smiled at this charismatic young man. "Yes, I thank you for your concern, Mr. Mackenzie."

The brush of his lips and scent of fresh air and heather sent images racing through her mind in a state of primordial chaos. Words fell from her mouth heedless of the consequences. "I must say, you appear to be very strong. Do you have the occasion to spar often, Mister Mackenzie? The majority of the fellows here appear to be likewise."

The vivid conception of men bare to the waist in kilts, fighting with great swords filled her mind. Such bold fancies sent a most uncomfortable wave of heat rushing up her neck to burn her cheeks.

Jamie's brows raised and he flicked an enquiring glance at Drew before offering her a quizzical gaze.

"Aye, I practiced with Drew this morning. Mayhap the noise we made entered your dreams, aye?"

Adrianna caught Drew's annoyance and brushing it aside smiled at his brother. "Oh, most certainly but due to the constant conflict in Scotland, I am sure Highlanders have a pressing need to hone their skills?" She glanced around the Great Hall at the gathering of hostile Scotsmen and the anger vibrating from them stifled her. Swallowing her apprehension, she inclined her head. "Being so close to the coast must be quite a change. Do you enjoy the invigorating sea air?"

"It is all verra well, being close to the sea but we are eager to return to the Highlands." Jamie smiled warmly. "A man goes mad, aye, being cooped up in this old castle for so long a time." He dropped her hand and grinned. "Ye will have noticed how cranky the men are, aye?"

"Well, I shall not hold you up a moment longer." She caught the glint of amusement in his eyes and inclined her head. "But before we leave, may I ask your indulgence for one question? Why do your friends refer to you as Dubh Jamie?"

"They call me Black Jamie because we have another Jamie in the clan, a cousin wi' red hair." Jamie grinned. "And ye are Lady Beachwood, aye?"

"Have ye forgotten ma orders? Her name is Adrianna and best ye remember and not be acting as if she were the bloody Queen of England." Anger flashed in Drew's eyes. He turned toward her with a determined and yet somewhat exasperated expression. "Have I not informed ye to refer to us by our Christian names or risk undue attention." He waved Ian forward. "Ian has filled a flask with the ptisan. Drink some now and more if the pain returns." He turned his attention to Betty. "Ye will ride wi' Ian on one of the carts. Go wi' him now and collect your things."

Adrianna took the silver flask and smiled at Ian. "Thank you." She opened the top then sipped the thick spicy liquid. The ptisan warmed her from the inside and heat spread throughout her limbs easing the pain. She replaced the cap and pushed the flask inside the pocket of her skirt. Drew stepped closer and his fresh musky scent engulfed her making her heart race. He tucked a strand of hair inside her cap with the tips of his freezing fingers then offered his arm.

"Ye will ride with me. I dare say my lap will be more comfortable than sitting on the seat of one of the carts." He led the way to the horses walking at a slow pace. "We will go slowly until ye are better." He bent his head and lowered his voice to a whisper. "Ye did fine and nayone kens we have feelings toward each other. I will allow them to witness a growing fondness between us on the trip."

Seated in a most precarious position across Drew's muscular thighs, with one of his strong arms wrapped around her waist, Adrianna turned her attention to her surroundings. Trickles of daylight with dancing dust motes fell through the arrow slits to the floor, to illuminate an arrangement of stone slabs laid out in the shape of an oak leaf. With a pang of regret, she recalled the dilapidated tapestry hanging in the solar and the wall sconces bearing the same design. "One moment if you please."

"What is it?" Drew examined her face. "We have not gone more than a few steps, are you indisposed?"

"No, I am sure I will manage but I ask your indulgence." The chance to discover more about the history of the castle lay in the oak leaf motto. "There is a fragment of a wall hanging in the solar. Would you allow me one moment to examine it?" She smiled. "I could not see it clearly in the candlelight and it appears to be quite ancient."

"Sassenach's are verra strange. Why would ye have the need to see an old piece of cloth?" Drew snorted and turned his horse around. "Verra well. Do ye mean to take it wi' ye?" He urged the horse into the small room and riding close to the wall grabbed the scrap of dust-covered material and handed it to her. "There. Now can we leave?"

"Yes. I thank you." She touched the delicate fabric and wished she could discover more about the women who had taken part in sewing such a fine tapestry. The castle had once been home to a clan of proud bearing. She could imagine weapons and fine tapestries gracing the thick walls now covered with damp patches and moss. A shiver ran down her back. If the many rooms divided by Romanesque archways could speak, what would they tell of bygone days? Death, murder, and betrayal? She smiled at him. "Do you have a library where I might discover more about this ruin?"

Drew splayed one large hand across her waist.

"Aye, we do but I believe this castle was once owned by the Grants, their land is close to here, aye, but when ye get to Badenoch speak wi' Father Dougal, he is verra knowledgeable."

She leaned back into his arms. "It seems such a romantic time. Knights in shining armor defending their queen."

"I dinna believe it was such a good time. Look at the state of this castle. It must have seen many sieges." He pulled her closer. "Are ye as comfortable as maybe?" He did not wait for her reply before urging the horse back into the Great Hall and issuing commands to his men in Gaelic. The clan moved out in silence leaving not one trace of occupancy inside the castle. He bent close to her ear. "I will give ye a break when needs be."

In truth, her leg ached and the ptisan muddled her thoughts. "Thank you. Yes, I am comfortable enough, although I must admit I have not ridden before in such a compromising position." She ignored his angry sound of derision and clung onto the horse's mane. "My leg is much better and the draft you concocted has eased the pain considerably."

"Ye must speak up if ye need a rest, aye?" His thigh muscles contracted under her bottom and the horse moved forward.

She gasped at the intimacy of his hard thighs beneath her bottom then covered his hand and squeezed. "Of course."

The horse clattered out of the Great Hall and they burst into early morning sunlight. A blast of freezing air cut through her clothes and she tightened the cloak about her. Behind her, Drew mumbled something incoherent and wrapped his thick woolen plaid around her tucking it beneath her legs. The heat from his body surrounded her suffused with his rich masculine scent and she bit back a sigh of pleasure.

Outside they paused in the ruins of the bailey and she turned to take one last glimpse at the once proud building. To be sure, the castle ruins held the violent history of Scotland. How much damage had the English kings brought to bear on the Scots over the centuries? She had studied the history of this land, from the pillaging of Catholic Churches during the Reformation by Henry V111 to the Jacobite rising of the '15 led by John Erskine, Earl of Mar. Although, her reasoning had brought condemnation from her tutor, she had gained an acute understanding of the Scottish preference for a Stuart king on the throne rather than a Hanover.

Her father had insisted she be fluent in German to accommodate King George, but he annoyed her with his arrogant and unyielding ways. She refused to condone the loss of life in pointless wars and could not fathom the way of things. Perhaps King George's son would be a king the Scots would accept. She turned to Drew. "Did any of your clan become involved in the rising of '15?"

"Och aye, Lord Lovet is kin o' mine on ma mother's side and many Mackenzies were involved."

She sighed. "Do you think there will ever be true peace between Scotland and England?"

"Not while the English refuse to accept the true king." Drew moved the horse to the head of his men and led the group out onto the road. "The Scots are not a verra forgiving people." He sighed. "The English nay doubt have their reason's to place a German on the throne rather than King James. I verra much doubt any of the Hannover kings will be happy until all of us are in our graves." He snorted.

She patted his hand absently. "Yes, I understand, perhaps a little more than you realize."

Drew growled deep in his chest, the sound reverberating through her back. He guided the horse from the ruins and along a road high above the sea.

"I am glad, lass, verra glad that ye do."

The journey ahead would be dangerous and the roads filled with thieves and excise men. She glanced over one shoulder at Drew's determined expression and the tension curling inside relaxed. *Whatever happens, I am where I want to be, safe in his arms.*

Chapter Two

The way ahead snaked around the shoreline for as far as the eye could see. The aroma of seaweed filled her nostrils and a strong gust of salty wind near blew her cap off. She turned to gaze at him and the strong muscles of his thighs tensed beneath her bottom. "I am educated and although you may not believe it, because of Rupert's wonderful tales of Selkies and Clooties I made a point of studying the history of Scotland."

"Och aye." Drew snorted. "Nay wonder your father wanted ye gone from his house. Ye father does nay think too kindly of the Mackenzies."

She squinted at him through the sunlight. "What a strange thing to say. He has never mentioned your clan in my company."

"I have discovered the reason he did not want me calling on ye." He shrugged in a dismissive way then smiled wickedly. "Angus told me last eve that ma grandsire refused him permission to call on ma mother. When I showed interest in ye, Lord Bracken nay doubt went straight to him being his best friend, aye." He chuckled in a most disarming way, full of positive glee. "An eye for an eye."

Shocked, she swallowed hard. "Are you saying he would see me dead rather than married to a Mackenzie?"

"Aye, and I was not going to trouble ye with this information. At first, I thought your refusal to marry any of his friends had his wame in a knot but I have thought on Angus's story and now believe he might still have romantic feelings for ma mother and could not face seeing her again or meeting the clan after being considered an unsuitable match." He squeezed her gently. "Dinna fash, at least now ye ken the way of things, aye? Try not to worry, tell me what ye ken about Scottish history."

Her thoughts wandered to the lessons delivered in an austere manner by her tutor, Mister Horacio Brown, who told of the Roman invasion and Hadrian's Wall built to separate Scotland from England in the year 122. The Roman army could not defeat the Picts because their spirit was so great Hadrian admitted defeat and returned to Rome. She cleared her throat. "The Picts defeated an army that had conquered the world. You are descended from them, are you not?"

"Aye, many clans do, but the Mackenzies have Viking blood from the Norsemen. The Romans had armor and the Picts with claymores or axes had naught but a targe to protect us." He grimaced. "I fear there will be another rising against the English. They have cannons and their armies outnumber us by many. I canna risk ma men in a war we canna win. Ma clan is depleted enough as is."

She swallowed hard at the thought of a bloody battle. "Why would you think such a thing?"

"Och, lass, there is talk but the king is in France, aye and nayone has the funds to pay for another rising. War costs a great deal in gold and lives." He moved the horse ahead of the others. "I have something to ask ye and I would appreciate an honest answer."

She swallowed hard. He must know she had already bared her soul to him and nodded meekly. "Of course."

"What would ye have done if I had not rescued ye?"

Drew could hear the clink of harness and the soft thud of the horses' hooves over the pounding of waves on the beach, but Adriana had suddenly lost her inquisitive tongue and his question remained unanswered. He cleared his throat and beneath his palm, her stomach muscles tightened. "It is a simple question, aye?"

"I knew you would come for me. You gave me your word."

He lifted her chin, turning her to face him, and swallowed at the sight of tears spilling unrestrained down her cheeks. His heart squeezed with compassion and with a sigh, he forced back the need to kiss away her pain. "I would have moved Heaven and Earth to find ye."

"I am glad you found me but knowing the truth of my father is distressing." She blinked and huge tears spilled from her lashes and ran over his fingers. Her eyes opened and she stared at him with an expression of such devotion he could not breathe. "It would seem I have always been a burden to him."

His heart missed a beat then raced. He dropped his hand from her damp face and memories of his wonderful childhood pushed into his mind. She had needed him to remove her from an impossible situation and perhaps destiny had a hand in his attraction toward her. He squeezed her gently to encourage her to confide in him, for how else would he be able to help her. "Tell me what your father did to ye. I am verra good at keeping secrets."

"Oh, it is nothing really." She sighed and brushed the tears from her cheeks in an agitated dash. "I wanted to learn a little about healing, after our discussion on how I should pass the time during your absence." Her eyes welled again with tears. "The very notion of this disturbed my father and when he discovered my visits to the poor and the brothels, he became irrational. I have reason to believe he made plans for my betrothal to Baron du Court before Rupert informed him of his plans to leave London."

Drew shook his head in disbelief. Lord Beachwood was indeed a fool to cast this precious and educated beauty from his hearth. "Your father is a verra strange man. He dinna want me calling on ye and yet would give ye to a murderer rather than have ye remain under his roof." He sighed. "I dinna understand why he treated ye so badly or why he discouraged ye from becoming a healer."

"Does it make a difference to *you* that I offered assistance to whores and visited the sick children of paupers?"

Taking time to think on her situation and how best to console her, he did not reply at once. She flashed him an indignant look, but her voice quivered.

"I am sure your opinion of me has diminished. However, if you decide to abandon me in this unforgiving land, would you allow me to throw myself into the sea b–because I hear drowning is a more p–peaceful death than starvation?" She bit her bottom lip and met his gaze. "Although, I would beg an indulgence? If you would p–please extend your protection to Betty, she has been a loyal servant to me and indeed a friend."

The lass had a death wish. Did she have no other plan than to commit self-murder the moment things went amiss? He snorted. "I dinna give a fig who ye helped, lass. I have never turned away anyone who needs ma skill as a healer and ye should be proud ye helped the less fortunate." He examined her tortured expression. How many times had Lord Beachwood chastised her? "I gave ye ma word of honor to protect ye. Does ma word mean nothing to ye, lass?"

"I know you are a man of honor." She turned on his lap to face him and her bottom lip quivered. "And I know Angus would rather see me dead than anywhere near you or your clan. Have you not noticed the way he glowers at me?"

"Aye, he has nay love for Sassenachs but he cares for your well-being." He pulled her against him. "And so do, I."

He swallowed hard. God help him, nothing mattered but Adrianna. His attention went to the small white teeth pressing into her bottom lip. He drew a deep breath and met her gaze. "I would have returned and saved ye all this pain if I could have, ye must believe me. There was nay time to write afore Rupert left London. The moment I received his letter explaining your position I moved Heaven and Earth to arrange a meeting wi' *The Black Turtle*. Ye have been on ma mind every moment since the masquerade ball and I have not lain with a lass since meeting ye. Your father's warning did not prevent me coming to ye, because I am a stubborn man and usually get what I want. I would have come for ye had ma father not died."

"Oh, Drew, I had no idea."

"Afore, I received Rupert's letter, I had planned to get ma clan settled afore I returned to London. As laird with considerable land and position, I would have sought your father's permission to call on ye." He touched her cheek. "I canna do that now we ken the truth of his objections toward me, but I *am* an honorable man. Will ye allow me to start afresh and court ye in the manner befitting a lady, ma bonnie Adrianna?"

Tears welled up in her eyes and ran down her flushed cheeks.

"I would like that of all things, but your clan? If my father discovers the truth I doubt he will let this matter go."

He rubbed his chin in an effort to put his mind in some sort of order. She trembled against him and he drew his cloak tighter around her. She had trusted him with her most guarded secrets and had been correct in assuming Lord Beachwood would pose a problem for his clan. He lifted his chin. He had made his decision, no man or Sassenach king would come between him and the woman he loved. As Laird Mackenzie, he would have many clans willing to fight by his side if needs be.

"Then we will follow our hearts, lass, and if all is well between us, I will deal with your father—and King Geordie." He smiled to reassure her. "Ye need not be afraid. Ma clan will follow my orders and protect ye. If ye will allow me to speak of ma desire to court ye and tell how ye have been mistreated by your father, most will agree ye are in need of ma protection."

She brightened and smiled at him.

"Perhaps you should mention I am an heiress. I have a small fortune with me and an estate in England with a good income."

He laughed. "Aye, I will. Ma clan has not been verra lucky of late."

"Why did you become a smuggler?" She sniffed. "Did your father condone such a dangerous way to make your fortune?"

Pain of losing his father tied knots around his heart. He drew a deep breath and stared along the ragged cliff face far into the distance. He tasted salt on his tongue and lifted his head to catch the breeze in an effort to control his emotions. As laird, he did not have the luxury of being maudlin. With his thoughts ordered, he swallowed the lump in his throat, and forced out the words. "Ma clan was growing faster than we could provide for them. We had a glut of whisky, but when I sold it in Scotland, the taxes took most of our profit."

He maneuvered the horse around a tree stump and lifted his face into the fresh breeze. "I have connections, in King Louis's court they ken me as *Monsieur* Alexander. Ma father thought it prudent for me to remove to France and I took fifty barrels wi' me and stored them in a warehouse on the docks. I marked the barrels as vinegar to avoid suspicion. I sold a small portion to the privateers along the French coast and soon had a warehouse filled with goods." He sighed. "I remained in France and sent the goods to Jamie to sell in Inverness. Soon I had the French nobility seeking out *Le Diable Noir* to procure merchandise for them. With goods I could trade legally in Scotland, ma clan prospered but I missed Scotland, aye. I sent one last cargo of French brandy to Inverness afore I left France."

"I find it hard to believe you did not enjoy the lavish indulgence of the French court." She gave him a meaningful stare. "I hear King Louis is extravagance personified."

He rolled his shoulders. Christ, he would admit less in a confessional, but she deserved to know every detail of his past.

"The French court is indeed an indulgence of food and lust, but I missed the sound of the Gaelic and the smell of mist on the heather. I am a Highlander and the call of the mountains is in ma blood. I saved enough coin to finance shares in an established wine business and have ensured ma clan has a constant income from the next quarter profits." He smiled. "I said, *au revoir* to *Le Diable Noir* and then I met you."

"What happened to make you to return to smuggling?"

The sight of his father's death mask came vividly to mind. "Ma father was poisoned along with two-thirds of ma clan. I arrived home to find ma father on his deathbed, ma tenants' homes ransacked by our neighbors, women and stock gone, and our fields afire." He grimaced. "I am a smuggler, aye, but I dinna usually risk moving goods off the coast of Scotland. I had nay choice because ma clan will not make it through the winter if I canna buy supplies."

"I have more than I need and will be most happy to help your clan." Adrianna's enthusiastic smile warmed his heart. "You are welcome to all I have with me, and the moment I employ a man of affairs I will have my funds transferred to a Scottish bank." She gripped his arm. "You are courting me, so there is no shame in taking my offer of assistance."

She had a small fortune in gold and jewels, but he would not touch a penny. He shook his head. "Nay, and have people say I am wooing ye for your fortune? Nay, lass, that would never do. I am a proud man, aye."

"Well, pride be damned." She drew herself up and gave him a rebellious stare. "You have admitted your clan is in desperate need and declining my willingness to help is ridiculous." She sighed. "If you refuse my assistance because of male pride then we must come to some other arrangement. As I do not intend to return to England, I might as well sell my estate in Surrey. I could build a house in Scotland." Her lips quivered into a smile of sorts. "It would be a simple matter of selling me a portion of Mackenzie land."

The idea sounded feasible and she had enough gold in her stays alone to feed his clan for a year or more, but he could not make a decision without consulting the terms with his clan. "Verra well, I will put your most generous offer to a meeting of the clan."

His clan would be more than happy to take her money, but heaven forbid if she decided not to marry him. As an unwed Sassenach lady with a holding on their land, her connection to King George would place her in constant danger. As his wife, she would be a Mackenzie and his clan would embrace her as the new Mistress of Badenoch.

He inhaled the feminine scent of her mingled with the herbal essence of the comfrey and his groin heated. No other woman attracted him to the point of madness. *I want her.*

Fate had thrown them together and beyond doubt, either God or the Ancient Ones had chosen her for him. She had two attributes he greatly admired; she glowed with inner strength and championed the less fortunate. To be sure, as the new Laird of Badenoch, the future offered him no surety. It would take time to rebuild his clan to its former glory and he would face a constant battle to keep his land in Mackenzie hands. Saint's willing, with her as a shining talisman by his side, he might shed the shroud of death and destruction in his path.

Lulled to sleep by the rocking motion of the horse, Adrianna woke enclosed in Drew's strong arms. Darkness surrounded her and a freezing wind buffeted her causing the horse's mane to fly in all directions. She blinked convinced the herbal concoction had caused her delirium. Had his request to pursue her and gentle kisses been a wonderful dream? She gazed at him and her heart raced with desire. His mouth had set in a determined line, but then he noticed her and his full lips turned up in a smile. He bent and brushed a kiss as soft as butterflies wings across her cheek then with exquisite tenderness, kissed the corners of her mouth, and traced the tip of his hot tongue over her lips. Tingles of awareness from his touch exploded into desire and she smiled. "Hello."

"Ye are awake." He pressed his lips to her forehead and sighed.

She glanced around suddenly embarrassed. "Will the clan make comment of your attention toward me?"

"Nay lass, I am wooing ye and as Laird I may chose ma own bride." He frowned at her moan of discomfiture. "We will stop in a few minutes to rest and have a bite to eat." He cupped her chin. "Are ye in verra much pain, lass?"

She wet her lips, tasting him and shook her head. "No, although I am a little stiff from sitting in the saddle so long." She gazed into his intent green eyes and smiled. She would be bold and tell him the truth of the matter. "Although, I will regret leaving your arms for more than a moment."

"That, ma sweet Adrianna, is music to ma ears." Drew bent to claim her mouth in a possessive kiss.

She melted into him and fell into bliss. His kiss curled her toes and she grasped great handfuls of his plaid to pull him closer wanting more of him. Innocent in the skill of such delightful pursuits, she opened her mouth to the demanding tongue pressing against her lips. As he explored every inch of her mouth, branding her with the taste of him, explosions of delight burst in white spots behind her eyes. Coming to her senses, she dragged her mouth away from him and her attention went to his full wet lips. She cleared her throat. To be sure, she had not expected such a reaction to her boldness but she craved more of him. "Your kisses, stir me to madness. I am quite undone."

"That is good and as it should be." He held up one hand pulling the line of carts and men behind him to a halt. He turned his horse around and addressed his men. "We will rest here, grab a bite to eat, and a couple of hours sleep. We will need to leave again afore dawn."

She smiled up at his weary expression. "I really have no need of sleep but I am willing to keep watch if needs be."

"I have men to keep watch." He rode toward the perimeter of the woods. "I will have a tent set up for ye. It will only be a blanket over a bush, but it will give ye some privacy. I will find Betty to change your dressings. It would not be seemly for me to attend ye, when your maid is at hand." He dismounted then held up his arms for her. "Take more of the ptisan if ye are in pain."

She slid down the length of him, her mind in turmoil. Such feelings of wantonness had never assailed her before and her boldness toward him astounded her. When he held her against him, safe in his strong arms, her legs weakened. She clung to him and fought to find reason in the madness swirling her emotions into erotic chaos. She blinked up at him and forced her mind back to his question. "Betty? Yes, I do need her. It would seem I have become a little unsteady on my feet."

"Aye, riding for six or more hours will do that to a grown man too." He helped her toward a tree stump. "Bide here and I will fetch your maid then I must speak to ma men."

Heart racing, her attention fixed on the solid strength of him. Moonlight filtered through the trees and bathed him in heavenly light. His hair fell about his shoulders and framed a handsome face with an expression of compassion. Her attraction to toward him had increased tenfold and from his ardent kisses, he truly wanted her. "Thank you." She met his gaze restless for more of him. "May I have one more kiss before you tend to your duties?"

Drew's smile glistened in the moonlight. In two strides, he had lifted her into his arms. "It would be ma pleasure to kiss ye and never stop."

She slid her fingers into his thick glossy hair and dragged him down to her. He groaned like a trapped animal and took her mouth in a deep, savage kiss, his tongue exploring every inch of her willing mouth. She moaned and thrust her hips against his muscular thighs in a primal demand. He lifted his head for one second, regarded her closely then cursed in a long string of Gaelic. His arousal pressed hard and firm against her hip and without thought of the consequences, she rubbed cat-like against him.

"Christ, Adrianna, ye will be the death of me."

He grasped her bottom in his large hands and massaged, sending streaks of erotic delight deep inside her. Then he slid his damp mouth over her lips, down her neck, and lavished kisses over the top of each breast. The next moment, he stiffened, his eyes shot open and he pressed a finger to her lips.

His voice dropped to a whisper and he thrust her into a bush.

"Hide—now. If anyone speaks to you, say nothing." In a swirl of tartan, he strode to his horse then leaped into the saddle. He swung the mount around and headed back to his men.

The sound of horses galloping toward them vibrated the ground. From beneath a prickly bush, she peered into the darkness to find shadows moving swiftly. All about her, horses snorted and stamped their feet. As the men unsheathed their swords, the sing of metal cut through the air chilling her to the bone. Drew's voice rang out above the din issuing orders. Men surrounded the wagons, weapons drawn, ready to defend their possessions. She held her breath, ducked low into the shadows and waited.

A group of men rode out of the darkness, moonlight glistening on swords and dirks. The leader reigned up his mount and held up a hand. Adrianna caught Drew's name in the fast Gaelic speech and her heart pounded. When Drew rode to greet the strangers, she caught a gleam of white teeth and a shout of greeting. *Thank God!*

She stood and pushed a few errant stands of hair under her cap. In the process of straightening her skirts, she heard a twig crack and whirled around to face a tall young man. He grasped her arm and pulled her roughly against him expelling the breath from her lungs. She gasped out a cry of protest but made a soundless squeak. His gripped tightened and he thrust his hips toward her in a lewd fashion. Caught in his grasp, she raked at his eyes and gagged at the smell of whisky and stale sweat. What could she say? Drew had given her strict instructions not to speak to a stranger less she divulge her nationality. *But I can scream.*

Gasping in a painful breath of air, she screamed.

The stranger laughed, grabbed her bottom, and let out a stream of Gaelic then bent his foul mouth and attempted to kiss her.

The next moment the man flew from her and landed a few paces away but rather than fall, he rolled to his feet and went for his dirk. Disorientated, she stared at him swaying and staggered a few steps before regaining her balance. Drew's voice came from behind her. He stepped between her and the man then addressed her in French.

"Apologies for this oaf's disrespect, Angelique." He stood rigid before her. "This is Con, the Macgregor's son. He understands French fine so before I speak with his father, he had better have a good excuse for attacking you or I will kill him."

The Macgregor, the one known as Rob Roy? She curtsied then dragging her skewed thoughts into some order, replied in her best Parisian accent. "The brutish lout is a barbarian. Is this what I am to expect in this vast wasteland?"

"No, in fact, the Macgregor is famous around these parts for protecting those less fortunate. The locals call him 'Rob Roy.' Have you by chance heard of him?"

"I have not. If he is a gentleman as you say, will you introduce me to him?"

"All in good time. Are you injured?" Drew examined her face with slow deliberation. "*Madame* Josephine will have my balls if you are damaged."

"Ah, so she *is* a whore." Con touched the scratches on his face and grinned. "Then why must I make an apology to her, no doubt she is with you for your men's amusement?" His French had a strange accent.

"No, she is *Madame* Josephine's sister and on her way to meet her betrothed. She paid me well to accompany her to Scotland." Drew tipped his head toward her. "Do not worry. I will see you safely delivered to your sister."

"I thank you kindly, Laird Mackenzie."

"Well then, I am sorry to put you in such a compromising position." Con bowed and gave her an impish grin. "If you find your suitor not to your liking inform your sister to contact me, Con Macgregor." He turned and said something to Drew is Gaelic then strolled toward the group of men sitting around the campfire.

She stared up at Drew and noticed a nerve twitching in his cheek. Anger tensed his stance and she laid a hand on his arm. "What did he say?"

"Ye dinna want to hear." He glared after Con, his fingers restless on his dirk.

"I rather think I must."

His head moved slowly toward her and he set a gaze as black as night on her face.

"Verra well. He said ye have the finest arse he has ever had the pleasure of holding."

His expression had become hard lines in the moonlight, unreadable, and under her palm, his muscles hardened.

"I told ye to hide and I find ye in the arms of another wi' his hands all over ye. Why did ye disobey ma orders and allow him to see ye? Now I have to lie to the Macgregor and we have been friends for many a year."

"When I saw you greet the men as friends I thought it was safe to come out of hiding." She smiled trying to reassure him. "He no doubt thought me a camp follower and in any case, Con will look a fool with the scratches on his face once his father knows of his mistake. Although you may have to lie to him again, when you inform him, I decided on a match with you in preference."

"A match wi' me?" Drew grinned and his shoulders relaxed. "Are ye making me an offer, ma lady?"

She giggled and leaned into him. "That is a gentleman's prerogative but perhaps a lady's suggestion."

"Aye, lass, it is to be sure and one I will give ma attention too at the earliest convenience." He led her toward the group of men weaving around the bushes and fallen logs. "Well, I had better introduce ye to Rob Roy, aye? He would be the one wi' the red hair. We will say ye are a lady–in–waiting from the Palace of Versailles if he should ask but keep ye head down and dinna get involved wi' the conversation. Mind ye keep Betty well away from the men, I dinna want her saying one word."

She did not have to worry. The Macgregor cast a disinterested eye over her then turned his back to listen to a story Jamie was describing with great arm movements. She sat beside Betty and gave her an encouraging smile. Wrapped in Jamie's plaid, the girl's pale, drawn expression said volumes. Without doubt, Jamie had issued a warning to her about uttering one word in the company of Rob Roy.

In the short time since their arrival, the men had a pot of something simmering on a fire and the conversation in the camp was lively. She inhaled the aroma of pork stew and her stomach rumbled. One thing for sure, she would not starve with the Mackenzie clan. She cast her eye over the Macgregor's band of unwashed, unshaven men, all appeared to have not seen a bath for some weeks and the reek coming from them would ruin her supper.

She touched her thigh gingerly and winced. The excitement of Rob Roy's arrival had masked the pain of her injury but after walking a short distance, the throbbing had increased. She reached for the flask in her pocket and sipped the concoction. At once Drew's gaze fell upon her assessing her condition. She lifted the flask in a toast and sipped again. He inclined his dark head and turned back to the conversation.

She glanced at the sky, in an effort to determine the time. The moon sat low above, so many hours would pass before dawn. The shortness of the winter days surprised her. She understood the gloaming, the endless twilight that accompanied the summer months but in November night had dropped like a black curtain midafternoon and the freezing nights appeared endless.

Before long, Dermot arrived carrying two trenchers of stew and a wineskin tucked under one arm. She took her spoon from her reticule and set to work devouring the excellent fare. The noise around the campfire grew boisterous and Drew cast a glance her way then issued orders to Ian. The young man collected blankets from one of the wagons and with a jut of his chin indicated, they should follow him. He led the way to the foot of a small tree surrounded by undergrowth. The bare limbs offered not one bit of shelter, but the thick layer of autumn leaves at least made the ground soft. She waited for Ian to fashion a tent of sorts using one of the blankets and then Betty made a bed using the rest. Ian stepped closer, and the darkness did not hide the concern on his young face.

"Drew has set guards to watch over ye while ye rest. I will bide close by too. I dinna ken how the Macgregor's men will act in their cups. We will be leaving in nay more than a few hours. We plan to make the coach house well afore dawn and God willing, Rupert will be there to take ye to Inverness."

She gazed at him astonished. "Lord Rupert?"

"Aye, himself sent a messenger to him afore and asked him to take ye to Inverness, to avoid Lord Moreau, ye ken? The Macgregor brought word that Lord Moreau has offered a fortune in gold to anyone giving him information about your whereabouts." Ian hunched and dropped his gaze. "I ken Drew dinna want him to ken about ye, but the Macgregor is nay fool and Drew told him the truth of the matter. In confidence, aye. Rob Roy has pledged to fight beside us if the needs be to keep ye safe from King Geordie's men. I ken Drew has not had the time to inform ye."

"Not to worry." She put away the small niggling concern about leaving Drew and smiled. "Thank you, Ian." She took another sip of the ptisan, turned away, and crawled into the bed beside Betty.

No sooner had she closed her eyes than Betty shook her awake.

"It is time to go, milady."

She blinked into the darkness. "What? Have the plans changed?"

"No, but we have to leave now. The Macgregor left some time ago." Drew's voice pierced her befuddled brain. "Get ready. I have a dish of tea waiting for you by the fire."

She sighed with delight. "You have tea?"

"Aye, we have ten chests on the wagons. I will take five of them to Badenoch. My ma is partial to tea."

After eating a few stale bannocks and drinking the welcome dish of tea, she allowed Drew to place her on his horse. She winced in pain, her hip, worse now from sleeping on the hard ground. He gave her a concerned gaze and took a silver flask from his sporran.

"Drink some of this, it tastes like cow dung but it will help ye to sleep most of the way." He handed her the bottle then climbed up behind her. "Dinna fash, I will take care of ye."

She drunk a good portion of the foul liquid then relaxed into his strong arms and rested her head on his shoulder. The delicious scent of him enclosed her and yawning, she snuggled against the solid strength of him. "You are the kindest man I know."

Chapter Three

ord Rupert Bainbridge lounged in the taproom of the Glen Albyn Inn after an overindulgence of black pudding and pumpkin followed by a most excellent treacle tart. As he sipped a class of porter, he caught mention of his name and his attention went to a man conversing with the landlord. His knowledge of the Gaelic being somewhat rusty, he gathered the man had urgent business with him. He pushed to his feet and strode toward the bar to greet the dusty stranger. "Are you by chance looking for me?"

"Aye, if ye are Lord Rupert, kin of Laird Drew Mackenzie."

Rupert inclined his head. "Yes, I am he, and you are?"

"Duncan MacBride, your servant sir." He bowed and on straightening frowned at the landlord, who had moved uncomfortably close. "May we speak in private, ma lord?"

"Yes, I have rooms upstairs. Is something amiss with Laird Mackenzie?" Rupert led the way from the taproom then took the creaky wooden steps to a narrow corridor.

"I have a letter for ye. I am sure the laird will have explained matters."

"This is my room." Rupert turned the white porcelain handle to open the door and stood back for Duncan to enter.

Once inside he turned to his valet, who lifted his attention from cleaning boots to gaze at the filthy Scotsman with unbridled disgust. Rupert cleared his throat. "I wish to speak with Mister MacBride in private, if you please, Mister Bent."

"Very well, milord, but I will be right outside if you need me." Bent gave him a meaningful gaze and left the room.

With the door firmly shut behind Bent, he waved the exhausted man into a seat but Duncan remained standing head bowed.

"Whisky?" Rupert poured a generous amount into a glass and pushed both glass and decanter toward Duncan. "Do help yourself."

"Och aye, I thank ye kindly, ma lord." Duncan removed his hat and struck it across his knees sending great clouds of dust into the air. "I have not stopped since leaving the laird. I have an urgent message for ye." He reached inside his sporran and retrieved a letter. "I will answer any questions ye might have then if ye dinna mind I will be off to find a bite to eat."

Rupert strolled to the bedside table and opened a drawer. He took out a plate of bannocks still fresh from breakfast and handed them to Duncan. "Here this will help. Do sit down man before you drop." He pointed to a seat at the table. "Give me a moment to read what Laird Mackenzie has to say then I will go downstairs and speak to the landlord about supplying a room for you. I am sure you would appreciate a hot bath and a good meal?"

"I would, sir." Duncan offered the crumpled document to Rupert.

He took the letter with his direction across the front in Drew's familiar handwriting. Breaking the seal, he moved to the fireplace to avail himself of the light from the candle on the mantelpiece.

> *To Lord Rupert Bainbridge,*
> *Glen Albyn Inn*
> *Inverness*
>
> *Dear Rupert,*
>
> *I find myself in a quandary regarding your dear friend, Lady A. As you advised, I organized a rescue and I am pleased to inform you the lady in question is now under my protection.*
>
> *You mentioned Lord M and I gather you will have recollection of this person. You may*

recall meeting him during the discussions regarding my mares. The gentleman, and I say this through gritted teeth for to utter such a falsehood for a man who would kill his own mother to gain the coin to support his addiction to the opium, will give you some idea of the state of mind the lady suffered on her arrival. She suffered injuries to the point and I had doubts for her survival.

Well, cousin, I have no doubt Lord M believes a certain smuggler had a hand in her escape and will be waiting anxiously for her arrival in Inverness. If my identity is exposed, we will face arrest, leaving him free to remove her to France.

Would you indulge me by bringing a carriage to meet me with all haste and accompany her and her maid to the safety of the establishment where you celebrated your eighteenth birthday? I believe this is the last place Lord M will search for her. I bid you explain the circumstances and inform the proprietor I will make significant recompense for the inconvenience upon my arrival.

To err on the side of caution, my clansman will give you my direction and any other information you require.

Your most affectionate cousin,
D.

Christ! Rupert read the missive twice then balled the paper and strolled across the room to toss it into the fire. Mind reeling, he watched the letter burst into orange flames then disintegrate into silver gray ashes. He bent and taking the poker, stirred the embers until no trace remained. He straightened slowly and clasping both hands beneath the tails of his jacket turned to Duncan. "Where exactly is Laird Mackenzie?"

Duncan blinked and his Adam's apple bobbed in an attempt to swallow a mouthful of bannock. He scratched a mass of dark brown hair.

"He is traveling along the coast from Burghead. It is verra slow going with the loaded wagons so I would say by the time ye reach him he will be closer to the coach house at Nairn but not as far as Culloden Moore." He lifted his chin and sighed. "I would wait for him at Nairn, he will bide at the coach house there to rest the horses. I will be more than happy to take ye to him."

"What were your orders?"

"To give ye the letter and wait for the laird here." Duncan lifted his glass of whisky sniffed the contents then sipped. He sighed. "But if ye dinna ken the way, I am sure the laird would want me to take ye to him."

Rupert stared through the grimy windowpane, over the rooftops of Inverness, and into the distance. Drew would expect him to slip out of Inverness without notice and Duncan would with all probability, be well known as one of his men. He turned his attention back to him and smiled. "That will not be necessary, but I thank you, Mister MacBride. I am familiar with this part of Scotland."

He lifted the gold watch from the pocket of his waistcoat and peered at the enameled Roman numerals. Nine hours before dawn and it would take at least one hour to arrange a carriage and supplies for the round trip. Nairn lay approximately fifteen miles north of Inverness; a fine pair of horses would make the distance in three hours at a trot, but the old nags he had seen in the Inn's stable would be more likely drop dead on the journey back if he pushed them too hard. Unless, the coaching inn at Nairn was prepared to swap the team. He searched his mind for the current phase of the moon and could not, for the life of him remember. He cleared his throat. "Is there a moon tonight do you know?"

"Aye, a quarter moon is enough to see the way and the storm clouds have moved off to sea so they will not be bothering ye. Stick to the coast road because it is well marked. The stable has ten o' more horses here used for the mail coach swap. They may be slow, but they will not be afraid of traveling the roads at night." Duncan placed his empty glass on the table and his gaze wandered to the decanter of whisky. "They have a carriage for hire, but I gather ye will be needing a coachman?"

"No, I am sure I can manage." He strolled to the door and removed his cloak and hat from a peg on the wall. He donned his hat and turned to Duncan. "I will make the necessary arrangements. If you would accompany me downstairs, I will speak to the innkeeper and ensure he supplies you with everything you need." He opened the door and paused to speak to Bent. "Be a good chap and order me a coach and four. I must leave at the earliest convenience." He rubbed his chin. "Oh, and unpack my pistols on your return. I will be back within the hour. I have some business to attend to before I leave."

"Right away, milord." Bent bowed. He straightened and a frown crossed his young face. "Do you want me to accompany you?" He shrugged. "I mean, perhaps you will need me to protect you, seeing that a bunch of Highland brigands might well hold up the coach and kidnap you for ransom. You being a lord and all."

Across the room, Duncan's eyes narrowed, his broad shoulders stiffened, and one hand flew to the silver handled dirk at his waist. Stepping toward him, Rupert laid one hand on the shoulder of the indignant Highlander. Although in all honesty, he could do little to prevent the massive man slaughtering his servant for the breach of etiquette. He squeezed the rigid muscle under his palm and glared at his valet. "Mister Bent, must I constantly insist that you mind your tongue?" He dropped his hand. "I spent many of my tender years in the Highlands with *my* clan. I may have the appearance of an English lord but my mother, God rest her soul, was a Mackenzie." He raised both eyebrows. "Which I believe makes me a 'Highland brigand' as well." He cleared his throat. "I am sure you did not intend to insult Mister MacBride with your careless attack on his character?"

"Oh no, sir. I beg pardon I do." Bent pale as a ghost and visibly shaken bowed to Duncan. "I was, you see, trying to protect my master from any unsavory occurrence."

"Och aye, well ye will find yourself split from neck to arse, if ye continue to spread unfounded gossip wi' that loose tongue of yours." Duncan glared with malice at Bent. "Highlanders do not take so kindly to Sassenachs making groundless accusations about their character. It is a matter of honor, aye?"

"Yes, I thank you, sir, for your patience." Bent's face had gone a peculiar shade of green.

"That will be all, Mister Bent." Rupert waved Bent away and the young lad scampered off toward the servants stairs at the back of the building. He raised both brows at Duncan. "He may speak his mind at the most inopportune moments, but he would give his life to protect me and he *is* a damn good valet."

"He is young and lacking the skill to keep ye from harm, ma lord. Most likely he will cause ye more trouble." Duncan gazed after Bent. "Ye will do well to allow the laird to train him so he may offer ye better protection."

"Yes, I will give that idea some consideration." Rupert smiled and waved a hand toward the hallway. "I had better arrange a room for you."

Leading the way along the corridor, he took the steps to the taproom. After speaking with the landlord, he bid Duncan farewell then stepped out of the warm, noisy taproom and into a blustery night. He turned and gazed toward the ocean. The storm had brought the chill of winter in its wake and he shivered at the freezing wind cutting through his clothes. The journey to Nairn would be most uncomfortable and he would require a basket of food for Lady Adrianna and a good quantity of blankets. He made a mental note to ask Mister Bent to arrange the necessities. Throwing his cloak about his shoulders, he moved into the quiet street and headed in the direction of *Madame* Josephine's brothel.

He pulled the flapping black woolen cloak tighter around him and bent his head into the wind. Turning the corner into Hog's Lane, he inhaled the scent of cheap wine and perfume from the molls overflowing from the bawdy houses into the street. The smell ignited a glowing memory of his first encounter with the famous *Madame* Josephine. *Christ, had it been eight years?* Unceremoniously dragged by his cousins to the brothel, as an untried lad of eighteen, *Madame* Josephine had literally taken him to her bosom. Of course, being foolishly ignorant in the ways of the world and deeply armored with her, he had visited her boudoir daily for more than a week depleting his entire month's allowance.

His cheeks grew uncomfortably hot recalling the foolish act of kneeling before her and declaring his undying yet penniless love. She, having experience in such matters of the heart had taken pity on him and had insisted he take pleasure in the other delights her house had to offer. Penniless and as randy as a bull he had little choice but to acquiesce.

He laughed, gaining the immediate attention of a group of red-lipped harlots and waved them away too engrossed in his memories. Indeed, he often recalled the romp with Angelique, a petite blonde temptress and the client, a delectably muscular young man who went, if he recalled by the name of Roman—a gladiator of love to be sure. After such an encounter, his outlook on life and indeed all things pleasurable had changed dramatically.

He paused in front of the brown door with the brass lion's head knocker and rapped twice. The door swung open to reveal a footman dressed in fine livery and wearing a white wig. Stepping over the doorstep, he removed his cloak and handed it off to a servant girl. He turned to the footman. "Tell Madame, Lord Rupert requests a word in private."

"At once, milord." The footman bowed, straightened then marched toward *Madame* Josephine's private receiving room.

Moments later the great woman herself breezed into the hallway hands extended in welcome. "Lord Rupert, how wonderful to see you again. You have stayed away too long, you naughty boy."

He bowed over her hand then met a gaze dancing with mischief. He lowered his voice to just above a whisper. "I have come on a private matter."

"Oh, I see. Well then, *cher*, come this way." *Madame* Josephine turned her billowing skirts and strolled down the corridor. Pausing beside a door, she turned to him. "We will have privacy in here." The door opened revealing a study and he followed her inside. "Shut the door and tell me what is troubling you."

"I recently requested Laird Mackenzie's assistance in helping me save a friend from certain death." He cast a glance at the door and lowered his voice. "She was traveling on *The Black Turtle*."

"Then I think you are too late, Drew would have concluded his arrangement with Captain Jacques by now, *non?*" She met his gaze and a small frown creased her extravagantly powdered brow. "Or has he fallen foul of the beast Lord Moreau?" She turned and spat into the fire.

Astounded by her venomous reaction toward the man, he stepped forward and patted her arm to calm her. "I do not believe Laird Mackenzie is capable of being hoodwinked by the likes of him, but unfortunately that reprobate is the reason I am here, *Madame*."

He explained Lady Adrianna's delicate position avoiding Drew's romantic involvement with her and reached for his pocketbook. *Madame* Josephine's expression softened at the overly large amount of pound notes, he pressed into her hand. He smiled. "Lady Adrianna is a particular friend of mine and I would see only the very best for her." He glanced toward the door. "She will require complete privacy, her safety is essential."

"For how long?"

Rupert waved a hand dismissively. "A few days, four at the most before I am able to leave Inverness with her." He met her gaze with a tight smile. "It is imperative there is no hint of Laird Mackenzie's involvement or Lord Moreau will discover he is *Le Diable Noir*. Many lives depend upon your absolute discretion."

"Very well, his secret is safe with me as always." *Madame* Josephine went to the desk, took out a small box, and dropped the banknotes inside. "But you do understand, Lord Moreau and Jacques are frequent visitors here, and I cannot guarantee her safety if she wanders from her room. Both these men will recognize her, *non?*" She tapped her chin with the tip of one finger. "Come with me to the parlor and choose which of my girls is similar in size as Lady Adrianna."

He rubbed his chin. "She comes with a maid."

"Then you must select two girls, *cher.*"

Intrigued, Rupert inclined his head and studied the carefully painted face for a few seconds. For a woman in her forties, she appeared as voluptuously appealing as she had to him as a youth. He dismissed the thought and raised a brow picturing Adrianna in his mind. "Yes, I do believe I could estimate her size and her maid is but a slip of a girl. Why, may I ask?"

"Oh, you silly man." She laughed and the sound sent shivers of awareness to places he wished would remain dormant. "How do you hide a straw of hay in a haystack? We must dress your fine lady and her maid like whores then they will slip in unnoticed. So, my friend, you will let them down from your carriage in the main street and have your valet escort them along Hog's Lane, down the alley to my back door. I will take them through the kitchen up the servants' stairs to the loft. Should they be seen, I will say they are 'special' girls for the more unusual clients, *n'est-ce pas?*" She smiled beatifically. "Then if you wish to visit them, you may do so through the front door as usual." Laughter filled the small room. "Am I not resourceful, *cher?*"

He returned her smile. "Indeed you are, *Madame*. If we may conclude our arrangement as soon as possible, I have to travel some way to collect Lady Adrianna but I will return before daybreak."

"I will be waiting." She wet her lips and stepped closer, her skirts wrapped around his legs and the heat of her burned through his breeches. "I hope you will spend a little time with me on your return, *cher.*" In a bold gesture, she cupped him and ran the tip of her pink tongue over his bottom lip. "You will have the choice of three *very* handsome young men who will be more than happy to join us if you have the inclination." She gave him a knowing smile. "Or I will give you one of them free of charge if you prefer?"

Christ! On the brink of agreeing, for the notion of a night of unbridled passion with her and a young virile man was almost too much to bear, he dragged his mind away from such diversions, and forced his attention back to Lady Adrianna's plight. He took a step backward away from her allure. To his dismay, his knees encountered the edge of a chair and he sat down in a most ungainly fashion. His face heated and he found the need to push to his feet to relieve the pressure his tight breeches had inflicted to his groin. Embarrassed by his behavior, he bowed. "I thank you kindly and will take you up on your most generous offer on my next visit."

"Very well, *cher.*" She moved toward the door, her hips swinging provocatively. "Come now and chose a girl and I will find you some clothes."

Heaving a sigh, he straightened his waistcoat and followed her into the hallway. Entering the salon the aroma of aroused female and rose perfume accosted his nostrils. He strolled into the welcoming warmth and stopped at the disturbing sight of Lord Moreau leaning casually against the wall. Dear God, he had stepped into a quagmire of deceit and the need to play a convincing role was paramount. He returned *Madame* Josephine's encouraging smile, but his passion had faded like an autumn rose in the winter's first frost.

Damnation! Why did she not inform me he had arrived? The pernicious cadaver of a man raised a brow and observed him through sunken eyes. Gathering his wits, he turned his back refusing to acknowledge the gentleman's presence.

With luck, Lord Moreau would not remember their brief encounter at Lord Bradshaw's stables in London. What in Christ's name was he doing here anyway? Surely, *The Black Turtle* had not yet docked in Inverness. He had not spied the vessel on his walk earlier, and could not have missed a ship, painted black with matching rigging although, being a privateer the captain would anchor off shore. His expression must have displayed his disquiet because *Madame* Josephine gave him a meaningful look and moved to the center of the room, her long red skirts brushing the exquisite Chinese rug. She narrowed her gaze and clapped her hands.

"Attention, *ma petites.* I have a very particular gentleman here to view you."

Silently giving thanks to his father's insistence of tutoring his sons in the discipline of remaining calm when all about them had gone to hell. He ignored his palpitating heart and the sweat trickling an itchy path down his back and took a nonchalant pose. He dropped his lashes and allowed his gaze to drift in casual abandon around the large room. It would seem nothing had changed to any degree since his last visit. Although, the elaborate blue velvet curtains held back with gold fittings appeared new as did the glossy white marble statues of entwined couples.

His attention moved to the chaise lounges dominating the remainder of the room draped in scantily clad bodies. At his appearance they, both men and women, made an attempt to lock eyes with him and all moved in a provocative fashion to display their attributes to the best advantage. He swallowed hard and openly admired white globes tipped with rose pink or flat brown nipples offered for his devotion. He hardened at the brazen invitation from thighs spread to give him glimpses of curls in a variety of tempting colors made unashamedly visible beneath sheer chemises or pantaloons. He swallowed hard and forced his mind to concentrate for indeed the whores in this room left nothing to his imagination.

The smell of opium gave advance notice of Lord Moreau moving to his side. He ignored him and set his attention on the women before him. He selected a girl approximately the size of Adrianna and chose a skinny girl of about fourteen.

"Appearances are deceiving, *non?*" Lord Moreau chuckled. "I would have thought you would have preferred a sweet young boy in your bed."

Rupert rounded on him and dropped his voice to a menacing whisper. "Are you insinuating I am a sodomite, sir? For I tell you, if we were not inside a Scottish brothel, I would call you out."

"You English are so, how you say, 'pretentious,' *non?* There is nothing wrong with tasting all the temptations a brothel has to offer. No one cares what happens inside the bedchamber."

"Gentlemen." *Madame* Josephine moved between them. "This is a place of *love,* not duels. Come now." She rested her fingertips on Rupert's arm. "I will show you to your room."

Outside in the hallway, he turned to her. "I beg you to collect the dresses with all speed. I must leave at once."

"I understand, *cher.* Go now and collect your carriage. Wait in the main street well away from Hog's Lane and send your valet to the back door. I will have the dresses ready for him. You will require powder and rouge as well. I suggest you insist your ladies make good use of it. This is a whorehouse, *non?*" *Madame* Josephine pushed him toward the door. "God's speed, *mon ami.*"

Lord Moreau sidled closer to the door in an attempt to catch the conversation between *Madame* Josephine and the English Lord but only muffled words came to his ears. He had met the fop before and searched his memory for the more than familiar name hovering in the corner of his mind. *Lord Rupert Bainbridge.* Ah, yes the popinjay had intervened during his purchase of a stallion for Baron du Court and procured a number of mares for a business partner he referred to as Mackenzie. What business had brought Lord Rupert in Scotland and particularly Inverness? The delivery of the mares? He rubbed his chin and stared sightlessly at a nude statue. Pieces of the puzzle of exactly why Lady Adrianna had escaped *The Black Turtle* without his knowledge fell into place with a resounding jolt.

During his interview with Lord Beachwood before leaving London, the lord had detailed concerns regarding one of her suitors, coincidentally by the same name and duly sent Lord Rupert away with a flea in his ear. Concerns indeed, if Lord Rupert had organized Lady Adrianna's escape from *The Black Turtle.* It was no wonder Lord Beachwood had insisted he remove his daughter from England with all haste to avoid complications.

He drew in a deep breath to clear his head. He needed to think. The slave who had escaped with Lady Adrianna was a Mackenzie too and now Lord Rupert had arrived with mares to deliver to a man with the same surname. To find him in Inverness, so soon after Lady Adrianna's disappearance from *The Black Turtle* was more than a little coincidental. *Mon Dieu!* Had Lord Rupert organized the Mackenzie lad to board the ship and aid in Lady Adrianna's escape? Would a lord of the realm conspire against Lord Beachwood, and indeed her godfather King George?

Too many coincidences accosted his brain. He pushed through the miasma of opiate to command his fleeting thoughts. Why had Lady Adrianna jumped ship at Burghead if not to meet Lord Rupert? She could not possibly have knowledge of the notorious *Le Diable Noir*, nor would the Mackenzie slave, although she could have overheard the conversations regarding their scheduled meetings and used it to her advantage. He had to be correct in his assumption for the Burghead rendezvous was the sixth along the British coastline and Mackenzie came aboard on the fifth. Yes, it made sense because if Lady Adrianna had wanted to escape previously, she could have stowed away in any one of the boats carrying cargo at one of the earlier rendezvous. So why Burghead unless the meeting was preordained?

Anger shivered through him and he flattened his lips. If Lady Adrianna was indeed under the protection of Lord Rupert, the game had changed. Mackenzie was a common name and if Lord Rupert had paid for the protection of a clan, he would have little hope of retrieving his master's prize alone. A Frenchman kidnapping a lady from the Scottish Highlands would be a receipt for disaster. Nevertheless, discovering Lord Rupert's direction should not be a problem and he had more than enough money to hire a band of Lowlander yahoos to do his bidding.

The Black Turtle would have to weigh anchor a little longer than expected but no matter. He touched the bulging purse at his waist and glanced around *Madame* Josephine's parlor. Pointing a finger at a thin wastrel of a girl with large eyes and an expression of terror, he smiled. The need to inflict pain and relieve the anger boiling within consumed him. She and perhaps one or two of her friends would do nicely for his pleasure this evening.

Chapter Four

Drew breathed a sigh of relief as the lights of Nairn came into view. The tortuous journey with a warm, feminine backside pressing against his arousal had near driven him insane. Holding Adrianna's voluptuous body in his arms had caused him to make lists of merchandise or recite Latin, anything to distract from the desire she evoked in him. He gazed down at her, her head rested on his shoulder and her face tipped up giving him access to her soft pouting lips. He pushed back the need to crush her mouth in a deep kiss and thanked God the ptisan and the rocking of the horse had lulled her into a deep sleep. Indeed, apart from two stops to rest the horses and eat, she had slept most of the trip.

He pulled the horse to a stop to allow the carts to catch up to him and gazed into the distance. With luck, Rupert would meet him within the hour and take Adrianna to safety. Although, the lass was none too pleased with the idea of leaving him, he had convinced her to go with Rupert and avoid the chance of meeting Lord Moreau on their arrival in Inverness.

He had made plans with the owner of the Dunbar Inn to trade the variety of meat his men had bagged in exchange for a selection of the locally made cheeses. He would seek a bed in the inn for the night. After an arduous journey, his men required a decent sleep but he would set men in shifts of two hours duration throughout the night to guard his precious cargo. Once they reached Inverness, he would send Jamie and Angus with a wagon each to deliver the merchandise and collect the goods or cash. He would take a few of the bolts of silk and cambric to Lady Josephine to fill her order plus one or two bottles of his finest whisky by way of thanks.

In his arms, Adrianna stirred and moaned. Although, she claimed to be without pain, he knew better. Changing her dressings at the side of a road buffeted by a freezing wind, with only whisky to clean the wound had turned him into a blithering idiot. The sight of unrestrained tears spilling down her cheeks and the intense pain caused by his ministrations had not only shaken his hands but had near undone him. His jaw ached from grinding his teeth in despair of Adrianna's agony.

Jamie moved his horse beside him and his brow wrinkled into a frown.

"Christ, ye look like ye have just walked off a battlefield."

Drew shrugged. "Aye well, it is the lass. It would seem I bring her to tears each time I tend her."

"Why are ye blaming yourself?" Jamie indicated toward Adrianna. "Ye had nothing to do wi' her injury and ye have done your best to help her." He frowned. "I ken ye well enough, brother, ye appear to have more than the weight of the world upon your shoulders."

"I care for her, aye." He stroked Adrianna's ashen cheek. "I ken it is not in the best interest of the clan, but she holds ma heart. I told Da the truth of it and now being with her, I ken I have wanted her from the first time I kissed her."

"Then have her." Jamie gave him a wry smile. "Ye can deal wi' the clan later."

He gazed down at Adrianna's beautiful face and sighed. In her waking moments, she had clung to him, accepted his offered words of comfort, and buried her face in his neck. Oh God, no other woman had captured his heart then dissolved his emotions into a rambling mess. The journey, with her in such close proximity, had bonded them to be sure. However, had her response to his advances been a true indication of her feelings? A man such as he had the way to lure a maiden into his arms. She lusted after him, but the love he required from her needed to last a lifetime.

I cannot let her go. I want her for my wife. He met Jamie's concerned expression. "I thank ye for your support but now is not the time. She is vulnerable and I will need time to convince her my intentions are honorable. When I wed, it will be for love, and forever." He sighed. "I ken she cares for me, but she is innocent, and I am well skilled in seduction."

He cleared his throat. "It must have been a fine shock to her seeing me as a smuggler and to make thing worse, I accused her of enslaving Ian."

"Aye, but I ken she thinks well of ye now. I see the way she looks at ye." Jamie sighed and his gaze narrowed. "Nay man could have done more for the lass. In truth, many would have bedded her and left her on the side of the road to fend for herself. I can see ye care for her, so take your time. Woo her and she will see the good in ye, aye?"

"She encourages ma kisses, but I canna undo what I am. She expected a finely dressed gentleman to rescue her, not a Highlander." He stared into the distance and forced words over the lump in his throat. "Such things come between a man and a woman to be sure. She may worry I will turn into a barbarian or worse an adulterer the moment we are wed."

"Then ye will have to convince her otherwise." Jamie chuckled. "I dinna think ye have had much trouble convincing women in the past to your way of thinking, have ye now?"

Anger crawled up his spine and he glared a warning at him. "Dinna speak like that about Lady Adrianna. She is a maiden and worthy of respect, not bawdy discourse."

"I am sorry, brother, but ye have to admit ye *do* have somewhat of a reputation." Jamie raised both eyebrows then turned his horse around and headed down the line of weary travelers.

Drew gathered Adrianna closer and wrapped his plaid tighter around her. He stared into the distance and made out a smudge of white picked out by the moonlight and recognized the turnpike. Within the half hour, they would reach the inn on the boarder of Nairn. God willing Lord Rupert had received his missive in time and would be on his way with a carriage to take her to Inverness.

He touched her clammy white skin and frowned. Although, he had mixed more of the ptisan and given her a large dose at their last stop, the fever had returned. If Betty followed his orders and administered more of the mixture, Adrianna should sleep for most of the journey to *Madame*

Josephine's establishment. He grimaced at the thought of exposing her to the indecencies of a brothel but had little choice. He had good reason to expect Lord Moreau, even in his constant state of oblivion, would have the capacity to relate Adrianna and Ian's escape to *le Diable Noir*'s dealings with *The Black Turtle*. If his clan arrived in Inverness with the two women, the jig would be up. As Laird Mackenzie, and with his men wearing their dull-colored hunting plaids, they should blend into Inverness without notice.

At the turnpike, he urged his horse toward the welcoming lights of the Dunbar Inn. The beast pricked his ears and danced sideways no doubt excited with the notion of a stall brimming with fresh straw and a manger filled with oats. Moments later, the horses hooves clattered over the cobblestones and stable lads rushed out to greet him.

"Do ye have room for all of us?" He waved a hand toward his men.

"Aye, laird, that we do." The familiar weathered face of old Tom Braddock came into view. "I will send one of the lads inside to see to your rooms."

"Thank ye, kindly." He waved his men forward then glanced down at Adrianna. "I will need a room for the lasses."

"I think not." Rupert stepped out of the shadows, his grin white in the darkness. "I have arranged more suitable accommodation."

Immaculate as usual, Rupert appeared to have stepped from his club rather than from the seat of a coach and four driven at full gallop in the dead of night. With not one hair out of place, he strode toward him. The healthy glow to his cheeks from the biting chill was the only hint of discomfiture. Drew grinned down at him and shook his head in disbelief at the flicker of the stable lantern's reflection in the high shine on Rupert's riding boots. Indeed, he never failed to appear perfectly attired from top to toe. Relief at seeing Rupert relaxed the tension in his jaw. *Thank God, she will be safe now.* He rubbed the stubble on his chin and drew her tighter against his chest unwilling to let her go. Lord Rupert would not be amused with the condition of her. In truth, if Rupert had presented him with a fine lady in such disarray, he would have just cause to call him out.

"Och, I kenned you would be here afore me." He turned his attention to Tom. "Just the men then, aye?"

"Aye, laird." Tom ambled off toward the stables.

He gave Adrianna a little shake to wake her. "Wake now, lass, I have a surprise for ye."

"I beg your pardon?" Adrianna blinked and straightened then catching sight of Rupert, her full luscious lips curled into a wide smile. "My dear Lord Rupert. How good to see you again."

"Your most obedient servant, my Lady Adrianna." Rupert bowed. "I am here to escort you to safety."

Drew squeezed her with gentle care and brushed a kiss on her cheek. "Aye, lass, he will take ye to a safe place. Bide a few days and I will get word to you when I have concluded ma business."

"I still cannot understand why I cannot remain with *you*?" Her eyes had widened into great bottomless pools. "What if Lord Moreau has raised a battalion and they kill Rupert the moment we arrive in Inverness? Do you to expect him to give his life to protect me?"

"Lord Moreau has no army, he is quite alone." Rupert smiled. "And I am most capable of protecting you, my lady and *I* have my valet."

"M—must I go?" She gripped his arm with considerable force.

His stomach cramped at the thought of losing her for even a few days. As much as it pained him, he had to insist she leave with Rupert. "Aye, lass, and not because I want to be rid of ye but ye ken full well it would be better for all concerned if the French weasel dinna discover ye are wi' me. I canna risk ma clan being recognized. Already he has seen Angus and kens Ian well enough." Drew sighed and rubbed her back. "Dinna fash, Rupert will keep ye safe. I would trust him wi' ma life and he will protect ye in ma stead."

"How long am I expected to wait for you this time?" She grabbed handfuls of his shirt and gazed at him wild-eyed. "I am afraid Lord Moreau will find me and take me to France."

Lord Rupert moved closer, his face set in a mask of concern. "I am afraid Lord Moreau is indeed in Inverness. He is presently at a brothel and the very one where you will be hiding, but I am certain he will not discover your direction." He grimaced at Adrianna's gasp of horror. "You can be sure Lord Moreau will not be searching the brothels for you. Both of us have the utmost confidence in the proprietor to guarantee your safety."

She turned her mournful expression on Drew. "Give me your word you will not abandon me in Inverness. Your word of *honor*, if you please, Laird Mackenzie."

He wanted to offer his heart and soul, but instead, he smiled. "You have ma word of honor." He bent and brushed a chaste kiss over her lips. Her dark lashes dropped and her lips parted in invitation. As she pressed closer boldly demanding more of him. His attention flicked to the disapproving stare from Rupert. He pulled away regret clutching at his heart and gazed into her big sad eyes. "Now go wi' Rupert, I will see you as soon as I am able."

Adrianna shook her head tumbling brown curls from beneath her cap. "But—"

"Do stop arguing, Adrianna. If you do not trust the word of my honorable cousin, trust mine." Lord Rupert opened his arms to hand her down. "Come now, you will have to change in the carriage before we leave." He met her gaze. "There are clothes in the portmanteau inside the coach. If you have any belongings, I suggest you bring them with you."

"I beg your pardon, did you say you required me to *change* my clothes?" Lady Adrianna gripped Rupert's arms and her mouth turned down. "In the *carriage*?"

"Yes, my lady. You cannot possibly arrive in Inverness wearing the Mackenzie tartan." Rupert flashed Drew an apologetic gaze. "For this ruse to work, you and your maid are to disguise yourselves as harlots."

"Harlots?" Lady Adrianna glared at Rupert. "Why must I do such a deplorable thing, may I ask?"

"So not to attract undue attention on entering the establishment, my lady. My valet will escort you to the back entrance, he is not known to Lord Moreau." He took her arm. "You will be taken up the back stairs to lodgings in the loft well away from the goings on below." He glanced up at Drew. "I will make frequent visits to ensure her safety."

"Aye, that is sound reason." Drew dismounted and turned to Adrianna. He cupped her face, not giving a fig about Rupert's disapproving glances and covered her warm mouth in a long lingering kiss. He lifted his head and held her trembling body away from him. "I will send more supplies for your injury. Do as Rupert says and we will be done with the likes of the gomeral Moreau and be on our way before ye ken it." He sighed. "Dinna fash, ye have ma word, Lord Moreau will not be able to remove ye from Scotland while I live." He bit back the overwhelming desire to kiss her again, dropped his hands, and stepped back. "Go wi' Rupert and do exactly what he says." In a rush of panic for her safety, he screwed the signet ring off his little finger and thrust it into her hands. "I ken ye are afraid, lass, so take this and should our plans go asunder run for your life. Make your way to the Glen Albyn Inn and find Rupert or if ye canna, go to any of the taverns in Inverness and show the proprietor ma ring. Tell him to keep ye safe and to send a man to fetch me or Rupert." He swallowed hard as despair cramped his wame. "Do ye understand?"

Adrianna's blue eyes held an expression of undisguised relief. She squeezed his arm in a surprising gesture of comfort. Christ, had his expression betrayed his emotion at the thought of losing her?

"Yes, I understand and I thank you." She gave him a hesitant smile and pushed his ring into her reticule. "I am as you say *braw* and if I am able to escape a pirate ship to be sure a brothel will be a piece of cake." She dropped her hand and inclined her head. "Safe journey, dearest Drew. I will wait in anticipation of our next meeting."

He smiled to offer encouragement. "Safe journey to you too, lass. I will send Betty wi' your things, but I will be keeping your stays and petticoat safe until we meet again."

Her lips twitched and her cheeks pinked with embarrassment, but the heat from her gaze warmed his heart.

"I trust you will. You are an honorable man, Laird Mackenzie, but I fear Lord Moreau is a despicable man, and I beg you to be careful."

He lifted her hand and placed a lingering kiss on her palm. "Go with Rupert and put away your fears. I will be fine. I have ma men."

"I will pray for you." Adrianna pulled on a pair of gloves and placed one hand on Rupert's arm. She met his gaze and her lips twitched into a tremulous smile. "I am ready, Lord Rupert, lead on."

As he watched her limp toward the carriage with Betty close on her heels, a lump formed in his throat. *Dear God keep her safe.*

* * * *

Hours later, Adrianna peered from the carriage window searching the dark misty streets for her first peek of a Scottish city. The smell was not so different from London and it would seem this city awoke well before dawn too. She caught sight of housemaids with baskets filled with fresh bread or carrying pails of milk and scurrying in all directions, others scrubbed the ice from the steps of their master's houses.

Her attention moved over Betty and she could not disguise her disgust at the girl's slattern appearance but had to admit, the bright pink dress she had squeezed into was little better and cut so low at her bosom it left nothing to the imagination. She wrinkled her nose at the smell of the previous occupant a combination of heavy rose fragrance, stale sweat, and men's seed.

She removed her gloves then lifted Drew's ring from her reticule and pushed it onto her finger. It fit snugly on the third finger of her right hand and she wiggled her fingers admiring the large sapphire. The gem cut with his initials was set in an intricate weave of gold. She ran the tip of her finger over the design and her stomach flipped in a most unusual fashion. How silly of her to miss him already but she would have liked it of all things to remain by his side. Although, riding astride his thighs had stiffened her back, she missed the solid strength of him wrapped around her, the heat of his body, and his scent. In truth, she could linger in his arms for a lifetime.

She closed her eyes, bathing in the memory of his comforting embrace. With his warm hand splayed across her belly, his thumb had brushed the undersides of her breasts and her nipples had hardened aching to be touched. She had aroused him too for sitting across his thighs, she did not fail to notice his hard length pressed against her bottom. Snuggling so intimately against him, she had brazenly offered him encouragement, but he had kept his advances to a few delightful kisses. His admission of his desire and his intention to call on her had made her giddy with joy.

She sighed and turned the ring around her finger. Dear Lord, she could feel his large hands cupping her face and her lips still tingled deliciously from his kisses. Staring down at her outrageous attire, she swallowed hard and doubt clouded her mind in a wave of panic. Drew may well have offered to woo her, but many things stood in the way of a match between them. He had admitted to not bedding a woman for some time, perhaps his attention toward her had been nothing more than his need for female company. She caught sight of her reflection in the carriage window and her excitement wilted. Doubt clouded her mind. What would become of her if he chose not to return?

A man like him could have any woman. Why would he want me?

The carriage jolted to a stop, and rather than Lord Rupert jumping down from the seat, his valet came to the door, dropped the steps then handed her down. Apprehension sent a shiver the length of her spine at the sight of the dark alley adjacent to the coach. The smell was abhorrent. She rested her fingers on Mister Bent's arm and holding her skirts higher than was decent, stepped gingerly around the piles of muck. A window opened in the red brick wall and she barely missed the steaming cascade from the contents of a chamber pot dumped unceremoniously into the street without so much as a warning.

She pressed one hand over her nose, and wished she had thought to take the fragrant handkerchief from the pocket of her other dress. The thought of visiting a bordello did not upset her, but Lord Moreau in close proximity made her heart race in terror. She stepped around a pile of rotting cabbages draped with dead rats and shook her head with incredulity. Why did men debase themselves by walking through such filth to slake their desire with a whore? Had they no shame or fear of contracting the French disease? To think many such men took their pleasure with a light skirt then returned to bed their wives. Did they not know they would likely cause their wife to lose their heir or worse sire a deformed child due to the syphilis?

At the end of the alley, Mister Bent acting as businesslike as one could in such circumstances, bid her to stand to one side, lifted the knocker of the establishment and rapped three times. The door opened and a woman dressed in a blood-red gown with an ample bosom smiled benevolently at her and greeted her in a thick French accent.

"Come inside, I have a room ready for you." She inclined her head as if she held a position in society. "I know who you are, *cherie*. I am the proprietor, *Madame* Josephine." She examined Adrianna with consideration and made a clicking sound with her tongue. "I can see the journey has not treated you well." She turned and waved a footman forward. "Carry her to the attic."

"I am quite capable of w—"

"You will keep your mouth shut, *non?*" *Madame* Josephine scowled at her and dropped her voice to a conspiratorial whisper. "Do you intend to announce your arrival to Lord Moreau because, *Cherie*, he is occupied above, as is another man who will recognize you, one Captain Jacques?"

Swung into the footman's arms and carried effortlessly up three flights of stairs, she found herself inside a room of reasonable size. The man deposited her beside a large bed and brushed past Betty to leave the room. *Madame* Josephine surrounded by an overindulgence of cheap perfume breezed inside with a swish of skirts and shut the door behind her.

"You must remain here and not leave this room." *Madame* Josephine waved a hand toward the chest of drawers. "Lord Rupert insisted I supply you with the necessities and I have gathered a few items for you on his behalf. I am sure a fine lady such as you will not be happy wearing a harlot's shift, *non*?" She grinned showing remarkably good teeth. "I will have a bath sent up for you."

Adrianna forced her mouth into some semblance of a smile. "I thank you for the bath but fortunately, I will not require any clothes. I have a few of my own gowns in my portmanteau."

"Ah, yes but on the occasion one of my servants brings food to you or empties your chamber pot, you must appear to be one of my girls, *n'est-ce pas*? So if you insist on dressing in your own clothes, cover yourself before you open the door." *Madame* Josephine smiled. "Lord Rupert will wish to call upon you, *non*? I will not always be on hand to escort him to your room. I will inform my girls, you are here for my special patrons and I have placed you in the attic so no one will hear your screams." She giggled. "They are already aware your gentleman has exotic tastes."

Exotic tastes? Dearest Rupert? I think not. The niggling thought of Drew visiting this establishment came to the front of her mind. She had to discover the truth of it. "I understand my coming here was organized by my particular friend Lord Rupert. Do you know Laird Mackenzie by chance?" Her heart hammered and she pressed one hand to her stomach to calm her nerves. "I heard mention he frequented this establishment."

"I have had the pleasure of knowing both Rupert and Drew since they were pups." She winked. "As Rupert is your *particular* friend you would know why he enjoys his visits to my premises but Drew, well, as he is *my* particular friend, I am not at liberty to discuss our relationship."

Her particular friend? Drew mentioned young widows, yes, but not a harlot old enough to be his mother. *Have I fallen in love with a whoremonger?* A wave of nausea gripped her at the possibility of Drew in this woman's arms. She straightened her skirts in an effort to cover her indisposition and lifted her chin. Deciding not to divulge her involvement with him, she forced her lips into a smile. "How interesting. I know very little of Laird Mackenzie."

"He would be a good match for a lady in your position. He is a fine specimen, and very large in all the right places." *Madame* Josephine gave her a knowing smile.

Her face grew uncomfortably hot. *Damn her eyes for peering into my soul.* The need to discover the truth about him became unbearable. "I understand Lord Rupert holds him in high esteem." She touched *Madame* Josephine's arm and smiled as if drawing her into her confidentiality. "Although, I have heard whispers that Laird Mackenzie has many mistresses and I cannot fathom why he would have the need to frequent a brothel?"

"We have other business, *cherie*. Drew does not enjoy the fruits of my establishment, as you say he has a variety of mistresses to warm his bed."

"Ah, as I thought." Relief curled her lips into a smile. "And I thank you, *Madame,* for your hospitality." She dropped her hand and met her inquisitive gaze.

"Very well, but remain well hidden if you value your life." *Madame* Josephine pursed her red lips. "Lord Moreau is a danger to all of us. That brute has ruined many of my girls and if not for my business with Captain Jacques, I would not allow him in my establishment." She wagged a finger at Adrianna. "Mark my words, if he finds you, he will punish you severely." With a snort, she swung open the door. "And he will extract great personal pleasure from doing so." In a swish of scarlet taffeta, she left the room closing the door behind her.

Betty's expression did not hide her fear but the girl straightened and went about the business of unpacking the bag.

"I will lay out some clean clothes, milady. I only packed two of your outfits in case we had to leave the bag behind." Betty stared at the door as if listening for footsteps. "I expect someone will bring a tub soon enough and you can have a nice soak." She went to the small bag and removed a few garments.

Adrianna smiled. "You may have a long soak for once, Betty. I am concerned if my wound becomes wet, it will fester again. I will wash my hair, but I think a bath will have to wait." She sighed. "Never mind, a good scrub will do just as well and I am looking forward to sleeping in a real bed for a change." She eyed the lumpy bed. "At least the linen appears clean and it is large enough for both of us."

"Oh, no, milady, I will sleep on the floor by the fire." Betty smiled. "But I will accept the offer of a bath. I am filthy after sitting on that wagon."

"We are for the moment in the same boat, as it were." She waved a hand around the room. "We may well have to flee this establishment without notice, so will need our rest. You *will* share the bed with me and I will not hear another word about it."

Chapter Five

Early the following morning, Lord Moreau buttoned his waistcoat and moved toward the small window. Frost had formed a floral pattern on the windowpane to obscure his view of the street below *Madame* Josephine's brothel. He shrugged into his jacket and turned his attention to the two whores tied to the bed. They had disappointed him and although their flesh bore signs of the thin strip of birch, he used for discipline, he had not enjoyed the thrill of watching them die. His taste had changed considerably since his involvement with Baron du Court's ritualistic orgies. Now, he found he could not inflict *enough* pain on *Madame* Josephine's whores, even the young ones did not offer him the satisfaction he craved. He grimaced. Scotland had laws to prevent the killing of whores and he could not risk incarceration not when he had to find Lady Adrianna.

She would pay dearly for escaping him and when he informed Du Court of her ungrateful behavior, her death would be brutal indeed. He stroked his growing erection and smiled. Mayhap after breaking his fast, he would return and slake his lust on the new girls he overheard arriving late last eve. His ears had pricked at the sound of *Madame* Josephine's explicit orders to her servants that the two newcomers had been reserved for her special patrons. Yes, indeed perhaps she had heeded his advice and offer of substantial coin to procure a couple of virgins for his pleasure. After all, surely he had time to indulge his desires. Even if the English bitch had procured a horse, she would not have reached the coach house at Nairn before last eve, which meant, he had the best part of a day to enjoy the delights *Madame* Josephine's brothel had to offer.

He slipped from the room leaving the door open for all to see his magnificent work and took the stairs to the front door. Stepping with due care through the debris-laden alleyway, and into the main street, he strolled toward the ordinary overlooking the docks. His stomach growled at the aroma of fresh bread and oyster soup drifting on the breeze. As he approached the door, a man seated before the window with magnificent blond curls caught his attention. He smiled. Not many men displayed a head of hair quite as well as Lord Rupert. Indeed not many owned a wig of such quality. He moved toward the table and bowed. "Ah, it is good to see you again, Lord Rupert. Your servant, sir."

Lord Rupert's intense green gaze flicked over him and the spoon in one hand paused midway between the bowl of soup and his mouth. Returning the spoon to the table, Lord Rupert inclined his head.

"Lord Moreau."

Something intangible about Lord Rupert fascinated him, perhaps his foppish attire and manner had perpetuated a desire to discover more about him. Indeed, Lord Rupert's angelic countenance, gave him the impression the man was a sodomite. He had not only called on Lady Adrianna but at *Madame* Josephine's brothel had the choice of a number of young men, had taken two whores to his bed. *Perhaps, you desire the attentions of both sexes. A man after my own heart.* He smiled at him and waved toward the table. "May I join you? It is lonely, is it not dining alone?"

Lord Rupert forced his expression to remain disinterested and hoped Lord Moreau could not see the pulse pounding in his temples. The heavy stink of sweat and whores wafted toward him and he fought the overpowering need to stand and walk from the ordinary into the fresh air. Clearing his throat, he met his amused gaze. "In consideration of your opinion of me last eve, I think not."

"Oh, it was said in jest, was it not?" Lord Moreau twisted the silver tipped ebony cane in his thin fingers with practiced skill and had the audacity to grin at him. "Come now, we are acquaintances of sorts and in the situation such bawdy talk amongst men is not unusual." He sighed dramatically and bowed low. "My humblest of apologies, *Monsieur* if I caused offense."

Rupert leveled his gaze on the disgusting Frenchman, gave him a curt nod, and waved him into the seat downwind from the salty breeze blowing through the open door. *What do you want?*

"I thank you." Lord Moreau sat down and caught the attention of a serving girl. After ordering his meal, he smiled at Rupert. "Do you speak French?"

Lord Moreau's smile reminded him of a laughing skull and appetite gone, repressed a shudder. "I do." He continued in French. "Is there something in particular you wish to discuss with me about the horses I acquired?" He refilled his teacup from a pot on the table averting his gaze from the gaunt visage before him. "Before you ask, they are not for sale at any price."

Lord Moreau leaned on the table and his black beady gaze narrowed.

"Horses, no they are the last thing on my mind." He paused to allow the girl to place a bowl of soup and a loaf of bread before him. He inhaled the soup's aroma and sighed with obvious relish. "I wondered if you had the acquaintance of Lord Beachwood, I believe he is King George's physician?"

Deciding truth would be the best option, he shrugged. "I do have his acquaintance, yes. Lord Beachwood tended my mother during her illness."

"Ah, well I do hope she is recovered." Lord Moreau tore the loaf of bread into small pieces then dropped a few into his soup.

Rupert stiffened. "She died."

"It would seem I am constantly offending you. Apologies." Lord Moreau moved around uncomfortably in his seat. "And his daughter, Lady Adrianna, have you made her acquaintance too?"

Did the despicable man have thoughts of involving him in his search for Lady Adrianna? On the other hand, had someone caught sight of him driving the coach and four? He lifted his cup and allowed his irritability with the man to show. "Get to the point man." He eyed him over the rim of his dish of tea. "I move in the same circles as Lord Beachwood so obviously I am acquainted with his daughter." He placed the cup on the table and lifted his chin. "Now, I have a question. Why would a man such as you, who does not have the where with all to move in such circles, be asking after a bluestocking?"

"Bluestocking? You have me at a disadvantage, I an unfamiliar with that term. My interest in Lady Adrianna is not for myself. You see, she is betrothed to Baron du Court and I was charged with the task of accompanying her to France aboard *The Black Turtle*."

Rupert raised an eyebrow. "A bluestocking is a highborn lady with learning my dear man. Surely you have such women in France?" He snorted. "And I find it hard to believe Lord Beachwood would commission *you* to accompany his daughter to France. Good God, think of the scandal, Lady Adrianna is King George's goddaughter. I do believe you think I am a fool to believe such nonsense."

Lord Moreau's thin lips curled into a confident smile.

"Perhaps you should read this announcement." He pulled a folded broadsheet from his pocket and tossed it on the table. "Lord Beachwood has announced Lady Adrianna's betrothal to Baron du Court of Muzon." He raised a brow and his dark gaze narrowed. "A lady she may be by birth but not by her actions."

Ignoring the document, Rupert dropped his voice to a whisper, leaned across the table, and glared at him. "How dare you cast aspersions, sir?"

"Oh, I have good reason. The *lady* eloped with a slave by the name of Ian Mackenzie. A Scottish slave of no more than sixteen years. I have reason to believe she is this very moment making her way here in his company." Lord Moreau shrugged. "I do understand the way of the Scottish clans and have reason to believe Mackenzie has connections with the Mackenzie *you* represented in the sale of the mares. I gather *you* are here to deliver them in person and that is somewhat of a coincidence. Do you not agree?"

Laughter bubbled out from the incredulity of the situation. "How utterly absurd. What a vivid imagination you have." He waved the serving girl to the table and requested a cup of mulled cider then turned his attention back to Moreau. "However, you are correct on one point. I did purchase horses on Laird Mackenzie's behalf, but the idea that Lady Adrianna would abscond with a young lad is outrageous. Indeed, to imagine Laird Mackenzie would involve himself in such a scandal is quite ridiculous. In fact, he is at home and sent word to me yesterday. I am quite sure he would have made mention of the Lady Adrianna arriving unannounced, as he is fully aware of my connection with her family."

Keeping the air of hilarity to cover his abhorrence of the man's astute deductions, he took the drink from the girl, gave her his best salacious wink, and waved her away.

"As to the slave you mentioned, I am sure the entire Clan Mackenzie would be crawling over *The Black Turtle* in a demonstration of violence never before seen on the high seas if such a thing were true. How do you know if the lad gave his correct name?" He sipped the mulled cider and regarded Lord Moreau over the rim of the tankard. "Laird Mackenzie is journeying to Inverness to sell his goods, but I can assure you, he would not allow an English lady within a mile of him or any member of his clan." He chuckled. "Surely you understand the current politics? Laird Mackenzie would not compromise an English lady and risk being leg shackled to her." He sipped again and the tart spiced liquid danced over his tongue clearing the taste of oysters from is palate. "To be sure, his clan would more likely kill her than rescue her."

Lord Moreau's eyes flashed in anger and his mouth turned down. "If this is true then I will wait as long as it takes for her to arrive in Inverness." He pushed to his feet and the next moment, his mood brightened with significance as if he had remembered something of a pleasing nature.

Rupert considered Lord Moreau with interest. Perhaps the opium pipe had addled his brain after all. The hairs on the back of his neck raised at the thought of this brute anywhere near Lady Adrianna. *A dangerous man indeed with such sudden changes of mood.*

"If she is traveling alone as you say, I will make enquiries to discover her direction. I find it difficult to believe the lady would accept the Baron du Court's offer then elope with a sixteen-year-old boy and a slave to boot. If this is indeed true then she must be in dire straits and require my assistance. Lady Adrianna is no fool and may well be traveling back to London." He sighed. "I dare say she would keep well away from the ports, in anticipation of your arrival."

"You may be correct, but I will find her eventually. You see it is of no consequence to her betrothed if her reputation is in tatters. My master seeks the alliance by the marriage nothing more." Lord Moreau's dark eyes flashed with menace. "Fortunately, I have experience in breaking strong willed, ungrateful women, and so does Baron du Court."

He bent toward him in a confidential manner and a sickly smile curled his lips.

"I am prepared to wait. A lady of her standing will not be content in a village and will require more suitable accommodation. This suits me well because I will have plenty of time to attend *Madame* Josephine's establishment. She has a batch of girls newly arrived from Spain." He winked. "Mayhap you will have your chance later, although they will not be as fresh after my visit." He straightened. "Good day to you, sir." Taking the silver snake's head cane in one hand he strolled purposely out the door, and headed in the direction of *Madame* Josephine's brothel.

Rupert ran a hand down his face. It would seem the opium had not dulled Moreau's reasoning after all and obviously, the vile substance gave him the stamina of a bull. He breathed in the gust of fresh salty air pouring through the door and stared after the man. Discussing Drew had been a risk but he had at least convinced him Lady Adrianna was not in Drew's company. He glanced enquiringly at the girl waiting patiently beside the table and sighed. The bastard had left without paying for his meal.

* * * *

The following morning, Adrianna paced the small room in an effort to come to terms with her situation. At least, she had risen free of the fever with not more than a twinge of pain in her leg. The treatment Drew had administered had worked in an astonishing rate. *Drew.* She lifted his plaid from the back of the chair and pressed it to her nose to inhale his scent. His bergamot smell made her heart ache for him and a moan escaped her lips. Embarrassed by her lack of control she glanced at Betty. Her maid sat beside the fire mending a pair of stockings. The girl cleared her throat in a slightly judgmental manner and returned to her work. Abashed, Adrianna folded the plaid neatly and placed it atop of Jamie's.

All thoughts of Drew vanished at the sound of footsteps on the stairs. Fear of discovery clenched her stomach and she grabbed a blanket from the bed to toss over her head then turned toward the window to conceal her face. A soft knock came at the door and *Madame* Josephine's French accent drifted to her ears.

"Open the door."

Betty shot a worried gaze in her direction.

"Shall I open the door, milady?"

Adrianna turned and tossed the blanket onto the bed. She straightened the skirt of her plain woolen dress and lifted her chin. "Yes, you may."

Madame Josephine entered in a cloud of perfume and pint taffeta. She raised her penciled eyebrows and smiled.

"Ah, you appear quite different without the rouge, younger, and innocent." She gave her a long appraising look. "Are you sure you would not like to join my establishment? You would be *very* popular with my patrons."

Me, join this band of reprobates? Has the woman lost her wits? Trying to breathe through the miasma of rose scent, she smiled. "I think not, but I thank you for your most generous offer."

The sentiment seemed to appease *Madame* and she smiled showing rouge smudged teeth.

"Ah well, perhaps after living here for a few days you will change your mind." She patted her hair and frowning tapped her temple. "Ah, *qui,* now I remember why I came up here. Captain Jacques returned to his ship last night and Lord Moreau left this morning so your maid will be able to do for you. Send her to the kitchen for a tray and I will have one of my servants to show her where we keep the linens."

She cast a critical gaze over the plaids folded neatly on a chair.

"I am surprised Drew gave you his plaid as he has taken such great pains to distance himself from you. Do you want me to have one of my footmen deliver them to the tavern where he is staying?"

The Glen Albyn Inn, with Rupert? She smiled. "Ah, no I think politeness requires I return them to him in person. I do, after all have to thank him for his most generous assistance." She met the woman's intuitive gaze. Indeed, it would be difficult to hide her feelings from her but she would do her best. "I am sure Lord Rupert will call on me as soon as arrangements have been made for my departure then I will request a meeting with Laird Mackenzie at his convenience."

"As you please." *Madame* Josephine turned to Betty. "Bring the chamber pot and follow me. You will have to complete your duties in haste. I have no idea when Lord Moreau will return. He prefers to dine elsewhere so he may well be back within the hour." She ushered Betty from the room.

At the sounding of his name, fear shivered down her spine in a trickle of doom. Indeed, Lord Moreau haunted her every waking minute. Hiding right under his nose might have been prudent but having him so close chilled her to the bone. How could she slip away unnoticed when he frequented the brothel so often? *I wonder how many times he attends this establishment.* She cleared her throat occasioning *Madame* Josephine to pause in the doorway and turn an inquiring eye on her.

"Do you require anything else, *cherie*?"

"Is it Lord Moreau's usual practice to bed whores in daylight too?" Her face grew hot. "I assumed men acquired the urge to do such things at night."

Madame Josephine's eyes danced with mirth.

"Lord Moreau has an insatiable appetite and he is brutal. Men, in general, *ma petite,* always have, how did you say, 'the urge' that is why they have mistresses and visit brothels, to keep the myth that they are in control of their cocks." She laughed raucously and left the room shutting the door behind her.

Adrianna glared at the floor, her mind in turmoil. To be sure, she had not heard a whisper about such things occurring in daytime. How often did a man find it necessary to bed a woman? She chewed on her bottom lip. More than once a month, a week, a day? *No, not a day, surely.* She would have to ask Drew that particular question. After all, he had been very forthcoming during their recent conversation and he was indeed *au fait* in such matters. With a sigh, she turned back to the window of her prison.

Condensation clouded the windowpane and she drew the outline of a heart placing Drew's name within. She cared for him deeply and wrapped in his arms on the journey had given her a wonderful feeling of belonging. In truth, he made her restless for more of his erotic delights. She yearned for the security of his strong arms and fear gripped her at the notion of Lord Moreau finding her before Drew arrived.

A creek on the stairs followed by heavy footsteps prickled the hairs on the back of her neck. Heart pounding, she turned and stared at the slow turn of the doorknob. Frozen in fear, her attention fixed on the inward swing of the door. "Is that you, Betty?"

A dark figure moved into the room and in horror, she stared into the black gaze of Lord Moreau. He gaped at her openmouthed for some moments before a smile curled his thin lips. He spoke to her in French in a cajoling manner, but his expression had turned intent and dangerous.

"Lady Adrianna, if I had been made aware of your requirements, we may have spent a more enjoyable voyage."

He removed his hat with a flourish and placed it on the washstand then proceeded to remove his gloves.

"You certainly had me fooled and my master will be most disappointed you are not a virgin."

She forced air through a throat closed in terror and used the only weapon in her arsenal—her station. Straightening, she took a threatening step toward him. "Damn your impudence, sir. How dare you address me in such a manner? Do I have to remind you, I am the goddaughter of King George? You overstep your place. Remove yourself from my presence this instant."

Instinct had her reaching for the window catch. Turning away from him, she flung the casement wide glancing down into the street below and judging the distance to the ground. The alley appeared surreal and distorted through the early morning mist.

"You will not fit through that window and do you really think I would allow such a thing?" Lord Moreau inclined his head. "Remove your clothes, now if you please." His thin lips curled into a demonic smile. "Or I will tear them from you, either way it makes no difference."

Gathering her wits, she lifted her chin and stared down her nose at him. "I fear you are gravely mistaken. I am not a prostitute and you are compromising me by being in such close proximity. I am sure Baron du Court will be most displeased if I inform him of your outrageous behavior."

Lord Moreau chuckled and his long pale fingers went to the buttons of his jacket.

"Ah, you are in no position to threaten me. You see, I understand the ways of women, as does my master. I am sure you have retained your maidenhead to ensure a profitable marriage, after all there are many ways a man may seek his pleasure, are there not?" He raised a dark eyebrow and gave her a meaningful stare. "Although coming to this particular establishment was a mistake if you intended to forgo Baron du Court's most generous proposal and become a whore. If you must know, I have had the pleasure of frequenting this establishment for many years. Indeed, *Madame* Josephine and I have an understanding. It was she who informed me she had two virgins for my pleasure and here I am." He bowed low flourishing one hand in the manner of the French court.

Before he had time to rise, Betty rushed into the room, and swinging a chamber pot high in the air brought it down smartly on the back of his head. A loud gonging sound echoed in the room and Lord Moreau let fly a stream of French expletives then pitched forward onto his knees moaning and clutching his temples. Betty gave a warrior battle cry and struck him again. Lord Moreau crumpled to the floor and his head hit the carpet with a dull thud.

"Run!" Betty's voice quivered, but she stood over Lord Moreau, her expression wild-eyed and determined. "Go now and do not worry, milady. I will hit him again if he attempts to rise."

Adrianna's mind slowed and she examined her predicament with amazing clarity. "He is unconscious and will not recover for some time. Go and inform *Madame* Josephine then hide in the kitchen. I will find Lord Rupert and send someone for you."

She gazed without one jot of compassion at Lord Moreau's corpselike form and slid her reticule over one hand. Taking hold of Drew's plaid and tucking it firmly under one arm, she drew a deep steadying breath then stepped around Lord Moreau's twitching feet. She squeezed Betty's arm. "Go now before he regains consciousness."

"No, milady. He is only stunned and will recover soon enough then he will be hot on your heels. It would be better if I stay here and hit him again should he try to follow you."

Lord Moreau moaned and Betty raised the chamber pot high above her head again. Her lips trembled into a small smile.

"You go and be quick about it, milady. Do not worry about me, *Madame* Josephine will help me, I am sure."

"I will kill you for this." Lord Moreau made an unsuccessful grab for Adrianna's ankle. "Both of you and I will enjoy every slow minute."

"You will not touch my mistress." Betty swung her thin arm and dropped the chamber pot on his head then it slipped from her grasp and shattered on the floor sending shards of white stained porcelain spinning across the polished wood. She turned, cheeks flaming and hair tumbling from her cap.

"Run, milady."

Adrianna lifted her thick woolen skirts and fled toward the stairs. She grasped the handrail and sped toward the front door, her retreat catching the attention of a variety of patrons, and whores ascending to the boudoirs. The blue floral carpet wavered unnervingly before her and one of her ankle boots slipped on the pile. She regained her balance and chanced a glance behind her. Thank the stars Lord Moreau was not following, not yet. Ignoring the inquisitive gazes of a few men stepping from doorways, she rounded the landing to the final flight of stairs. Behind her, Lord Moreau's distinct voice bellowed a tirade of vulgar expletives in French and Betty screamed.

"Help! Murder!"

Two burly men burst from a doorway and barged past her taking the stairs in great leaping bounds. Legs cramped with fear, she stumbled down the steps, jumping the last four in a most unladylike fashion, and stumbled into the foyer to the astonishment of a small group of wide-eyed housemaids. With Lord Moreau's threats ringing in her ears, she reached the entry in two strides. She glared at the gorilla of a footman, who gaped at her open-mouthed before flinging the door wide open.

Bounding outside and into the filthy alley, she ignored the icy wind cutting through her gown, lifted her skirts, and ran toward the main street. As she rounded the corner of Hog's Lane, sleet stung her cheeks and dribbled down the neck of her gown. Gasping a great lungful of freezing air, she dashed down the main street frantically searching the shop fronts for a tavern or any open doorway.

Her attention went to a young girl a few paces before her trying desperately to cover a basket of bread with her cloak. *A bakery*. Gasping for breath, she headed toward the girl and the aroma of fresh bread came to her like a sign from God. She examined the red brick buildings and spied a sign above a door, *Macgregor's Fine Fare Bakery.* Slowing to a dignified swiftness, she cast a wary glance over one shoulder. To her relief, Lord Moreau had not yet turned the corner.

She moved toward the shop and tugged at the bitterly cold brass handle on the door. The bell above the entrance tinkled and she staggered inside to blessed warmth. Disheveled and gasping like a charging bull, the customers turned to stare at her as if a mad woman had entered their midst. To be sure, only a fool would venture out in this weather wearing nothing but a day gown.

She pasted an affable expression on her face, inclined her head in a respectful manner and requiring time to gather her wits, strolled into the crowd to give the impression of examining the display of fresh bread, rolls, pies, and bannocks. Moving her attention from the bread to the people strolling along the pavement outside the shop, she took a few deep breaths, and composed her features. Lord Moreau would recognize her in an instant if he glanced through the window. Under one arm, Drew's plaid pressed warmly against her freezing flesh reminding her of its presence. She opened the plaid and wrapped the thick woolen cloth around her like a cloak. Thank goodness, Betty had pinned up her hair and her mop cap was in the pocket of her skirt.

Betty.

Dear God, what had the brute done to her? Morbid thoughts assailed her until a woman's voice in Gaelic jerked her attention. She forced her frozen lips into a smile. "I am sorry. I do not have the Gaelic."

"May I help ye, madam?" The rotund woman with rosy cheeks smiled at her from behind the counter.

Lost in thought, she had not noticed the people in the line before her had made their purchases and left. Desperately trying to act in a calm fashion, she glanced at the display. "You have so many choices and I have yet to make up my mind."

"I have a nice tray of pasties straight from the oven." The shopkeeper smiled. "Or some bannocks."

Avoiding the need to glance over one shoulder and into the street, she took a few coins from the purse in her reticule and handed them to her. "Yes, a few bannocks would be very nice. In a linen sack if you please, I seem to have mislaid my basket this morning." She chanced a glance behind her and gasped. The shop was deserted and she stood in full view of anyone passing in the street. Lord Moreau might walk by at any moment. In sheer panic of being recognized, she reached into her pocket for her mop cap.

The shopkeeper narrowed her gaze at her and glanced past her into the street. In an effort to make some excuse for her behavior, she smiled and waved her hand in a distracted manner. "Do forgive me. I completely forgot to wear my cap this morning." She dragged the obnoxious white linen hat with floppy lace edging over her hair and pulled it down to cover her ears. "I seem to be getting forgetful of late."

"Are ye in trouble, lass?" The shopkeeper's expression changed from suspicion to honest concern as she handed her the package. "Come now, ye can confide in me and I may be able to help ye." She drew in a deep breath. "Ye will not be the first lass to run from *Madame* Josephine's establishment and end up in ma shop. Dinna fash, there are many kind folk in Inverness that will offer ye honest work. I will be happy to make enquiries on your behalf and in the meantime, I have a cot in the back ye can use."

"I thank you kindly for your most generous offer of assistance." She glanced over one shoulder then back to the woman. "Unfortunately, I do find myself in a delicate situation. I need to find a friend staying at the Glen Albyn Inn." She swallowed hard. "Laird Drew Mackenzie or Lord Rupert. You see there is a gentleman trying to kidnap me and take me to France." She met the woman's gaze. "Would you be so kind to give me the direction of the Glen Albyn Inn?"

The shopkeeper's gaze widened and her voice dropped to just above a whisper.

"I think it may be too late, lass, but I will see the laird gets your message. I have kenned him since he was a lad. I will send ma lass with a message the moment she returns from delivering this morning's orders." She frowned staring past her to the doorway. "What name do you go by?"

"Adrianna."

The bell above the door tolled like a death knell to announce the arrival of Lord Moreau. Good Lord, he had taken the time to put on a cloak and to her dismay, the ivory handle of a pistol stuck out from the belt of his britches. The sickly smell of him wafted over her and she turned to meet a gaze straight from Hades. Anger radiated off him in almost visible waves and a nerve in his sunken cheek twitched. He strode toward her and his face contorted into a hideous mask of fury made worse by the trickle of blood smeared across one gaunt cheek. He moved closer and his mouth formed a feral grin. He screamed at her in French.

"You whore! I will make you pay for escaping me."

Pain shot though her face and she staggered. The display of bread swum before her eyes and colors flashed across her vision. The brute had struck her! She staggered and grabbed the counter for purchase, but he lashed out again. The metallic taste of blood coated her tongue and somewhere in the sea of pain, clarity of thought prevailed. *He has broken my nose.*

"You canna treat a lady in such a fashion." The shopkeeper's voice seeped through the buzzing in her head.

"I will treat her as I wish. She is my property. Mind your business, madam."

Lord Moreau closed his steel-like grip around Adrianna's arm and dragged her from the bakery. Nausea roiled her belly and a red sticky mess blurred her vision. She swiped at the annoyance and her fingers came away dripping with blood. The horrid man had tried to kill her! Using every ounce of strength she possessed, she pushed hard at his chest falling to her knees in the effort.

Agony tore up her injured leg in a ripping sensation and she gasped in pain. The sound of his laughter steeled her resolve. Damn him, she refused to die on the side of a road beaten and bleeding. She sucked in a blast of freezing wind to clear her head and rolled away from him. Lord Moreau was not a large man and she should be able to escape him if only she could get to her feet. She dashed a sleeve across her eyes and struggled to stand staring around for someone—anyone to offer assistance. People had stopped to stare, but not one moved to intervene. She glared at them. "Help me! This man is assaulting me."

Lord Moreau, his face twisted in a hideous grin thrust her into the wall expelling her breath in a painful rush then with one hand pressed indecently on her breast, turned to face the crowd.

"I find my wife lifting her skirt and have every right to beat her, she is an adulterous whore. Now mind your business and leave me to mine."

"No! Do not believe him, *please,* I beg you to help me." She gasped for air under his crushing force and twisted away but not quick enough, he gripped her hand grinding the small bones together and pressed his erection hard into her belly. She stared into his expression of enjoyment and fear stilled her heart for a second before it raced on at an alarming rate. *He gains sexual pleasure from hurting me.*

"Come with me or I will have no choice but to render you unconscious." He dragged her forward.

She hung back digging her heels into the pavement. "Let go of me, I say. I am not your wife and will not go with you." She glanced around frantically, but the people in the street had turned and scuttled away. *Dear God, they think I am an errant wife.* She aimed a kick at his shin. "I am not your property, you—you scoundrel."

"Your life is *mine.*"

He wrenched one arm behind her back and with his icy fingers digging into her flesh, dragged her against him. His oily hair brushed her cheek and his voice exuded a deep sexual innuendo.

"I will make you pay well for the trouble you have caused me, English whore, and I will enjoy every second."

Lord Moreau's foul breath washed over her and she heaved. The next moment, searing pain jarred her teeth and the edges of her sight sparkled in an array of fireworks before darkness fogged her mind.

Chapter Six

With every muscle aching, Drew urged his tired horse forward. He rasped a dry tongue over his cracked lips and shook his fist at the first drops of rain. *Sleet is all I need.* He had proceeded at a fast pace since leaving Nairn an hour or so before daybreak and had not stopped once on the road to Inverness for fear of leaving Adrianna alone, albeit in the care of *Madame* Josephine. He sighed with relief and rode into the courtyard of the stables at the Glen Albyn Inn. His horse's hooves clattered over the cobblestones paving the entrance announcing their arrival. The beast let out a piercing whinny so pleased was he to see an end to the grueling journey. He patted the silken neck.

"Aye, I am pleased to rest for a while too. Nay worry, I will be riding ye brother to Badenoch. Ye have done me proud." He beckoned to a stable lad watching his clan's arrival with interest. "It is good to see ye again, Johnny. I hope ye have been taking care of ma stallion. Do ye have enough room for all of us fore by? We can tend to our own mounts." He dismounted and pushed a coin into the boy's hand.

No sooner had his feet touched the ground, than a woman's voice called from behind him.

"Would ye be Laird Drew Mackenzie of Badenoch by chance?"

He sighed too exhausted to deal with local squabbles but as a Highland laird, he had many clansmen living in Inverness. He turned to see a young lass, red-faced, and agitated. Christ, the child was trembling with fear. He inclined his head and smiled at her.

"Aye, I am Laird Mackenzie."

She bobbed a curtsy and her words came out in a rush.

"Oh, I beg pardon, laird, but I came here to bring a message to ye or indeed, Lord Rupert, but I could not find either of ye at the inn." The lass gripped great handfuls of her crisp white apron and stared at him with wide brown eyes. "The innkeeper said ye were expected so when I saw the lot of ye coming down the road I waited for ye to arrive."

Oh God, Adrianna. He straightened and with concentrated effort, forced his expression to remain calm. He did not want to alarm the lass. "What message do ye have for me, lass?"

"Oh, laird, it was such a stramash. A French gentleman was cursing and bleeding and then he chased the woman into the street. Ma—"

Drew swallowed hard. He grasped the girl's shoulder and her thin frame wilted under his touch. "What woman would that be?"

"Ma said her name was Adrianna, laird, and ye needed to come quickly."

Fear clenched his wame and he stared at the girl with disbelief. How could Lord Moreau have found Adrianna in such a short time and where in God's name was Rupert? This child held the truth of it, *if* he could extract the information from her before she ran away in fear of her life. He released his grip, dropped his voice to a coaxing whisper, and patted her lean shoulder.

"Ye are doing fine, lass, now tell me exactly what happened and do ye ken which way they went?"

"Well, after I delivered the bannocks to *Madame* Josephine's, I heard the screaming. I could not believe ma eyes for they were outside the bakery, fighting in the gutter, and she was bleeding something awful." The lass made the sign of the cross. "Then the Frenchman hit her so hard I think he may have killed her."

She bit her trembling bottom lip then drew a deep breath.

"He c—carried her off toward the docks." Her eyes welled with tears. "Over his shoulder like a sack of maize and she leaving a trail of blood on the pavement with her hair hanging loose." She produced a soiled mop cap, stained with blood and held it out to him between shaking fingers. "I picked up her cap. Ma came out and sent me to tell ye or Lord Rupert what had happened."

He recognized the lace on the cap and anger raged blackening all thought but to take Lord Moreau apart. Oh, Christ could that beast of a man have killed Adrianna? No, Lord Moreau would have no reason to carry a corpse to *The Back Turtle*. With his heart racing at the implications of the girl's story, he turned his attention back to the child. "How long ago did this happen, lass?"

"Not more than a few minutes. I ran straight here to tell ye, laird."

He handed the girl a coin. "Thank ye kindly."

He leaped back into the saddle and yanking his horse around bellowed at Jamie. "Moreau has Adrianna and he is heading for the docks. Tell the stable lad saddle the stallion and ready a coach and four. I am going to get her and will leave for Badenoch at once." He glanced at Ian. "Find Rupert and have him wait here. I will send for him the moment I have found Adrianna."

"Aye, I will see to the carriage and a fresh horse for Rupert too. He will have to accompany ye as chaperone, ye ken?"

Drew nodded toward his brother. "Aye, he will and Angus too."

"I am coming wi' ye." Jamie, his face stricken vaulted into the saddle and grabbed the reins.

"So am I." Angus reined up beside him. "What has happened?"

"There is nay time to explain and I dinna ken the truth of it, aye." Drew moved his horse toward his brother. "We have a Frenchman to deal wi' and a maiden to rescue." He kicked his horse into a gallop and with its hooves slipping on the damp cobblestones, charged down the main street.

He weaved his mount at speed between carts and carriages plodding along the busy road barely missing the people crossing. Steam rose from his mount's nostrils and white globules of foam flowed like soapsuds from his open maw. Drew's hat flew off in a gust of wind and sleet bounced off his forehead sending icy raindrops splattering across his lashes. He bent close to the horse's neck and urged him faster uncaring of the patches of ice forming on the wet road. His horse responded without more than a grunt of protest. Thank the Lord his father had bred a mount such as this.

Soaked hair stuck to his face blinding him and he dashed it away to stare through the pounding rain to search the busy dockside for any glimpse of Lord Moreau. He could make out nothing but shadows in the downpour. Panic gripped his wame at the thought of arriving too late to save Adrianna. He had sent her away and broken his oath to protect her. *Dear God, keep her safe.*

He glanced behind him to see Jamie thundering down the street behind him. His brother veered off taking a laneway between the warehouses at full gallop. Drew urged his horse down the quay. His faithful steed leaped over crates of tea and bolts of wool, sure-footed in the melee of people yelling abuse and scattering in all directions. He rounded a stack of wooden boxes and spotted Lord Moreau dockside. The filthy pig was waving a wet scarf in a frantic gesture toward a black shadow in the mist. *The Black Turtle* was sitting at anchor out to sea.

He shuddered with rage at the sight of Adrianna lying so still over Lord Moreau's shoulder with her hair a mass of brown sodden curls. He pulled his mount to a stop and slid from the saddle hitting the ground at a run. Lord Moreau turned and had the gall to smile before addressing him in French.

"Ah, if I am correct in my assumption *your* name is *Mackenzie,* is it not, and you are in business with Lord Rupert Bainbridge? I believe you had a hand in stealing Baron du Court's betrothed from *The Black Turtle.*" Lord Moreau's brow wrinkled into a frown. "A clever ploy indeed to use an illegal transaction to cover your involvement. I am sure *Le Diable Noir* will seek you out for retribution. He will not be at all happy to discover you used his dealings with Captain Jacques to commit a crime against Baron du Court."

Drew refused to admit to anything and glared down his nose at the despicable man. "Speak English, man. I dinna ken what ye are prattling about but I can plainly see ye have a member of ma clan over your shoulder and one I am told wants nothing to do wi' ye."

Lord Moreau flicked a dark gaze over him, squinted as if trying to place him then shrugged.

"I would have sworn—oh, never mind." He laughed and raised a dark eyebrow. "This is not a member of *your* clan, fool. This is Baron du Court's betrothed. Now be on your way, this matter does not concern you."

Enraged by the blood dripping from Adrianna's nose and pooling on the ground, he placed one hand on his dirk and moved closer. "Ye are correct, I dinna ken the woman, but she is wearing ma plaid, so is under ma protection." He lifted his chin and met the man's hawk-like eyes. "Put her down and allow her to speak so I may ken the truth of the matter."

Lord Moreau rubbed Adrianna's bottom in a lewd manner and smiled.

"Unfortunately, the lady is indisposed from a night of lust. You will have to accept my details of the situation."

Anger roared in Drew's head. He strode toward him. "I said, put her down—now."

He heard a strangled shout of warning from Jamie then caught sight of the pistol, shielded under Lord Moreau's cloak. The man had raised the barrel and casually pointed it at him. He ducked to avoid disaster. Lord Moreau laughed and a flash of gunpowder turned his world into shattered chaos. White and red flashes danced over his vision and through tears, he caught sight of Lord Moreau's yellow grin widened into an expression of glee.

He staggered a few steps and reached for Adrianna, but his hand closed on emptiness. The ground swirled and his legs would no longer support him. He caught sight of Jamie's mouth moving in silent protest, his face twisted in anger. He wanted to tell his brother to forget him and save Adrianna, but the words would not come. Blackness surrounded him and he fought to open his eyes against a strange fog enclosing him in a cocoon of nothingness.

A loud noise shocked Adrianna into consciousness. She opened her eyes and wondered why the world had tipped upside down. Her head throbbed and something sharp dug into her ribs. She blinked at the waves hitting the dock and to her disgust found Lord Moreau's bony shoulder was causing the pain in her ribs. The stink of him and blood filled her nostrils. Gathering her strength, she tried desperately to slide free. "Put me down, I say."

"Put her down, ye wee arse wipe. She is our clanswoman and ye have nay claim on her."

Was that Drew's voice? She squirmed to catch sight of the figure moving in her periphery. Not Drew but his brother, Jamie.

Lord Moreau tightened his grip on her.

"I do not care what she is wearing. This woman is English and not a member of any clan. Come one step closer and I will break her neck." He dropped her to her feet and pulled her hard against his chest. "It would seem I have nothing to lose."

A pistol clattered to the ground and spun at her feet. Dizzy, she squinted through heavy, painful eyelids and ice filled her veins at the sight of Drew's crumpled body sprawled motionless and bloody on the ground. Ice-cold dread gripped her heart. "No! Dear God! No!" She turned to glare at Lord Moreau. "Sweet Jesus, what have you done?"

"I will kill anyone who tries to stop me from returning you to your rightful place." Lord Moreau's grip tightened around her neck. "Now you will come with me and complete your obligation to Baron du Court or do you want more blood on your hands?"

Using every ounce of strength she possessed, she twisted to get away but the grip on her neck tightened. Tears blinded her and she stared down at Drew's lifeless body in despair. *Oh no, please God, no.* Blood trickled from his head. His eyes, his beautiful green eyes, dear Lord, stared blindly into nothingness. He lay motionless with one arm outstretched toward her, his large palm turned upward. She glanced at Angus. "Do something, help him I beg you."

Angus, his face twisted in rage ripped the shirt from his back and bent to stanch the bleeding.

"I would suggest you inform these men to whom you belong, my lady. The rowboat is almost here to take us to *The Black Turtle*. Do this and I will not mention your behavior to Baron du Court." Lord Moreau growled deep in his chest. "Disobey me and I will have great pleasure in breaking your pretty neck, *n'est pas?*"

Pain gripped her heart and her knees trembled. Drew had given his life to protect her and if she went with Lord Moreau, it would have been for nothing. Once on board *The Black Turtle* she would be a pawn in a game she could never win. At his insistence, she stumbled forward a few paces and noticed a rowboat some distance from the shore. She had time to escape and with Jamie and Angus at hand, Lord Moreau might not be able to take her. She met Jamie's unflinching gaze. "I would rather die than return to that ship. I beg you. Do not allow him to take me.

Jamie's attention did not leave Lord Moreau's face. He walked backward keeping in step with her halting progress. With a slide of metal, he drew his sword.

"I would not do that if I were ye. The lady has made her wishes known." A grim smile etched his lips. "I am a wee bit bigger than the lass, aye?" He moved forward grasping the sword in both hands. "If ye harm one hair on her head, I will take great pleasure in feeding your corpse to the fish."

She did not care if Lord Moreau killed her. Her heart ached and life would mean nothing if she lost Drew. Without warning, Lord Moreau moved closer to the dockside and she fell, his arm tightened around her neck cutting off her air. She batted at his arm fighting to remain conscious.

"Let her go." Jamie swung his sword and it cut through the air with a whine.

Lord Moreau's evil breath brushed her cheek.

"Why would *you* want to save her? She is nothing but a worthless whore." He chuckled and his grip slackened allowing her to take a few precious breaths. "I have had the pleasure of lifting her skirt and slipping between her white thighs many a time."

I am going to kill you. She stamped down hard on his foot grinding her Cuban heel into his toes.

"Filthy English whore." He tightened his grip around her neck again, and lifted his snake's head cane. "You will feel this across your back the moment we are on board *The Black Turtle.*"

Jamie tossed his head sending trickles of water from the ends of his soaked hair to the front of his green velvet jacket.

"Stay still, lass." He turned his grim expression on Lord Moreau. "If ye think for one second ye are going to get away wi' shooting ma brother, ye can think again." Jamie glared at him. "We have our own justice in the Highlands ye ken, and we dinna take too kindly to anyone assaulting a laird."

"I have the trump card, *n'est pas?*" Lord Moreau chuckled and wrenched her hard against him. "You will not risk harming he—Arrrr."

A loud thud came close to her ear and Lord Moreau loosened his grip and slid with elegant grace to the ground. Free from his hold, she staggered and the edge of the dock came perilously close.

Warm breath brushed her cheek and Drew's familiar scent wafted over her.

"I dinna think, ye should be going for a swim right this minute." He wrapped one large hand around her arm to steady her. "You are safe and you are well." He sheathed his dirk and pulled her into his arms. "Rest your head on my shoulder for a wee while." He lifted his chin. "Jamie, send a lad for Lord Rupert's carriage, she will need tending and dry clothes."

Numb with shock she stared at his blood-splattered, ashen face. "I thought you were dead. Oh, Drew, are you badly hurt?"

Drew touched the top of his head gingerly and winced.

"Nay but a scratch but it addled ma brains for a bit. Just as well we arrived when we did or the misbegotten toad would have had ye on that rowboat." He rubbed her back in slow circles. "I am sorry for not getting here sooner. I believed ye would be safe with *Madame* Josephine for a day or two."

She rested her head on his damp plaid and sighed. "You are here now and that is all that matters." Glancing down at the crumpled figure of Lord Moreau, she frowned. "What did you hit him with?"

"The handle of ma dirk. He will be wi' the fairies for a while yet." Drew's full mouth twitched up at one corner.

She touched her face and winced in pain. "I want to kick him for breaking my nose."

Drew held her away then examined her face with gentle care.

"Nay lass, leave the fighting to me, aye? Your nose is not broken, but ye will have a nasty bruise on your cheek and mayhap a black eye to boot." He grimaced and pointed his chin toward Lord Moreau. "Angus will deal wi' him. I need to get ye away from the docks. The rowboat from *The Black Turtle* is minutes away and we will need to be gone afore anyone can identify us."

She lifted her attention toward *The Black Turtle* and a small boat with two pirates rowing frantically toward shore. "How will we ever be safe while he lives?" She pointed at Lord Moreau.

Angus's mouth twisted into a rueful smile.

"Dinna fash about him, lass. I will remove him from your presence." He bent, lifted Lord Moreau over one shoulder and grinned. "Go now. I will be more than happy to deal with him. I have a wee surprise for him in mind, ken?" He slung Lord Moreau across his broad shoulders like a carcass of beef and strode off down the dock.

She stared after him in disbelief for some moments before turning back to Drew. "Where are we going?"

Before Drew had a chance to reply, a carriage and four came thundering up the road and stopped a few paces away.

Lord Rupert, hair untied, and flowing lose about his shoulders, jumped from the door.

"What is amiss?" His attention went to Drew then to her and his blue eyes widened. "Dear God, Adrianna, who did this to you?"

"I will explain later." Drew handed her into the carriage. "Take her to *Madame* Josephine and see she is tended and dressed for travel then meet me back at the tavern. I will go there now and inform Bent to pack your bags. We are leaving for Badenoch without delay." He pushed a lock of black hair from his blood-splattered cheek and smiled at her.

"Go now, *mho creagh*. We are going home."

Lord Rupert slipped into the coach and gave her a speculative gaze.

"I am to blame for this injustice. I should have visited you at first light." He pulled a clean handkerchief from his sleeve and handed it to her. "Will you ever forgive me?"

The coach rattled down the street and she leaned back into the squabs. "There is nothing to forgive." She dabbed at her nose. "I am more concerned about Betty." She pressed one hand to her stomach and met his intent gaze. "She may be dead. I heard her screaming as I fled the brothel. She remained behind to prevent Lord Moreau following me. She hit him over the head with a chamber pot. God knows what he did to her in my absence."

"I doubt Lord Moreau would risk killing her." Rupert grinned. "Was the chamber pot full by chance? Although one would hardly notice, indeed the man has the foulest odor."

She smiled, the action made her face ache, but she did not care. "No I do not believe so, but a good part of me wishes it was full to the brim."

* * * *

Drew bit back a groan and grasped his head convinced it would tumble off his neck and roll across the dock into the sea. He leveled a gaze at Angus from beneath heavy eyelids. "Dinna tell me ye let the ugly piece of dung go free?"

"Well, I did and did not." Angus held up both hands as if warding off a raging bull and grinned. "I sold the worm-riddled dog shit for two shillings to a captain sailing for the Indies. I thought it would be an appropriate punishment for enslaving Ian. The ship is due to sail on the next tide, so I dinna think he will be bothering ye again."

He returned the smile, but the small action sent needles of agony through his head. "I thought ye would have tossed him into the sea, although drowning is too good for that pig of a man."

Angus reached behind him and pulled Lord Moreau's snake's head cane from his belt.

"I kept ye a wee souvenir. I thought ye might want to spit on it and burn it on Samhain."

Drew shook his head and needles of agony pierced his brain. "Nay, I dinna want any reminder of the wee pest. Throw it into the sea and let the fish have it."

His focus cleared and he noticed the concerned expression on Jamie's face and his pallid appearance. He forced his lips into some semblance of a smile to reassure him of his well-being. "Ye did well, Jamie. Da would have been proud of ye and so am I." He squeezed his brother's arm. "I am glad ye had ma back as always." He met his gaze. "Ye ken I must take Adrianna away now and I will need Angus to drive the coach so *you* will have to visit the merchants in ma stead and sell our goods. Can I trust ye and Ian to bring ma mares safely to Badenoch?"

"Aye, have nay fear. I will treat them like gold sovereigns." Jamie chuckled.

"See that ye do. Visit as many merchants as you can today. I dinna want ye more than a day behind me. Now, I would be much obliged if ye would fetch ma horse, ma balls are frozen, and if I stand here a moment longer, I may never sire a bairn."

Chapter Seven

Snug and warm, Adrianna stared aimlessly out of the window and waited for Rupert to return. Rain glistened on the rooftops of Inverness and mist bathed the mountains in the distance. Somewhere, hidden in those rugged but beautiful mountains lay Badenoch, Drew's home. His bloodied face filled her mind and her heart twisted. *Dear God, he very nearly died saving me.*

She *loved* him, indeed, had *craved* him from the first moment she set eyes on him, and knowing him so intimately had locked him in her heart forever. She delighted in the solid strength of him, his unfailing sense of honor, and the way his unique scent of male musk and bergamot ignited her arousal, as if he belonged only to her.

At the sound of a soft knock on the door, she turned her head.

"That will be Lord Rupert, milady." Betty rose from a chair by the roaring fire and moved to open the door.

Lord Rupert had dressed in his traveling cloak. He smiled at her from the hallway.

"Well, I must say you appear to be much better." He removed his hat and bowed. "The carriage awaits. I have obtained a basket of food and blankets."

She smiled at his earnest expression. "How long will the journey take?"

"Two days perhaps." He waved Mr. Bent inside to collect her belongings. "Come now, we must make haste and remove you from Inverness without delay. Drew is, as we speak discussing a plan with Jamie to explain Lord Moreau's disappearance to Captain Jacques." He offered his arm. "If this ruse is a success you will not have to worry about being discovered at Badenoch."

Swaddled in warm serenity by his words, she smiled at him. "That is wonderful news." She took his arm and lifted her skirts. "I cannot wait to see Foiseil Castle. Is it a large holding?"

"Indeed, and is fit for a queen, my lady." Rupert led her toward the stairs.

* * * *

On the evening of the second day of the journey, Drew moved his horse beside the carriage and leaned his dark head toward the window to speak to Adrianna.

"See there." He pointed to a large castle in the distance. "Ma home. Does it please ye?"

Adrianna dropped down the window and squinted at the formidable fortress wedged on the side of Badenoch Mountain. Rising above a wide river snaking its way south, Foiseil Castle appeared to grow from the rock face, as a dark smudge on the pristine snow covered peaks. The walls rose up, impenetrable, black slabs of rock topped with barbed spikes. Arrow slits sat in a line some ten feet below, the faces of guards evident. A reinforced wooden door, six horses wide, was set in the middle of the building and appeared to be the only crack in the building's defense. Flying high above the magnificent building waved a flag, no doubt the standard of the Mackenzie.

"I will signal the guards to open the door." Drew withdrew his sword and standing in his stirrups waved it in the air. "We are home at last."

Small patches of snow lay on the ground and icy wind blew through the window chilling her to the bone. The carriage rattled across a bridge over the river and continued down a well-worn road toward the castle. As they approached, voices rang out in Gaelic and Drew responded. Moments later, the massive gate swung open with a whine, and the horses clattered over the flagstones into a courtyard.

To her disappointment, Drew dismounted and walked away to speak to his men. Finally, Lord Rupert opened the carriage door and let the steps down.

"Hand me Fru Fru. He took the dog then offered his arm to her. "Come along, my dear. It is much warmer inside."

She gathered her skirts and took his arm alighting from the carriage. "This is a fortress."

"Indeed, and just as well." Lord Rupert led her toward the keep. "This part of the castle is cut from the rock face."

She gazed around the huge area. The walls showed the marks of the tools used to hone the rock. Crystal glittered in small patches amid the lines of orange and black running in waves throughout the dark blue walls. In places, trickles of water flowed over green swatches of lichen and moss. Fat candles sat in rusty iron sconces dripping wax in a constant flow.

The courtyard held a blacksmith at one end. The clang of metal followed by the hiss of steam percolated through the noise of men's voices. She strolled with Rupert through a pair of massive oak doors and into the keep. Her attention went to a group of men busy inside a well-stocked armory. Rows of guns, with long oiled shafts, rested in racks beside swords, the lethally sharp blades glistening in the candlelight. Along one wall, barrels of arrows had been set in a row before a long bench piled high with bows.

The scent of gunpowder mingled with the heavy musk of sweaty male hung in the air. She swallowed hard, frightened at the extent of the brutal weaponry. She had never seen such instruments of death. Outside the armory sat a man sharpening swords. Heavens above, the flying metal sparks barely missed her. She flinched away and Rupert patted her hand.

"Have no fear, my lady. We are at a safe distance." He moved swiftly guiding her toward a pair of closed doors. "You will be more comfortable waiting in the Great Hall. I am sure Drew will not keep you long." He smiled at her. "After what had been happening here over the past few months, you must appreciate he needs to discuss any current threats with his men."

She held her breath as a guard pushed open the massive doors to the Great Hall and a wave of delicious heat brushed her legs. "Yes, of course. He is laird and no doubt will have to explain why he has brought an English lady to his home too."

"Hmm, I am sure once they set eyes upon you, they will be charmed." Rupert strolled toward a fireplace. "Warm yourselves. I will ask one of the servants to bring you some mulled cider."

Betty moved to her side and her eyes widened.

"Goodness, milady, do you think all these people live here?" She placed a bag at her feet. "A fine place to get lost. I have never been in such a huge place. You will need to ask the laird for a map to be sure."

She waved Betty into the chair opposite. "Sit down and warm yourself. It will be some time before someone takes me to a room. I was not expected. No doubt they will have to find a place for me to stay."

Glancing around the massive hall, she noticed all within had jobs to do. Housemaids changed the rushes on the stone floors and others busied themselves by placing trenches on the long wooden tables. A procession of serving girls followed with goblets, pitchers of wine and plates of bannocks.

A rosy-faced older woman came bustling toward her and gave a bob of a curtsy.

"I am Ellie, ma lady. I am the housekeeper for Laird Mackenzie. I will get ye settled in a room and have a bath sent up and some food." She smiled. "Ma Lady Badenoch will be along shortly to speak wi' ye."

Adrianna followed the large rotund woman from the hall and up a spiral staircase along another hallway and up another flight of stairs. At a door with a guard standing outside, the woman paused and turned to her.

"The laird has given ye his chambers for now." She opened the door and stood to one side. "The guard will keep ye safe. Dinna leave the room, aye." She waddled down the hallway without a backward glance.

Hmm, well at least she speaks English. She examined the room and sighed. The laird's room to be sure with fine furniture and a huge bed with a swan's down cover displayed crisp, clean linen. A newly set fire heated the room and on one side of the fireplace, a fine bookshelf filled to bursting with leather bound volumes. She wandered around the room admiring the swords and targes adorning the walls and the painting of stags in a forest of green leaves.

A knock sounded at the door and it opened to reveal a small woman, with a pretty face and engaging blue eyes.

"Ah, you must be Rupert's visitor." She spoke in French. "Welcome to Badenoch. I am sorry I do not have a room ready, I had no idea he would be bringing a fine English lady home with him." She held out her hands. "I am Lady Badenoch, Drew's mother."

Rupert's guest? "I am most pleased to meet you Lady Badenoch. I am Lady Adrianna Beachwood." *Heaven's above Drew has not informed her about me.*

* * * *

Drew dropped into the chair in his solar and leaned back stretching his legs. Two days of hard riding in the freezing cold had stiffened his muscles. He glanced at his mother's inquisitive expression and smiled. "What is amiss?"

"Why did ye put Lady Adrianna in your chamber? It is not seemly for a laird to do such a thing. If she is not betrothed to Rupert why may I ask have you brought a Sassenach to Badenoch?"

He reached for the bottle of whisky and half-filled his glass. *Ah well, I suppose I will have to get it over with.* "The truth is, Ma, she is the lass I mentioned to Father. I plan to make her my wife." He held up a hand to prevent the tirade he expected going by his mother's beet-red face. "I *love* her and the fact she has a considerable fortune will nay doubt sway the clan to ma way of thinking." He sipped his drink hoping the clenching in his wame would ease. "I would ask your blessing because I plan to marry her first thing in the morning." He snorted. "If she wi' have me."

"If she wants ye or nay, I will not have ye marrying wi' out your family to witness the union." She glared at him. "And shame on ye for not giving a fine lady time to prepare for her own wedding or for the housekeeper to prepare a feast in your honor."

Drew rubbed his chin dismayed at the thought of waiting another hour to make Adrianna his own let alone another two days. "Jamie and Ian will arrive tomorrow. I will not wait more than an hour after they arrive home so you will need to make sure Father Simon is here in the castle and not out visiting ma tenants."

"Verra well but until that time, ye will not step one foot inside your bedchamber or go near the lass. Proprieties will be observed, ye ken?" She gave him a gimlet eye. "I will inform the lady, ye are verra busy wi' clan business and will call on her in a day or two. Then ye can ask her if she will have ye but afore ye do, I suggest ye call the clan to the Great Hall and inform them of your decision." She turned and in a swish of tartan left the room.

He rubbed both hands over his face and stared after her hoping their conversation had not been overheard. His ears grew hot with embarrassment. *Will I ever be a grown man to ye, Ma?*

* * * *

He waited for his clan to sit down to supper then banged on the table to get their attention. With all heads turned in his direction, he cleared his throat. "Afore ma father died, I made him a promise to marry and I told him about a bonny lass I met in London. He gave me his blessing and now I ask for yours. I will wed Lady Adrianna Beachwood the day after tomorrow. She is the goddaughter of King Geordie and I am marrying her against her father's wishes, but it will be a marriage of the heart. What say ye?"

Angus got to his feet and his mouth twisted into a semblance of a smile. He lifted his goblet.

"To the new Lady of Badenoch."

To his delight, his men raised their goblets in a toast to his future. He emptied his drink and grinned. *Now all I have to do is to convince Adrianna to have me.*

Chapter Eight

Adrianna sat in the huge bed and stared at the smoldering peat fire unsure of her future. Lady Badenoch had sent seamstresses to make her a new gown but had not permitted her to step one foot from her room and insisted she take to her bed. Her feeble excuse for Drew's absence worried her. *Has he changed his mind about me after all?*

A knock on the door had Betty rising from her seat at the hearth to answer.

"I would like a word wi' your mistress in private, aye." Drew stepped inside the room.

Adrianna bathed in the sight of him and her heart raced with joy. He had shaved and wore his long black hair tied in a neat queue. Dressed in full Highland regalia, with ruffled shirt, blue velvet jacket, and the end of his plaid tossed over one shoulder attached by a silver brooch, he was magnificent.

With some difficulty, she found her tongue and cleared her throat. "Yes, of course. You may wait outside, Betty." She met eyes of the finest emerald and smiled. "You are looking very handsome today, Laird Mackenzie?"

"*Laird Mackenzie* is it now?" Drew's dark lashes dropped shuttering his expression and he bowed. "Your most obedient servant, my Lady Adrianna."

He rose and she caught a flash of annoyance in his intent stare.

"Your hesitance to use ma Christian name causes me confusion after our recent fondness for each other." He straightened keeping a good distance from her. "Do ye not want me, Adrianna?" He held out both arms at his sides palms up. "I thought we had an understanding, aye?"

Her heart raced in anticipation. She pushed down the desire to leap into his arms and smiled. "Yes, we do have an understanding."

His wide lips twitched into a smile.

"That is just as well."

Her heart squeezed with joy. She slid from the bed and faced him. "Drew ... what have you done?"

Making a feral sound deep in his chest, he went to her encircling her in his strong arms and pressing her against him. A tremble shuddered through him, so slight if she had not been wearing a thin chemise she may not have noticed.

"I love you *mho creagh.*" He stroked her hair. "I wanted to come to ye, but I have been busy organizing a few things ye ken."

Her nostrils filled with a scent as familiar as breathing. His hot breath brushed her neck before he found her lips and plundered her mouth in a possessive kiss, deep and savage. She melted against him, opening to his probing tongue, and tasting whisky. She clung to his broad shoulders and kissed him back unable to contain her desire. Her breasts brushed against his jacket, and she gasped at the delicious sensation. She squirmed against him needing to be closer to ease the throbbing tips.

She wanted him.

Drew dragged his mouth away from paradise and gazed into Adrianna's flushed face. So bonnie, with her long brown curls all about her scandalously bare shoulders and framing a face with skin like the finest French china. When she moaned and wriggled against him, his attention dropped to her full breasts with erect rosy nipples pressing hard against the thin muslin of her nightgown. He inhaled the familiar feminine scent of her infused with a hint of roses. *Christ give me strength.* He cupped her chin rubbing the pad of one thumb in slow circles over her cheek and strengthened his resolve. He came to speak with her and speak with her he would. "Adrianna. Look at me, lass."

Eyes as blue as a loch in summer, flitted open. Tracing one finger over the bruise on one cheek and the red tip to her long aristocratic nose, he swallowed hard. *Christ, I nearly lost her.* The speech he had practiced vanished from his mind like last winter's snow. He brushed a soft kiss over her lips. "I want you, *mho creagh.*"

"I want you too." She gripped his shirt and with a determined expression lifted her chin. "Now."

Nothing mattered, not the eloquent speech, he had concocted to persuade her to wed him, because love shone in her beautiful eyes, love for *him*. He swallowed hard then held her away and noticed her bottom lip quiver from rejection. He smiled and stroked her soft curls. "I will not take ye now, maybe later after we are wed, aye?"

Adrianna blinked and her astonished expression made him sigh. He cupped her cheeks and hot tears splashed over his knuckles. "Och lass, dinna cry. I love ye wi' all ma heart." He rested his forehead very carefully against her brow. "Will ye have me, ma bonnie Adrianna, to be ma wife, and stay by ma side, forever?"

"*Yes*, oh, yes, I would love that of all things but what about your clan and my father's threat to murder you all?"

Her expression of concern warmed his heart. He shrugged. "Aye, well ma clan has welcomed ye as ma bride and your father is not the only threat to clan Mackenzie in the Highlands. There are many things afoot and probably more to deal wi' since my absence. We must form new alliances wi' other clans. I will hold a calling of the clan to bring the Mackenzie men from across Scotland to join us." He smiled. "There are many like Lord Rupert, Mackenzie by birthright who will come."

"How wonderful, Rupert is like a brother to me." Adrianna returned his smile. "But if my father discovers my direction and takes issue, he may convince King George to send troops to avenge his honor."

He met her gaze. "Aye, he might but I have not disrespected your father. Although, he might seek revenge by complaining to King Geordie. I ken there is talk of another rising to place a Stuart on the throne, so being a Scotsman will not bode well with any English king. Ye will become Scottish by marrying me."

He shrugged and regarded her closely. "Then there is the matter of my life as *Le Diable Noir*." He took a deep breath and sent up a silent prayer. "In consideration of everything I have told ye. Would ye still want to take me as your husband?"

"Yes, I do. I believe your notoriety is exciting, indeed thrilling." Adrianna cupped his face and smiled. "You are an honorable man, a great leader, and the Mackenzie clan will be strong again. Whatever the future holds for us we will face it together because *I love you*, Drew, and that is all that matters." She leaped into his arms. "Thank you."

Relief flooded over him and he sighed. "Dinna thank me, lass. I have wanted ye since the first time I laid eyes upon ye." He kissed her again and reluctantly stepped away. "I have something for ye, but I dinna want ma men to see ye in your nightgown." He lifted his spare plaid from the back of a chair and wrapped it around her. "Good, now sit yourself by the fire for a bit, aye."

He moved to the door and swung it open then motioned for his men to carry her chests from *The Black Turtle* inside and set them on the floor. He noticed with some pride, all of them kept their attention firmly on the floor and not one as much glanced in Adrianna's direction.

"How did you collect my belongings?" She jumped to her feet and rushed toward the chest then one of his men placed a small leather covered box on the table and all color drained from her face.

"Adrianna?" He rushed to her side. "What is amiss?"

"The box ... it was my mother's." She lifted her face to him. "Where did it come from?"

He held her against him and rubbed her back to comfort her. "Jamie sent men to *The Black Turtle* wi' a letter from Lord Moreau, a forgery, of course, to collect your belongings. They searched Lord Moreau's cabin too. The wee box contains a marriage contract and what I assume is left of your dowry, a goodly portion but nay doubt nibbled by Lord Moreau for one of the purses is near empty."

She made a sound of distress.

"I had forgotten about the agreement. Burn it and there will be no proof of the arrangement between my father and Baron du Court. You are my betrothed now and the dowry belongs to you."

He let out a long sigh. "I dinna ask to marry ye for your dowry, and aye, I will burn the document. I have a marriage contract I need ye to sign afore we wed and once the priest has bound us your father will not be able to part us."

"Then burn it now and give me your contract to sign before anything else happens to prevent our happiness." She broke free of his arms and moved toward a small desk. She held out one hand. "Now if you please."

He took the folded document from his sporran and handed it to her with a smile. "God, I love a braw woman." He opened the small box, removed Baron du Court's contract, and tossed it into the fire watching with relish as the parchment curled, darkened then burst into flames.

"There, I have made my mark. When will we be married?" Adrianna held out the document to him. "Is there a chapel here?"

"Aye there is and a priest waiting to join us." He folded the paper and placed it back in his sporran. "Get dressed in the gown ma mother had sewn for ye, *mho creagh* and become ma wife."

He pulled her into his arms and the plaid fell from around her shoulders. With her soft skin pressed against the length of him, he kissed her, savoring her tempting mouth. Her arms came around his neck and she pulled him down to her demanding more of him. He could lay her down on the bed and take her now. The thought of burying his aching shaft inside her virgin folds consumed him. He broke the kiss gasping. Christ, she tempted him beyond reason. He gazed into eyes fogged with passion and stepped away.

"I will send Betty to help ye dress. Then when I have made an honest woman of ye, we will take this further, aye?"

He turned and headed for the door then stopped to gaze upon her again still caught in her spell.

"Ye are so verra beautiful. Dinna take too long, *mo nighean donn*. I miss ye already."

He threw open the door startling Betty waiting outside. He waved the girl into the room then strolled down the passageway. He grinned so wide it hurt and pushing one hand inside the pocket of his jacket closed his fingers around his great grandmother's silver wedding band.

Chapter Nine

Standing before the altar in the small bitterly cold kirk, Adrianna, arranged the skirts of the thick tartan gown, and gripped Drew's hand. She repeated the vows spoken first in Gaelic and then in English. As Drew spoke the words to bind them together, she gazed into his handsome face and his vulnerable expression filled her heart with love. She had found her knight in shining armor, the Highland warrior who would love and protect her forever.

When the time came and he slipped a beautiful silver ring on her finger, the third finger of the right hand, as was the custom in Scotland, his warm hand trembled slightly but lips curled into a beatific smile.

"We are wed, lass. Ye are *mine.*"

"Ye may kiss the bride." The priest closed his prayer book and grinned.

To her delight, Drew gathered her against him, surrounding her with warmth and his enticing lips moved across her mouth in a slow embrace. She clung to him drinking in his flavor, tasting whisky, and kissed him back. In his embrace, time and all around them melted into insignificance.

"Carry her to your chamber, afore we all die of the cold." Angus's voice drifted into her consciousness and she dragged her mouth away. "Ye canna consummate your wedding here, man."

The clansmen cheered and Lord Rupert stepped forward and slapped Drew on the back.

"My most heartfelt congratulations to you both." Lord Rupert bowed low over her hand. "I am very glad to see you well after your ordeal."

"I thank you, Lord Rupert." She smiled at him. "As you can see, I am fine and extremely happy." She glanced down at the small dog at his feet complete with a Mackenzie tartan bow on its head. "Hello Fru Fru, I see she is now one of the clan."

"Indeed." Lord Rupert scooped up the ball of fluff and tucked it neatly against his side.

Drew's mother gave her a bright smile and came forward holding out her hands. She addressed her in French.

"Welcome to our family, Adrianna. I am sure we are going to be great friends. I will teach you the Gaelic and you may teach me English." She met her gaze, her blue eyes dancing with happiness. "I can see how much Drew loves you and to see him happy means so much to me. I hope you will do me the honor of calling me Mother?"

Adrianna took her hands and squeezed. So happy to be accepted, she returned her smile. "I would enjoy your company very much and I promise to keep Drew happy, *Mother*."

She slipped under Drew's arm and snuggled against him then waited patiently for the priest to make his mark. Lord Rupert and Angus witnessed the marriage contract she had signed earlier, her name set below Drew's bold hand.

"Good, now we can eat." Angus rubbed his hands together." I have been looking forward to the wedding feast."

"Ah-hum." Drew glared at him. "Will ye not be welcoming your new mistress to our clan?"

"Oh aye, beg pardon. My Lady Badenoch, may I be the first to welcome ye to Clan Mackenzie?"

He had greased down his unruly red hair and bowed before her in such a formal fashion, she smothered a giggle. "You may. I thank you, Angus."

She leaned into Drew soaking up the heat radiating from his body and sighed. "Do we have to go to the wedding feast? Our room is so much warmer than the Great Hall."

He gave her such an abashed look, she laughed. "What is it, husband? Did I say something inappropriate?"

He raised one black eyebrow and bent close to her ear.

"Ah, lass, I *love* ye being bold and I canna wait to bed ye." He chuckled. "But I dinna want ma mother overhearing your wicked intentions toward me, aye?" He pulled her against him and led her from the church.

* * * *

Drew waited with agitated patience for the numerous toasts and good wishes to end. The feast had gone past supper and his men were well into their cups although, he had partaken of one tankard of ale all evening. His bride, God bless her endurance, had started to wilt at his side like a parched rose. He banged his empty tankard on the table to hush the noise. "I will be taking ma leave now, ma wife needs her rest."

Rowdy jeers greeted his announcement and he glared around the table but to no avail. He grinned and shrugged then pushed to his feet. He offered his arm to Adrianna. "My Lady Badenoch."

"Husband." She stood smiling at him then wet her lips in an invitation he could not ignore.

To be sure, the small action sent blood rushing to his groin and he cleared his throat. "Ye will not need Betty tonight." He led her from the Great Hall and toward the stairs. "I have moved her into a maid's chamber down the hall, so ye will have her nearby to tend ye."

"I thank you." She smiled up at him. "There is one thing I would like to discuss with you."

He patted her hand, and pulled his thoughts away from the temptations ahead. "Aye?" He opened the door to his bedchamber and stood to one side to allow her to pass. "What is it?"

Adrianna strolled into the room and moved around running the tips of her delicate fingers across the backs of the chairs.

"I know you are aware of the gold and gemstones I have in my stays" She turned and smiled at him. "All I have is yours now, husband, but there is more. Betty is carrying an amount in silver and I have a substantial income from my estate in Surrey." She sighed. "In truth, I hope it is enough to sustain Badenoch. The thought of you putting your life in danger by smuggling again is a worry to me."

"I am verra glad you care for my safety, but I am canny and will use ma business in France to account for my whereabouts." He smiled and cupped her chin. "I will not risk ma life, not now I have ye."

His attention went to the curve of her hips and the way her rounded bottom swayed provocatively with each step. Desire flamed in his groin. He would not wait one second longer to possess her. "Whatever the future holds, we will face the problems and the joys together, aye?"

His mouth watered to taste the pale, smooth skin hidden beneath the layers of her skirts, to cup each breast, and suckle her tempting pink nipples. He rubbed a hand down his face. Christ, she was innocent of the ways of men and the sight of his erection might frighten her. He cleared his throat pushing the need to ravish her to the back of his mind.

"Betty laid out a nightgown for ye. Do ye trust me wi' your laces?"

She turned and gave him a slow sensual smile and pulled the pins from her hair. Long silken locks tumbled down her back.

"Oh, I trust you to do for me, husband." She turned her back and lifted her curls over one shoulder. "Then perhaps, if I may be so bold, might I be permitted to undress you too?"

Oh, Christ! He fumbled over her laces and his face grew hot with frustration. The sight of the creamy skin exposed slowly to his sight near undone him. He sighed in relief as the dress fell into a mass of fabric at her feet. She kicked it aside then turned her head to gaze at him from beneath hooded eyelids. If she continued to look at him in such a lustful fashion, he might well drop dead of an apoplexy.

He drew a deep breath to calm his nerves and started on her corset. Damnation, he could unlace a woman's stays with his eyes closed but apparently, his fingers had lost dexterity. After an embarrassing few moments, the lace slipped through the final eyelet and he eased the stays away from her voluptuous curves dropping them to the floor. He inhaled the delicious scent of feminine arousal mixed with the rose soap she used and sighing, slid one hand around her waist. He would wait to remove her thin muslin shift, stockings, and slippers. He turned her to face him. "Are ye ready, wife?"

"No, not yet. I want to undress you too." She unfastened the brooch attaching his plaid then slid her hands under his jacket pushing the garment away from his shoulders. She blushed and her eyes rounded. "Oh, I am not sure how to unfold your plaid or remove your sporran."

"I think it better if I undress maself tonight." He grinned. "I will teach ye later, aye?"

He shrugged off his jacket and sat in a nearby chair to remove his boots and stockings. He stood to take off his belt and sporran, allowing his kilt to fall to the floor. He observed her face for any sign of fear, but her eyes glowed with passion. He drew a deep breath and pulled his shirt over his head. Standing naked before her he waited anxiously for her reaction.

Adrianna bit down hard on her bottom lip. Her attention moved over her husband's naked flesh and the magnificence once hidden under his clothes. Smooth skin clung to a wide muscular chest and rippled over his ribs to a flat belly. She had a little understanding of male anatomy but seeing the line of dark hairs running from his chest to navel as if pointing the way to his crowning glory astounded her. Rising from a nest of dark curls, a solid length, its tip wet with moisture twitched a welcome to her. She moved her attention higher and trailed her fingertips over each silvery scar on his solid torso and arms. He had the body of a seasoned warrior, hard, powerful, and glorious. She stared down again at his engorged cock and swallowed hard. *Oh my, it would seem Highlanders are large in all areas.* She glanced back and met his concerned expression.

"Do ye approve wife?" He stepped closer and the heavy musky scent of him filled her nostrils.

She placed one hand on his shoulder and the skin burned hot against her palm. "You are the first naked man I have seen."

"And the last." He chuckled. "Dinna be afraid, lass, the first time may hurt but after, I promise I will only give ye pleasure." He scooped her into his strong arms and carried her to the bed. "Just relax and let me do all the work, aye."

The cool sheets hit her back and she smiled. "I am not afraid. I *want* you." She sat up, pulled her shift over her head and tossed it to the floor. "Do *you* approve, husband?"

Drew's mouth widened into a brilliant smile.

"Oh aye, but then I have already had the pleasure of seeing ye naked." He kneeled on the bed and ran his hand from knee to ankle, then removed her slipper. "Ye do, I hope remember the masquerade ball?" He caressed her knees, her calves then removed the other slipper.

She bit back a moan. He moved slowly sliding down her stockings. Each touch was a gentle caress then he cupped her heel, lifted her foot to his mouth, and proceeded to kiss her toes. *Oh my.* Goose bumps prickled her bare flesh and her mind went into disarray. She could not form a logical thought. She had to respond to his question and forced the words out in a gasp. "I remember everything."

"Uh-huh." His kisses moved up her calf pausing at the inside of her knee. "Your skin is so soft, I canna wait to taste ye again, wife." He trailed his tongue up the inside of her thigh then rose above her. "We will go verra slow, aye?"

She pushed her hands into his hair, feeling the place where the bullet had scraped his scalp and a shiver ran through her at the memory of how close she had come to losing him.

As if, taking her reaction as one of fear, Drew's handsome face creased into a frown.

"I will not hurt ye. I promise."

She pulled the blue ribbon from his queue, and shook free his long silken locks. "You will never hurt me. I will trust you forever." She dragged him down to her and found his lips.

His bare chest brushed her aching nipples and one small point between her folds throbbed deliciously.

Drew groaned in pleasure and took her mouth in a passionate embrace. To his delight, she needed no coaxing and kissed him back, her tongue timid at first then growing bolder. He nibbled across her bottom lip and moved down her long elegant neck to suckle the throbbing vein. She squirmed beneath him rolling her hips and demanding his attention. He chuckled. She was a bold lass and reacted well to his touch, but he would not destroy her desire for him by rushing her the first time. He cupped one deliciously full breast and scraped his thumb over the taut nipple. She arched toward him in an offer he could not resist and he bent to suckle one rosy tip then the other. Lost in the taste of her, he nibbled swirling his tongue around each tight bud.

"Please, Drew, I cannot stand much more pleasure." Her fingernails raked his shoulders.

He lifted his head and brushed a chaste kiss over her lips. "I have not started to pleasure ye yet, ma love."

"Oh, I am not sure I can survive more of such delights."

Sliding down her body, he gazed at the brown curls glistening with moisture and pressed a kiss to her mound. "Aye well, I hope ye do because I am going to taste every inch of ye like I did afore I left London."

"Oh!" She undulated beneath him and gripped the sheets.

He kissed her mound then parted the soft curls and used his tongue to circle her hard nub. She bucked beneath him and he took a firm hold of her rounded hips and lapped. She tasted so sweet and the scent of her made his shaft throb with the need to be deep inside her. *Soon, my love, you will be mine.*

Adrianna gripped the sheets and rode the waves of erotic sensations. Her legs shook and something burst inside her followed by delight so profound she cried out. "I am undone."

Drew crawled up her body, his mouth glossy from licking her and smiled.

"Nay, lass, all is as it should be."

When he gazed down at her, she noticed the black in the center of his eyes had grown huge and only a sliver of green remained. He kissed her slowly, languidly then murmured against her lips.

"Lift your knees up for me lass and wrap your arms around me." He smiled encouragingly. "Ye are so beautiful. Nay other has stirred me so."

Restless, she tossed her head, but the now familiar urges pushed her onward, she wanted him in every way. Her tender nipples rasped against the fine hairs on his chest and her core quivered from his touch. She complied and the hot tip of his cock slid over her entrance, once then twice before easing inside. Holding her breath, she waiting for the pain, but he stilled and pressed kisses to the corners of her mouth.

"Relax, *mho creagh*. I will take care of ye." His damp breath brushed her lips. "Look at me and ken that I will love ye forever."

"I love you too."

When he surged forward, she gasped at the pain. He moved deep inside spreading her to an impossible limit. She relaxed. Indeed, his intrusion had not hurt more than a slight pinch. She took a deep breath but before she could exhale, he filled her completely. The heat from their intimate joining surprised and delighted her. Tingles of erotic euphoria exploded into curls of unimaginable fervor. He growled deep in his chest and made a rolling motion with his hips. Waves of delicious sensation tilted the room and she closed her eyes drunk with passion.

The curl of desire she had experienced before grew strong once more, building, building until she could stand no more. Gasping, she dug her fingernails into his shoulders and lifted her bottom to meet each delicious plunge lost in sensual oblivion. His pace quickened and she opened her eyes to see his attention locked on her. His face set in a mask of concentration.

"Let go, *mho creagh*." He lifted her legs onto his shoulders then thrust hard.

"Oh, my head will surely explode."

She clung to him trapped in a world of pleasure. Flames of desire ignited nerve endings and sent shooting stars of delight from nipples to toes. Waves of exquisite release consumed her. Somewhere in the confusion of sensation, Drew shouted her name, trembled, and her core heated with the release of his seed. Her legs hit the damp sheets and she pulled him to her cradling him to her breasts.

"*Mine*, ye are *mine*." Drew closed his eyes and sighed.

After some time, he lifted his sweat-soaked face and smiled at her. He looked so funny, with a serious expression and hair stuck to his face that she chuckled.

"I hope that is not your opinion of ma bedding skills?" His cheeks reddened.

She pressed kisses over his chest. "Of course not. You were wonderful." She pushed the mass of damp hair away from his eyes. "You look so serious as if contemplating going into battle."

"Well that is good, about the bedding, I mean. I will admit ye had me worried for a bit." He rolled to one side and cupped her face. "Are ye alright, *mho creagh?* Did it pain ye too much?"

She smiled wanting more of this fine sport of bedding. "No more than a pinch but I do have one question to ask if I may?"

"Oh aye, well then ask away." He pushed a lock of hair behind her ear and raised one perfect eyebrow.

"How often does a man require to bed a woman? If I am to understand, men would be much the same as horses and need a certain amount of time to recover, do they not? I mean before they um…?" Her face grew hot at his broad grin. She cleared her throat. "I mean *it* is very enjoyable. Is it not wonderful for you too?"

"Aye it is, but some wives find it a might distasteful." He cupped her breast and made swirling motions around her nipple with his thumb. "A man's desires are often ruled by his wife, unless o' course he takes a mistress or two."

Her mind centered on the movement of his thumb and his full tempting lips moved so close to her nipple she moaned with delight. "I find it quite delightful, so you will have no need of a mistress."

"Aye well then, it will be ma pleasure to bed ye as often as ye desire, *mho creagh.*"

He bent his dark head to kiss her again and she sighed with pleasure. To think, she had escaped her dull London life and now her future promised to be a wonderful adventure, safe, and loved in the arms of her Highlander—*Le Diable Noir.*

Author Biography

H.C. Brown is a multi-published, bestselling, award-winning author of Historical, Paranormal, Sci-Fi, Fantasy, BDSM, Time Travel, Action Adventure, and Contemporary Romance.

In 2015, she was delighted to be named Luminosity Publishing's Bestselling Author of 2014.

In 2015, *Highlander in the Mist* was placed 3rd in Historical and *Rock 'n' Leather* was placed 3rd GLBT in the Easychair Bookshop Competition.

In 2011, she was delighted to receive nominations in three categories in the 2011 CAPA Awards: Favorite Author, Best GLBT Romance, and Best Science Fiction Romance.

She was nominated for Best Historical M/M in the 2013, Goodreads Book of Year Awards.

H.C writes about strong alpha male heroes and girl next door heroines in complex settings, and all her stories have happy endings.

H.C. welcomes feedback from her readers.

Connect with H.C.

http://www.hcbrown-author.com/

H.C. BROWN

LUMINOSITY
PUBLISHING